AURORA RISING

ALSO BY AMIE KAUFMAN AND JAY KRISTOFF

Illuminae (The Illuminae Files_01)

Gemina (The Illuminae Files_02)

Obsidio (The Illuminae Files_03)

ALSO BY AMIE KAUFMAN

The Starbound Trilogy (with Meagan Spooner)

The Unearthed Duology (with Meagan Spooner)

The Elementals Trilogy (for children)

ALSO BY JAY KRISTOFF

The Lifelike Trilogy

The Nevernight Chronicle (for adults)

The Lotus War Trilogy (for adults)

AURORA RISING

AURORA CYCLE_01

—

AMIE KAUFMAN & JAY KRISTOFF

ALFRED A. KNOPF
NEW YORK

THIS IS A BORZOI BOOK PUBLISHED BY ALFRED A. KNOPF

All rights reserved. Published in the United States by
Alfred A. Knopf, an imprint of Random House Children's Books,
a division of Penguin Random House LLC, New York.

Knopf, Borzoi Books, and the colophon are registered
trademarks of Penguin Random House LLC.

Visit us on the Web! GetUnderlined.com

Educators and librarians, for a variety of teaching tools,
visit us at RHTeachersLibrarians.com

Library of Congress Cataloging-in-Publication Data is available upon request.
ISBN 978-1-5247-2096-4 (trade) — ISBN 978-1-5247-2097-1 (lib. bdg.) —
ISBN 978-1-5247-2098-8 (ebook)

Book design by Heather Kelly

Printed in the United States of America
May 2019
10 9 8 7 6 5 4 3 2 1

First Edition

If your squad was hard to find,
or you're still looking,
then this one is for you.

PART 1

THE GIRL OUT OF TIME

1

TYLER

I'm gonna miss the Draft.

The *Hadfield* is disintegrating around me. Black arcs of quantum lightning are melting the ship's hull to slag. My spacesuit is screaming seventeen different alarms, the lock on this damn cryogenic pod still won't open, and *that's* the one thought blaring in my head. Not that I should've stayed in my rack and gotten a good night's sleep. Not that I should've just ignored the damn distress call and headed back to Aurora Academy. And not that this is a really stupid way to die.

Nope. Looking death right in the face, Tyler Jones, Squad Leader, First Class, is thinking one thing, and one thing only.

I'm gonna miss the damn Draft.

I mean, you work your whole life for a Thing, it's only natural the Thing be important to you. But most rational people would consider getting vaporized inside a derelict spaceship drifting through interdimensional space just a little more important than school. That's all I'm saying.

I look down at the girl sleeping inside the cryopod. She

has shortish black hair, with a strange white streak running through her bangs. Freckles. A gray jumpsuit. Her expression is the kind of blissful you only see on babies or the cryogenically frozen.

I wonder what her name is.

I wonder what she'd say if she knew she was about to get me killed.

And I shake my head, muttering over the scream of my suit alarms as the ship around me begins to tear itself into a million burning pieces.

"She better be worth it, Jones."

. . . . .

Let's back it up a little.

About four hours, to be exact. I know they say to start your story at the exciting bit, but you need to know what's going on here so you can actually care about me getting vaporized. Because me getting vaporized is totally gonna suck.

So. Four hours ago, I'm in my dorm at Aurora Academy. I'm staring up at the underside of Björkman's mattress and praying to the Maker that our training officers throw some kind of grav-failure or fire drill at us. The night before the Draft, they'll probably just let us get some rest. But I'm praying anyway, because:

(a) *Even though he never snores, Björkman is snoring now, and I can't sleep.*
(b) *I'm wishing my dad could be there to see me tomorrow, and I can't sleep.*
(c) *It's the night before the Draft, and I. CAN'T. SLEEP.*

4

I dunno why I'm so worked up. I should be cool as ice. I've aced every exam. Finished top of almost every class. Ninety-ninth percentile of all cadets in the academy.

Jones, Tyler, Squad Leader, First Class.

Goldenboy. *That's what the other Alphas call me. Some throw it as an insult, but I take it as a compliment. Nobody worked harder than me to get here. Nobody worked harder once they arrived. And now all that work is about to pay off, because tomorrow is the Draft and I've earned four of the top five picks, and I'm gonna have the best squad a senior class in Aurora Academy has ever seen.*

So why can't I sleep?

Surrendering with a long sigh, I climb out of my bunk, drag on my uniform, drag my hand through my blond hair. And shooting a look at Björkman that I wish could kill—or at least mute—I slap the door control pad and stalk out into the corridor, cutting off his snores behind me.

It's late: 02:17 station clock. The illumination is set low to simulate nighttime, but the fluorescent strips in the floor light up as I mooch down the hallway. I ping my sister, Scarlett, on my uniglass, but she doesn't answer. I think about pinging Cat, but she's probably asleep. Like I should be.

I wander past a long plasteel window, looking at the Aurora star burning beyond, gilding the frame's edge in palest gold. In old Terran mythology, Aurora was the goddess of the dawn. She heralded the coming of daylight, the end of night. Someone back in the day gave her name to a star, and that star gave its name to the academy now orbiting it, and the Aurora Legion I've given my life to.

Five years I've lived here. Signed up the day I turned

5

thirteen, my twin sister right beside me. The recruiter on New Gettysburg Station remembered our dad. Told us he was sorry. Promised we'd make the bastards pay. That Dad's sacrifice—all our soldiers' sacrifices—wouldn't be for nothing.

I wonder if I still believe that.

I should be sleeping.

I don't know where I'm going.

Except I know exactly where I'm going.

Stalking down the corridor toward the docking bay.

Jaw clenched.

Hands in my pockets to hide the fists.

.　.　.　.　.

Four hours later, I'm pounding those same fists on the cryopod's seal.

The chamber around me is filled with a hundred pods just like it, all rimed with a layer of pale frost. The ice cracks a little under my blows, but the seal isn't opening. My uniglass is running a wireless hack on the lock, but it's too slow.

If I don't get out of here soon, I'm dead.

Another shock wave hits the *Hadfield,* shaking the whole ship. There's no gravity in the derelict, so I can't fall. But I'm hanging on to the cryopod, which means I still get whipped around like a kid's toy, smashing my spacesuit's helmet into another pod and adding one more alarm to the seventeen already blaring in my ears.

WARNING: SUIT INTEGRITY BREACH. H_2O RESERVOIR COMPROMISED.

Uh-oh . . .

The girl in the cryopod frowns in her sleep like she's

6

having a bad dream. For a moment, I consider what it's gonna mean for her if we make it out of this alive.

And then I feel something wet at the base of my skull. *Inside* my helmet. I twist my head and try to spot the problem, and the wetness sloshes across the back of my neck, surface tension gluing it to my skin. I realize my drinking tube has ruptured. That my hydration tanks are emptying *into* my helmet. That even if this FoldStorm doesn't kill me, in about seven minutes, my helmet is gonna fill with water and I'm gonna be the first human I've ever heard of to drown in space.

If we make it out of this alive?

"No chance," I mutter.

· · · · ·

"No chance," the lieutenant says.

Three and a half hours earlier, I'm standing in Aurora Academy Flight Control. The flight deck lieutenant's name is Lexington, and she's only two years older than me. A couple of months back at the Foundation Day party, she had too much to drink and told me she likes my dimples, so I smile at her as often as possible now.

Hey, if you've got 'em, flaunt 'em.

Even at this hour, the docks are busy. From the mezzanine above, I can see a heavy freighter from the Trask sector being unloaded. The huge ship hangs off the station's shoulder, her hull battered from the billions of kilometers under her belt. Loader drones fly about her in a buzzing metal swarm.

I turn back to the lieutenant. Dial my smile up a notch.

"Just for an hour, Lex," I plead.

7

Second Lieutenant Lexington raises one dark eyebrow in response. "Don't you mean 'Just for an hour, ma'am,' Cadet Jones?"

Whoops. Too far.

"Yes, ma'am." I give her my best salute. "Apologies, ma'am."

"Shouldn't you be getting some rack time?" she sighs.

"Can't sleep, ma'am."

"Fretting on the Draft tomorrow?" She shakes her head, finally smiles. "You're the highest-ranked Alpha in your year. What's to worry about?"

"Just nervous energy." I nod to the rows of Phantoms in Bay 12. The scout ships are sleek. Teardrop shaped. Black as the void outside. "Figured I'd put it to good use and log some time in the Fold."

Her smile vanishes. "Negative. Cadets aren't allowed in the Fold without a wingman, Jones."

"I've got a five-star commendation from my flight trainer. And I'm a full-fledged legionnaire as of tomorrow. I won't go farther than a quarter parsec."

I lean closer. Push my smile into overdrive.

"Would I lie to you, ma'am?"

And slowly, ever so slowly, I watch her smile reappear.

Thank you, dimples.

Ten minutes later, I'm sitting in a Phantom's cockpit. The engines heat up and the dock systems load my ship into the launch tube, and with a soundless roar I'm soaring out into the black. Stars glitter outside my blastscreens. The void stretches as wide as forever. Aurora Station lights up the dark behind me, swift cruisers and lumbering capital ships moored at its berths or cutting through the dark around it. I shift course, feeling a

rush of vertigo as gravity drops away, replaced by the weightless-
ness outside the station's skin.

The FoldGate looms in front of me, about five thousand
klicks off the station's bow. Huge. Hexagonal. Its pylons blink
green in the darkness. Inside it, I can see a shimmering field,
shot through with bright pinpricks of light.

A voice crackles in my headset.

"Phantom 151, this is Aurora Control. You are clear for
Fold entry, over."

"Roger that, Aurora."

I hit my thrusters, pushed back hard in my velocity couch
as I accelerate. Auto-guidance locks on, the FoldGate flares
brighter than the sun. And without a sound, I plunge into an
endless, colorless sky.

A billion stars are waiting to greet me. The Fold opens wide
and swallows me whole, and in that moment, I can't hear the
roar of my thrusters or the ping of my navcom. My worries
about the Draft or the memories of my dad.

For a brief second, all the Milky Way is silence.

And I can't hear a thing.

. . . . .

I can't hear a thing.

The blob of water creeping up the back of my head has
reached my ears by the time I get the cryopod unlocked,
muting my suit alarms. I shake my head hard, but the liquid
just slips around on my skin in the zero grav, a big dollop
pooling on my left eye and half blinding me. Doing my very
best not to curse, I pop the cryopod's seals and tear the
door open.

The color spectrum here in the Fold is monochrome, everything reduced to shades of black and white. So when the pod lighting switches to a slightly different kind of gray, I'm not sure what color it's actually turning until . . .

RED ALERT. STASIS INTERRUPTED. POD 7173 BREACHED. RED ALERT.

The monitors flash a warning as I plunge my hands into the viscous gel, wincing as the chill penetrates my suit. I can't imagine what dragging this girl out prematurely is going to do, but leaving her for the FoldStorm is *definitely* gonna kill her. And if I don't get this show on the road, it's gonna kill me, too.

And yeah, that's still really gonna suck.

Luckily, the *Hadfield*'s hull looks like it was breached decades ago, so there's no atmosphere to leech the remaining heat from this girl's body. Unfortunately, that means there's also nothing for her to breathe. But the drugs they pumped into her before they froze her will have slowed her metabolism enough that she can survive a few minutes without oxygen. With my water reserves still leaking into my helmet, I'm more worried about myself in the whole Not Being Able to Breathe department.

She hangs weightless above the pod, anchored by her IV lines, still encased in freezing cryogel. The *Hadfield* trembles again, and I'm glad I can't actually hear what the FoldStorm is doing to the hull. A burst of jet-black lightning crashes through the wall beside me, melting the metal. The water leaking into my helmet is creeping closer to my mouth every second. I start scooping handfuls of goop off the girl's face, slinging it across the chamber to spatter against yet more cryopods. Row upon row of them. Every one filled with this same freezing gel. Every one with a shriveled human corpse floating inside.

They're all dead. Hundreds. Thousands.

Every single person on this ship is dead, except her.

The holographic display inside my helmet flashes as lightning liquefies another piece of hull. It's a message from my Phantom's onboard computer.

WARNING: FOLDSTORM INTENSITY INCREASING. RECOMMEND IMMEDIATE DEPARTURE. REPEAT: RECOMMEND IMMEDIATE DEPARTURE.

Yeah, thanks for the advice.

I should leave this girl here. Nobody'd blame me. And the galaxy she's going to wake up to? Maker, she'd probably thank me if I just left her for the storm. But I look around at those corpses in the other pods. All these people who punted out from Earth all those years ago, drifting off to sleep with the promise of a new horizon, never to wake up again. And I realize I can't just leave her here to die.

This ship has enough ghosts already.

. . . . .

My dad used to tell us ghost stories about the Fold.

We grew up on 'em, my sister and me. Dad would sit up late into the night and talk about the old days when humanity was taking its first baby steps away from Terra. Back when we first discovered that space between space, where the fabric of the universe wasn't quite stitched the same. And because we Terrans are such an imaginative bunch, we named it after the single, magical thing it allowed us to do.

Fold.

So. Take a sheet of paper. Now imagine it's the whole Milky Way galaxy. It's a lot to ask, but you can trust me. I mean, come on, look at these dimples.

Okay, now imagine one corner of that paper is where you're sitting. And the opposite corner is alllll the way over on the other side of the galaxy. Even burning at the speed of light, it'd take you one hundred thousand years to trek it.

But what happens when you fold the paper in half? Those corners are touching now, right? One thousand centuries of travel just became a stroll to the end of the street. The impossible just became possible.

That's what the Fold lets us do.

Thing is, impossible always comes with a price.

Dad would tell us horror stories about it. The storms that spring up out of nowhere, closing off whole sections of space. The early exploration vessels that just disappeared. That breath-on-the-back-of-your-neck feeling of never being alone.

Turns out the effect of Fold travel on sentient minds grows worse the older you get. They don't recommend it for anyone over twenty-five without being frozen first. I get seven years in the Legion, and after that, I'll be flying a desk the rest of my life.

But right now, it's a little over an hour ago and I'm flying my Phantom. Crossing the seas between stars in minutes. Watching those suns blur and the space between them ripple and distance become meaningless. But still, I'm starting to feel it. That breath on the back of my neck. The voices, just out of earshot.

I've been in here long enough.

The Draft is tomorrow.

I should be getting my zees.

Maker, what am I even doing out here?

I'm prepping a course back to Aurora Academy when the message appears on my viewscreen. Repeating. Automated.

SOS.

My stomach drops as I watch those three letters flash on my display. The Aurora Legion's charter says all ships are duty-bound to investigate a distress call, but my sweep detects a FoldStorm near the SOS's origin that's about four million klicks wide.

And then my computer translates the distress call's ident code.

IDENT: TERRAN VESSEL, ARK-CLASS.

DESIGNATION: HADFIELD.

"Can't be . . . ," I whisper.

Everyone knows about the Hadfield *disaster. Back in Earth's early days of expansion, the whole ship disappeared in the Fold. The tragedy ended the age of corporate space exploration. Nearly ten thousand colonists died.*

And that's when my computer flashes a message on my display.

ALERT: BIOSIGN DETECTED. SINGLE SURVIVOR.

REPEAT: SINGLE SURVIVOR.

"Maker's breath . . . ," I whisper.

. . . . .

"Maker's breath!" I shout.

Another arc of quantum lightning rips the *Hadfield*'s hull, just a few meters shy of my head. There's no atmo and my ears are full of liquid anyway, so I can't hear the metal vaporizing. But my gut flips, and the water filling my helmet suddenly tastes like salt. It's covering my mouth now—only my right eye and nose are still dry.

It had taken me a while to find her. Trawling through the *Hadfield*'s lightless innards as the FoldStorm rushed ever closer, past thousands of cryopods filled with thousands of corpses. There was no sign of what killed them, or why a single girl among them had been left alive. But finally, there she was. Curled up in her pod, eyes closed as if she'd just drifted off. Sleeping Beauty.

She's still sleeping now, as the tremors throw me into the wall hard enough to knock the wind out of me. The water in my helmet sloshes about, and I accidently inhale, choking and gasping. I've got maybe two minutes till I drown. And so I just drag the breather tube out of her throat, rip the IV lines out of her arms, watch her blood crystallize in the vacuum. The whole time, she doesn't move. But she's frowning, as if she's still lost somewhere in that bad dream.

Starting to know the feeling.

The blob of water covers both my eyes now. Closing in on my nostrils from both sides. I squint through the blur, hold her close and kick against the bulkhead. We're both weightless, but between the *Hadfield*'s tremors and the water near blinding me, it's almost impossible to control our trajectory. We crash into a cluster of pods, full of corpses long dead.

I wonder how many of them she knew.

Bouncing off the far wall, my fingers scrabble for purchase. The belly of this ship is a twisted snarl, hundreds of chambers packed with pods. But I aced my zero-grav orienteering exam. I know exactly where we need to go. Exactly how to get back to the *Hadfield*'s docking bay and my Phantom waiting inside it.

Except then the water closes over my nose.

And I can't breathe anymore.

Which might sound bad, I know . . .

Okay, it really *is* bad.

But not being able to breathe means I don't need my oxygen supply anymore, either. And so I aim myself at the corridor leading away from cryo. Reaching to the back of my spacesuit, I find the right set of cables and rip them loose. And with a burst of escaping O_2 acting like a tiny jet propulsion unit, we're flying.

I'm holding the girl tight to my chest. Guiding us with my free hand, squinting through the water filling my helmet. My lungs are burning. Lightning shears through the wall, carving the titanium like butter. The ship shudders and we bounce off walls and consoles, my boots kicking, somehow keeping us on course.

Out.

Away.

We're in the docks now, my Phantom sitting on the far side, just a dark blur in my underwater vision. Vast, swirling clouds of the FoldStorm wait just outside the bay doors. Black lightning in the air. Black spots in my eyes. The whole galaxy underwater. I'm almost deaf. Almost blind. One thought building in my mind.

We're still too far from the ship.

At least two hundred meters. Any second now, my respiratory reflex is gonna buck and I'm gonna inhale a lungful of water, and within sight of salvation, I'm gonna die.

We're both gonna die.

Maker, help us.

Lightning crashes. My lungs are screaming. Heart screaming. The whole Milky Way, screaming. I close my eyes. Think of my sister. Pray she'll be okay. There's a rush of vertigo. And then I feel it under my hand. Metal. Familiar.

What the . . . ?

I open my eyes and there we are, floating right beside my Phantom. The entry hatch under my fingertips. It's impossible. There's no way I—

No time for questions, Tyler.

I tear the hatch open, drag the pair of us inside, and slam it closed. As the tiny airlock fills with O_2, I rip my helmet loose and paw the water from my face, breath exploding from my lungs. I'm curled over, floating, gasping, dragging great heaving lungfuls of air into my chest. The black spots burst in my eyes. The *Hadfield* rocks and lurches, tossing my Phantom about in its docking brackets.

You've got to move, Tyler.

MOVE, DAMN YOU.

I claw open the airlock, pull myself into the pilot's chair. Lungs still aching, tears streaming from my eyes. I slap at the launch controls, hit the burners before the couplings are even loose, blast out of the *Hadfield's* belly like my tail is on fire.

The FoldStorm swells and rolls behind us, my sensors all in the redline. The thrust pushes me back in my chair, gravity pressing hard on my chest as we accelerate away. Oxygen-starved already, it's more than I can take.

I manage to activate my distress signal with shaking

hands. And then I'm sinking. Down into the white behind my eyes. The same color as those stars, twinkling out there in all that endless black.

And my last thought before I pass out completely?

It's not that I just saved someone's life or that I have no idea how we covered the last two hundred meters back to my Phantom's airlock or that the both of us should most definitely be dead.

It's that I'm gonna miss the Draft.

2

AURI

I'm made of concrete. My body's carved from a solid block of stone, and I can't move a muscle.

And this is the only thing I know. That I can't move.

I don't know my name. I don't know where I am. I don't know why I can't see or hear, taste or smell or sense anything.

And then there's . . . input. But like when you're falling and you can't tell which way is up or down, or when a jet of water hits you and you can't tell if it's hot or cold, now I can't tell if I'm hearing, or seeing, or feeling. I just know there's something I can sense that I couldn't sense before, so I wait, impatiently, to see what happens next.

"Please, ma'am, just let me have my uniglass, I could tune in to the Draft remotely from here. I might be able to catch the last few rounds, even if I can just—"

It's a boy's voice, and in a rush I understand the words, though I don't know what he's talking about—but there's a note of desperation in his tone that kicks up my pulse in response.

"You have to understand how important this is."

·　·　·　·　·

"*You have to understand how important this is, Aurora.*" *It's my mom's voice, and she's standing behind me, wrapping an arm around my shoulders.* "*This is going to change everything.*"

We're in front of a window, wisps of cloud or smog visible on the other side of the thick glass. I lean forward to rest my forehead against it, and when I look down, I know where I am. Far below, there's a glimpse of muddy green. Central Park, with its brown patchwork quilt, the roofs of the shantytowns and the little fields carved out by its residents, the gray brown of water beside it.

We're on West Eighty-Ninth Street, at the headquarters of Ad Astra Incorporated, my parents' employer. We're at the launch of the Octavia III expedition. My parents wanted us to understand why they were going. Why we were looking ahead to a year of boarding school, breaks spent stranded with friends. This was about two months before they told Mom she was bumped from the mission.

Before Dad told her he was going without her.

Then, as I watch, the trees of Central Park start to grow, shooting up like Jack's magic beanstalk. In seconds they're the height of the skyscrapers all around them. Vines leap across to twine around our building in fast-forward. They squeeze like boa constrictors, and the plaster on the walls starts to crack, fine dust drifting from the ceiling.

Blue flakes fall from the sky like snow.

But this part of the memory never happened, and the sight is painful—unwelcome and unpleasant in a way I can't put my finger on. I shy away from it, shove myself free of it, stumbling back toward consciousness.

Back toward the light.

. . . . .

The light is bright and the boy is still talking, and as I return to the confines of my body, I remember my name. I am Aurora Jie-Lin O'Malley.

No, wait. I'm Auri O'Malley. That's better. That's me.

And I definitely have a body. This is good. This is progress.

My senses of taste and smell are back, and I'm immediately wishing they weren't. Because holy cake, my mouth tastes like two somethings crawled in there, fought a battle to the death, and then decomposed.

There's a woman's voice now, from farther away. "Your sister will be here soon, if you'll just wait."

The boy again: "Scarlett's coming? Maker's breath, is the graduation ceremony over already? How much longer do I have to wait?"

. . . . .

How much longer do I have to wait?

I'm in a vidchat with my dad, and that's the question doing laps around my brain. The uplink delay is dragging on my very last nerve, the broadcast system making me wait a couple of minutes before my replies reach him on Octavia, a couple more before his bounce back.

But Dad's got Patrice sitting beside him, and there's no reason she'd be here except to break the news herself. I think I'm

20

about to hear that the wait that has dominated my life for two years is nearly over. I think that all the work I've put in is about to pay off, that I'm about to be told I'm slated for the third mission to Octavia.

Today's my seventeenth birthday, and I can't think of a better present in all of time and space.

Patrice hasn't spoken yet, though, and Dad's rambling on about other stuff, grinning like his Megastakes numbers came in. His tent is gone—they're sitting in front of an actual wall, with a real live window and everything, so I know the colony must really be progressing. On Dad's lap is one of the chimpanzees he works with as part of the Octavia bio program. When my sister and I misbehave, he teases us by calling them his favorite children.

"My adopted family is very well," he laughs, petting the animal. "But I'm looking forward to having at least one of my girls here in person."

"So will it be soon?" I ask, unable to hold the question in any longer.

I groan inwardly, tipping my head back and resigning myself to a four-minute wait for a reply. But my heart drops when I see my question finally arrive at their end. Dad's still smiling, but Patrice looks . . . nervous? Worried?

"It'll be soon, Jie-Lin," my father promises. "But . . . we're calling about something else today."

. . . Wait, did he actually remember my birthday?

He's still smiling, and he lifts his hand up into view on the screen.

Mothercustard, he's holding Patrice's hand. . . .

"Patrice and I have been spending a lot of time together

21

lately," he says. "And we've decided it's time to make things a little more official and share quarters. So it'll be the three of us when you arrive." He keeps talking, but I'm barely listening. "I thought you could bring rice flour when you come. And tapioca starch. I want us to have just one meal that didn't come from the synth to celebrate being together again. I'll make you rice noodles."

It takes me a moment to realize he's done, that he's waiting for my reply. I'm looking at the pair of them, their hands interlocked, Dad's hopeful smile and Patrice's pained grin. Thinking of my mom and trying to process what this will mean.

"You've got to be kidding," I finally say. "You want me to . . . celebrate?"

Arguing back and forth with a four-minute delay doesn't really work, so I keep my transmission on. Saying everything I need to before he gets a chance to answer.

"Look, I'm sorry you have to hear this, Patrice, but obviously Dad wasn't considerate enough to tell me in private." I turn my stare onto my father, my finger pressing the Transmit button so hard my knuckle turns white. "First off, thanks for the birthday wishes, Dad. Thanks for the congratulations about winning All-States again. Thanks for remembering to message Callie about her recital, which she nailed, by the way. But most of all, thanks for this. Mom couldn't get clearance for Octavia, so what . . . you just replaced her? You're not even divorced yet!"

I don't wait to hear their delayed reply. I don't want to hear new versions of the same old excuses or apologies. I stab a button to kill the transmission. But before I can rise from my seat, the frozen image of the two of them wavers.

I see a flash of light.

It's so bright, the whole world burns to white. And as I squint against it, put my hands out in front of me, I realize I can't see anymore.

I can't see.

. . . . .

I can see.

I'm lying on my back, and I can see the ceiling. It's white, and there are cables snaking across it, and somewhere above me is a light that hurts my eyes. I hold up my hands in front of it like I did in my dream, almost surprised I can see my fingers.

But weird dreams aside, I have my name now. And I remember my family. I was part of the third shipment of colonists to Octavia III. Progress!

Maybe I'm on Octavia now, and this is cryo recovery?

I stare up at the ceiling, eyes half-closed against the light. I can feel more memories hovering just out of reach. Maybe if I pretend I'm looking *this* way, away from them, they'll come creeping out. And then I can pounce.

So I focus on something else and decide to try and turn my head. I pick left, because I think that's where the guy's voice is coming from. I feel like one of those strongmen you see in vids trying to tow a whole loader drone by hand as I strain against the inertia, putting every atom of myself into the effort. It's the weirdest sensation—immeasurable exertion without feeling a thing.

I'm rewarded with a view of a glass wall, frosted to about waist height. The guy's on the other side of it, pacing like a caged animal.

My brain goes haywire, trying to process too much information at once.

Fact: He's hot as all get-out. Like, chiseled jaw, tousled blond hair, brooding stare with a perfect little scar through his right eyebrow, this-is-just-ridiculous hot. This fact takes up quite a bit of my mental real estate.

Fact: He's not wearing a shirt. This is now making a play for Most Important Fact and currently seems very relevant to my interests.

Whatever those are.

Wherever I am.

But wait, wait a minute, ladies and gentlemen and everyone both otherwise or in between. We have a new contender for Fact of the Century. All other facts, please step aside.

Fact: Though the frosted glass obscures all the interesting details, there can be no doubt about it. My mystery man is not currently in possession of pants.

This day is looking up.

He frowns, making the very most of that scarred eyebrow.

"This is taking forever," he says.

.   .   .   .   .

"This is taking forever."

The man in front of me is whining again. We're lining up for cryo, hundreds of us, and the place smells like industrial-strength bleach. There are butterflies in my stomach, but they're not nerves—they're excitement. I've trained for this for years. I fought tooth and nail for my apprenticeship. I've earned this moment.

24

I said goodbye to my mom and my little sister, Callie, yesterday, and that was by far the roughest part of leaving. I haven't spoken to Dad since the Patrice Incident, and I don't know what either of us will say when we're reunited. Patrice herself has been okay—she's sent through a few briefing papers she needs me to read, kept it friendly and professional. But of all the people he could've picked, my father had to start boning the woman who was going to be my supervisor?

Thanks again, Dad.

I shuffle a little closer to the front of the line. In a minute it will be my turn in the showers, and I'll scrub myself within an inch of my life, don my thin gray jumpsuit, and step into the capsule. They knock us out before they get the breathing and feeding tubes in.

The girl in line behind me looks about my age, and nervous as all hell, gaze flickering around the place like it's ricocheting off everything it lands on.

"Hi," I say, trying on a smile.

"Hi back," she replies, shaky.

"Apprenticeship?" I guess, aiming for distraction.

"Meteorology," she says, her grin a little sheepish. "I'm a weather nerd. Hard not to be, growing up in Florida. We get all the weather."

"I'm Exploration and Cartography," I say. "Going where no one has gone before, that kind of thing. But I'll be back at base a lot, too. We should hang out."

She tilts her head like I've said something strange, and the whole scene shakes, shivers, a bright light flickering somewhere like a strobe. The girl closes her eyes against the flashes, and when she opens them again, her right eye has changed. I can

25

still see the pupil, the black edge of the iris, but where her left
eye is brown, her right has turned pure white.

"Eshvaren," she whispers, staring at me like she doesn't
see me.

"... What?"

The whiny man in front of us in line whispers the word.
"E-E-Eshvaren."

When I whirl around, I see that his right eye has turned
white, too.

"What does that mean?"

But neither of them replies. They just whisper the word
again, and it spreads up and down the line like a forest catch-
ing fire.

"Eshvaren."

"Eshvaren."

"Eshvaren."

Eye burning, fingers trembling, she reaches out to touch
my face.

· · · · ·

Oh, hello, touch. I see you've decided to join us. And now
you're here, I can tell every single part of me is hurting in
ways I didn't know had been invented yet.

Another wave of pain hits me, sweeping away the last of
that creepy memory-that-wasn't-a-dream thing and reminding me my body seems to be just as messed up as my head
is right now. I'm reduced to panting, to whimpering with a
raw throat that catches and gags at the effort, to just *existing*
until the hurt starts to ebb away. But with pain, and touch,
comes proper mobility. And that means I can push up onto

my elbows and look across for the guy once more. His lower half has turned dark gray, and from this I deduce he is now, unfortunately, wearing pants.

This day really *is* turning out to be a bust.

The pants discovery prompts a tickle of a question in my head, and I look down beneath the light, silvery sheet that currently covers me to check what *I'm* wearing. Turns out that the answer is "nothing at all."

Huh.

I look back at the boy, and at the same moment, he turns to me, his eyes widening as he realizes I'm awake. I draw breath to try and speak, but I choke, my throat stinging like someone's ripping out my vocal cords one by one.

"Are you okay?" he asks.

"Is this Octavia?" I wheeze.

He shakes his head, blue eyes meeting mine. "What's your name?"

"Aurora," I manage. "Auri."

"Tyler," he replies.

And I should ask him where I am. If we're on the *Hadfield* and I was pulled out early, or if I'm on Earth and they aborted the mission. But there's something in his gaze that makes me shy away from the question.

He lets his forehead rest against the glass between us with a thunk. Like I did at that window on Eighty-Ninth Street. The memory catches me unawares, bringing with it a sharp wave of I-want-my-mom. This boy looks just as lost as I feel.

"Are *you* okay?" I whisper.

"I missed it," he finally says. "The Draft. I missed the whole thing."

And I've got no idea what a Draft is or why it's so important. But I ask anyway.

"Had somewhere else to be?"

He nods and sighs. "Rescuing you."

Rescuing.

That's not a good word.

"Who knows who I got," he says, and we both know he's changing the subject. "I was supposed to have four of the first five picks, and now I'm stuck with the bottom of the barrel. The dregs. And I was just following reg—"

"The news isn't *all* bad, Ty."

The low purr comes from somewhere outside my field of vision. A girl's voice.

Tyler swings away from me like I'm yesterday's news, plastering himself against the front of his holding tank. "Scarlett."

I carefully turn my gaze that way—it still takes thought and strategy, my body refusing to do anything without a plan—to see who he's greeting. There are two girls standing there in blue-gray uniforms, the same color as the pants he seems to have acquired. One has flaming red hair—orange, really, amazing dye job—cut in a sharp asymmetrical bob that swings around a chiseled chin just like his. She shares his full lips, too, his strong brows. Her uniform's skirt is impressively short. She's tall. And she's gorgeous. Presumably, this is Scarlett.

The second girl has a narrow face and a soaring phoenix tattooed right across her throat (ouch). Black hair, longer and spiked on top, shaved to fuzz down the sides with more tattoos underneath. I can tell she has dimples and that her smile would be huge, but I have to deduce it all without seeing the

28

real deal, because right now she looks like somebody killed her grandmother.

"Cat?" Tyler says to her. His voice is low, pleading.

"Ketchett tried to draft me," Cat says. "And a bunch after that. I told them I already had an Alpha, he just couldn't make it."

"Told them, huh? Is Ketchett still breathing?"

"Yeah," the girl smirks. "Next time you go to chapel, you might wanna say a prayer for his testicles, though."

He exhales slowly and presses his palm against the glass, and she lifts hers to press it back in return.

The girl with the orange hair watches them. "I didn't have to insist *quite* as hard," she says, wry. "But I could hardly leave you out there alone. You'd probably get yourself killed without me to talk our way out of trouble, baby brother."

Tattoo Girl pulls up her uniform sleeves, revealing more ink. "Speaking of getting yourself killed, you wanna tell us what you were doing Folding by yourself? Thinking with your other head again?"

Scarlett nods in agreement. "Rescuing damsels in distress is *very* twenty-second century, Ty."

. . . *Say what?*

Tyler holds up his hands, like, *What do you want from me?* and the girls turn to look at me on my slab with curious eyes. Checking me out. Weighing me up.

"I like her hair," Scarlett declares. Then, as if remembering I'm an actual *person*, she speaks to me, louder, a little slower. *"I like your hair."*

The second girl sniffs, obviously less impressed. "Did you tell her the bad news about her library books yet?"

"Cat!" the other two snap in chorus.

An adult voice cuts in before they can get any further. "Legionnaire Jones, your quarantine has cleared, you're free to go."

Ty looks across at me, and our eyes meet. He hesitates.

Did you tell her the bad news?

"You can call in the morning to find out when you can visit," the voice says.

He nods reluctantly, stepping out of his holding pen as the door hisses open in front of him. With a last glance at me, the trio leaves the room, Ty's voice fading out of hearing as he disappears from sight.

"Hey, can I get a shirt?"

My brain's starting to assemble more facts now, agitation creeping in as the lethargy of cryo slips away.

Where am I? Who are these people? They're in uniforms—is this some kind of military facility? If so, what am I doing here, and am I safe? I try to croak out a question, but I can't make my voice work. And there's no one to ask anyway.

And so I'm left alone in silence, every nerve throbbing in time with my heartbeat, my head swimming with half-asked questions, trying to wade my way free of the confusion I didn't know came with cryo.

· · · · ·

I don't know how much time has gone by when I hear voices again. I'm in the middle of another strange dream-thing, this one of a world thick with grasping green plants, blue snow drifting down from the sky, when—

"Aurora, can you hear me?"

With effort, I push away the image of the place I've never

seen and turn my head. I must have been dozing, because there's a woman beside me in the same blue-gray uniform as everyone else.

She's perfectly white. And I don't mean I'm-half-Chinese-and-you're-whiter-than-me white, I mean pure-as-the-driven-snow white. Impossibly white. Her eyes are a pale gray—the whole eye, not just the iris—and they're way too big. Her bone-white hair is pulled back into a ponytail.

"I am Greater Clan Battle Leader Danil de Verra de Stoy." She pauses to let me digest that mouthful. "I am pleased to meet you, Aurora."

Great Clan what now?

"Mmmm," I agree, not game to risk a different kind of sound.

Nobody ever calls me Aurora unless I'm in trouble.

"I imagine you have many questions," she says.

She's evidently not expecting a reply. I nod a fraction, willing my focus to stay with this moment.

"I'm afraid I have bad news," she continues. "I know of no way to break this to you gently, so I'll be frank. There was an incident while your ship was en route to Lei Gong."

"We were traveling to Octavia," I say quietly, but I know the name of my colony isn't the point. I can tell from the careful reserve in her voice that there's something much bigger coming. There's a pressure in the air, like the moments before a storm breaks.

"You were removed from your cryopod improperly," she continues, "which is why you're feeling like you've been turned inside out. That will improve soon. But the *Hadfield* was the subject of an incident in the Fold, Aurora."

"It's Auri," I whisper, stalling.

Incident in the Fold.

"Auri."

"What kind of incident?" I ask.

"You were adrift for some time. You may have noticed I don't look like you."

"My mom always said it wasn't polite to point out that sort of thing."

She has a sad kind of a smile for that. "I'm a Betraskan. I'm one of many alien species Terrans have encountered in the time since you boarded the *Hadfield*."

My mind flatlines with one long *beeeeeeeeeeeeeeep*, all coherent thought shutting down.

Alien species?

Many?

Does not compute, please reboot.

"Um," I say, very carefully. My brain's trying its best to throw out possibilities and getting nowhere good. Are these people conspiracy theorists? Have I been kidnapped by psych cases? Maybe they *are* military and they've been keeping first contact from us civilians?

"I know this must be difficult to process," she says.

"We encountered aliens?" I manage.

"I'm afraid so."

"But the Fold to Octavia was only supposed to take a week! If we didn't even get there, it's only been a few days, right?"

"I'm afraid not."

Something's trying to creep across the corners of my vision, like water seeping in, only this water's phosphorescent, pricked with a thousand points of turquoise light. I shove it back and focus my attention on the woman at my bedside.

"How . . ." My throat closes over. I can barely whisper the question. "How long was I gone?"

"I'm sorry, Aurora. Auri."

"How *long*?"

". . . Two hundred and twenty years."

"What? You've got to be kidding me. This is—" But I don't even have words for what this is. "What are you *talking* about?"

"I know this must be difficult," she says carefully.

Difficult?

Difficult?

I need to speak to someone who's making sense. My heart's thumping wildly, trying to burst out of my chest, matching the pounding in my temples. I clutch the silvery sheet to myself and sit up, setting the world whirling. But I manage to swing my legs over the edge of the bed and haul the sheet around me like a toga as I stagger to my feet.

"Aurora—"

"I want to speak to someone from Ad Astra, someone from the Octavia expedition. I want to speak to my mom or dad."

"Aurora, please—"

I stumble my first few steps, and momentum carries me to the door, which slides open as I approach. Two women in blue-gray uniforms swing around to face me, and one steps forward.

I try to dodge, but I nearly fall over sideways and she grabs me by the shoulders. My hands are busy holding up my sheet, so I just kick her in the knee. The woman yelps, her hands tightening painfully on me, fingers digging in.

"Let her through." It's Battle Leader White Lady's voice behind me, and in total contrast to my panic, she sounds calm. Kind of resigned.

The woman releases me, and my legs are shaking as I totter forward, my throat tight, as if someone's squeezing it.

And then I see the windows across the hallway. I see what's outside them.

Stars.

My brain tries to understand what's happening, flipping through options and discarding them at top speed. The view outside the windows isn't a wall. It's not a building. It's a huge sweep of metal, studded with bright lights, stretching away from me in a long curve.

Those are spacecraft zipping around it, like a school of tiny fish darting around a shark.

This is a space station. I'm in *space*. This place is impossible—it makes the Cid Shipyards that the *Hadfield* launched from look like a gas station somewhere out in the boondocks.

This place is impossible.

Unless that lady really is an alien.

Unless I'm really in space.

Unless this really is the future.

Beeeeeeeeeeeeeeeeeeeep.

Does not compute, please reboot.

I'm 237 years old.

Everyone I know is dead.
My parents are dead.
My sister is dead.
My friends are dead.
My home is gone.
Everyone I know is gone.
I can't.

The next wave of the vision comes for me.

And this time I let the glowing waters sweep over my head.

And they pull me under.

3

SCARLETT

This is such crap.

That's what my baby brother is thinking. I can see it all over his face. He won't actually *say* it, because Tyler Jones, Squad Leader, First Class, doesn't curse. Tyler Jones doesn't do drugs or drink or do anything we mere mortals do for fun. But if my eighteen years in this strange little galaxy have taught me anything, it's this:

Just because you're not saying it doesn't mean you're not thinking it.

We're sitting on a mezzanine above the arboretum . . . well, Cat and I are sitting, anyway. Tyler's pacing back and forth, trying to come to grips with the thought that his last five years of work just got flushed into the recycler. He drags one hand through his golden blond hair, and as he walks past me for the seven hundredth time, I notice a small scuff mark on his normally immaculate boots.

Yeah, he's really taking it hard.

The dome above us is transparent, letting in the light of a billion distant suns. The garden below is a mix of

36

flora from across the galaxy: swirls of Rigellian glassvine and orbs of Pangean duskbloom and blossoms of singing crystal from the stillsea on Artemis IV. The arboretum is probably my favorite place in the whole academy, but the splendor seems kinda lost on my dear baby brother right now.

Can't blame him, really.

"It's not the end of the 'Way, Ty," I venture.

"Yeah, but you gotta admit it's bloody close," Cat replies.

I look at Cat sidelong and give her my best *shut uuuuuup* smile, speaking through gritted teeth. "We should look on the bright side, Cat."

"Come on, Scar," Cat says, ignoring my smile's *shut uuuuuup*–edness. "Everyone knows Ty got robbed. He's the most decorated Alpha in our year. And now he's stuck with the jank and chaff no other squad leader wanted to touch."

"Not to feed that rampant ego of yours," I sigh, "but you're the best Ace in the academy, Cat. You may be counted as neither jank nor chaff."

"Cheers," she smirks. "But I was talking about you and the others."

"Oh, stop." I clutch my chest. "My poor heart."

"Aw. Hug?"

"Kiss."

"No tongue this time."

Catherine Brannock is my bunkmate here at Aurora Academy. She's the yin to my yang. The half-empty glass to my half-full. The mint chocolate chip to my strawberry triple ripple. She's also Tyler's and my oldest friend. Ty pushed Cat over on our first day of kindergarten, and she broke a chair over his head in retaliation. When the dust settled, my baby brother ended up with a nice little scar on his right eyebrow to go with his killer dimples—and a friend whose loyalty is pretty much unquestionable.

She's totally not into him, in case you were wondering.

"That O'Malley girl was stuck in the Fold for two hundred years," Cat continues. "The brass should be pinning a bloody medal on Ty for rescuing her, not saddling him with a squad of no-hopers."

"No-hopers?" I say. "You know, you're lucky I'm such a soulless shrew. Otherwise you might be at risk of quite possibly *maybe* hurting my feelings."

Cat scowls. "The Aurora Legion is the best chance we have of bringing stability to the Milky Way. How're we gonna be of any help out there with a squad of psychos, discipline cases, and gremp fondlers?"

"People fondle gremps now?"

"I mean, I've heard rumors. . . ."

"Who *does* that?"

"She's right," Tyler says.

Cat and I look up at my brother. He's stopped with the pacing and is staring down at the garden. He reminds me of our dad for a minute. And though I'm doing my best to keep up my Queen of Bitch routine, my shriveled black heart *does* sort of hurt for him.

"She's absolutely right," Tyler sighs again.

"Damn right I am," Cat growls. "We should go talk to de Stoy. Lodge an official complaint. You earned those points, Ty, it isn't fair—"

"I mean Scarlett's right," Tyler says.

". . . She is?"

". . . I am?"

Tyler turns to us, leans against the railing, and folds his arms.

"I shouldn't have been out in the Fold in the first place. It was my mistake."

"Ty, you risked your—"

"No, Cat," Ty says, looking at his bestie. "I know you had your pick of squads, and I won't ever forget that you stuck with me. But the Draft is done. It wouldn't be fair to ask for special treatment. I've gotta go the way."

Sigh.

Know the way.

Show the way.

Go the way.

That's what all good leaders do, according to our dad—the great Jericho Jones. And those are the words Tyler lives by. They're the reason he's spent his whole life looking after me and everyone around him. They're the reason he joined the Aurora Legion in the first place. And normally, hearing him say them makes me want to kick my dear baby brother right in his sanctimonious junk. But every now and then, they remind me just how much I love the little jerk.

Tyler takes a deep breath, nods to himself.

"The Legion stands for something real. There's people out there who need our help, and we're not helping any of them by sitting here feeling sorry for ourselves. I've still got the Legion's best pilot in my squad." He smiles at Cat, giving her a double shot of dimples. "That's a start, right?"

Cat doffs an imaginary cap. "Bloody great one, if you ask me."

Ty winks in my direction. "And my diplomat isn't *totally* incompetent."

"Respect your elders, brother mine."

"You're three minutes older than me, Scarlett."

"Three minutes and thirty-seven point four seconds, Bee-bro."

"You know I hate it when you call me that."

"Why do you think I do it?" But I stand up slow and offer him a wry salute. "Legionnaire Scarlett Isobel Jones, reporting for duty, sir."

Tyler salutes back, and I just roll my eyes.

"The highest-ranked Alpha in Aurora Academy," he says. "The best Ace. A killer Face. That sounds like the makings of a squad to me. I mean, we're part of an elite military school with the best students from across the galaxy, right? How bad could the rest of the crew I've been saddled with actually be?"

Cat and I exchange an uneasy glance.

"Um, yeah. About that . . ."

. . . . .

"She's a psychopath," Tyler declares.

"Technically, she's more of a sociopath," I reply.

"Look at these disciplinary actions, Scarlett."

"Um, I read them when I compiled the file for you, thanks for noticing."

Cat, Tyler, and I are walking down C-Promenade through the early-morning crowd. The place is always a hive, but today it's especially busy with all the newly promoted Legion squads being shipped out to their first assignments. Everyone in the crowd is military—Betraskans and Terrans mostly, rubbing shoulders in our scandalously drab uniforms.

I swear, the person who designed these things must have considered *boring* an interstellar sport. I'd rather give the Great Ultrasaur of Abraaxis IV a foot rub than wear one. The cut is okay, I suppose, padded and plated and formfitting. But the color is an ugly shade of blue gray, with a shiny Aurora Legion logo on the chest and a single bright strip across our shoulders and cuffs to denote our divisions:

Blue for the leadership corps.

White for Cat and her fellow Aces.

Green for the Brains in the Science Division.

Purple for the Gearheads.

Red for the Tanks.

And lucky me, a bright, sunny yellow for the diplomatic corps to match my bright, sunny disposition.

I do what I can to liven things up—my hemline is five centimeters higher than regulations technically allow, and my bra probably defies Newton's law of universal gravitation. But pushing the envelope any further is a good way to get a disciplinary citation from one of our instructors, and who needs another one of those, honestly. I've already collected the set.

It's twenty-four hours since Tyler pulled his white knight routine out in the Fold. Battle Leader de Stoy and Admiral Adams have debriefed him, so aside from the novelty of him pulling a two-hundred-year-old orphan from the most famous derelict in Terran history, we're back to business as

41

usual. First missions are being assigned by the hour, and the sooner we meet the rest of our squad, the sooner we hit the black. We've worked five years for this, and I'm so sick of this place I can actually taste the vomit. School is most definitely *out*.

Tyler is still looking over the digital dossier on his uniglass. "Zila Madran. Terran. Age eighteen. Science Division."

"She's clever," I say. "Her academic record is flawless."

"She's had thirty-two official reprimands in the last two years."

"Well, we aren't all perfect little snowflakes, brother mine."

"Speak for yourself," Cat grins, smacking her butt. "I'm bloody brilliant."

Tyler looks over the uniglass in his hand, shaking his head. "Says here Cadet Madran locked two fellow cadets in a hab room and exposed them to the Itreya virus so she could test a serum she'd concocted."

"Well, it worked," I point out. "They didn't go blind."

"She shot her roommate with a disruptor pistol."

"Set to Stun."

"Repeatedly."

"Maybe she didn't stun so easy?" Cat offers.

"Et tu, Brannock?" Tyler asks.

We salute a passing instructor, dodge a gaggle of younger cadets (who whisper in appropriate awe at the sight of the famous Tyler Jones), and step into the elevator leading down to the squad briefing rooms. As the station spins past the transparent plasteel, along with all the hustle and bustle twenty thousand people can provide, Tyler flips to the dossier on our next squaddie.

"Finian de Karran de Seel. Betraskan. Age nineteen. Tech Division."

"He's smart," I say. "Top tenth percentile. If you're into that sort of thing."

"Says here he failed Fold dynamics."

"Otherwise he'd be top two percentile," I say. "See? *Super* smart."

"Also says here he wears an exosuit," Tyler continues.

"Yeah," I nod. "He has nerve damage, muscle weakness, and impaired mobility. He caught the Lysergia plague as a kid. The suit compensates."

"Fair enough," Tyler nods. "But if he's so smart, why'd he fail Fold dynamics?"

"The final exam was a group exercise."

". . . So?"

"So, you'll see," Cat sighs.

We step out of the elevator, work our way through the crowd, and a few corridors later, arrive at our allocated briefing room. The walls are aglow with displays—star maps denoting galactic territories, daily feeds about the Syldrathi civil war, news footage of the refugee fleets amassing on the edge of Terran space. A smartglass table dominates the room, the sigil of Aurora Academy projected on the surface, along with our motto.

We the Legion
We the light
Burning bright against the night

And on opposite ends, literally as far apart as they can possibly be, are two of our new squadmates.

Zila Madran is Terran. She's even shorter than Cat, with dark brown skin and long, tight black curls. The green stripe of the Science Division across her shoulders does nothing for her complexion, but if cute could be weaponized, she'd be a pretty good candidate. There's something about her stare, though. Like there's no one home behind those dark eyes of hers.

But hey, at least she's not carrying a disruptor pistol today. . . .

Leaning against the far wall, our second squaddie is almost the mirror opposite of our first. Like all Betraskans, his skin is the white of bleached bone. The only bright color on him is the purple stripe of the Tech Division on his uniform. His eyes are bigger than a human's, and the protective contact lenses he wears over them are totally black. His bones are the kind of long and thin you get growing up in zero gee, and that makes him unusual. Betraskans love to travel, but almost all of them are reared on their home planet of Trask. Finian's file says he spent a lot of his childhood on offworld stations. He has short, spiky hair with just enough product to make it look like he might not use product at all. But he doesn't fool me.

The most notable thing about him is the light exosuit mentioned in his file. It's made of a silvery metal, a half-shell covering his back, his arms and legs fitted with articulated sleeves, gloves, and boots. It's state-of-the-art tech, and his movement is fluid, almost soundless. But even if I hadn't read his background, I'd still be able to tell the suit is handling most of the hard work for him.

Tyler looks at the pair, offers them a picture-perfect salute.

"Good morning, legionnaires."

They both just stare at him, Zila as if she's counting all his atoms one by one, and Finian as though he just got served a dish that looks *nothing* like the pretty picture on the menu. Still, he's the one who moves first, lifting one hand in a half-assed salute.

"Sir." The honorific doesn't sound like a compliment.

Zila keeps staring. When she finally speaks, she sounds quiet. Polite, even.

"Good morning."

Tyler turns to me, eyebrow raised. "Aren't we missing someone?"

"Your guess is as good as mine, dear brother."

"He's going to miss the briefing."

"Hmm." I make a show of patting down my uniform, peering down my tunic. "I seem to have left the part of me that cares in my other pants."

Please note: I love my brother very much and I know he's having a tough day, but I was up really late last night pulling together his dossier and I haven't had my caffeine yet and I'm normally not this mean to him.

. . . Wait, who am I kidding.

Ty makes a face and gets down to business.

"All right, first off, apologies for the unusual circumstances. I'm not sure what you've heard about how the Draft played out, but it looks like we're going to be working together for the foreseeable future. Our official designation from Aurora Legion Command is Squad 312. My name is Tyler Jones. I'll be this squad's Alpha. This is our Face, Scarlett Jones, and our Ace, Cat Brannock."

Cat sits and leans back in her chair. "Call me Zero."

"As in zero chance of success?" Finian asks, all innocence.

"As in most cadets miss twelve to fifteen percent of targets on their pilot stream exam," Tyler says.

"Guess how many I missed, Skinnyboy," Cat smiles.

Said Skinnyboy stretches, his suit making a hum and a series of soft clicks. "Finian de Karran de Seel. Just Fin if you wanna be lazy about it. Gearhead. You break it, I'll put it back together. Can't promise a hundred percent success rate on anything but my dashing wit, though."

I nod hello, turn to our second squaddie. She's hunched in her chair, knees drawn up to her chin. She's got this puzzled look, as if the idea of introductions doesn't quite compute. And I get it—meeting new people can be tough. Especially since she knows she wasn't Tyler's first, fifth, or even last choice.

"Zila Madran," she finally says. "Science officer."

"I love your earrings," I say, trying to put her at ease.

Well, that gets a reaction. Zila's gaze snaps back to me, and she lifts one hand to the band of beaded gold as if she wants to hide it.

Hmmm. They're the sort of thing you wear so they can be admired. But she doesn't like it when people do.

Iiiiinteresting.

"So," Finian says, turning his black gaze on Tyler. "Gotta say, I'm impressed, Goldenboy. There was a pool running on how long you'd be crying in your bunk before you pulled it together and gave us a rousing speech. To be honest, I had you down for this time tomorrow."

Testing the water. Trying to push Ty's buttons.

"How much did you bet?" my brother asks.

"Fifty creds."

"Gambling is against academy regulations," Tyler points out.

"And only a bloody idiot bets against Tyler Jones," Cat adds.

Finian blinks at Cat, glances back and forth between her and Ty.

"What is he, your boyfriend or something?"

Uh-oh. Bad move.

Cat's eyes grow a little wider. Standing slowly, she starts to pick up her chair.

"At ease, Legionnaire Brannock," warns Tyler.

Finian looks unimpressed. I'm not sure he quite understands the damage Cat can do to a guy's important bits with a piece of furniture. But Tyler is her commanding officer now, and with Cat, at least, that carries weight. So with one last scowl, she sits, giving our new Gearhead a glare that could melt plasteel.

Fin grins at Tyler. "Hey, is it true what they're saying about you?"

"Probably not," Tyler sighs. "What are they saying?"

"That you blew your spot in the Draft rescuing some civilian out in the Fold?"

"That's classified," Tyler replies. "I'm not allowed to talk about it."

"So it *is* true," Fin snickers. "You're just a regular . . . what is it you Terrans say . . . Boy Scout? A regular little Boy Scout?"

Zila, it seems, has had enough of the conversation. She picks up her uniglass, swipes the surface, and taps out a quick rhythm with her fingertips. Checked out. Despite my lack of sleep and caffeine, I feel sorry for Ty. As far as dream picks go, these two sure aren't it. But my brother isn't fazed.

"I remember you now," Tyler says to Fin. "You're the cadet who irradiated the propulsion labs so he could get out of his spatial dynamics exam."

"Technically, *everyone* got out of their spatial dynamics exam."

"You were that frightened of failing, huh?"

"Are we bonding right now?" Fin asks. "I feel like we're bonding."

"You're also the kid I see sitting alone in the mess hall every chow break." Tyler turns to Zila. "And *you* I don't see at all. But like it or not, I'm your CO now, and we're stuck together for the next twelve months. So you can buckle up and enjoy the ride, or play the tough guy and spend the next year cleaning latrines. Your choice, legionnaire."

Ultimatum. Nice play, baby brother.

Finian stares just long enough to save face. But really, he's got no other move here and he knows it. So slowly, and as sloppily as he can, he salutes.

"Sir, yessir."

"And what about you, Legionnaire Uniglass?" Tyler asks.

Zila looks up from the device in her hand. Tilts her head and blinks once.

"I understand, sir."

Tyler nods, all business. "All right, then. I don't know

48

where our Tank is, but I've got reports to file. Our mission briefing is at 08:00 tomorrow—with any luck, Command will send us somewhere we can do some good. Don't be late. Squad dismissed."

Tyler stands, and I shoot him a wink to show my approval. He's not as good at reading people as I am, but then again, not many people are. I'm not sure what to make of Zila Madran yet. But I've met guys like Finian de Seel a thousand times. Chip on his shoulder, and an open invitation for the whole Milky Way to take a big old bite.

He's gonna be trouble.

We file out into the corridor. Cat is chatting to Tyler about tomorrow's briefing, wondering which sector we might be assigned to. Zila and Finian follow quietly. I'm walking in front, uniglass in hand, shooting a query to our missing squadmate. So I'm kinda surprised when a hundred kilos of bleeding boyflesh crashes into my boobs.

"Scar!" Tyler shouts.

We hit the floor. Boyflesh is sprawled on top of me in a decidedly unflattering pose and I'm starting to regret the five centimeters missing off my hemline.

"Ow?"

Ty moves to haul the lump off me, but the guy's already up and charging down the corridor, back toward the knock-'em-down, punch-'em-out brawl he came from.

"You're gonna pay for that, pixie," Boyflesh growls.

There's five of them slugging it out at the end of the hall. All young. The red stripes on their uniforms mark them all as Tanks. Four are Terran—the kind of burly lumps you'd expect to find in the academy's Combat Division. The fifth

Tank is taller. Agile and lithe. He has olive skin and his long ears taper to gentle points. Silver hair is tied back from his face in five long braids, spilling down over his shoulders. His eyes are the kind of violet you only read about in stories and his cheekbones are sharp enough to cut your fingertips on, and he'd be beautiful if it wasn't for the blood spattered on his fists and face.

Still, there aren't many in the academy, so it doesn't take long to realize . . .

He's Syldrathi.

"Ne'lada vo esh," he says calmly, raising his bloody hands.

"Speak Terran, Pixieboy!"

One of the Terrans aims a punch at the Syldrathi's head, and I realize the fight is four on one. The Syldrathi easily blocks the strike, locks up his attacker's arm with the sort of crunch you never want to hear your own elbow make, and flings him at a girl built like an armored troop carrier, sending them both tumbling.

"Esh," he says, backing up a step. "Esh ta."

"Hey!" Tyler shouts in his best voice of authority. "Knock it off!"

Tyler's voice of authority is pretty good, but still nobody listens. The Syldrathi takes a punch to his jaw, lashes out with his fingertips into his assailant's throat. The guy drops with a gurgle, and in a move that makes even Cat wince, the Syldrathi stomps him right in the fun factory, eliciting a high-pitched scream. His face totally serene, the Syldrathi weaves below a punch, drops another cadet with a kick to his knee. And even though it's four on one, I start to realize . . .

"Maker's breath," Cat murmurs. "He's *winning.*"

The Syldrathi gets smashed against the bulkhead, opening up his brow. Dark purple blood spills down his face. He strikes back, moving like he's dancing, those long silver braids streaming out behind him. Tyler roars "Break it up!" and wades in, pulling one of the bleeding Terrans back. Never one to miss a brawl, Cat jumps in as Finian helps me to my feet.

"Well, it's nice to know station security are on the job," he says cheerfully.

The brawl dissolves into chaos, flying fists, and bilingual curses. The Syldrathi drops the last Terran with a flurry of strikes to his face, chest, groin, and as the guy falls, Tyler claps a hand on the taller boy's shoulder. It's a rare mistake on my baby brother's part—Syldrathi don't like to be touched without permission, as a general rule.

"Hey, ease up!"

Three things happen pretty much simultaneously here.

First up, the actual SecTeam finally arrives. They're kitted in tac armor and armed with stun batons—affectionately known as "sicksticks," since you tend to puke when you get shocked with one.

Second, the Syldrathi punches Ty right in the face. Ty's eyes widen in surprise, and he tackles the taller boy to the ground in retaliation. The pair go at it, the Syldrathi trying to knock Tyler out of his not-so-shiny boots, and my brother trying to lock him up while shouting "At ease! At ease, Maker's sake!"

And third, beneath the blood, I finally recognize the Syldrathi's face.

"Oh, this is not good," I whisper.

"I dunno," Finian smiles, first studying the Syldrathi, then taking a look at me. "Looks pretty good from here."

"Oh, *please*," I reply, rolling my eyes.

The SecTeam guys hit everyone moving with their sick-sticks. Copious vomiting ensues. As Cat protests, they start slapping combatants in mag-restraints. Finian doesn't move from my side, and Zila stands behind us, watching with a blank expression as the team gets ready to haul everyone off to the brig.

But holding my bruised ribs, I step forward with my best smile to defuse things. I didn't spend my diplomacy classes sleeping, after all.

(I took my afternoon nap in astrometrics instead.)

"Hey, Mr. Sanderson," I smile.

The SecTeam leader glances up from securing Tyler.

"I mean, *Lieutenant* Sanderson," I say, smiling wider.

"Well, well. Scarlett Jones. Should've known you'd be caught up in this."

"Are you implying I'm a troublemaker, Lieutenant?" I put a hand on my hip and pout. "Because I'm offended."

Relax, it's not what you're thinking.

And ew, by the way.

"How's Jaime doing?" I ask.

"He's good. Back on Terra with his mom."

(Jaime Sanderson. Ex-boyfriend #37. Pros: good kisser. Cons: likes jazz.)

"Tell him I said hi."

"Shall do."

"Um, so listen," I say, glancing at my brother, the carnage

around us. "None of this was Tyler's fault. He was trying to break it up. Do you need to lock him down?"

"Standard procedure." The lieutenant shrugs, back to business. "Security footage of the incident will be reviewed, and if what you say is true, Squad Leader Jones here will be out in time for dinner."

I give Lieutenant Sanderson my best pout. "But, Lieutenant—"

"It's okay, Scar," Tyler groans, trying to hold back his vomit. "I'll be fine."

The officers pull everyone to their feet, careful to avoid getting puke on their uniforms. The cadet with the broken arm is whimpering with pain, the guy whose soft parts got stomped on isn't even conscious. As Lieutenant Sanderson cuffs him, I see the Syldrathi's pretty face is glistening with dark purple blood. Tyler's blood is smudged on the Syldrathi's knuckles, bright red.

"That was a cheap shot," Tyler says to him.

The Syldrathi says nothing. His expression is ice-cold, and there's not a hair out of place on his head.

I glance between the pair, wondering if my smile looks as forced as it feels.

"Ummm . . . so this is awkward. . . ."

"Meaning what?" Tyler blinks.

I look pointedly at the Syldrathi. "Welllll . . ."

"No," Tyler says.

"Afraid so, Bee-bro."

"Nooooo."

"Squad Leader Tyler Jones," I say, glancing at my uni-glass, "may I present your combat specialist, Legionnaire

53

Kaliis Idraban Gilwraeth, firstson of Laeleth Iriltari Idraban Gilwraeth, adept of the Warbreed Cabal."

The Syldrathi glares at my brother with those amazing violet eyes.

Spits a mouthful of purple blood on the floor.

Speaks with a voice like melting chocolate.

"It is Kal for short."

4

ZILA

Hmm.

My current situation could be adequately described as . . .

. . . suboptimal.

5

AURI

Screaming.

Someone's screaming right near me.

My eyes flash open and I lurch upright, pulling my bedsheets with me.

There's a guy standing in the middle of my room. Glaring straight past me like he's trying to burn a hole in the wall. He has long silver hair tied back in five braids and seems around my age, but he kind of looks like something straight out of Middle-Earth central casting. Pointy ears like a freaking *elf*, beautiful violet eyes, stupidly tall and stupidly graceful. There's some kind of small tattoo on his forehead.

"*Cho'taa,*" he says. "*It has nothing to do with my blood.*"

"Uh, w-what?" I stammer, wincing inwardly as I stumble over just two syllables.

I hear a loud thump, the grinding screech of metal. A cold voice.

"*I will see you in the Void, Warbreed.*"

There's a flash of energy, violet like his eyes. The boy

cries out and falls. I feel something warm on my hands and look down to see they're covered in blood.

Purple blood.

I can feel a scream of horror building in my throat, but a beat later it all starts to fade. Dissolving the way my visions have been. And past the surging of my heart, the ice in my stomach, I realize that's exactly what he is—yet another vision of something I've never seen.

I stare at the spot where he stood, my pulse climbing down from the ceiling.

"What the hell . . ."

When are these visions going to stop?

Is my brain trying to recalibrate after what it went through?

I push my knuckles into my eyes to clear the image away, waiting for my heart to stop racing. Wondering if this is another symptom of being stuck so long in cryo.

Wondering if I'm losing it completely.

Looking around, I realize I'm in a different room from yesterday. My glass walls are gone. Now I have four gray ones, which make a nice match for the gray carpet and the gray ceiling. My new room is small, dim light coming from hidden fixtures where the walls meet the ceiling.

My memory's a patchwork of doctors coming and going, and somewhere in there is a meal that was surprisingly normal. Of course, that's the only normal thing I can really point to today. Because it's the *future*. And I'm two hundred years old. And I'm seeing things. And there are freaking aliens here, wherever *here* is.

I think I'd like to be unconscious again, please.

I'm lying in a bed, still tangled in soft white sheets, and

as I sit up, I find I feel a little better. My heart's still pounding, but I'm not dizzy, or fuzzy. And *score,* there are clothes waiting for me at the bottom of the bed, folded in a neat gray pile.

I lean toward them, and with a soft patter, two drops of red land on my perfectly white sheets.

Blood.

I touch my nose, bring my fingers away smudged with red. There's a mirror over a small sink in the corner, and I wobble over to it to clean up. There's blood smeared across my upper lip in a gross mustache, and . . .

. . . holy cake, what's happened to my *hair?*

The cut's still the same messy pixie as it's always been, but looking at my reflection, I can see there's a wide streak of white through my bangs. I run my fingers through it, wondering if maybe it's another symptom of my long-term cryo. Wondering if I'm sick. Maybe I should mention it to someone. Though I suppose it'll be a miracle if I get out of two centuries in suspended animation on a malfunctioning ship with nothing more than a bloody nose and a few white hairs.

Well, a bloody nose and a few white hairs and *hallucinations.*

I wash my face, then focus on getting dressed. I trade my white pajamas for what looks like a cross between a school uniform and some kind of sports gear. There's underwear, a bra that's a little optimistic given my assets, leggings, and a long-sleeved tunic with a logo I don't recognize on the chest.

I spot a pair of boots by the door, which is when I notice a small red light on a panel beside it. I allow myself a minute to wonder if that means it's locked and debate whether there's any value in confirming this.

Not really. Where would I go?

Up in the corner is a second red light, probably a camera. As I'm looking at it, there's a soft knock at the door, and when it slides open, it reveals Captain Hotness—the guy who rescued me from the *Hadfield*. He's in the same blue gray as me and my imaginary visitor from earlier, and he's got a faint bruise along his jawline, just a shadow. He's carrying a little red package with a bow on top, the only real spot of color in the room. Unless you count my blood, I mean.

It's the gift that makes me think he's probably another hallucination, because it's so out of place. At least no one's bleeding or screaming in this one, I guess. I wonder if I'll get to find out what he brought me before he fades away.

"Can I come in?" he asks.

When I don't answer, he makes his way to the end of the bed and sits, keeping a polite distance between us. I'm staring at him and he's staring back, looking a little bit worried. My heart's going *thud-thud-thud* in my throat, and I'm going to panic if I'm not careful.

The visions are getting more frequent, and more real.

". . . Are you okay?" he asks. "It's Tyler, remember?"

"I remember," I say. "Are you going to vanish, or what?"

His brows lift, and he looks over his shoulder toward the door, like he's checking if I'm talking to someone else. "Um, vanish?"

And that's when I realize the mattress is bending a little under his weight.

Wait, is he real?

I poke at his chest, encountering solid muscle. I yank my finger back, scrambling for an explanation and desperately hoping I got rid of every last trace of the creepy cannibal blood mustache.

"What the hell are you keeping under that shirt? Rocks?"

Oh, son of a biscuit, did I just say that out loud?

"I brought you a present," he says, saving me from myself, and holds out the package. "I figured you might be ready for something to break the monotony."

Peeling the wrapping away—the fact that he's gone to the trouble to wrap it makes the gesture extra sweet—I find a slim plate of tempered glass about the size of my palm, edges rounded.

I turn it over in my hands, then hold it up to the light to look through it. "I think I'm going to need an instruction manual," I admit.

"It's a uniglass. Portable computer, hooked into the station net," he says, holding out his hand for it. "I'm going to hold it up to your eye so it can register that you're its new user."

He lifts it level with my face, and I stare as a thin red line travels down its length. A message flashes to life in the same red on the glass.

Retina scan complete.

The thing lights up like someone dropped a match on a pile of fireworks. Holographic menus are projected to either side of it, data scrolls across the screen, displays spring to life and vanish again. I can see a list of offerings across the bottom of the glass plate.

DIRECTORY	STORAGE	NETWORK
MESSENGER	MAP	SCHEDULE

"Happy birthday." He grins, and heaven help me, those dimples of his should have their own fan sites. "I mean, I know today's not technically the date you were born, but I figured you deserved a present. Seeing as how you've missed a few."

My birthday.

My dad forgot to wish me a happy birthday.

That was the last thing I said to him. I basically told him he was the worst and hung up on him.

And now he's—

But I'm not ready to think about that yet—about what I've lost. On top of everything else that's happened, it's just too much. So I push the thought away, take the uniglass. I turn the device over to rest on one palm, and the displays flip so they're still facing me. I try pressing the lit-up section labeled MAP, because once a cartography nerd, always a cartography nerd.

A detailed holographic display flickers to life above the uniglass, showing several floors above and below me, my own location marked with a blinking red beacon. A little icon says DIRECTIONS?

The detail is amazing, and I'm left gawking. I saw prototypes of stuff like this when I went to trade shows with my father in Shanghai, but compared to this thing, they were tricycles alongside a Harley.

"Wow," I say. "Thank you."

The glass beeps at me three times, then speaks in a high-pitched, robotic voice. "YOU AIN'T SEEN NOTHING YET."

I nearly drop it, juggling wildly for a second, then grabbing hold of it with both hands. I only barely resist the urge to say, *Did that thing just speak to me?*

Auri, you're an ambassador for your whole century. Captain Hotness probably thinks you're a complete bumpkin. Get it together.

"This thing might be smarter than I am," I murmur.

"Aw, don't feel bad, boss. You're only human."

"I wasn't talking to you."

"I'm top-of-the-line, new-gen uniglass technology, available nowhere outside the academy," it shoots back. "I'm seventeen times smarter than him. And three times better-looking. You should be talking to me—"

"Silent mode," Tyler orders.

The uniglass falls quiet, and I look at the boy sitting on the end of my bed.

"It's my old unit," he explains with one of those killer smiles. "It only has access to info in the academy archives, but it's better than nothing."

"It's amazing," I say. "Do they all . . . talk at you like that?"

"Not like that, exactly. The older models came equipped with a 'persona' in the operating matrix. They don't do that anymore—the techs never got it right. So, fair warning, these models were a little buggy. And sort of . . . unrelentingly chirpy."

"I think we'll get along," I say. "I—I really appreciate it."

A kind gesture when you don't know anybody—it's water in the desert, I'm realizing. He chews his lip, a little uncertain.

"So, how are you doing with it all?" he asks.

I stare down at my uniglass, at the blinking box that says directions?

"I'm okay," I say eventually.

I'm deciding to focus on the physical, because I don't think we know each other well enough to go with *I'm scared and alone, and as if I don't have enough to deal with in reality, my brain's conjuring up its own version as well, and I'm having trouble telling them apart.*

That's more a third- or fourth-date disclosure, right?

"I feel a little weak," I say, sitting on the bed beside him. "Tired. I guess I was on the *Hadfield* so long, nobody really knows how I'm meant to be doing. I don't know if it's still dangerous, but back when we launched, we couldn't spend a long time in the Fold. You'd start hallucinating, get paranoid . . ."

I trail off, because of course hallucinating is *exactly* what I've been doing.

Is paranoia next?

"It's still dangerous," Tyler nods. "Though it turns out Fold travel affects young minds far less. Our technology is a little different from your day, too. Back when the *Hadfield* launched, humans could only travel through naturally occurring gates. Weak spots in the Fold. Now we can build our own entry and exit points anywhere we like. There's a big one right outside the station we're on, matter of fact."

"I saw . . ." I shake my head, remembering the sight of the station when I stormed out of my room. "So, if humans can go anywhere, where are we now?"

"That's kinda funny, actually," he says, nibbling his lip again.

". . . What do you mean?"

"You heard of a star system called Aurora?"

I blink. "Are you messing with me?"

"We're orbiting Gamma Aurorae, the third star in the cluster," he says, spreading his arms to take in the station around us. "Aurora O'Malley, welcome to Aurora Academy, training facility for the Aurora Legion."

". . . I have a legion now?"

He shrugs and gives me one of those smiles, and I swear, I don't know whether to be charmed, amazed, or completely freaked out right now.

"I went to sixteen different schools," I say. "There was always another girl in my class called Aurora. Now I have to share my name with a star?"

"Space academy, too."

I shake my head, find my thoughts drifting back to . . .

"My mom would have said it was fate."

"The Maker had an eye on you," Ty agrees.

I bite my lip. I have to keep looking for answers instead of more questions.

"So humans are on more than two planets now. And . . . we discovered aliens. I met one last night. I think she said she's in charge?"

"Yeah, that's Battle Leader de Stoy," he says. "She's Betraskan. Their homeworld is Trask in the Belinari system. They live mostly underground, and they don't process vitamin D like us, hence the lack of melanin and the contact lenses. Biologically, we're pretty similar, though. They were the first species humans ever made contact with. We were at war a couple of hundred years back, but they've been our strongest ally for generations."

I think of the boy who appeared in my vision. The hot, angry-looking one with the pointed ears, the long silver hair.

"Are there other, uh, species on the station? Maybe some with . . ." I can barely say it out loud, one finger lifting to touch the curve of my own ear. I'm going to sound like an idiot if I completely imagined him.

"Syldrathi." He nods, his smile gone completely. "We were at war with them for a couple of decades, too. Terra only struck a peace accord two years ago."

His hand lifts, fingers curling around the chain I can see around his neck. He tugs it free of his neckline—I don't even think he's doing it consciously—and I catch a glimpse of a ring before his fist swallows it up, squeezing tight.

He finds his smile again, though it's weak.

"But that's a history lesson you don't need right now. Point is, yeah, we've discovered a *lot* of other species. Some we get along with, some we don't."

"So what do you do here?"

I mean, I'm assuming the dimples aren't a full-time gig.

"I'm a legionnaire," he says. "There was a thing back in your day called the United Nations, right?"

I nod. "That's you?"

"More or less," he says. "We're the Aurora Legion. We're a coalition between Terrans—humans, you'd say—and Betraskans. Some Syldrathi joined us two years ago when our war ended. We're an independent peacekeeping legion. We mediate border conflicts, police neutral zones of space. I'd say we're humanitarian." His mouth quirks to a proper smile. "Except a lot of us aren't human."

"And something happened yesterday, with the cadets? I heard the nurses talking about squads?"

And just like that, I've killed his beautiful smile stone-dead.

Farewell, dimples. I miss you already.

"In our final year, we form squads," he says. "Six legionnaires, encompassing the six specialty streams here at the academy. Yesterday was this big annual event called the Draft. It's where the squads are formed."

"Big day. But you look like somebody ran over your cat."

I was trying to coax his smile into returning, and I sort of succeed.

"The Alphas pick their team members in the Draft, and those with the highest exam results get to pick first."

"Except you were rescuing me instead." My heart sinks as it all slots into place. "I'm sorry, Tyler."

He's quick to shake his head, his voice firm. "No. Don't be sorry. I did what any legionnaire would have done, and I'd do it again. I'm glad you're here, Aurora."

"Auri," I murmur.

"Auri," he echoes, softer.

And we're both quiet a moment, because I guess the whole rescuing thing creates some kind of bond between you, and we both jump a little more than we should when the door opens to admit a grumpy-looking nurse.

"That's it for today, Legionnaire Jones," she says.

Ty hesitates a moment, then comes to his feet. "Can I—"

"You can visit her tomorrow," says the nurse.

"I'm shipping out today, ma'am."

"You're leaving?" I blurt, quietly panicking.

"I'll be back, don't worry," he smiles. "But yeah, those humanitarian missions I told you about? My squad has its first briefing in twenty minutes."

"Then you'd best get moving, legionnaire," the nurse says.

Her tone is no-nonsense, her manner terse. So Tyler gives her a brisk salute, then hits me with those dimples one more time.

"I'll come see you as soon as we get back, okay?"

". . . Okay."

But somehow, it's really, really not.

And with a small, sad wave, Captain Hotness walks out the door.

The nurse fusses about me, poking and prodding with various instruments I don't recognize. I fold over the white sheets so she won't see the blood and take it to a whole new level.

As I wait her out, I remember I'm sitting on a space station, tens of thousands of light-years from Earth. Totally alone.

How did this become my life?

Why did I get another chance at life at all, when ten thousand other people aboard the *Hadfield* lost theirs?

The nurse finally leaves, and I find myself alone for real. My head's a mess, and now, without distractions, the reality of my situation's pushing to the fore.

Even if my parents recovered from my loss and lived long, wonderful lives, they've been dead for over a century. I'll never see them again.

I'll never see my sister, Callie, again either.

Everyone I knew is gone.

My home, my stuff.

I can hardly wrap my mind around it, and I push at the idea like I'm wiggling a loose tooth, trying to find the point at which it hurts. There are little twinges for the most ridiculous things. My running shoes. My trophies. The fact that two centuries later, I'll never find out what happened on my favorite series.

I look down at Tyler's present in the palm of my hand. A small, glowing prompt is pulsing on the screen.

PLEASE NAME YOUR DEVICE.

And after a little bit of thought, I type a single word in response.

MAGELLAN.

Because he was a pretty epic explorer . . . well, except the bit where he died horribly, far from home. Before that, though, did he ever see some stuff. And that's why I trained in exploration. Because I want to see *everything*.

Maybe now I will. And honestly, I could use some of Big M's mojo.

After a moment or two of processing, the device lights up and speaks.

"HELLO! NEED SOMETHING, BOSS?"

"Yeah." My mind's ticking over slowly. "Can you research things for me?"

"SAY THE WORD," it replies.

I know that once I've seen this, I won't be able to unsee it. But I know just as surely that I don't have a choice. Someone will tell me if I don't ask.

"The colony the *Hadfield* was headed for," I say slowly, remembering Battle Leader de Stoy had a different name for it. "Can you tell me about that?"

"NO PROBLEM," Magellan chirps, with a cheery little beep for punctuation. "LEI GONG COLONY, COMING RIGHT UP."

Yeah, that's what she called it. They must have changed the name. . . .

Magellan projects a 3-D solar system above his screen, the planets slowly orbiting the sun at the center. But I find myself frowning.

"Wait a minute, Magellan. That's not Octavia."

"No," it agrees. "It's Lei Gong."

"Okay, do you have an Octavia system in your database?" I say slowly.

Magellan throws a different solar system up above its screen, and this one is immediately familiar. I jab a finger at the third planet. "Zoom in on this one. Rotate."

And there it is. I see the familiar stretch of coastline, the spot inland, up the river, where the Butler settlement was founded. Where I was supposed to be.

"I don't want to rain on your parade," says Magellan, sounding completely cheerful about doing exactly that, "but there's never been a settlement on any planet in this system. It's under Interdiction."

". . . What's Interdiction?"

"It's a total ban on system entry. Interdicted systems represent a risk to at least twenty-five sentient species and are marked with a planetary warning beacon. The penalties for entering an interdicted zone are zero fun."

"But Octavia was fine," I protest.

"Nope," Magellan contradicts me. "The planet was deemed unsuitable for habitation by carbon-based life, and no colony was ever established. Can I interest you in more information on Lei Gong's imports and exports, or festival season?"

My gut clenches, but I make myself ask the question anyway.

"Can you search the colonial records for me? I want to know what happened to a Zhang Ji. Born 2125. He was my father."

The wait stretches forever, but in a way, it's far, far too soon when Magellan beeps, like it's clearing its throat before it gives an answer.

"THERE IS NO RECORD OF THAT NAME IN ANY TER-RAN COLONIAL DATABASE."

My throat's tight, and my breath's coming quick again.

Maybe this is just a mix-up?

But before I can press any further, there's a soft knock at the door, and it opens to admit the Betraskan woman, Battle Leader de Stoy. She's in a blue-gray uniform related to Ty's, though hers is far more formal.

"Good morning, Aurora," she says, closing the door. Her gaze flicks up to the camera but settles on me as she joins me on the bed. "I'm glad you're up and dressed. I see you've acquired a uniglass."

Magellan is smart enough to keep its sass to itself, and I set it aside on my pillow. "I did," I say, trying to marshal my most reasonable tone. If I let her hear my grief, let her think I'm not holding it together, she'll start treating me like a child. I don't want decisions made *for* me right now. I need to understand what's happening.

"And how are you feeling?"

"I'm okay," I manage.

"It's not unusual to feel side effects from prolonged exposure to the Fold." When our eyes lock, I find that blank gray

70

stare totally unnerving. "The effects can be serious, even on young minds. Your mood and memories may take time to settle."

Do I tell her about the nosebleed? That a chunk of my hair wasn't white before? About the hallucinations?

Why *aren't* I telling her?

I decide to start with a question instead. Feel out her willingness to be straight with me. "I was just trying to look up what . . ." My voice wavers, and I let it. "I was trying to look up what happened to my father. But our colony records seem to have been changed. And all records of my dad have been . . . lost."

Such a small word for such a big thing.

The silence before she replies is just a beat too long. "Is that so?"

"That's so," I agree. "Which is kind of upsetting, because I'd like to know how things turned out for the people I care about."

"Of course," she says. "We'll have someone look into it."

Total brush-off.

"*When* will someone look into it?" I press. "It isn't like these are old paper records you somehow lost. This stuff should be stored somewhere digitally, right?"

"I expect so," she agrees. "In the meantime, I have good news. The Terran government is sending a ship for you. Top priority, direct from the Global Intelligence Agency. Once their operatives arrive, they'll escort you home. It will be perfectly safe."

Safe? That's a weird reassurance to offer.
Why wouldn't it be safe?

And where is home, anyway? My house will be long gone—nobody I know is back on Earth. I don't know what home means anymore.

And that's when I realize she's twisted to sit with her back completely to the red camera light in the corner. And as she speaks, she's shaking her head—very slowly, almost imperceptibly.

As if she's contradicting her own words.

"R-right," I stammer, frustration fading away as a shiver goes through me. "So I should go with them?"

"Absolutely," she says, reaching for my hand. "The GIA operatives will be here soon. I'm sure you'll be more comfortable on your birth planet."

When she withdraws her hand, there's a tiny slip of paper in the palm of mine. I make a fist around it.

"Got it," I say, my heart beating a mile a minute. She's warning me, that much I know. But against what? What should I do instead?

"It's been good to meet you," she says, pushing to her feet. "Good luck, Aurora O'Malley. I mean that sincerely."

And with military precision, I'm dismissed. She turns for the door, and I sweep Magellan off my pillow and let myself fall back onto the bed, trying to keep it natural as I curl up on my side, back to the camera.

I make myself lie still as I count to thirty, and then, carefully, I check the slip of paper hidden in my hand. There's a message written on it.

Docking Port 4513-C. Passcode: 77981-002.

I glance at Magellan. The menu still glowing across the bottom.

MAP.

DIRECTIONS?

I curl my hand around the paper again, glancing across at the door. And that's when I realize the little light on the lock isn't glowing red anymore.

It's switched to green.

I'm being lied to, and I don't know who to trust. But I have one source of information I can try.

"Magellan?"

"HEY, BOSS, I MISSED YOU TOO! WHAT'S UP?"

"I want you to tell me everything you know about this station I'm on. Start with the basics."

And as it begins talking, I'm already heading out the door.

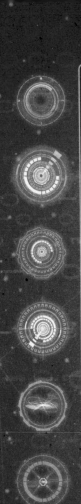

AURORA LEGION SQUADS

▶ **SQUAD MEMBERS**

▼ **STREAMS**

IN THEIR THIRD YEAR, CADETS SEPARATE INTO STREAMS AND TRAIN FOR THE FOLLOWING ROLES WITHIN SIX-MEMBER SQUADS, WHICH CAN BE DEPLOYED ANYWHERE IN THE GALAXY AT A MOMENT'S NOTICE. THEIR VERSATILITY MEANS THERE'S NO CHALLENGE AN AURORA LEGION SQUAD CAN'T CONQUER.

ALPHAS: RESPONSIBLE FOR LEADERSHIP AND PLANNING

FACES: RESPONSIBLE FOR DIPLOMACY AND NEGOTIATION

ACES: RESPONSIBLE FOR PILOTING AND TRANSPORT

GEARHEADS: RESPONSIBLE FOR REPAIRS, MAINTENANCE, AND MECHANICAL WORK

TANKS: RESPONSIBLE FOR TACTICAL COMBAT AND ENGAGEMENT STRATEGY

BRAINS: RESPONSIBLE FOR SCIENTIFIC AND MEDICAL DUTIES

6

CAT

"Join Aurora Academy, they said. . . ."

"Cat . . . ," Tyler warns.

"See the 'Way, they said. . . ."

"Cat."

We're sitting on the bridge of our brand-new Longbow with our brand-new squad in our brand-new flight gear. Our seats face each other around a broad circular console, studded with glowing controls and monitors. The holographic display floating above the console is currently showing the view from our forward cams: the long run down the launch tube to a small spot of black beyond.

Scarlett and Finian are across from me. Zila and our new Syldrathi combat specialist are to my right. Kaliis Whatchamacallit, firstson of Laeleth Something-Something, has some nice bruises from yesterday's brawl, and a nice smoldering glare in those purple eyes of his. He hasn't spoken since we bailed him out of the brig this morning. Zila hasn't squeaked either, come to think of it.

Well, at least they're bloody quiet.

From my seat at main control, I glance to the copilot's chair on my left. Tyler's studying his displays. His hair is tousled and his eyes are blue as oceans, and the scar I gave him when we were kids cuts through one brow. And even though he looks as tired as I've ever seen him, Maker, help me, I can't stop the butterflies in my—

"Preflight check complete," he reports. "Take us out, Legionnaire Brannock."

"Sir, could I just say this is a complete waste of our bloody time, sir?" I ask.

Finian looks up from his displays, blinks at Tyler with blank black eyes.

"I find myself agreeing with the short annoying one," he says. "Sir."

"Nobody's talking to you, Finian," I growl.

"Funny, I get that a lot."

I'm still glaring at Tyler, all my frustration at this jank squad and this jank mission boiling in my chest. After five years of academy training, all the hours, all the hard work, we were given our first assignment this morning, and it's turned out to be a bloody *supply run*. I can't believe it. I'm the best pilot in the academy, and I've been relegated to nothing but a damn courier. An automated drone could do this job for us. Tyler knows it. I know it. Everyone on the damn ship knows it.

But our Alpha just stares back at me, all business.

"Orders are orders," he says. "This is what we signed up for."

"Speak for yourself," I say. "I didn't slog my guts out for five years so I could lug med supplies to a couple of refugees in the arse end of the bloody galaxy."

"Color me confounded," Finian says. "But again, I find myself agree—"

"Shut up, Finian."

"Look, this is the job," Tyler says, looking around the bridge. "I know we all hoped for more, but we can't expect to save the whole Milky Way on our first trip out. It may not be the most high-profile mission, but these people need our help."

"And I get that, sir," I say. "But you don't think there's a better way for the Aurora Legion to utilize my highly trained, supremely skilled, and totally spankable tail section than as a glorified delivery girl?"

Scarlett grins. "It *does* seem a shameful misappropriation of Legion resources."

My eyes are still locked on Tyler's.

"I could've had any squad I wanted, you know that, right?"

"And I love you for sticking with me, you know that, right?" he replies.

Hmm.

There's that word.

Pretending not to hear it, I reach into my flight jacket, pull out Shamrock, and prop him beside my displays. His fur is soft and green, and stuffing is leaking from a split in his stitching. I should get around to fixing him. . . .

"What's that supposed to be?" Finian asks.

"It's a dragon," I reply. "Present from my mum. He's for luck."

"It's a stuffed toy, how is it supp—"

"Shut *up*, Finian."

". . . Okay, are you hitting on me? It feels like you might be hitting on me."

"I'll be hitting on your face in a minute, you fu—"

"Legionnaire de Seel, can it," Tyler says smoothly. "Again, Legionnaire Brannock, preflight check is complete. Pretty please with sugar on top, would you be so kind as to take us out now, thank you."

I glance at Ty and he raises that scarred eyebrow and his lips curl in that infuriating lady-killer smile, and dammit, I realize mine are doing the same.

"I'll be your best friend?" he offers.

And just like that, my smile falls away. I exchange a glance with Scar, then turn to the console and stab in my commands. Our Longbow purrs like a new kitten and the vibration of her engines shakes us in our seats, and for a moment it's easy to forget the impulse to punch those dimples right off Ty's face.

My arse, this is what we signed up for.

I tap my throat mic. "Aurora Control, this is Squad 312, requesting permission to launch, over."

"Permission granted, 312. Good hunting, over."

I glance over my console to the members of my squad.

"Right, hold on to your undies, kids."

Our thrusters fire, pushing us back hard into our seats. The walls of the launch tube rush past us and the beautiful black opens up in front of us, glittering with tiny pinpricks of white. And all of a sudden, it doesn't matter that I'm on this jank mission with this jank squad, doing a job a trained gremp could do. Because I'm home.

Sailing out from Aurora's arms, I look into my aft-view monitors. They show another dozen Longbows, silver and arrowhead shaped, rocketing through the dark. I can see the academy in all her glory: a cityport of smooth domes and twinkling lights and impossible shapes, floating on nothing at all. The g-force from our thrust keeps the weightlessness away, but I can feel it anyway, just outside our Longbow's skin.

The big empty.

The place where I'm the best at what I do.

"Squad 312, gate beacon has you locked. You are cleared for Fold entry."

"Roger that, Aurora. Pour me a shot, I'll be back for last call."

My fingers flit over the controls, guiding us toward the huge hexagon floating off the academy's shoulder. I can see the Fold waiting inside the gate's flashing pylons—that beautiful swath of black, punctured by a billion tiny stars. Speeding toward it, I'm lost in the moment. Feeling the ship beneath me, around me, inside me. Slicing the empty like a knife.

"Course programmed," Tyler reports. "Feeding to navcom."

His voice brings me back to reality. I remember who we are.

Where we're going.

Where we've been.

I'll be your best friend?

We push past the gate's horizon and into the colorless sea of the Fold. The ship shudders as the impossibility of distance becomes meaningless.

The colorscape around us shifts to black and white. Signal beacons light up my scopes—thousands of FoldGates blinking out there in the brightness. Like a room full of hexagonal doors, with a new sun behind every one. A 3-D map flickers to life on the central console above our stations. Tiny readouts, scrolling data, a small pulse indicating our current position.

"Horizon's clear," I report. "No FoldStorm activity. Should be smooth sailing to Juno. Navcom is estimating . . . six hours, twenty-three minutes."

"Roger that. Walk in the park."

Tyler unbuckles his safety harness and stands, stowing his flight jacket behind the copilot seat. His T-shirt sleeve isn't long enough to cover the tattoo of the academy's Alpha Division on the swell of his right bicep. Along with my full sleeves of dragons and butterflies, and the hawk across my back and the phoenix across my throat (yes, it bloody hurt), I have a similar tatt to Ty's.

Mine is the Pilot Division sigil, of course. But we got them in the same place. Same time.

I find myself thinking about the night I convinced Tyler to get inked with me. Shore leave on Cohen IV. The last time I ever saw him have a drink. The pain of the fresh design on our arms and the liquor in our veins and the thrill of graduating into our final year crackling in the air. Just you and me, Tyler. Staring at each other across that barroom table and all those empty glasses.

Best friends forever, right?

The colors around us are monochrome, because that's just how it goes in the Fold. Tyler's once-blue irises have turned to gray, and he's staring at the main viewscreen with a totally weird expression.

Probably thinking about the last time he was in here.

That girl he found, floating in all this nothing.

She was a pretty one, too. . . .

"All right, let's go over the mission again," he says.

Finian sighs, his exosuit whispering as he massages his temples. "We've been over it already, sir. That's what our briefing this morning was for, right?"

Tyler glances at Pixieboy. "Legionnaire Gilwraeth was incarcerated by academy security during that briefing, so I thought we could run over it again."

"Well, do the rest of us have to hear it? Sir?"

I fold my arms and glare. "Are you, like, a professional arsehole or . . . ?"

"More a hobbyist," Finian replies. "Hoping to go pro next season."

He's smirking, waiting to see what I'll lob back over the net. Skin already white and eyes already black, Finian's the only one of us unchanged by the Fold. I keep a lid on it, but deep down, I'm just as frustrated as our new Gearhead is. I heard Ketchett's squad got sent to Beta Fushicho to eliminate a pirate fleet. Troile's squad landed a sweet detail escorting ambassadors to the Sentanni peace talks. For an Alpha with the grades Tyler got, this mission is nowhere. This squad is nothing. But again, and as always, he keeps it professional. He's good like that.

Except when it comes to the pretty ones.

"We have six hours and twenty-two minutes till our destination, Legionnaire de Seel," Tyler says flatly. "You can spend it scrubbing the latrine floor until you can see your face in it, or you can spend it going over our mission. Up to you."

The Betraskan purses his lips in thought. "Well, if you put it like that . . ."

"I do."

Tyler taps a series of commands into his console, and the miniature map of the Fold is replaced by a hologram of a big lump of rock, floating in a sea of other big lumps of rock. It's an asteroid. The ugly mother of all asteroids.

A glance at the specs tells me it's about a thousand klicks across, hollowed and pitted like wormy fruit. I can see the domes and pylons of a large factory, clinging to its side like a barnacle.

"This is Sagan Station in the Juno system," Tyler says. "It was an ore-processing rig, owned by the now-defunct Jupiter Mining Corporation, abandoned in 2263. Since the Syldrathi civil war broke out twelve months ago, Sagan has seen an influx of refugees from Syldrathi space, who've claimed the abandoned facilities as their own. AL Command now estimates the population at seven thousand."

I'm watching our new Syldrathi squaddie while Tyler talks, but Pixieboy has a good poker face. His stare is piercing, cold. He's radiating that traditional Syldrathi aloofness. That "I'm-better-than-you-and-that's-just-Science" attitude. But there's not a silver hair out of place on his head, his face is like a model from a fashion zine, and even with the bruises from his brawl, I've gotta agree with Scar. You wouldn't kick him out of bed for snoring.

"The Juno star is situated in a neutral zone," Tyler continues. "With the Terran and Betraskan governments still refusing to accept Syldrathi refugees, their welfare is the Aurora Legion's responsibility."

"Which I don't understand," Scarlett says.

"We're a neutral relief organization, Scar, we're sup—"

"Yes, thank you, Bee-bro." Scar rolls her eyes. "I know what the AL is. What I mean is, I don't understand why the Terran and Betraskan governments won't open their borders and *help* these people. Their home system has been decimated by one of their own Archons. Why are Terra and Trask leaving them out in the cold?"

"This is wartime." Finian shrugs. "If they open their borders up, who's to say some of the refugees they let in won't be a danger themselves?"

"That's such crap, Finian," I growl.

"I'm not saying I *agree*, I'm just telling you what they're thinking."

"So we just leave these poor people out here to rot?" Scarlett asks.

"Obviously not," Tyler says. "We've got a cargo bay full of medtech for them."

Scar starts sniping at her brother about that being no better, and Finian weighs in with his two cents, and the bridge devolves into brief chaos before a deep, warm voice cuts through the clamor.

"They fear."

Silence falls, and all eyes turn to Kaliis Thingywhatsit, firstson of . . . Whoever.

"Your governments," he says. "They fear the Starslayer."

That brings quiet to the bridge. We all glance at each other, unnerved. As if saying the name has somehow given it even more power.

"They are right to fear," he continues. "The Starslayer has declared all free Syldrathi his enemies. And those who offer them refuge become his enemies also."

Tyler stares at Kal, and even our illustrious leader looks a little uneasy. "Since you weren't there for our briefing, Legionnaire Gilwraeth, maybe you'd be so kind as to give us your insight now. These are your people we're bringing aid to. What can you tell us?"

"I would have thought you well acquainted with Syldrathi, sir," Kal replies, his voice smooth as silk. "Given the fate that befell your father."

Scarlett's eyes narrow at that. Tyler's voice draws tight.

"And what do you think you know about my father, Legionnaire Gilwraeth?"

"That he was a war hero. A senator who argued for peace with my people long before peace ever came. And that he died fighting them in the Orion Incursion."

"Remember Orion," I say softly, touching the Maker's mark at my collar. Across the table, I see Finian mirror the movement.

"Del'nai," Kal replies, scoping me with those glittering eyes.

"I don't speak Syldrathi, Pixieboy," I mutter.

"It means 'always,'" Scarlett says. "'Ever and always.'"

Pixieboy inclines his head to Scar, looks back to Tyler. "I know of the great Jericho Jones. I know how he died. So you have my apologies, sir. I imagine the presence of a Syldrathi in your squad is . . . unwelcome."

"Is that the kind of person I seem to you?" Tyler responds. "The kind who decides to hate an entire species because one of them killed his old man?"

"Given the particulars of the Orion attacks, I imagine most people would have difficulty with it, yes."

Tyler stares into Pixieboy's eyes. "Well, it's a good thing for you I'm not most people."

Kal holds Tyler's stare, that infuriating arrogance radiating off him in waves. I know Syldrathi can live for a couple of centuries if you let them, and even though Kal is only nineteen, he looks at us like we're some passing irritation. Here today and gone tomorrow. I can see the mark of his sucker punch on Tyler's jaw. The bruises and cuts from his brawl with those cadets yesterday.

All of them Terran. Four on one, and he kicked the living crap out of them.

Remember Orion. . . .

Kal finally nods to the holograph of Sagan Station.

"Syldrathi are a proud people," he says. "The refugees will be suspicious of our presence. They will not want our aid and will not trust us easily."

Tyler glances at his sister. "Well, Scar speaks fluent Syldrathi. Between you and her, I have every confidence you can convince them we're only here to help."

Kal blinks. "You cannot mean to send me aboard?"

"Why wouldn't I?"

Pixieboy points to the small tattoo on his brow. Three crossed blades.

"I assume you know what this is, sir."

"A glyf," Tyler nods. "It denotes which of the five Syldrathi cabals you belong to."

Kal nods. "And this is the glyf of the Warbreed Cabal."

"So?"

"Why do you think I was the last cadet to be picked in the Draft? Why do you think not even other Syldrathi wanted me

85

in their squads?" Kal looks around at the rest of us, answering his own question. "Because the Starslayer is Warbreed. And his Templars are Warbreed. And his Paladins are Warbr—"

"Not every Syldrathi in the warrior cabal joined the Starslayer," Tyler said. "Not all of you are responsible for his crimes."

Kal looks at Ty with clear disdain. "And I am certain the starving, desperate spirits aboard that station will be all too ready to have a *Terran* explain that to them."

"Um, excuse me." Finian raises his hand, looking at Pixie-boy. "But between me and Red over there, I think this squad already has its sarcasm quota filled."

"Right." Scarlett smiles sweetly at Kal. "And *I'm* the Face of this outfit. So maybe stick to punching things until they fall down? You seem good at that."

Scar looks to her brother and nods.

"We'll make it work, sir."

"Right," Tyler says. "The Starslayer's fleets are hunting any Syldrathi who haven't sworn to his new universal order. But a blip as small as Sagan is probably too unimportant to get anyone's attention, which I presume is why the refugees are hiding there. The odds of any interference with our mission are low."

"Approximately eight thousand seven hundred and twenty-five to one."

We all stop, surprised to hear Zila speak. I'd almost forgotten she was on the bridge, to be honest. She's sitting at her station, sucking on a lock of curly black hair, her dark brown skin illuminated by the displays as her fingertips fly over the keyboards.

"Eight thousand seven hundred and twenty-five to one?" I repeat.

"Approximately," she replies, not looking up.

"How'd you figure that out?" Finian asks.

Zila cocks a finger, points at her head. "With my brain."

Tyler clears his throat in the uncomfortable silence that follows.

"Okay," he finally says. "Regardless, I want you all on high alert. This is our first opportunity to prove our worth. So if you're of the opinion that you're more than just a glorified courier"—Ty glances at me—"now's your chance to step up. Our governments might be afraid of getting the Starslayer offside, but we're the Aurora Legion. We don't bow to tyrants, and we don't back down from a fight."

Even with the colors in monochrome, I can see the fire in Tyler's eyes. There's a passion in his voice that raises goose bumps on my skin. For all the griping, all the crap, listening to him speak, I remember why he was the top-ranked Alpha in our year. I remember why, staring at each other across that barroom table and all those empty glasses, I thought we might've had a chance.

"Squad 312, this is Aurora Flight Control, over."

I tap my comms to reply. "This is Squad 312, over."

"I have Aurora Command here for your Alpha, 312, over."

I blink at that. Frown at Tyler as he taps the Receive button on his console.

"This is Legionnaire Jones."

A holograph of Battle Leader de Stoy materializes above our displays. She's in full dress uniform, hair drawn back in a harsh ponytail. I can see Admiral Adams standing beside her, also in dress, cybernetic arms folded over his barrel-broad, medal-studded chest, washed black and white and gray by the Fold.

Adams and Ty go way back. He and Ty's dad were best friends back during their pilot days in the Terran Defense Force. Adams took Ty and Scar under his wing when their old man was killed. He and Ty go to chapel together every weekend, and Adams has always shown Tyler a little more attention than other cadets.

But still, I look into my Alpha's eyes and see he's just as confused as me.

"*Good morning, legionnaires.*" Adams salutes.

We salute back and murmur our good mornings as de Stoy speaks.

"*We wanted to wish you and your squad good hunting, Legionnaire Jones.*"

"Thank you, ma'am," Tyler replies.

"*This is your first step onto a much bigger stage,*" Adams says. "*The challenges that await you may be unlike any you've imagined. But we have every faith in your ability to see it through. No matter what may come. You must endure.*" Adams looks directly at Ty as he speaks. "*You must believe, Tyler.*"

This is just weird. No matter how tight Adams and Ty might be, the senior brass don't directly brief grunts like us. We're so far down the chain of command we're practically invisible, and this mission counts for nothing at all. But here's *both* academy commanders addressing us like we're a First Class squad on a top-tier gig.

And then Adams looks directly at me, speaking the academy motto.

"We the Legion. We the light. Burning bright against the night."

". . . Yessir," I reply.

"Burn bright, legionnaires," de Stoy says. *"The cargo you carry is more precious than any of you can know."*

"Maker be with you." Adams nods.

"Um . . . ," Tyler says. "Thank you, sir. Ma'am."

Their images hang there a moment longer, like they're trying to burn us into memory. I wonder what the hells is going on. But with a final salute, the projections fade, replaced with the rotating projection of Sagan Station. We're all staring at the place our commanders were a moment before, a little dumbfounded. And into the quiet, Zila Madran speaks a single word that sums all our feelings up spot-on.

"Odd . . ."

Tyler drags his hair back from his eyes, takes a seat. He's all business once again, though I know he has to be asking himself the same questions I am.

"Right," he says, leaning down to rub an imaginary scuff off his immaculate boot. "Kal, I want strategies if we come across hostile Syldrathi out there. Scar, I want diplomacy options with the refugees. Zila and Finian, you're studying Sagan's systems. We have six hours. Let's get to work."

"What about me?" I ask.

Tyler glances at me and raises that scarred eyebrow and his lips curl in that infuriating bloody smile.

"Keep us flying, Zero."

Just you and me, Tyler.

Staring at each other across that barroom table and all those empty glasses.

We'd known each other since we were five years old.

I turn to my controls and plug in our course.

"Yessir," I sigh.

Best friends forever, right?

AURORA LEGION SQUADS
▶ **SQUAD MEMBERS**
  ▼ **TANKS**

THEY'RE BIG, THEY'RE BAD, AND THEY'LL HIT YOU WHERE IT HURTS MOST. TANKS ARE THE MEMBERS OF **AURORA LEGION (AL) SQUADS** TRAINED TO BRING THE PAIN, AND I SUSPECT A DISTURBING PERCENTAGE OF THEM ENJOY IT.

TANKS SPEND ENDLESS HOURS IN GYMS, DOJOS, AND FIRING RANGES, HONING THEMSELVES TO PHYSICAL PERFECTION. GIVEN THE OPTION, THEY'LL SHOOT FIRST AND LET THEIR **FACE** ASK QUESTIONS LATER.

TANKS ARE SPECIALISTS IN **MARTIAL ARTS** AND ARE REQUIRED TO MASTER FIGHTING UNDER VARIED GRAVITY AND PLANETARY CONDITIONS. BENEFICIAL TRAITS INCLUDE DETAILED KNOWLEDGE OF **MULTI-SPECIES ANATOMY**, A TOLERANCE FOR PAIN, AND A RECREATIONAL INTEREST IN HURTING **SMALL FLUFFY THINGS**.

TANK'S INSIGNIA

7

KAL

The song is always the same.

It is two hours since we returned to realspace through the decrepit FoldGate near Sagan Station. Ninety minutes since the Syldrathi refugees aboard began negotiations. One minute since Scarlett Jones finally broke the news that a member of the Warbreed Cabal was present aboard our ship. Ten seconds since Sagan's defense grid locked missiles on us.

Humans are such fools.

Well-meaning fools, sometimes.

But fools, always.

". . . And I respect that, sir," Scarlett Jones is saying, trying to ignore the large MISSILE LOCK flashing on our displays. "But Legionnaire Gilwraeth is our combat specialist. If we're to fully examine your defenses—"

"No member of the Warbreed Cabal will set foot upon this station while I am First Walker!" comes the reply. *"By the spirits of the Void, I vow it!"*

I study the holographic projection Scarlett is speaking to.

Taneth Lirael Ammar is an elder—at least two centuries old by the look. His skin is marred by faint wrinkles, and the silver sheen in his hair is darkened by age, swept back from the small sigil of the Waywalker Cabal etched on his brow. The glyf reminds me of my mother. How far I am from home.

What is left of it, anyway.

It is often said among other races that we Syldrathi are arrogant and aloof. That we hide our feelings behind walls of ice and stares of stone. But still, Taneth is clearly outraged at my presence. His violet eyes flash as he speaks, and a faint flush of anger shows at the tips of his tapered ears.

Tyler Jones raises his hands in supplication, trying to calm him. "First Taneth, Legionnaire Gilwraeth is a member of the Aurora Legion, and I can—"

"He is Warbreed!" Taneth glowers. *"He is not welcome here!"*

I look at my squad leader and bite down on the words *I told you thus.*

It has been two years since the war between Syldra and Terra ended. Twenty months since I tried to forge a new future as a member of the Aurora Legion, despite my mother's protests. I have studied among the Terrans. Lived and worked and fought among them. And I still do not understand them.

They are like children. The youngest race among the galactic milieu. Oblivious in their righteousness. Firmly convinced that any problem can be solved with enough faith or good hard work or, when all else fails, bullets.

But they have not seen their sun die. Their people burn. Their world end. And they do not know, yet, that there are some breaks that cannot be fixed.

"Maybe there's a compromise?" Scarlett Jones suggests to Taneth, running one hand through her flame-colored hair. "If you're willing to let Legionnaire Gilwraeth into the cargo bay, he can deliver the medical supplies while the rest of us see to Sagan's onboard systems?"

Hmm.

I look at the human who would speak for me.

A wise one.

First Taneth remains silent, stroking his brow in thought.

"Honestly, sir, the faster we work, the sooner we'll be out of your business," Tyler Jones assures him. "I give you my word, Legionnaire Gilwraeth will follow all AL protocols while aboard Sagan Station."

I look at the human who would be my leader, eyes narrowed.

A trusting one.

Despite our diplomat's assurances, I still do not believe Taneth will agree. Syldrathi are a noble and ancient people. The warriors who followed the Starslayer, who refused to accept peace with the Terrans, named themselves the Unbroken in their hubris. Even those of us who accepted the peace still felt our pride stung by the treaty. Though we Syldrathi are fallen far from what once we were, we do not accept charity from others. Especially not those who made their first stumbling steps into the Fold only a few hundred years ago.

And so I am surprised when Taneth purses his lips and bows his acquiescence. Looking at the shadows under his eyes, the desperation on his face, I realize their situation must be more dire than I imagine.

All is not as it seems here.

. . . . .

Our Longbow's airlock hisses open, and I immediately taste stale oxygen and old sweat. Faulty lighting flickers in the cargo bay, and I see half a dozen Syldrathi waiting for us. They wear traditional robes, glyfs of the Waywalker Cabal etched in the flowing fabric, Void crystals strung on silver glass about their necks. They are tall and graceful. But thin. Haggard. Many have centuries behind their stares, and aside from a psi-blade at the waist of their youngest, none are armed.

Physical contact is an intimacy among my people. Syldrathi do not touch strangers, but I know it is custom among Terrans to shake hands upon meeting others. And so I am surprised when Scarlett Jones walks forward to Taneth, raising her fingers to her eyes, then her lips, then her heart in perfect greeting.

The First Walker repeats the gesture with a small, puzzled smile, obviously pleased to see a Terran so well versed in our ways.

Scarlett Jones introduces the other members of our squad. "Tyler Jones, our commander. Zila Madran, science officer. Finian de Seel, engineer. Catherine Brannock, pilot. And finally, Kaliis Idraban Gilwraeth, combat specialist."

One by one, the Syldrathi close their eyes and turn their backs on me, until only Taneth remains facing us. And he does not spare me a glance.

"The five of you are welcome here," he declares to the others. "Though we do not ask it, we will gratefully receive any assistance the Aurora Legion offers."

Tyler Jones looks about the cargo bay, notes the fluctuating power, the wires and circuitry spilling from tears in the walls, the staleness of the air. He sees their plight as swiftly as I do. This station was abandoned by its original owners years ago, and without money and maintenance, it is falling apart. The people here are in obvious need. But still, a part of me is saddened to see those of my race lunge so eagerly for help. To prostrate themselves like beggars before children.

Once we walked the dark between the stars, unequaled.

What have we become?

"Where are the rest of your people?" Tyler asks.

Taneth blinks. "The rest?"

"Legion Command told us there were close to seven thousand refugees here."

"We are a hundred at most, young Terran."

Tyler Jones shares an uneasy glance with his sister. Zila Madran simply blinks, like an automaton storing data for later inquiry. Finian de Seel has the same question in his large black eyes as Cat Brannock does. As I do.

Why travel so very far, risk so much, for so few?

"Do you have a command and control center?" Tyler Jones asks. "We need a better look at your systems so we can prioritize repairs."

"And a chapel maybe?" our Ace mutters, peering about the bay. "So we can ask the Maker what the hells we're doing here?"

"We have a central control," Taneth nods. "Please, follow me."

He turns to the youngest among them—the female with the psi-blade at her belt. "Aedra, please oversee the delivery of the medical supplies. And watch"—a glance at me—"*that.* Carefully."

The female glares at me with cold violet eyes. She replies in our own tongue. "Your voice, my hands, First Taneth."

Tyler Jones looks at me with one eyebrow raised in question. I bow in reply, assuring him all will be well. My squad accompanies the Waywalkers into an elevator that looks older than Taneth, and twice as decrepit.

"You kids play nice, now," Finian de Seel smiles.

The elevator rises slowly to the upper levels, clunking as it goes. It shudders to a brief stop for no apparent reason, and our Gearhead thumps the control panel to get it moving again. Finally, my squad disappears from sight.

I find myself alone with the female.

She is tall, willowy. Her skin is tanned, her hair silver, tied back from her brow and spilling in gleaming waves over her shoulders. Now that we are out of sight of the Terrans, she allows her disdain for me to show more openly, curling her lip, hatred glittering in her eyes. I know she is scanning me telepathically—my mother was also of the Waywalker Cabal, and she taught me the signs. I can feel the gentle press of Aedra's mind on my own as she skims my surface thoughts.

I glance down to the hand on her psi-blade, see the glyf encircling her forefinger. She seems young to have answered the Pull. And yet, from the single teardrop inside the circle, I know her lifelove has already died and returned to the Void.

"May the spirits guide him home," I offer.

She moves. Swift as a sunbeam. An arc of energy springs from her psi-blade's hilt—mauve, crackling, reflected in her eyes as she raises it to my throat.

Something surges inside me as she brandishes her weapon.

The call in my blood.

The Enemy Within.

But I push him back. Forcing myself to be calm.

"You may have deceived those childlings you call your comrades," she growls, "but I see your soul. You are born to brutality. Drenched in the blood of our homeworld. You and all your wretched kin."

I know this song. Every Syldrathi cadet at the academy sang it. Every Syldrathi I have met since our star was burned to ashes. The glyf at my brow tells them who I am before ever I have a chance to speak. But I speak anyway, hoping the tune will be different this time.

"The Unbroken are no kin to me," I say. "The Starslayer betrayed us all when he destroyed our homeworld. I bleed as badly as you."

"Not yet, Warbreed," she spits. "But speak to me again, and you shall."

I look into her eyes, fighting the urge to meet rage with more rage. To succumb to what I was raised to be. The call is so strong, the anger so real, it feels like a flame in my chest. Threatening to burn me alive. Screaming for release.

Instead, I bow slowly, my palms upturned. Slower still, she lowers her blade. And turning to the Longbow's airlock behind me, I clomp inside, busying myself with unloading our medical supplies.

I do not blame her for hating me.

I try to speak every time.

But the song is always the same.

. . . . .

"Kal, this is Tyler, do you read?"

The voice crackles from my uniglass as I step back into the cargo bay for the fifty-third time, placing the med container on the loading ramp with a thud. The containers are large, almost too heavy for me to carry. The work would pass twice as swiftly if Aedra would deign to help me, but she simply follows as I work, one hand on her psi-blade's hilt, eyes on me at all times.

"I read, sir."

"How's it going down there?"

I glance at Aedra, who is studying the wall and trying to appear as though she is not listening to my every word. Her lip curls to hear me call a Terran "sir."

"Slowly," I reply.

"Well, take your time, we're gonna be a while. Zila is getting life support back up to speed. Finian and Cat are checking defenses."

Cat Brannock scoffs on her channel. *"Such as they are."*

"It's not exactly state of the art down here," Finian de Seel agrees. *"Their missile grid has been cobbled together from the skiffs they flew here in, so the good news is they probably couldn't have shot us down even if they wanted to. But that's also the bad news. Short-range scanners should be back online any second, though."*

"I will be finished unloading the supplies within the hour," I say.

"Roger that," my Alpha replies. *"Anything you need in the meantime, sing out."*

"I would like to ask a question, sir."

Scarlett Jones pipes in. *"Is it the one about where babies come from?"*

"No."

"Someone's going to have to explain it to you sooner or later, Spunky. . . ."

I suppose she is trying to be funny.

"Since Syldra's destruction, there are millions of Syldrathi refugees scattered over the galaxy. All of them in need. All without home or succor."

"I'm not hearing a question, legionnaire," Tyler Jones says.

"Of all the places they could send us, why would Legion Command choose here? A derelict station in a nowhere system, with only a hundred people aboard?"

I can tell from the silence over the feed that my comrades were all asking themselves the same question. We may be the dregs of Aurora Academy. Most of us are in this squad because nobody else would have us. But it seems we are being punished for something we haven't done yet.

"I don't know, Legionnaire Gilwraeth," comes our Alpha's reply. *"But I do know you and I swore an oath when we joined the Legion. To help the helpless. To defend the defenseless. And even though the—"*

"Um, sir?" Finian de Seel says. *"We might have a problem."*

"You mean aside from you interrupting my speech? Because I'd been practicing it in my head for an hour and it was gonna be great."

"And I can't tell you how distressed I am about that, sir, but I got scanners online as promised, and you know how Legionnaire Madran and her brain told us the odds of the

Unbroken stumbling across us out here were eight thousand to one?"

"Eight thousand seven hundred and twenty-five," Zila Madran corrects. *"Approximately."*

"Well, maybe 'approximately' means something different on Terra, because a Syldrathi war cruiser just dropped in from the FoldGate. Fully armed. Wraith-class. They're flying Unbroken colors. And they're headed this way."

Aedra looks at me across the cargo bay, her eyes growing wide.

"Um, totally unrelated question," Scarlett Jones says. *"But did anyone bring a spare pair of pants, perchance?"*

"Yeah," our Gearhead replies. *"But I think I'm going to need mine."*

"Knock it off." Our Alpha's voice is hard with command. *"Finian, I want those missiles hot. Zila, you're on comms. Kal, I need you up here. Move!"*

Adrenaline kicks me in the stomach, and I heft my crate of medical supplies, shuffle over to the perfect stack I've been building. We have perhaps ten minutes before that Unbroken ship is in range. A Wraith-class cruiser is small, with a crew of twenty-seven adepts. But still, with only our Longbow and this station's crude defenses, we are outgunned and outmatched. The promise of violence tingles in my blood.

The Enemy Within, awakening.

Aedra is looking at me with fury in her eyes, fists clenched.

"This was *your* doing," she spits.

I feel my lip curl. "What?"

"We have hidden here for six months, undiscovered. You arrive, and barely an hour later, the Unbroken follow?"

"Obviously others know you are here," I say. "Legion Command, for one. But you immediately assume *I* betrayed you?"

"You are Warbreed," she hisses.

I try to bite down on my reply, but the Enemy has the better of me now.

"And you are a fool," I hear him say.

Aedra's eyes widen, and with a snarl, she draws her psi-blade again. And though her form is swift, smooth, splendid, she was not born as I was.

I was born with the taste of blood in my mouth.

I was born with my hands in fists.

I was born for war.

The violence within me unfurls, full and hot and pounding. The thing I was raised to be takes hold. I step aside as she swings, thought and motion becoming one, stabbing her neck with outstretched fingers. Quick as silver. Hard as steel. All too easy. The nerve strike numbs her arm and she gasps, stumbles into my neat stack of medical crates. The containers topple to the deck, the latches on the largest springing open with the sharp song of snapping metal.

And out of it spills a girl.

She is slender as a lias tree. Her hair is dark as midnight, with a streak as white as starlight running through it. Her skin is a light brown, and the freckles across her cheeks are perfect constellations. Her gasp is thin and pained as she tumbles along the deck, and still, it sounds like music to me. And as I look at her face, I feel a stabbing in my chest, bright and sharp and real as broken glass.

A feeling I thought I might never feel.

But . . .

But then I see she is . . .

Human?

"Um," she says, looking at Aedra. "Hi."

She pushes herself up on her elbows and finally looks at me. And behind the pain and the shock and the surprise, I see another color in her eyes.

Her thoughts are a kaleidoscope.

Her voice is a whisper.

"I've seen you before. . . ."

8

ZILA

The bad news is that the life-support system I have been trying to revive belongs in a museum. I'm certain the comms system is worse.

The good news is that their condition may not matter much longer.

Finian peers at me from inside the terminal he is fixing.

"You know what I don't understand?" he asks.

"Probably," I reply.

9

AURI

It's the guy from my vision. Mr. Middle-Earth.

Only he's real.

And he's standing right here in front of me.

And I—

"Treachery," a voice snaps behind me. "When were you going to tell us there were seven of you?"

I tear my eyes away from the guy from my vision, twisting around to check on the speaker. She's the same species, tall and slender, with the same olive skin, the same long silver hair. The small tattoo in the middle of her forehead is different, though—his is three crossed blades, but hers is an eye crying five tears.

"I did not know." The guy behind me sounds uncertain, but less like he wants to cut me open and see what's inside, so I edge closer to him, sliding on my butt. My arms and legs are still cramping from the tight space of the cargo crate, my eyes aching from all the reading I've been doing on Magellan's tiny screen. Also, I need a bathroom break. Why does that never come up in spy movies?

"She is Terran," the girl says, gripping a slender black cylinder in a way that makes it seem like a weapon. "She is wearing the uniform. She is yours."

"She—" He glances at me, clenches his jaw. "She is beneath our concern."

. . . Wait, what did he just say?

We're in a huge room—part of a space station, I'd guess—and the whole place looks like it's held together with spit and good luck. Gaping holes in the walls reveal a tangle of fire-hazard wiring, the lights flicker like they're about to give out, and the only new things here are the crates I stowed away in. I followed Battle Leader de Stoy's instructions, so I'm guessing this is where she wanted me to be? I just wish I knew why.

I wish I knew anything at all.

In reply to the tall boy's edict, the girl raises the stick, and suddenly *holy cake, that thing's definitely a weapon.* Purple energy crackles to life, sprouting from it like a long, curved blade, and I scramble backward so fast I crash into Middle-Earth's legs behind me.

"Control yourself, Aedra," he says, voice cool. "You shame yourself, acting so, in front of a human. Should we survive, we can argue about the girl later."

I both do and don't want to know why our survival is in question, but apparently I don't get a vote—he reaches down and lifts me to my feet like I weigh nothing at all, holding me in place while I get my balance. My knees are still singing a protest at being straightened as the girl kills the juice on her weapon, glaring one last time before stalking across the room like she expects to be followed.

"My name is Kal," the guy says quietly.

"Aurora," I reply, still miffed about the Beneath Our Concern crack.

"You are the girl Tyler Jones discovered in the Fold."

". . . How do you know about that?"

"You were found on an infamous derelict after being lost for two centuries and you have the same name as the academy I have lived at for the past two years."

Okay, good point, well made.

"Yeah. Look, sorry but I—"

"Explain when the danger is over," he says, cutting me off. "For now, stay beside me and do not stray."

His eyes are the same purple as the energy the girl called Aedra was wielding a minute ago. When I saw the vision of him in my room, I thought his hair was silver because of the light, but no—it really *is* that color, pulled back from his face and spilling down his back in five long, perfect braids. I can even see the same bruises on his jaw.

I remember the sound of screaming.

The blood on my hands.

When he looks at me, a shiver runs straight up my spine so hard the muscles cramp. It's like a fear response, except it's something else, too. There's a coldness to him. Something entirely . . . well . . . *alien*, I guess. He scares me, but despite his crappy manners, he scares me slightly less than everything else in the galaxy for now. So as he turns and stalks away, I match his stride.

"What's happening?" I whisper, just in case I understand the answer.

He looks at me with distant eyes.

"This is an abandoned mining station," he finally says as we step into an ancient elevator. "I am part of an Aurora Legion squad sent here with relief and supplies. A warship manned by . . . by a violent faction of my people is nearby."

"It was summoned," Aedra says, and though her voice is calm now, she still gives the boy a glare that's almost pure murder.

"It is dangerous," he says, as though she didn't speak, turning away from me. "But do not fear, human. You are among friends now."

"Could've fooled me . . . ," I mutter.

The elevator shudders to a stop and the doors slide open and we're in a control center. Large screens show flickering images of the stars and incomprehensible graphs and graphics, and half-dismantled control banks line the edges of the room, the middle taken up by a central bank. The room is full of people, shouting and rushing about.

"Aurora?" Someone's saying my name over in the middle of the room, incredulous. It's Captain Hotness. Ty, I mean. He's standing with his sister, the one with the bright orange hair, Scarlett, and a guy with paper-white skin. He must be Betraskan, just like Battle Leader de Stoy. Except this boy is wearing a sort of exoskeleton over his uniform that hums and whirs as he turns to me.

All three are staring at me now, like Kal just pulled me out of his hat. I feel him shift his weight, fold his arms beside me.

"Hi," I say.

Solid opener.

Scarlett frowns at me. "Um, what's she doing here?"

"The Unbroken first," Kal says. "Questions later."

I'm guessing the Unbroken are the violent faction he mentioned, and the looks on the faces around me send a finger of ice curling down my spine.

Tyler simply nods. "Cat, I want you flying perimeter in the Longbow. Keep out of sight. Kal, you're on our defenses. That Wraith is gonna be on us in ten minutes unless we give them a reason not to be."

The girl with the tattoos that I saw in the infirmary brushes roughly past me, the elevator doors rattling closed behind her.

Kal glances at me, then strides over to a series of consoles. I want to ask what's going on, but considering the mood up here, I figure I should try to keep out of the way instead. So I back up against the wall near an older-looking Syldrathi man. My heart's beating a mile a minute, and a part of me wants to find a small space and hide. It's too much. I can almost cope with two centuries in cryo, if I don't think too hard about everything that entails. I can deal with stowing away aboard some ship with a bunch of strangers. Being lied to by everyone around me. But being *under attack* might be a bridge too far.

I wish I could say the room's full of trained operatives clicking together like a well-oiled machine, but they're anything but. The legionnaires are talking over one another, shouting questions without waiting for answers, their voices rising to a frantic note. If this is the squad Ty didn't want to lead, I see his point—nobody's listening, and from the outside, it's obvious how badly everybody should be.

I glance at the old man next to me, who's the only one

109

not doing something. "I'm Auri," I offer quietly. And then, feeling the need for more formality in the face of his perfect posture, I offer a small bow. "Aurora Jie-Lin O'Malley."

He looks at me quizzically, like I'm a dog that just performed an amusing trick. "I am First Walker Taneth Lirael Ammar, young Terran," he replies, his voice deep and cool. "You may call me First Taneth."

"The people on the warship . . ." I try to swallow, my throat raw and aching. "Will they kill us?"

"Most assuredly," he says, in the same voice he used to give his name.

Well, son of a biscuit. This is going from bad to worse.

The joke sounds weak in my own head, and my breath feels oddly shallow, as if someone's squeezing my chest. I can't die in the middle of a conflict I don't even understand, on a space station, two hundred years into the future.

Can I?

There are things I should have done before a moment like this came. I still haven't even tried to look up my mom, or Callie, to find out what happened to them. Through all the long hours jammed in that packing crate with Magellan, I never felt ready to see them reduced to names and dates on a screen. Or worse, missing like Dad. So I didn't try at all, and now I might never get the chance.

Kal's voice breaks over the noise around me, the chaos of the squad's shouted questions and instructions. "Station defenses will not be adequate to fend off the Wraith. We must break out all available weaponry and prepare for a boarding action. The Unbroken will show us no mercy."

The Betraskan boy replies, his voice dry, as though the

situation's somehow funny. "Our combat specialist's advice is to gather up the sharp cutlery and pointy sticks, then run face-first at certain death? You know, I like you, Kal."

The other boy raises one perfect silver eyebrow. "You have a better plan?"

"We could ask the Unbroken out to drinks, flirt a little, talk this thing out?"

"You are not much of a warrior, are you, Finian?"

"Well, you're not much of a—"

"Shut up, Finian," Scarlett says, exchanging a glance with her brother. She tilts her head and he lifts his chin, and something passes between them. They have the same language of siblings I have—*had*—with my sister.

I wonder if Callie went on to become the composer she dreamed of being.

I wonder what it was like to only have Mom there in the audience, trying to clap hard enough to make up for Dad and me.

Ty lifts his head to address the ceiling.

"Zila, are we anywhere on comms?"

Surprisingly, a voice from the ceiling answers him. "One minute, sir."

A pair of legs in the same blue-gray uniform we're all wearing appear through an open hatch, and a moment later they're followed by the rest of a girl about my age. She has dark brown skin and long curly black hair pulled away from her face in a loose braid that shows off big, gold hoop earrings. She looks like she could have been in any one of my high school classes. She types a series of commands into a console and nods.

"Signal strength is now sufficient to send a distress call into the Fold," she informs him. "We can also hail the Syldrathi vessel if you wish."

Kal shakes his head. "The Unbroken will not negotiate with the likes of us."

"We could all evac?" Scarlett asks. "Run for it through the asteroid field?"

The Betraskan boy, Finian, chimes in again. "We won't all fit in the Longbow. And the skiffs these people came in are in no shape to outrun a Syldrathi Wraith."

Ceiling Girl—Zila—speaks up. She's the only one without that hint of panic in her gaze, and she's still studying her station like she's doing a crossword. "Legionnaire Brannock could ram our Longbow into the Syldrathi ship. Impact would be fatal for her, but if she aimed right, she has an excellent chance to take out their reactor and weapons systems."

Cat's voice rings out over the loudspeaker.

"You know I can hear you, right?"

"Yes," Zila deadpans.

"Well, if we could avoid any orders that end with the words 'ramming speed,' that'd be just brill, thanks. Ty, I'm launched. Stealthing through the asteroid field right now. They dunno I'm here yet."

"Stay off their scopes," Tyler replies. "Zila, have a mayday ready to broadcast, but don't send it yet. This station looks like it's falling to pieces. If we don't do anything to attract attention, we might convince them nobody's home."

"Sir, I'm detecting a launch from the station's aft port bays," Zila reports.

"Visual," Ty snaps.

An image springs to life on the largest screen. It's a debris field in space, mostly chunks of rock, a few pieces of derelict machinery floating lifelessly among them. Like I'm watching a video game, the focus shifts and zooms as Zila adjusts it, and we get a close-up of a tiny shuttle weaving through the asteroids. First Taneth tenses beside me, whispering in a language I don't understand.

"De'sai . . ."

"One of the refugees making a run for it," Finian reports, hands on his hips. "Trying to save their own hindparts while alerting our new friends ab—"

He gets no further, his voice cutting off as the shuttle soundlessly explodes into a million glittering shards, spinning out into space. We all watch it, nobody even seeming to breathe, until Zila breaks the silence in her strangely calm voice.

"One Syldrathi war cruiser, Wraith-class, turning straight for us, sir."

"Maker's sake," Ty mutters.

"Transmission incoming," she reports.

"Onscreen," Ty orders, turning to his sister. "Scar, work some magic."

"Magic?" Scarlett raises one sculpted eyebrow in disbelief. "I left my wizard's staff in my other pants, Bee-bro."

Tyler meets her gaze squarely. "You got this, Scar."

An image blossoms to life on the main display. It's of a beautiful young woman, a Syldrathi like Kal, Aedra, First Taneth, like everyone here except the legionnaires. Her skin is olive, almost golden, her silver hair pulled back into a series of ornate braids. Black armor makes broad shoulders squarer,

113

and it's adorned with what might be blades. Her canines are filed into sharp points as well—or maybe they just come that way. She's speaking in what I assume is Syldrathi, but as she registers Scarlett's features, her scowl deepens, suspicion slipping into her icy tone.

"What are you doing here, Terran?"

"My name is Scarlett Jones," Scarlett replies smoothly. "My squad and I are representatives of Aurora Legion, here in neutral space on an aid mission."

"You are meddling in Syldrathi affairs."

"We're providing medical assistance to refugees, as per the provisos in—"

"Those who aid enemies of the Unbroken become enemies of the Unbroken."

Scarlett runs one hand through her red hair, widening her stance, bracing herself as though she's about to throw a punch. "With all due respect, the Aurora Legion is a neutral party in your conflict, ma'am. I advise you to withdraw. We are authorized to respond with force in the event our safety is threatened."

"Threatened?"

The young woman shakes her head and sneers.

"We make no threats, little Terran. Only promises. Ready your souls for the Void's embrace. In Caersan's name, you will be purged."

The screen drops into sudden black.

". . . That's your idea of magic?" Finian asks softly.

"Shut *up*, Finian!" Scarlett snaps in reply.

"They're accelerating," Zila says, calm as ever. "ETA four minutes."

"Zila, send the mayday," Ty commands. "Loud and wide as you can."

Scarlett's running her hand through her hair again, leaving it a mess. "Nobody'll respond. If the Terran or Betraskan defense forces hear it, it's policy *not* to. And if there was another AL ship within range, we wouldn't have been sent here in the first place. This is all us."

Ty simply nods and presses on. "Finian, you have the bridge. Keep working on those missiles. Zila, stay with him, keep on comms."

For once, no sass—the two of them simply murmur an acknowledgment and get to work. I think that scares me more than anything else has so far.

"Looks like we're going with your plan, Kal," he continues. "You, me, Scar, arms ready. We'll head for the cargo bay. First Taneth, gather up anyone among your people who has a weapon and meet us there."

Kal and the Syldrathi girl are already moving toward where the First Taneth and I stand by the door, and Tyler's eyes are on me as he draws close.

"I don't suppose you've had any combat training?" Ty asks softly.

"Um," I say. "I mean, I took a self-defense course at school?"

"You cannot intend to send her down there?" Kal says.

Tyler glances at the taller boy. "Give her a sidearm."

Kal bristles at the suggestion. "That is *extremely* unwise, sir. She will only be a liability."

"Hey, listen here, Lord Elrond . . . ," I begin.

"We face adepts of the Unbroken," Kal says to Tyler, not

115

even looking at me. "Syldrathi are faster and stronger than Terrans. And these ones are trained from b—"

"I appreciate the warning, legionnaire. But we're in it up to our necks here."

A small electronic chirp sounds from my breast pocket. "WELL, IF I MAY OFFER AN OPINION—"

"No, you may not," Tyler tells Magellan. "Silent mode."

My uniglass falls quiet as Ty turns to me. "Look, Auri, I'm sorry. I don't even know what you're doing here, but we need everyone in the ring or we're all dead. If you can pull a trigger, we could use you. Will you help us?"

My heart is in my throat and my palms are damp. And I'm a million light-years from home and two hundred years out of time, and none of this makes any kind of sense. But if we're all going to die anyway . . .

"Okay," I say quietly.

I find myself crammed in the cage elevator with the rest of the team. Kal holds out a dangerous-looking high-tech pistol, and the words *"She will only be a liability"* are echoing in my head as I snatch it from his hand.

"This locks on to your target," he says, pointing. "This will fire. In the unlikely event you actually hit someone, hit them twice more for good measure."

"Thanks," I say. "But I learned to use a flare gun in my colony training. I can shoot just fine, Legolas."

He blinks. "My name is Kal, human. Who is this Legolas you speak of?"

I roll my eyes and mutter under my breath, "Read a book sometime, you conceited sonofa . . ."

My grumbling trails off into nothing as I notice how quiet

everyone else is. And in that moment of silence, the truth I've been running from catches up and hits me like a freight train. I'm about to go into *combat* here. My hands are sweating, and I'm not sure I'm even going to be able to grip the gun. My body's still aching from hiding in that crate, and my lungs have gone all tight, so I can't even suck in a slow breath to try and calm myself. Truth is, the thing in my hands is to a flare gun what a full-grown lion is to a kitten.

All the stupid little routines I used to do before a big competition at home flash through my mind—the stretches, the breathing exercises, the pump-up songs—and they all seem so impossibly small and stupid. That version of me—the one who thought she had any idea what life-and-death stakes were—feels young and far away, even though, really, she was me only a few days ago.

I'd give *anything* to be her again. To be able to tell my mom this scares me and have her tell me to switch off the scary movie. To be able to tell my dad I don't feel ready and have him help me look up the answers in yet another training course.

Everything I ever learned, I learned from sims or books.

But this is *real*.

Finian's voice sounds from Tyler's uniglass as we spill out into the cargo bay.

"Fired the missiles, sir. They bounced off the Syldrathi like kebar balls. Their ship's in position, and they've got a shuttle preparing to dock. I'm trying to run a localized current through our hull to stop them from getting a seal, but I'm a little worried about the insulation in this place. I don't want to do their work for them and fry you all."

"Acknowledged," says Ty, grim, gesturing for us to take cover behind the crates. "Cat, as the boarding party's docking here, target their cruiser. They'll be as distracted as they're going to be."

"Roger that," says Cat over the comms, her tone crisp. *"Sucker punch for the mummy ship ready to go. I'll aim straight for the love factory."*

"They put those on cruisers now?" Scarlett asks.

"I mean, I've heard rumors. . . ."

The cargo bay elevator doors creak open again, and First Taneth appears with the Syldrathi girl, Aedra. A few dozen elderly Syldrathi are with them, all moving slowly, wearing long robes and clutching what even I can tell are weapons as old as they are. Kal is beside me behind a tall stack of crates, calling out as he sees them.

"Take the gantries around the bay. We will cover the ground."

"We do not take orders from you, Warbreed," Aedra glares. "Nor your Terran pets, for that matter. This is *our* station."

"We must stand united in this, Aedra," Kal replies calmly. "Or fall alone."

Aedra breaks away from the other Syldrathi, stalking toward the two of us. Kal shifts his weight so he's standing in front of me.

"You speak of standing united?" The purple blade in her hand crackles to life, matched by the fire in her eyes. "When your kind tore our entire world apart?"

"You know nothing of who I am," Kal says. "Or what it cost me to be here."

She holds up her hand, and I see a tattoo on her ring

finger. A circle with a single tear inside it. "I know my be'shmai is dead because of your kind, Warbreed. Him, and our whole world besides."

"Aedra!" Taneth calls. "Now is not the time for this!"

"We're about to die, Taneth!" she shouts. "What better time than now?"

She turns back to Kal, her lips curled in a sneer.

"Your path is littered with death, and your destiny is in your blood."

"Cho'taa," Kal says, his voice subzero. "It has nothing to do with my blood."

And all the breath goes out of me right there.

Because . . .

I've seen this before.

He stood just like this in my vision back on Aurora Station. Perfectly poised even when he's standing still, like a coiled weapon, bruises on his face and disdain in his tone. He spoke these exact words.

This can't be happening. . . .

This is my vision come to life.

Abruptly the room's filled with a loud thump, the grinding screech of metal. Nobody needs Finian to tell us that the boarding party's docked with the outer airlock. Kal turns his head, and all eyes shift to the bay doors.

The girl takes her chance, lifting the crackling purple blade.

"I will see you in the Void, Warbreed."

Everything slows down. It's like watching the world in freeze-frame, like a strobe light's going off and I can see each and every movement and moment.

What I'm seeing, and what I've already *seen*.

119

Aedra will raise her blade and swing it, a flash of purple just like in my vision, a killing blow in the making. Kal will begin to turn but he'll be too late. The blade will cut straight into him, and he'll cry out and fall in front of me, and my hands will be covered in blood. Purple blood.

His blood.

I can see it in my head.

Clear as the walls around me.

My hands in front of me.

And I know I can change it.

The cargo bay is suddenly lit by a flickering white light. I throw my hand up. And though I'm nowhere near her, Aedra goes flying backward. She slams into the wall, arms spread wide. As she crumples to the ground, a searing pain cuts through my right eye, lancing into my head. It's like a clamp around my temples, like it's squeezing, *squeezing,* and as I curl in on myself, my scream drowned out by the grinding metal of the cargo bay doors being cut open, blood drips from my nose again. Warm and salty on my lips, spattering on the metal at my feet.

And Kal's in front of me, his lips moving, his stare locked on my own.

"Spirits of the Void," he breathes. "Your eye . . ."

Aurora Legion Squads
▶ Squad Members
  ▼ Gearheads

Gearheads are the mechanics of **AL squads**, responsible for keeping machinery and equipment going in the field and for cobbling together anything their squads may need that wasn't brought along. Mad inventors, most of them.

They have a reputation for being ingenious, fascinated by **gadgets**, and often covered in **grease**. Frequent personal traits include missing eyebrows and an intense personal interest in **things that go boom**.

GEARHEAD'S INSIGNIA

10

FINIAN

The radio's a low murmur in my ears as I wrestle with this hunk of junk's systems. Somewhere off to my left, Zila is silently working on improving our comms range, and I'm locked in my own private battle with a computer grid that's older and uglier than my third grandfather. If this piece of chakk station was going to screw me this bad, it should have bought me dinner first.

The Unbroken have their docking clamps in place, and they're cutting through the outer hull now. If I can't find a way to divert their attention from making a new door through to the cargo bay, Zila and I are in line for a sudden—and probably very brief—promotion.

"The Maker better take into account that we died on a mercy mission." I plug my uniglass into a port, praying it's not too modern to interface with this pile of nuts and bolts. "Because I'm going to need a place to hide when my grandparents reach the afterlife. I'm never going to hear the end of this."

Zila doesn't reply, and when I glance over, she's got that

blank stare of hers fixed on her screen, as if she didn't hear me at all.

"My parents are dead," she says flatly.

Well.

That kills the conversation deader than we're about to be.

I don't get this girl. I don't get what makes that big brain of hers work or what the hells she's doing here or how she can remain calm when we're all about to become corpsicles floating in space.

And see, this is our problem. Right here. None of us are technically *bad* at what we do. Individually, we have the goods, at least on paper. It's just that half of us didn't volunteer to be here, and the other half don't have anywhere else to be. We should never have been drafted into the same squad.

We just don't . . . click.

I actually didn't think I'd be the last Gearhead picked, to be honest.

They all pretend the exosuit isn't an issue, but I know it is. It always has been. When people look at me, it's the first thing they see. Still, I'm damn good at what I do, so it was a kick when the incompetents were picked before I was. Gearheads who couldn't count past ten without taking their socks off got a gig, and I was left standing there with my tool in my hand.

Alone.

I was sent away from home when I was six years old— they said it would be easier on an orbital station with my grandparents. I could sleep in low grav there, have access to the best doctors. What they meant was that it would be easier for *everybody else.* You'd think I'd have learned to lower my expectations by now.

Not that I'll be moping about that—or anything—much longer.

My uniglass does the job, and a virtual screen springs up above the console. The rush of relief is like a drug. *This* is what I'm good at. Not people. This.

I step back and lift both my hands like I'm conducting an orchestra, burrowing my way into layer upon layer of ancient maintenance algorithms. I crunch them in my fist, sweeping aside safety protocols and delivering a surge of power to the couplings holding the Syldrathi shuttle in place. I hear a faint secondhand scream through Tyler's uni, and the nerve-jangling sound of the plasma cutters abruptly halts. That'll buy us thirty seconds.

I plunge into the dizzying mess of code for round two. I deliver a second shock to the couplings, but the Syldrathi techs are onto me now. Dismissing the display with a sweep of my hand, I ease my weight back onto my heels, my suit hissing softly as it compensates.

Maybe I can mess with their readings, make their computer think there's not enough atmosphere inside the cargo bay to equalize pressure. That's going to require something more hands-on.

I pop a multi-tool out from where it nests in the warm curve of metal at my ribs, yanking the cover off my bank of computers so I can crawl inside. I really hope my suit stays grounded, or I'm going to fry myself. But even if this works, I know I can't do it forever. And my hands are shaking. Usually they're fine, especially with the tiny lines of stimulators that run down to my fingertips—it's my legs that need the most help, my knee extensions and my hips.

But pump enough adrenaline through me and everything gets tougher, and right now, adrenaline's not in short supply. In my mind's eye, I can see the Unbroken bursting into the cargo bay, eating my team for dinner before heading up here for dessert.

Will I hold my nerve long enough to face them?

Or will I hide so they have to drag me out?

There are so many conversations I should have had. I should have been nicer to my grandparents. I should have apologized to my parents. Should have apologized to most of the people I've ever met, I guess, but my apologies always seem to make things worse.

Still, this is probably my last chance to try.

"Look, Zila," I say. "About your parents. I—"

"Sir, I'm getting a transmission from a Terran Defense Force destroyer," she says. "Ident: *Bellerophon*. They just dropped through the FoldGate in response to our mayday and estimate they're eleven minutes from weapons range."

Tyler replies down comms. *"Um, are you sure?"*

He sounds as lost as I feel. No way in hells is the TDF involving itself in a scuffle like this. No way they'd even be *out* here in the nowhere end of space, let alone willing to compromise Earth's neutrality with the Unbroken . . .

"Affirmative," Zila says without missing a beat.

"Put me on comms with the Syldrathi, Zila," Scarlett says.

"Broadcasting."

"Syldrathi invaders," Scar begins, in a don't-mess-with-me tone. *"Please be advised we have incoming support from the Terran Defense Force vessel you can no doubt see popping on your scopes. If you want to keep your pretty asses in your pants,*

I advise your immediate withdrawal. Or you can stick around to see if a Wraith-class Syldrathi cruiser is a match for a fully armed Terran destroyer. Your call."

Is it weird that this girl's don't-mess-with-me tone makes me want to tell her she can mess with me any day she wants?

We hold our breath. I stay where I am, on my hands and knees, half-inside an ancient bank of computers. Zila doesn't move a muscle above me, and through my audio I can hear the soft breathing and rustling of the team down in the cargo bay as they hold position.

And then, with a shuddering clunk, the Syldrathi shuttle pulls free.

"Sir, they're in retreat," Zila reports, in exactly the same tone she's used all through this near-death experience.

What is *with* this girl?

Tyler chimes in on comms. *"Cat, let the incoming TDF destroyer know you're there so they don't mistakenly blast you out of space. Zila, we need you down here for medical. Finian, you too."*

I crawl out backward, and Zila and I exchange a glance.

Why do they need medical when nobody made it on board?

When we reach the cargo bay, the Syldrathi refugees are standing together, doing a pretty good job of looking aloof and composed despite the fact they all just escaped certain and brutal murder. The Jones twins are crouching over the one young Syldrathi who's out cold on the floor, silver hair splayed around her like a halo, arms outflung. Kal's busy looming nearby, along with our stowaway. I remember her name now—Aurora—and I know where I've heard it before.

126

She's the one Goldenboy pulled off the *Hadfield*.

But what's she doing here?

Zila busts open a crate of medtech, and I help her carry a kit over to where the Syldrathi girl's lying. Someone's clearly punched her, and she's smacked her head but good on the wall behind. Might have been our Aurora, because now that I squint at her again, I see she's sporting a bloody nose. She looks wild, down on one knee, cheeks wet as though she's been crying, one hand trying to stanch the blood. Weirdest of the weird, her right iris has turned almost totally white.

"What has happened to her eye?" Zila asks.

I shrug, glancing at the bleached stripe running through Aurora's bangs.

"Matches her hair now, at least?"

Aurora ignores us both, looking up at Tyler instead.

"The Terran government's outside?"

"That's right," he says, speaking a little carefully.

"Please, don't tell them I'm here. I can't go with them."

He blinks, exchanging a glance with his sister.

"Auri," he tries. "That's *exactly* where you should go. I don't know how you ended up here, but you're a Terran, they'll take care of you."

"You don't understand," she insists, lowering her bloodied bandage. "Battle Leader de Stoy told me to avoid them. She *told* me to stow away with you."

Another twin-to-twin glance ensues while Auri tries her pleading eyes on me. Then she hisses, hand to her head as though it's hurting her. Pawing at her bloody nose.

Scarlett takes over from her brother. Apparently during their silent communion they decided this is a job for a diplomat. "Auri, there's no reason de Stoy would say that. Maybe you misunderstood her?"

"I can't go," Auri insists, eyes getting wilder, doing herself no favors at all. "You don't understand. *You don't understand.* They wiped away every trace of my colony. It's like Octavia never existed. They want to wipe me away, too."

Kal stares at her with cold violet eyes. Zila is looking at her like a bug under a magnifying glass. She's not coming off as any kind of reasonable, and her uneasiness is infecting me, if I'm honest. Maybe it's just nerves in the wake of a bunch of Unbroken almost getting close enough to barbecue me. Or maybe it's that from time to time, the Terrans make me uncomfortable, too. They're so complex, with so many languages, so many different clothes and colors, like a bunch of kazar birds, always picking fights and swirling into a blur. But I don't know if we should force this girl to go somewhere she doesn't want to be, either.

"Listen," she says, appealing directly to our squad leader. "I know this sounds crazy, but . . . I saw de Stoy before I ever met her, Tyler. I saw Kal in my hospital room, saying *exactly* what he said here just a few minutes ago. And I saw what they'll do to me. I can see it right now in my head and I can *feel* it, and . . ."

Ah. Oh. Got it.

This girl's spent too long in the Fold.

Our fearless leader has clearly drawn the same conclusion, because his voice goes very gentle. "They can help you, Auri. It's going to be okay."

Kal drops to a crouch, murmuring in her ear. She glares at him, and for a moment, her hand tightens around the pistol she's holding. But surprisingly, whatever he says seems to calm her, and she lets him slowly ease the gun out of her white-knuckle grip.

I can hear Scarlett talking over comms to the TDF crew as the destroyer draws close to the station. With a heavy clunk, their umbilical clamps onto the outer doors, and First Taneth disarms the airlock. Our whole squad's quiet. Auri's breath is audible, catching and huffing, as if she's trying not to cry.

"They've got no faces," she's whispering.

I blink. "What did you say?"

"They've got no *faces,*" she hisses desperately. "And they're going to wipe all this away, they're going to make it clean, they're going to paint it *black.*"

Kal comes to his feet as the airlock doors rumble open. I catch sight of the familiar khaki uniforms of the Terran Defense Force marching into the bay, heavy tac armor and heavy boots. None of them are over twenty-five.

The famous Ty Jones heads across to greet them, and though he's only a freshly instated legionnaire, he manages to look like he's in charge. Which is all the more impressive, because he has to be as confused as the rest of us about why the TDF's even involving itself here.

"We sure are glad to see you, Lieutenant," he says, offering a polite salute and one of those smoldering smiles he does so well.

"Of course." A young woman salutes back. "Glad we could help."

"I've gotta say, LT, we weren't expecting help," he admits. "If word gets out the TDF got involved in this, the Unbroken might consider the Terran government to have taken a side. There could be reprisals."

A voice comes from behind the group of soldiers, low and steely, as if it's coming through a speaker. "THAT RISK HAS BEEN NOTED, LEGIONNAIRE."

The soldiers part like a comb's running through them, and with heavy, deliberate footsteps, five tall figures make their way to the front.

What the . . . ?

They're clad head to toe in charcoal gray, and their faces are completely hidden behind featureless masks, like elongated grav-bike helmets. No eyes, no nose, no mouth. Just a dully reflective surface, concealing even the smallest hint of the individual behind it. With their electronic voices, you can't even guess at their age or gender.

"Holy *shit*," Scarlett whispers. "They're GIA."

I wonder if this would be a bad time to revisit that conversation with her about a spare pair of pants, because I might not be a Terran, but even I know operatives of the Global Intelligence Agency are *not* folks you mess with.

They've got no faces.

And here they are.

The five GIA agents are all perfectly identical except the one fronting the pack. The leader is dressed in pure white instead of gray, so spotless and crisp it's actually a little eerie. And I'm a Betraskan, so when I find too much white intimidating, you know it's really doing a job.

I figure maybe the lack of color is some marker of rank, because Goldenboy gives it a smart salute and stands at attention like he's on parade.

"Legionnaire Tyler Jones reporting."

The figure surveys us, breath hissing softly. I can't see its eyes, but I can tell it's looking right at our stowaway, addressing Goldenboy like an afterthought.

"You will refer to me as Princeps."

Tyler clears his throat, finally looking a little out of his depth. "Princeps, I don't mean to tell you your business, but if those Unbroken get—"

"Bellerophon has dispatched two full fighter wings," it interrupts, its voice flat and dead. "The Syldrathi wraith will be incinerated. There will be no evidence of Terra's involvement in this . . . incident."

"Forgive me for asking, Princeps, but how did you get to us so fast? We had no notification of a Terran vessel in this sector."

He's pressing just a fraction, and I can see Scarlett tense almost imperceptibly as she watches him. The operative turns to look Tyler in the face.

"The Global Intelligence Agency has one thousand eyes, Legionnaire Jones."

It holds out its hand to our stowaway.

"Aurora," it says. "We've come to escort you home."

They've got no faces. And they're going to wipe all this away, they're going to make it clean, they're going to paint it black.

"Don't make me go," she pleads.

She's looking at Tyler, Goldenboy, our fearless leader. Tears in her eyes and blood on her mouth.

"Please, Tyler," she whispers. "Don't let them take me."

Tyler glances at the TDF troopers, those blank GIA faces. He might be a legionnaire, but underneath it all, he's still a Terran. I can see it in his eyes. All those years of military training, all those years of *yessir, no sir, may I have another, sir*. You don't get to be top Alpha in the academy by rocking the boat. You don't get to be the Goldenboy by not following orders.

"You should go with them, Auri," he says.

Kal steps forward, hand on his sidearm as he stares Princeps down. "This station is under Syldrathi control, Terran. You have no authorit—"

The TDF troopers raise their weapons. Two dozen targeting lasers light up Kal like it's Federation Day.

"Control your man, Legionnaire Jones," Princeps says.

"Legionnaire Gilwraeth," Tyler says softly. "Stand down."

"Kii'ne dō all'iavesh ishi," the Syldrathi says, a tiny flash of anger breaking through the ice. "I will—"

"That's an order!" Ty snaps.

Kal smolders, but Syldrathi arrogance aside, the guns aimed right at that pretty face seem to give him pause. He backs down.

Auri looks around the group, tears in her eyes, but it's clear nobody else is going to step forward. No way I'm going to, anyway. Betraskans think in terms of the negotiation. The deal. And with a trade this bad, the smart move is to just walk away. My fellow legionnaires seem content to follow Tyler's lead, and he's not stepping in to save her, either. He risked everything for this girl once already, after all. And look where it got him.

Out here.

With us.

And so she lifts her chin and walks forward to join her escort like she's going to her execution.

The TDF troopers motion with their guns for us to follow.

Yeah, I don't feel good about this at *all*.

TERRAN LAW ENFORCEMENT

▶ **GLOBAL INTELLIGENCE AGENCY**
  ▼ **OVERVIEW**

TERRAN LAW ENFORCEMENT IS HANDLED BY THE FOLLOWING AGENCIES:

MILITARY OPERATIONS: THE **TERRAN DEFENSE FORCE (TDF)**

PEACEKEEPING: THE INDEPENDENT **AURORA LEGION (AL)**, ALSO INCORPORATING THE **BETRASKANS** AND **FREE SYLDRATHI**

AND THEN THERE'S THE GLOBAL INVESTIGATION AGENCY (GIA), THE INVESTIGATIVE ARM OF THE **TERRAN GOVERNMENT**. GIA AGENTS ARE THE SCARY BASTARDS RESPONSIBLE FOR KNOWING ALL YOUR SECRETS.

THEY CAN BE RECOGNIZED BY THEIR GRAY SUITS AND FEATURELESS HELMETS, WHICH, ALONG WITH VOICE SYNTHESIZERS, RENDER THEM IDENTICAL. THEY'RE ALSO RECOGNIZED BY THEIR ALMOST **UNLIMITED POWERS TO PURSUE AND DETAIN THOSE WHO DISPLEASE THEM**.

IF YOU EVER FIND YOURSELF ON THE WRONG SIDE OF THE GIA, I SUGGEST TERRIFIED AND ABJECT APOLOGIES. EITHER THAT, OR **PRAYER**.

11

AURI

I'm stumbling down a long hallway of burnished steel, the white-clad figure in front of me, the others in gray following behind. They walk in unison, their steps landing in the same instant on the metal grille, like soldiers on parade. I'm in the middle, messy and out of place, hurrying along to keep to their pace. My right eye is aching like there's glass in it. I can taste my blood on my lips.

And I'm repeating Kal's words to myself, whispered in my ear as he eased the gun out of my hand.

Go with dignity. You are more than this.

Though he spoke them like a rebuke, his words are enough to stiffen my spine. I spent years at competitions and championships, pushing myself, proving myself worthy of an Octavia berth. Now I reach with desperation for the composure that carried me through those times, though I can feel it slipping through my fingers as quickly as I grasp it.

The white figure stops outside a heavy sealed door, turns to the figures behind me. There's a short, uncomfortable pause and then, though no words were spoken, two of the agents nod and walk back the way we came. My head is aching, my eye is still burning. And looking at my dull reflection in that featureless helmet, I can see my right iris has gone completely white.

I want my mom. I want my dad. I want to run as far and as fast as I can, and hide somewhere safe, and never come out.

"Please," I whisper. "P-Pri—"

"PRINCEPS," the one in white replies, brushing imaginary dust off its lapel.

I can feel tears burning my eyes. "I w-want to go home."

"YOU ARE GOING HOME, AURORA. I AM ABOUT TO REPORT THAT YOU ARE ON YOUR WAY." Princeps waves one spotless gloved hand at the agents behind me. "MY COLLEAGUES WILL SEE TO YOUR NEEDS UNTIL I RETURN."

The white figure turns and marches down the hallway. One of the gray suits behind me touches a panel, and the heavy door beside us slides open with a whisper.

I begin to follow the agent through the doorway, then jerk to a halt two steps in, so suddenly that the faceless agent behind me nearly collides with me.

That stumble is the first truly human moment I've had from any of them.

I've seen this room before, and the shock of recognition was so strong, it stopped me in my tracks. An image of it flashed into my mind back in the cargo bay, the moment I heard the words *Terran Defense Force.* Another vision, arriving with a terror that completely displaced my panic about having thrown that Syldrathi girl into a wall with what I'm pretty sure was the power of my mind.

What the hell is happening to me?

I saw the same steel-gray walls I'm seeing now, the

same burning lights, the same single chair in the exact center of the floor, and me seated on it. My hands were bound in front of me with gray cuffs the same shade as my interrogators' suits, and the pain that was coming from those cuffs—the very memory of it has me trembling. It was melt-your-flesh-off-your-bones pain, cut-off-your-hands-to-escape pain, and on pure instinct I try to back up, bumping into my captor.

Two gray-gauntleted hands land on my shoulders, squeezing until my bones are fit to crack and fuse together, and my knees give, my vision swimming.

Those same hands grab my biceps and steer me, stumbling, toward the chair, twisting me around and dumping me in it. I remember that Syldrathi girl, remember throwing up my hands and pushing her away without ever touching her, and I stare up at my captors, half-blinded by pain and tears, desperately probing my mind for the part that knows how to throw them across a room, scrambling for anything that might help, and coming up short.

This was my vision. The cuffs, the pain, and the same words screamed over and over in a voice so hoarse I could barely recognize it as my own.

"I don't know. Please, I don't know."

It's only when two helmets tilt to look down at me that I realize I'm already whispering my reply. I'm already pleading, and they haven't even asked me the first of their impossible questions yet.

"Ms. O'MALLEY," one says quietly, voice perfectly even, perfectly neutral, cold as the vacuum outside the thin walls of this ship. "BELIEVE US WHEN WE SAY WE'D PREFER TO DO THIS THE EASY WAY."

Aurora Legion Squads

▶ **Squad Members**

　▼ **Alphas**

Alphas are the leaders of **Aurora Legion (AL) squads**, and almost without exception, they treat this as **Very Serious Business**. Alphas generally possess an encyclopedic knowledge of regulations and an intimidating work ethic, but most are also charismatic leaders. After all, it helps if your followers want to, uh, follow you.

Only the most talented academy cadets are accepted into the Squad Leader stream, and Alphas are ultimately responsible for the success or failure of any given mission, as well as the lives of their squad members.

No pressure . . .

ALPHA'S INSIGNIA

12

TYLER

"Well, isn't this cozy."

I glance up at Finian. He's leaning against the burnished steel wall, black eyes fixed on me. His exosuit gleams silver in the light of the fluorescents overhead, humming softly as he reaches down to the water cooler beside him.

"The decor's a little sparse for a 'meeting room,' though," he continues, sipping from a disposable cup and looking around. "I know you Terrans aren't the most stylish race in the Milky Way, but I swear this looks more like a holding cell."

"Oh, do go on," Scarlett says, leaning forward on our bench and batting her eyelashes. "Honestly, I could just listen to you bitch and moan all day, Finian."

Finian takes a bench and sighs. "I'm too old for this crap."

Zila tilts her head. "You are barely nineteen, Legionnaire de Seel."

"Yeah. And I'm too old for this crap."

"Knock it off," I growl. "All of you."

We're in a square room, five meters a side, benches

running along the walls. Scarlett's sitting next to me, Zila opposite, Kal as far as he can be from all of us and pouting like a goldfish. Everyone's on edge after almost getting flatlined by those Unbroken, and I've gotta keep a lid on it. But the thing of it is, I'm close to the edge myself. Finian's right. When they hustled us aboard the *Bellerophon,* a dozen troopers escorted us to a room to "await debriefing." But with the locked door and the blank walls, the box they've tossed us in *does* look an awful lot like a detention room.

I can feel the destroyer's engines thrumming through the seat beneath me, the massive ship plunging through the black, back toward the FoldGate. I'm trying not to remember the way Auri looked at me as they dragged her away, one white eye and one brown, both fixed on me like I was her last hope.

Please, Tyler. Don't let them take me.

Poor kid. Everyone knows staying too long in the Fold is bad for your brain, but I've never heard of exposure changing someone's *eye color* before. Whatever's happening to her, I didn't quite realize how bad she'd got it.

I hope they can help her somehow.

Maker knows I couldn't. . . .

"Get your bloody hands off me, you gremp-fondling sack of—"

The door hisses open, and a couple of TDF goons in full tac armor shove my Ace into the room, swearing all the way. Our escort told us she'd be brought to join us once she docked the Longbow, and it doesn't look like it was an easy ride. Cat's face is red, her fauxhawk mussed. She has her stuffed dragon, Shamrock, stowed inside her flight jacket, and she's looking about as mad as I've ever seen her. As she steps up to the bigger trooper, he slaps the door control and seals her in with the rest of us. Her boot leaves a scuff on the plasteel when she kicks it, shouting at the top of her voice.

"Yeah, you better run, you gutless *prick!*"

"Cat?" Scar asks, rising to her feet. "You okay?"

"Do I look okay?" she snaps. "No, I look ready to kick the crap out of the next"—another kick hits the door—"TDF *goonbag* who pops up on my scopes!"

"Cat," I say, standing up. "Take a breath."

"They *flatlined* them, Tyler!" she shouts, whirling on me.

I blink. "What? Who?"

"The refugees!" Cat snaps, arm flailing at the door. "Taneth and the rest! As soon as I docked in the Longbow, the TDF obliterated the entire station. It's *gone!*"

Finian's voice is a whisper. "Great Maker . . ."

I blink again, trying to make sense of what Cat is saying. Scarlett sinks back down to the bench, her face pale.

All eyes turn to Kal.

Our Tank's traditional Syldrathi cool doesn't shatter, but the line of his jaw is tense as steel as he stands and prowls across the room. He braces his hands against the wall, hangs his head, muttering beneath his breath. I don't speak Syldrathi half as well as Scar, but I know the words he's using are curses.

"Kal?" Scar asks quietly. "Are you okay?"

I can see the anger in his eyes as he turns on her. I can see the struggle inside him. But his voice is as empty and cold as the vacuum outside.

"A hundred of my people," he says. "A hundred songs now silenced. A hundred lives and thousands of years, lost to the Void. Not content to let us be butchered by our own kin, now Earth joins the Unbroken in our slaughter?"

"I'm sure there's some explanation," Scarlett says.

"They were Waywalkers," Kal says, stepping closer to my sister. "Sages and scholars. What explanation is there for that?"

"Ease off, legionnaire," I warn.

"De'sai!" he hisses, looking between me and Scar. "De'sai si alamm tiir'na!"

My jaw clenches as I recognize a few words. "Did he just say what I . . ."

"Shame," Scarlett translates, trembling with anger. "Shame to your father's house."

And that's it. The final straw. Losing my spot in the Draft. This nowhere mission. This nowhere squad. Being lied to by Command and the look in Auri's eyes as they led her away and now this pixieboy sucker puncher talking about my dad.

That's the spark that starts the inferno.

He blocks my first punch—turns out he's way faster than me. But I lock him up and hook his leg and we go down in a tumble where his speed will count for less, and Maker help me, when my second punch splits his lip, I find my own curling in a smile. All the frustration of the last couple of days boils up inside me as we wrestle and spit, as Cat shouts at me to stop, as Fin offers a small round of applause, as Zila begins typing into her uniglass as if bored to death. Kal's fingers close around my throat, I reach for his—

Cold water hits us, crashing over the back of my head.

I sputter and gasp, pulling Kal's hands away from my neck. Looking up, I see Scarlett standing over us, emptying the up-turned water cooler tank onto our heads. She shakes the last few drops onto us for emphasis before tossing the tank aside.

"Grow up," she says. "Sir."

My sister marches back to the bench, sits down with her legs crossed and her arms folded. Finian speaks into the quiet, one eyebrow raised.

"They teach you that in diplomacy class?"

"I improvised," Scarlett glowers.

Cat offers me her hand and I take it, standing with a grunt. Water puddles about my feet, soaking hair hangs in my eyes. My Ace looks up at me with a wry grin, shaking her head. Kal seems to glide back upright behind me, his uniform sodden, his eyes still full of fury, purple blood on his lip. He'd probably tear me to pieces now that I don't have the element of surprise, and I'm wondering if he's prepping for round two when our uniglasses all ping simultaneously.

I look down at the device on my belt. A single line of text glows on the display.

INCOMING MESSAGE, SQUAD CHAT. SENDER: ZILA M, SCIENCE OFFICER.

Scar and the rest of us tap our screens to open the message.

ZILA M: I AM ASSUMING THE TDF HAS NOT YET CRACKED OUR SQUAD NETWORK'S ENCRYPTION. THEY WILL CERTAINLY BE TRYING TO NOW. WE SHOULD SPEAK QUICKLY.

Cat looks at Zila like she's completely sideways.

"Um, something wrong with your tongue?"

Zila types some more, and moments later, my uniglass pings again.

ZILA M: THIS ROOM IS DOUBTLESS UNDER VISUAL AND AUDIO SURVEILLANCE. SPEAKING OPENLY WILL ONLY PROMPT THEM TO MURDER US SOONER. WE MUST GET OUT OF THIS CELL AND RESCUE AURORA FROM HER DETAINMENT. OR WE ARE ALL GOING TO DIE.

I frown, opening my mouth to speak. But Zila shakes her head in warning, setting her big gold hoop earrings jangling, and something in her eyes makes me type instead.

TYLER J: WHAT IN THE MAKER'S NAME ARE YOU TALKING ABOUT?

ZILA M: I ESTIMATE WE HAVE ONLY A FEW MOMENTS BEFORE THE TDF ARRIVES TO TAKE YOU AWAY FOR "DEBRIEFING," SIR. AT THE END OF YOUR INTERROGATION, YOU WILL BE KILLED. AND ONE BY ONE, THEY WILL THEN INTERROGATE AND KILL THE REST OF US.

Fin types quickly, eyes on Zila.

FINIAN dS: DID YOU FORGET TO TAKE YOUR HAPPY PILLS THIS MORNING?

ZILA M: NO. I AM ALWAYS LIKE THIS.

TYLER J: FIN, PUT A LID ON IT. ZILA, WHAT ARE YOU SAYING?

Zila sighs and begins typing in a flurry.

ZILA M: THE *BELLEROPHON*'S CREW JUST LIQUIDATED ONE HUNDRED INNOCENT SYLDRATHI REFUGEES. PRESUMABLY THEY ALSO DESTROYED THE UNBROKEN WRAITH, LEGIONNAIRE BRANNOCK?

Cat nods in reply.

Zila M: Ergo, we are the only witnesses left alive.

I type quickly, scowling in disbelief.

Tyler J: You're saying they're going to flat-line us to cover up the fact that they violated Terran neutrality with the Unbroken? Not that I don't value your input, Zila, but that makes no sense. Why save us only to kill us right afterward?

Zila M: They are not covering up their violation of neutrality, sir. They are silencing anybody who may know Aurora O'Malley is in their custody.

Scarlett J: Wait, what's Aurora got to do with this?

Zila M: Consider it logically. How is it that a TDF destroyer just happened to be within range when we sent our distress call?

Cat B: I told you Shamrock would bring us luck.

Finian dS: Didn't you hear, Legionnaire Madran? *spooky voice* The Global Intelligence Agency has one thousand eyes donchewknow.

Zila M: They were pursuing us. It is the only explanation for their proximity. Aurora said she was told to stow aboard our Longbow by Battle Leader de Stoy. De Stoy wanted Aurora with us, away from the GIA.

Cat B: Bollocks. O'Malley's spent WAY too

MUCH TIME IN THE FOLD. SHE'S GONE ALL THE WAY SIDEWAYS.

ZILA M: CONSIDER DE STOY'S WORDS TO US. *"THE CARGO YOU CARRY IS MORE PRECIOUS THAN ANY OF YOU CAN KNOW."* THE SUPPLY RUN TO SAGAN WAS NOT OUR MISSION. OUR MISSION WAS TO GET AURORA O'MALLEY AWAY FROM THE ACADEMY BEFORE THE GIA ARRIVED TO TAKE HER BACK TO TERRA.

FINIAN dS: THEY'VE GOT NO FACES.

CAT B: MAKER'S BREATH, FINIAN, HAVE YOU SNAPPED, TOO?

FINIAN dS: SCREW YOU, CAT.

CAT B: I'D RATHER SCREW THE GREAT ULTRASAUR OF ABRAAXIS IV, THANKS.

TYLER J: KNOCK IT OFF. FIN, EXPLAIN.

FINIAN dS: AURORA SAID THAT TO ME RIGHT BEFORE THE GIA ARRIVED. "THEY'VE GOT NO FACES." AND SHE MUTTERED SOMETHING ABOUT WIPING THIS CLEAN. PAINTING IT BLACK.

ZILA M: WHICH THE FACELESS GIA OPERATIVES ARE DOING RIGHT NOW. AURORA ALSO CLAIMED TO HAVE SEEN KAL IN A VISION BEFORE SHE EVER MET HIM.

CAT B: BECAUSE THE FOLD HAS MESSED WITH HER BRAINMEATS.

KALIIS G: THIS WILL SOUND LIKE MADNESS. BUT IN THE CARGO BAY, WHEN AEDRA ATTACKED ME, AURORA THREW HER INTO THE WALL WITHOUT EVER TOUCHING HER.

FINIAN dS: ARE YOU JOKING?

KALIIS G: I SWEAR IT ON THE SPIRITS OF THE VOID.

HER RIGHT EYE WAS GLOWING SO BRIGHTLY IT HURT TO LOOK AT. AND AFTER THE BATTLE, IT HAD CHANGED COLOR.

Scar and I look at each other then. I can see skepticism in her bright blue stare.

But Auri's eye *did* change color.

TYLER J: LISTEN, I DIDN'T MENTION THIS ON MY REPORT BECAUSE I DIDN'T REALLY WANT TO BELIEVE IT MYSELF. BUT WHEN I FIRST RESCUED AURORA ON THE *HADFIELD*, I THINK SHE

TYLER J: WELL, SHE MOVED ME.

SCARLETT J: MOVED YOU? LIKE IN A LOVE SONG WAY MOVED YOU?

CAT B: OH, SPARE ME.

TYLER J: LIKE I WAS ON THE VERGE OF PASSING OUT TWO HUNDRED METERS FROM MY PHANTOM. AND SUDDENLY WE WERE RIGHT OUTSIDE THE AIRLOCK.

ZILA M: TELEKINESIS. PRECOGNITION. INTERESTING.

CAT B: THIS IS TOTALLY BLOODY SIDEWAYS

SCARLETT J: I'M AFRAID I MUST CONCUR WITH MY PUNCHY BUT LEARNED COLLEAGUE.

CAT B: THANKS, ROOMIE.

SCARLETT J: ALL GOOD, GIRL. YOU'VE STILL GOT MY EYELINER, BTW.

ZILA M: IT IS COMMON KNOWLEDGE THAT PROLONGED FOLD EXPOSURE EXERTS EXTREME MENTAL DURESS ON TRAVELERS. I'D REMIND YOU THAT AURORA WAS DRIFTING IN IT FOR OVER TWO CENTURIES. NOBODY HAS EVER SURVIVED THAT KIND OF EXPOSURE BEFORE.

Finian dS: So what does the GIA want with her?

Zila M: An excellent question. But I think the far more pressing concern is our imminent and no doubt brutal murders at the hands of their operatives.

Finian dS: I admit that Princess guy didn't seem like a barrel of chuckles.

Scarlett J: PrincePs. It's Latin. Means "first among equals."

Zila M: I did not know you spoke Latin, Legionnaire Jones.

Finian dS: What in the Maker's name is Latin?

Cat B: Look, this still makes no bloody sense. If they want us dead, why didn't they just flatline us on the station?

Zila M: Perhaps they wish to speak to Tyler about how he found Aurora? Or to ensure we have not passed her location on to anyone else? Whatever their reasons, unless we find a way off this ship, we will never leave it alive.

Tyler J: This is the Terran Defense Force you're talking about.

Zila M: The Global Intelligence Agency is in command here, sir. The TDF is simply giving them a ride.

Tyler J: They're still Terran! Maker's sake, what are we supposed to do? Attack our own people?

Finian dS: As opposed to being executed by them?

A warning klaxon sounds across the destroyer's public address system, followed by a shipwide announcement.

"ALL HANDS, PREPARE FOR FOLD ENTRY. T-MINUS FIFTEEN SECONDS."

The thrum of the engines shifts in tone, and each of us takes a breath. There's a slow rush of vertigo, a brief sensation of weightlessness, and the colorscape shifts as the destroyer enters the FoldGate, everything around us dropping into black and white. I see my squad looking to me for a decision.

Impossible as it sounds, Zila is making an awful kind of sense. The lives of people who depend on me are on the line here. And the consequences of not believing her—and being wrong—would be fatal.

Problem is, if the TDF really means to flatline us, the only way I can see out of this is *fighting* our way out, and that means fighting fellow Terrans. My dad was in the TDF before he became a senator. If the Aurora Legion didn't exist, I'd probably be TDF myself.

I meet Scar's stare, and she tilts her head just a fraction.

It's a strange thing, being a twin. Dad told Scar and me that we invented our own language as little kids. Talking to each other in words nobody else could understand. Scar can tell me a story with a look. Write me a novel with a single raised eyebrow. And right now, I know exactly what she's saying, without her ever saying a word.

Show the way, baby brother.

The door hisses open, and four TDF troopers march into the room, clad head to foot in tac armor, carrying disruptor rifles. The young lieutenant I spoke to in the Sagan Station airlock is leading them. One eyebrow raised behind her visor, she stops to survey the puddle of water on the floor, and my soaking uniform.

"All right, legionnaire," she smiles. "If you'll come with us, we'll debrief you and have you and your squad back at Aurora Station in time for chow."

I glance at Scar again, looking for her impressions. I'm not exaggerating when I say she can read people like books. It's kinda scary sometimes. I haven't been able to fool her since we were five years old.

She looks the lieutenant up and down.

Glances at me.

Pouts.

Lying.

I can feel the tension around me. Cat's hands in fists. Kal's icy fury as he stares at these soldiers who just murdered a hundred of his people but are acting like nothing's wrong. I'm not sure how good Finian or Zila will be in a free-for-all, but there's six of us, four of them, and if they think I'm the kind to just march to my own murder, they don't know me too well.

I stand up with an easy smile, dimples on high beam.

"No problem, LT," I say.

And I bury my elbow right into her throat.

Her tac armor absorbs most of the impact, but it's enough to send her off balance. I kick her in the knee and she hits the ground, disruptor flying from her grip.

The room explodes into motion, the three other TDF troopers aiming their weapons at my chest. Kal rises up be-hind one and stabs with outstretched fingers behind her ear, and the trooper drops like she's been hit with a dose of Leirium rocksmoke. Cat tackles another, fighting for control of his rifle, and Scar hurls the empty water cooler bottle at the third's head, sending him back into Finian, whose exosuit whines as he grabs him like a vise.

I snatch up the fallen lieutenant's disruptor rifle, bring the butt down into her face, her helmet skewing crooked as the blow lands. We fall to wrestling, the LT knocking the rifle aside. She lands a knee in my crotch and the whole world burns white with the pain. Flipping me onto my back, she manages to draw her sidearm from her belt, raising it to my head.

A hand takes hold of her jaw and three fingers stab the side of her neck. With a sigh, the LT topples off me, eyes rolling back in her head. Above me stands Kal, his eyes narrowed. Not a single silver hair is out of place on his head. He's not even out of breath. Wincing at the ache in my groin, I look around the cell. The other three TDF troopers are scattered like broken toys.

They're all out cold. Battered and bloodied, bones broken. Scar, Cat, and Finian are looking at our Tank, half-awed, half-terrified, all silent.

"I don't want you to think this means I like you, Kal," Cat finally says. "But okay. I'm officially impressed."

"Did it just get hot in here, or is it me?" Scarlett asks.

"It's not just you," Finian mutters, fanning himself.

The Syldrathi offers his hand to me.

"We need to move, sir."

I realize this is the first time Kal has offered to touch me since he slugged me back at the academy. And knowing it's

151

a big deal for a Syldrathi to allow themselves to be touched at all, I figure I should accept the offer. I take his hand, and he hauls me to my feet. I'm trying not to look at the bleeding soldiers around me. The bleeding *human* soldiers. My mind is racing, looking for a way out of this.

We're outnumbered a hundred to one. The GIA has Auri in custody. They have our Longbow locked down. But I've studied Terran space vessels since I was six—I know the layout of a destroyer backward. And though this pack of losers and discipline cases and sociopaths might've been the last picks on anyone's mind during the Draft, turns out none of them are bad at their jobs. If I can hold this together, get us working as a team, we might even make it out of this alive. . . .

An alarm starts blaring, an announcement spilling over the PA.

"SECURITY TO DETENTION CELL 12A. SECURITY TO 12A IMMEDIATELY."

"That's for us," Cat warns.

"Okay, listen up," I say. "I've got a plan."

. . . . .

"FIRE ALARM, LEVEL TWELVE. EMERGENCY CREW TO LEVEL TWELVE IMMEDIATELY."

We're marching toward the elevators with the alarms blaring when the first TDF squad finds us. They round the corner, disruptor rifles raised, laser sights cutting through the sprinkler system's downpour. We're still Folding, so the colorscape is still monochrome, the water spray is silver, the squad sergeant's eyes are almost black.

"Don't move!" he barks.

Scarlett steps forward, her lieutenant's insignia gleaming on her collar, her fiery hair dulled to gray. My boots are too big, and I'm not bragging or anything, but the crotch in this tac armor just isn't sitting right. Still, considering we stole these uniforms off four unconscious TDF troopers, we're mostly pulling it off. Cat and Zila are skulking at the back, and Kal and Finian stand between us, mag-restraints around their wrists, looking appropriately cowed. Scarlett has more than enough swagger to fill in the gaps.

"We got two of 'em," she barks. "The other four made it to the air vents. Get your squad up to thirteen, we're taking these two to the brig!"

The squad sergeant frowns behind his visor. "The vents? We got t—"

"You get dropped on your head as a baby, soldier?" Scarlett snaps. "I just gave you an order! Move your asses before I flush 'em into the Fold!"

Say what you will about the military, but Maker bless, they don't teach you to think. They teach you to follow orders. No matter what uniform they're wearing, Legion, TDF, whatever, when a lieutenant starts yelling at the average sergeant to jump, their only question is gonna be "How high?"

Fortunately for us, this sergeant seems kinda average.

"Ma'am, yes ma'am," he barks, turning to his squad. "Level thirteen, move!"

The squad rushes past us. Scarlett starts yelling into her collar mic, demanding to know where the fire crews are at. We reach the turbolift, and I stab at the controls as the silver rain falls all around us, the lights flashing gray.

"Okay, Finian, how long before they get their cams back online?" I ask.

He glances down to his uniglass, shakes his head. "It was a pretty basic hack I threw in there. We've got about another minute, maybe two."

"Right. Every security squad is on their way up here to Level twelve. The docking bay is on five. Cat, you take Zila, Fin, and Kal down there and get the Longbow ready to launch. *Quietly*. If we're not aboard in five minutes—"

"Ty, I'm not taking off without you," Cat says.

"I was gonna say give us another five minutes, but no, you're right, you should totally take off without me."

"Where are you going?" Finian asks.

"Scar and I are gonna go get Aurora."

"I am coming with you," Kal says.

"No," I snap. "You're not. You stick out like a six-foot-eight pointy-eared sore thumb in here. Get to the docking bay. You might need to fight your way through."

"You will *definitely* need to fight your way to Aurora," Kal says, stepping forward. "And I am better at it than you."

"I just gave you an order, legionnaire," I growl.

Kal tilts his head. "Please feel free to put me on report, sir."

"For the love of . . . ," Scar sighs. "Will you two just kiss and get it over with?"

"I mean, I could think of worse things to watch?" Finian says.

The lift arrives and the doors hiss open as the alarms continue to scream. I wonder what the big deal is. Why Kal is so keen on rescuing Aurora when he was such a jerk to her back on Sagan. But looking up into his eyes, I can tell he's not going to budge unless I push, and Maker's breath, we just don't have the time.

"Scar, go with Cat. Five minutes, then you launch. That's an *order.*"

Scarlett looks at me, blinking in the silver rain. "Yessir."

The four board the turbolift, and I look Cat in the eyes as the door hisses closed. I turn to glower at Kal, met with a stare hard as diamond.

"Priority prisoners will be in the brig down on eleven," I say.

"Follow me," the Syldrathi replies. "Sir."

We dash to the stairwell, taking the steps four at a time to the level below. Out in the hallway, Kal walks in front, hands still held before him in the mag-restraints. I march behind, pointing my disruptor rifle at his back, hoping I look like a guard escorting his prisoner. A tech crew with fire-suppressant gear barrels right past us, followed close by a squad of TDF troopers. None of them spare us much more than a glance. The alarms are still blaring, the PA still shouting about the fire Zila set in the electrical conduits. I make a mental note to ask Fin exactly why he has a propane torch hidden in his exosuit, and what other surprises he has stashed in that thing.

Presuming we make it out of this alive, that is.

The brig is almost deserted—most of the troopers are upstairs looking for us. I see a hallway beyond the admissions area, lined with heavy doors. A junior officer is typing at a workstation, and a second sits behind the counter, shouting into a comms unit over the shipwide alarm. He holds up one hand at me, signaling I should wait.

And then it starts.

It's a weird prickling on the back of my neck at first. The air suddenly feels greasy—charged almost, like with static electricity. There's a noise above the thrum of the engines, below the shriek of the alarm. Almost . . .

Whispering?

I look to Kal, and from the slight frown on his face, I can tell he hears it, too. The brig officer blinks, glances in the direction of the holding cells.

Without warning, the lights flicker out, plunging us into darkness. The whisper gets louder, almost sharp enough to make out the words, and the room . . . *vibrates*. High-pitched screams sound out in the black, followed by a wet crunching noise, and every holding cell door buckles simultaneously, titanium crumpling like paper.

Every display on every console dies.

The engines and alarms are suddenly silenced.

The dull illumination of emergency lighting kicks in overhead.

Terran destroyers have four separate reactors, a hundred fail-safes and a dozen different backup systems. But impossible as it is, I realize the entire ship has suddenly and completely lost power. The silence after all that noise is deafening, and I look down the hallway, wondering what on Earth is going on here. Spilling from beneath one of those crushed doors is a long, dark, gray slick of what can only be—

"Blood," the brig officer whispers, reaching for his sidearm.

Kal takes his chance, sloughing off his mag-restraints

156

and slamming them into the officer's throat. The man falls back gasping, and Kal vaults the counter, strikes twice, and leaves him unconscious and bleeding on the floor. The junior officer turns with a shout, sidearm raised, and Kal has broken his wrist and his elbow and then knocked him senseless before I can squeeze my trigger.

The Syldrathi straightens, tossing his long braids back off his shoulders, his face as impassive as if he'd just ordered dinner.

Great Maker, he's good. . . .

I've no idea what just killed the power, but we've got no time to open a global inquiry into it. The overheads start flickering like strobes, and I come to my senses, leap the counter after my Tank. Dashing down the hallway, we skid to a stop at the blood-slicked door. I raise my disruptor rifle, heart beating quick, nod to Kal. Though he's stronger than a human, it's still a stretch for him, but finally he drags the cell door aside with a squeal of metal.

I step inside, weapon raised and ready.

"Maker's breath," I whisper.

Aurora is slumped in a single metal chair, restraints at her wrists. Her eyes are closed, blood dripping from her nose, spilling over her chin. The floor, ceilings, and walls are buckled outward, almost in a spherical shape. I see two faceless helmets on the floor, two charcoal-gray suits crumpled beside them, their contents smeared up the wall in a strange mixture of gray and black, textures unrecognizable. They go all the way up to the ceiling, like the people inside them were tubes of toothpaste and someone just . . . *squeezed.*

"Amna diir . . . ," Kal breathes.

"Grab Aurora," I say, fighting the churning in my gut. "We've gotta move."

He nods, his face grim. He kneels beside those shredded suits and rummages in the soggy pockets, finally producing a passkey. With a swipe, Aurora's restraints are unlocked, and Kal lifts her effortlessly, gently cradles her in his arms. Then we're moving across the bloody floor, out into the strobing light, wet footprints behind us. My disruptor rifle has a small flashlight slung under the barrel, a slice of light showing us the way through all that flickering gloom.

The elevators have no power, so we hit the stairs, barreling down as quick as we can to Level five. Slipping out through the door, I see four TDF troopers in a huddle around a wall comms console, trying to raise the bridge.

I know it's them or us, I know I've got no choice, but my stomach clenches as I take a knee and fire. They cry out and scatter into cover like the dummies in training exercises never did as I turn to Kal and roar.

"Go! *Go!*"

He dashes out from the stairwell and across the *Bellerophon*'s docking bay toward our Longbow with Aurora in his arms. Troopers around the bay turn at the sound of gunfire. Scar pops up from behind a stack of cargo crates and opens up with her own rifle, disruptor fire streaking white through the dark. Looking through our Longbow's blastshield, I see Cat has somehow managed to sneak aboard in the chaos. I breathe a prayer to the Maker that whatever killed the destroyer's power somehow hasn't affected our own ship, sighing in relief as she arcs the engines.

Sparks ricochet off the deck as troopers fire at Kal. I use

what's left of my disruptor's power on them, trying to give him cover. Cat opens up with our Longbow's gauss cannons, and the TDF troopers are forced back into cover as a barrage of supersonic shells explode across the bay.

Scar breaks cover and runs for the Longbow, and I take my chance, too, dashing after Kal, heart hammering in my chest. The Longbow's engines are growing louder, the ship rising off the deck. Finian's on our docking ramp, waving at me frantically as Scarlett leaps to safety. Kal bounds up onto the ramp in three long strides, I hit it close behind him as TDF fire whizzes around me, sprawled flat on my stomach as I roar, "PUNCH IT, CAT!"

The ramp shudders closed and our Longbow banks hard to port. There's a soft whine and bright *hisssss* as Cat fires two plasma missiles at the inner bay doors, melting them to slag. Bullets are pattering against our hull like hail as Cat fires again, this time breaching the plasteel on the outer hull, exposing the colorless void of the Fold beyond.

There's a burst of violent decompression, the atmo in the bay spilling out into the Fold and forcing the TDF to retreat or suffocate. Alarms are screaming, our engines roaring, Cat's voice crackling over the internal PA.

"Hold on to your undies, kids!"

We blast out from the bay, a handful of TDF bullets kissing us goodbye. The portside engines scrape against the melted bay doors as we rocket out into the Fold.

I look around to check on the others, and nobody seems to be hurt. Kal is crouching beside Aurora, making sure she doesn't slide around. She's out cold—her eyes are closed, lips

159

and chin smudged with blood, her expression as blissful as the moment I found her in that cryopod.

That was only three days ago.

"Everyone okay back there?" Cat asks over the PA.

I tap my uniglass to reply.

"Roger that," I sigh. "We're all okay."

Scarlett's looking at me across the Longbow's holding bay, eyes locked on mine. "You sure have a strange definition of 'okay,' Bee-bro."

Looking at my twin, I know what she's thinking. Sure as if she said it aloud.

We just undertook an armed insurrection on a Terran Defense Force destroyer.

We just violated a hundred or more Legion regulations before dinner.

We just attacked TDF personnel.

Great Maker . . .

The engines roar as we hurtle on through the Fold, farther away from the crippled *Bellerophon,* the scene of our crimes, on through all that glittering dark.

We might have gotten away alive, but we sure didn't get away clean. Not after what Aurora did in that cell. You don't murder GIA operatives and expect to keep breathing. It's only gonna be a matter of time before the Global Intelligence Agency and the entire Terran Defense Force are breathing down our necks. They were set on killing us, sure, but . . .

We're fugitives, I realize. *From our own people.*

Scar chews her lip and nods.

What would Dad say?

Finian looks around the bay, big black eyes finally settling on me.

"So, Goldenboy," he says. "What in the Maker's name do we do now?"

I take a deep breath, blow my hair back from my eyes.

"That," I sigh, "is an excellent question."

PART 2

A SKY FULL OF GHOSTS

Aurora Legion Squads

▶ Squad Members

  ▼ Faces

If you're dealing with an Aurora legionnaire smoother than a glass of **single-malt Larassian semptar**, then odds are you've just met a Face. Diplomats by nature and by training, their job is to deal with friends or foes—and a good Face can often turn the latter into the former with a few well-placed words.

Whether it's making **first contact**, **mediating** a local dispute, or talking their way out of a steaming pile of **alien dookie**, Faces are versed in the **cultures**, **traditions**, and **languages** of many species and have a reputation for being skilled negotiators.

Playing **cards** against one is *not* recommended.

FACE'S INSIGNIA

13

SCARLETT

Marc de Vries. Ex-boyfriend #29. Pros: built like a brick wall. Cons: brains like a brick wall.

"Mmmmmaybe," I murmur.

[STORE]

Tré Jackson. Ex-boyfriend #41. Pros: looks like Adonis. Cons: knows it.

"Nnnnope."

[DELETE]

I'm sitting on our Longbow's bridge, feet up on my console, my uniglass in hand. The ship is quiet except for the low hum of the engines, the occasional ping from the LADAR sweeps we've got running. We dropped out of the Fold through the gate at NZ-7810, and we're now cruising on low power through a random low-rent system out in a neutral zone. Cat programmed a course to keep us close to the gate before she retired to her boudoir. Just in case we need to run.

Everyone else is in quarters getting some sleep, but lucky me, I drew first watch. So I'm using the time to go through my contacts and delete some of my exes.

Memory was getting full.

Riley Lemieux. Ex-boyfriend #16. Pros: madly in love with me. Cons: MADLY in love with me.

[DELETE]

It might seem an odd time for the squad to take a nap. My hands are still a little shaky when I think about everything that's happened in the last day, and I can't imagine what comes next. But grabbing some beauty sleep is a good idea—everyone needed some rest after the chaos aboard Sagan Station and that TDF destroyer. Besides, Tyler thinks better after sleepy-bo-bos, and the decision he makes next will probably be the most important one of his life.

No pressure, baby brother.

We're outlaws. Probably wanted criminals. An Aurora Legion squad gone rogue. Though we're technically under Legion command, we still broke out of a TDF ship. Attacked Terran personnel. Our own people. And for what?

I chew my lip, eyes flickering over my uniglass screen.

Alex Naidu. Ex-boyfriend #38. Pros: biceps!!! Cons: unknown.

"Why did I break up with you again?"

[STORE]

I have to admit, when I signed up for Aurora Academy, this isn't exactly how I pictured my career panning out. To be honest, I didn't even really *want* to join the Legion. But Ty was hells-bent on "making a difference," and there was no way I was letting him join up alone. We grew up without a mom. Dad got killed at Orion when we were eleven. Damned if I was going to lose my twin brother, too.

I remember standing in line with Ty on New Gettysburg Station. Both of us thirteen years old, waiting to shuffle up for our turn with the recruiting officer. I remember asking Tyler if we were doing the right thing. If it would all turn out okay.

"I don't know," he'd said.

Then he touched the Maker's mark at his collar and shrugged.

"But sometimes you just gotta have faith."

I can cram with the best, so I did okay on my exams. I might've actually been good if I tried. The cadet guidance counselor once told me the phrase *if she applied herself* had appeared more times on my assessment sheets than on any cadet's in academy history. But I hated it.

Hated the rules, hated the routine, hated the station.

The boys were fun, though.

Jesse Broder. Ex-boyfriend #45. Pros: A$$. Cons: A$$hole.

"Hmmmm . . ."

[STORE]

What can I say, I'm a girl of simple tastes.

I hear the soft whisper of the bridge door opening, glance up expecting to see Zila come to relieve me from my shift. Instead, I see our resident stowaway, Aurora O'Malley. The girl out of time.

The girl out of bed?

"How'd you get up here?" I ask.

It might've seemed a little mean, but Ty had wisely insisted our young Ms. O'Malley be secured rather than be let loose to roam the ship. Whatever he'd seen aboard that TDF destroyer while rescuing this girl had my baby brother shaken

168

up good. So after she, Kal, and Ty cleaned up, Finian secured Aurora inside the hold with a blankie and extra encryption on the door, which apparently he forgot to lock, because she's totally standing here in front of me and she sure as hells shouldn't be.

I remind myself to give Finian some sass about that later. "Aurora?" I ask.

The girl doesn't reply. Her hair is mussed from sleep, that thick white streak through her bangs treading the fine line between chic and weird. Her eyes are almost closed. Lashes fluttering. Her right iris is the same bleached white as her bangs now, sadly falling off the line between chic and weird and tumbling right down into spoooooky.

Her movement is stiff, her body language *all* kinds of wrong, and my first thought is that she's sleepwalking. But that doesn't explain how she broke out of the hold. Unless Finian's encryption is so bad that a girl born two centuries ago can break it. In her *sleep*.

Yeah, I'm really gonna sass him about that one. . . .

Aurora turns her head, as if surveying the room. It's hard to imagine what's going through her mind. Two centuries out of time. Nowhere she was supposed to be and a galaxy gone all the way sideways. But she shouldn't be up here.

"Are you okay?" I ask.

She starts walking, making a beeline for Cat's pilot console. It's about now I decide that whatever the deal is here, our beautiful heroine, Legionnaire Scarlett Isobel Jones, has had just about enough of it.

My hand slips to the disruptor pistol at my waist, and I climb to my feet.

"All right, lovely lady, if you—"

Her right eye lights up with a soft, flickering glow, pale as moonlight. She raises her hand without looking at me, and an invisible blow to my chest slams me back into the wall. I gasp, trying to draw my disruptor, but Aurora curls her fingers into claws, her eye burns a brighter shade of white, and there's a force pressing on my wrist, stopping me from raising the weapon.

"Ezigolopai," Aurora says, in a voice that sounds nothing like her own. Hollow. Reverberating, like in an echo chamber. *"Emevigrof."*

I feel pain, as if some invisible grip were grinding my knuckles together. I let the disruptor go, and as it clatters to the deck, the pressure eases.

My heart's thudding in my chest and cold sweat is breaking out on my body. I realize I can't move a muscle, my throat compressing so I can't even speak. Aurora peers at the pilot's console, head tilted, lashes fluttering. Her right eye is still aglow, her hair is moving slightly, as if in a breeze. With her free hand, she begins typing commands, fingers blurring over the keyboards.

"Wh—" I wince, trying to force the words out of my crushed throat, my clenched teeth. "What . . . y-you . . . doing?"

Her nose starts bleeding. A thin line of red, rolling down over her lips. She doesn't stop typing to wipe it away, and I realize she's messing with the nav systems. Setting a new course. She's a novice, totally untrained, zero flight hours. Maker's sake, she's spent the last two centuries asleep in the Fold.

How does she know how a Longbow's nav systems work?

"Ytinretipmes," she whispers. *"Doogdoog."*

I hear the engines alter tone, the subtle shift of a course change. The blood's flowing down over Aurora's chin now, pattering on the console. She turns to face me, hand still outstretched. Her right eye aglow with a soft, warm light. My stomach's full of ice, fear hammering in my temples. But as much as I strain, it's like there's some hidden weight pressing me back into the wall.

I can't move.

I can't fight.

I can't even scream.

Aurora shivers, blood slicking her chin. Her brow furrows, lips moving slowly, carefully, as if she's straining to pronounce her words.

"T-t-ttrig-ggerrrrr," she says, pointing to herself. *"Trigg—"*

I hear the familiar *BAMF!* of a disruptor burst. Aurora's eyes widen, and she staggers. The pressure holding me in place relaxes, and I collapse to my knees. Zila's at the door, weapon trained squarely on Aurora.

One blast from a disruptor on Stun setting is enough to drop a full-grown Rigellian stonebull, but somehow Aurora's still standing. She turns and Zila fires again, pistol flashing. Aurora falls to her knees, groaning, raising one hand toward our science officer. Her right eye burns like a sun. And with the kind of callousness that earned her thirty-two disciplinary citations, Zila keeps firing—

BAMF!

BAMF!

BAMF!

—until Aurora crashes face-first onto the deck.

"Zila," I moan.

BAMF!

"Zila!"

BAMF!

Zila blinks, looks at me, finger still on the trigger.

"Yes?" she asks.

"She's d-down," I groan, my head splitting. "You can s-stop shooting her now."

Zila looks at her disruptor. Down at the unconscious Aurora, sprawled on the deck. And maybe for good measure, maybe just for fun, our science officer gives the comatose girl one more blast.

BAMF!

"Interesting," she says.

. . . . .

"We should just space this crazy slip right now," Cat spits.

We're gathered on the bridge, standing around the unconscious body of one Aurora O'Malley. She's seated in one of the auxiliary stations, mag-restraints around her wrists, though I'm not sure how much good that'll do if she wakes up. Cat, Zila, and I have our disruptors trained on her in case she decides on a repeat performance of her attack-the-gorgeous-yet-totally-down-to-earth-space-diplomat routine. I've got time to notice now that Zila's wearing a new pair of earrings—these ones are small golden chains with tiny charms in the shape of weapons hanging off them. There's a gun, a knife, a throwing star.

Did she stop for a wardrobe change before coming to my rescue?

Kal is standing silently by the doorway, a thoughtful pout on those oh-so-shapely Syldrathi lips. But at the mention of flushing Aurora, he looks at Cat.

"Do not be a fool," he says, voice dripping with disdain. "We cannot kill her."

"Screw you, Pixieboy," our Ace snaps back. "She nearly flatlined Scarlett. Head out of arse, please and thanks."

"Scar, are you sure you're okay?" Tyler asks.

"Yeah, I'm fine," I reply. "Just a little shook up is all."

"She really . . . held you in place just by looking at you?"

I nod, rubbing my neck. We're back in the Fold, headed on whatever course Aurora locked into the navcom before Zila knocked her flat. The bruises on my wrist are a dark and ugly gray. My skin is bleached to bone in the Fold colorscape— almost as pale as the glow that spilled from Aurora's eye as she crushed me against the wall.

"Tyler," Cat says. "We need our heads read, keeping this girl aboard. We have to either space her right now or sedate her hard and hand her over to the authorities before they court-martial us back to the stone age."

Kal looks ready to dish out some more insults, but before he can speak, a voice crackles over comms.

"Goldenboy, you read me okay?"

Tyler taps his uniglass. "We read, Fin, what's your status?"

"Well, I'm down in the hold, and I gotta tell you, this is about the scariest thing I've seen since I walked in on my third grandparents when I was twelve."

"Explain."

"Well, I had a med appointment that got canceled and I

173

came home early and found my grandmother and grandfather with a bowl of sagarine and a twelve-inch—"

"Maker's breath, Finian, I mean explain about the hold!" Tyler snaps.

"Oh," Finian replies. "Right. Well, I'm not sure how our little stowaway did it, but the inner doors have been peeled open like those things you dirt farmers eat. I can't remember what they're called. . . . They're round. Orange colored."

"You mean oranges?"

"Yeah, whatever. Point is, these doors are made from case-hardened carbite and titanium. And she bent them open like they were cardboard."

"Flush her, Tyler," Cat says.

Kal pushes off the wall, looming over Cat, his voice cold as ice.

"You will *not* hurt her."

I suck my bottom lip, noting the calm in Kal's voice versus the intensity in his eyes. Syldrathi body language can be tough to read beyond *We are soooo much better than you, and yes, we know it,* but Kal looks ready to tear Cat apart if she so much as blinks at the girl he was being a complete jackass to twelve hours ago.

Cat's a foot shorter than Kal—maybe a little more right now, with her fauxhawk flattened by sleep. But never one to back down, our Ace squares up against our Tank. "You heard what she did in the hold, Pixieboy! In case you flunked mecha-neering, our *hull* is built out of exactly the same material as those doors. *And* she buggered with my flight controls. How could she know how to do that if she's been drifting in the Fold for two hundred years? This girl is *not* what she seems."

"I agree," Kal says simply. "Which is *exactly* why you will not touch her."

Aurora groans and three disruptors immediately swing back in her direction. Kal steps in, eyes locked on Tyler.

"Sir," he says. "If Aurora wished your sister dead, she would be dead. You saw what she did to those GIA operatives."

"I surely did." Tyler looks at the stirring girl, and I can practically see the cogs turning behind his eyes. "What course did she lock into the navcom, Cat?"

Our Ace blinks, lowers her weapon. Turning to her pilot's console, she wipes off Aurora's nose-blood with a muttered curse, stabs in a series of commands.

"Sempiternity," she finally says.

"What's that?" I ask.

"You never heard of the World Ship?" Cat blinks.

"Astrography isn't my forte," I reply. "I remember sleeping through most of it."

"I remember you sleeping *with*—"

"SEMPITERNITY," a small, chirpy voice twitters, and Tyler's old uniglass lights up inside Aurora's breast pocket. "ALSO KNOWN AS THE WORLD SHIP. LOCATED DEEP IN A NEUTRAL ZONE, SEMPITERNITY IS A TRADING HUB, OUTSIDE ANY GOVERNMENTAL JURISDICTION, RUN BY . . . INTERSTELLAR ENTREPRENEURS."

"It means space pirates," Cat offers.

"I WAS TRYING TO BE POLITE," the device says.

"Silent mode," Tyler growls.

"Aw."

The uniglass falls silent as Cat calls up a 3-D schematic

175

of Sempiternity over the center console. It's an enormous collection of hundreds of thousands of ships, all different makes and models and sizes, bolted and welded and crushed together into a vast lopsided sphere. Beautiful. Hideous. Every kind of impossible.

"Sempiternity started as a single starport," Cat explains. "Run by a freebooter cartel. Pirate crews would unload there, sell their spoils, head out for more. But over the past fifty years it's accumulated more and more extensions. Ships that decide to stay and just attach themselves to the superstructure. Place goes on forever now. It's as big as a small moon. Hence the name. The World Ship."

I look at Aurora, still slumped in her chair. "So why does she want us to go there?"

As if she senses that I'm talking about her, Aurora groans and slowly lifts her head. Wincing with pain, she sees the three disruptors pointed at her face. Her mismatched eyes go wide, then narrow as she realizes she's in restraints. That she can taste blood on her lips.

"Um," she says. "If this is another vision, I'd like to wake up, please."

"You call that an apology?" I ask.

"W-what am I apologizing for?" She winces again, slowly rolling her shoulders and neck. "And . . . why do I feel like I was in . . . a c-car accident?"

"What, you don't remember slamming me against the wall without touching me? Or Zila hitting you with half a dozen disruptor blasts?"

A kaleidoscope of emotions cross her face. Fear. Dismay. Frustration. Genuine confusion as she looks around and realizes she's not in the room she went to sleep in.

"N-no," she says.

"Computer," I call. "Replay bridge security camera footage, 01:29 ship time."

The computer beeps, and the central display begins to play the sec reel. Aurora watches, going perfectly still when she sees herself walk onto the bridge, lift her hand as her eye starts to glow, and slam me back into the bulkhead.

"Ezigolopai," the recording says in that strange, warbling voice. *"Emevigrof."*

"I don't . . ." Aurora shakes her head, looks with growing panic to Tyler. "I don't remember doing *any* of that."

"How convenient," Cat says.

"Very," I say.

"Auri, why did you mess with the navcom?" Tyler asks, his voice flat and hard. "Why do you want to go to Sempiternity?"

She shakes her head and whispers, "What's Sempiternity?"

"Wait."

All eyes turn to Zila. She's playing idly with the tiny knife on one of her earrings, dark stare fixed on the security footage projection.

"Computer, replay footage in reverse. Real time. Include audio."

The computer complies with a small beep, and we watch the figure of Aurora at the pilot's console, typing backward. The rivulets of blood run back up her chin, into her nose. My dropped disruptor springs back up into my hand. And Aurora glances up at me and speaks in that strange, warbling voice. Only this time, the audio file is playing backward.

"Forgiveme," she says. *"Iapologize."*

Zila blinks at the recording. "Computer, replay sequence 02:43 to 02:52."

The footage skips to Aurora standing in front of me, pointing to herself, her face twisted with concentration.

"T-t-ttrig-ggerrrrr," she says. "Trigg—"

"Trigger," Zila repeats, head tilted.

"What does that mean?" Tyler asks her.

Our science officer turns to regard Aurora with her dark eyes.

"I have no idea, sir. But I am certain that Commander de Stoy placed Aurora in our keeping for a reason. In my opinion, we should maintain course."

Finian pipes up over comms. *For what it's worth, I think I agree with the tiny lunatic, Goldenboy. This is getting kinda interesting.*

"I'm sure the thought of the court-martial waiting for us back at Aurora Station has no bearing on your decision, Finian?" Tyler asks.

"None whatsoever, sir."

Tyler sighs, turns to me. It might sound like a little thing, but this is one of the main reasons my baby brother was the best Alpha in the academy. It's also one of the main reasons I never smothered him in his sleep. He's never afraid to ask advice when he needs it.

I think of the peeled-open door to the makeshift brig. Of the thin hull that protects us from the black waiting outside.

"We should go back to the academy," I say. "If we talk to Command, maybe there's some way to salvage this. We're in over our heads here."

"Damn straight we are," Cat growls. "I say give her to the G-men."

"Need I remind you all of Commander de Stoy's warning to us?" Kal asks. "She said, 'The cargo you carry is more precious than any of you can know.'" The Syldrathi looks Ty in the eye. "Admiral Adams spoke directly to you, sir. He said you must *believe*. What else could he have meant, if not this?"

Tyler chews his lip in thought.

But it's Aurora who speaks. "I want to g-go home," she says, her voice shaking. Tears begin welling in her eyes, and though she struggles to maintain her composure, it's crumbling anyway. She looks up at Tyler. "I'm not s-supposed to be here."

And even though she almost killed me, looking down at this poor girl, I can't help but feel a swell of sympathy for her. I put a hand on her shoulder, squeeze it gently as she hangs her head, tears pattering on her lap.

"It's okay, Aurora."

"I want to wake up," she whispers fiercely. "I want to wake up on Octavia III *l-like I was supposed to*."

Zila tilts her head. "The *Hadfield* expedition was bound for Lei Gong III, and—"

"No, it wasn't!" Aurora insists, a fire lighting in her tear-filled eyes as she glares at us. "I'm telling you, we were headed for Octavia! I spent years studying every centimeter of the planet, I know which one it was! I don't know why they're trying to wipe away any trace of it, any trace of *me*, but that's what's happening here."

Cat rolls her eyes at the outburst, drumming her fingers

on her console. Kal folds his arms, his customary Syldrathi callousness falling into place at the display of oh-so-human emotion. But Aurora doesn't seem to care.

"I w-want to go ho-ome," she repeats, the tears resurging as she abandons the attempt to hold herself together. "I want my family back. I didn't ask for any of this! *I didn't ask for any of it and I want to go HOME!*"

Tyler watches the girl break down, and I can see his heart in his throat. The questions in his eyes. Truth is, none of us know what the hells we're doing out here. De Stoy and Adams might have sent this girl with us for a reason. But Tyler was raised to play it by the book, and I can see how badly this is eating at him. The thought that we're wanted criminals, probably suspected of murdering our own people.

We're in deeper than we could've imagined.

"Three votes in favor of pushing on. And three against. Squad leader breaks ties." Tyler looks sadly at Aurora and sighs. "Cat, set a course for Aurora Academy. We're going home."

"Roger that," Cat smiles.

Kal sighs and shakes his head, but he doesn't dissent. Tyler drags his hand through his hair as Cat's fingers fly over her controls.

"Okay, course locked," she reports. "Should be back at station b—"

The Longbow shudders, sudden and violent. I reach out to steady myself when the ship bucks again, but I'm thrown into the wall, gasping in pain as I hit the titanium, then the floor. Brushing my hair from my eyes, I look around the bridge and see my squad scattered across the deck, groaning, wincing. Only Kal has managed to keep his feet. Finian's voice crackles over comms.

"What in the Maker's name was that?"

"Did something hit us?" Tyler demands.

"Nothing on scanners, sir," Zila reports.

"Cat, report," Tyler demands.

"We've . . ." Cat stabs at her console for confirmation. "Stopped?"

"Engines are offline?"

"No, I mean we've bloody *stopped*. Engines are at thrust, but it's like . . ." Cat shakes her head. "Like something is holding us in place."

"Not something," I breathe. "Some*one*."

The rest of the squad follows my eyeline, until we're all staring at Aurora. Our girl out of time has her head thrown back, her right eye burning with ghostly white light. Her body is trembling with effort, veins taut at her neck, in her arms. As we watch, another thin trickle of blood spills from her nose.

"Maker's breath," Tyler whispers.

"T-t-ttrig-ggerrrrr," Aurora says.

Up on her knees, Cat has her disruptor aimed at Auri's head, but smooth as silk, Kal steps in between our Ace and her target.

"Get out of the way!"

"You will *not* hurt her!"

Aurora turns her eyes on Tyler, her whole body shaking. The Longbow's shaking, too, violent, terrifying, as if the whole ship is trying to tear itself apart.

"Buh-buh . . . ," she stutters.

"What?" Tyler breathes, leaning closer.

"B-b-belieeeve . . ."

Another tremor hits, knocking me back to the floor. The hull groans around us, the rivets squealing as they start to turn. Tyler looks at me. At his squad. At the ship around us, convulsing so hard it might fly to pieces. I can see the wheels spinning behind his eyes. Weighing up the danger to his crew. The warning de Stoy and Adams gave us as we left the station. His hand goes to the lump beneath his tunic—our dad's Senate ring, hanging on the titanium chain about his neck. Ty's always played it by the book. Ever since we were thirteen years old on New Gettysburg, signing on the dotted line.

The cargo you carry is more precious than any of you can know.

"Believe . . . ," Aurora whispers.

Tyler clenches his jaw. His hand slips from Dad's ring to the Maker's mark at his collar. As the Longbow shudders and shakes all around us, Ty crawls across the bucking floor, up to his command console. And as I watch, he logs in to the navcom, sets us a new course.

Almost immediately, the Longbow stops shaking. The engines pick up, and I feel the press of thrust through our inertial dampeners.

The light in Aurora's eye flickers and dies like someone turned off a switch. She slumps down in her chair, blood dripping from her nose, out cold again. Zila runs to her side to check her vitals, Kal offering assistance. Cat's eyes are narrowed, shaking hands wrapped around her disruptor's grip. My eyes are on the navcom, the new course Ty just plugged in.

"Where we headed, Bee-bro?" I ask, already knowing the answer.

"Sempiternity," he says softly, looking around the cabin.

"You sure that's a good idea?" I ask.

"I don't know."

He touches the Maker's mark at his collar again, staring at Auri.

"But sometimes you just gotta have faith."

PLACES TO AVOID

▶ PIRATE ENCLAVES

   ▼ SEMPITERNITY

FOR A DETAILED HISTORY OF THE WORLD SHIP, CLICK **HERE**.

**MAPPING INCOMPLETE
DUE TO HOSTILE CONDITIONS**

HERE BE BAD THINGS

14

AURI

"Jie-Lin, wake up."

I open my eyes, wondering for a moment where I am. I re-member the argument on the Longbow's bridge. Tyler and Kal and Scarlett and Cat. Bright light. But now I'm lying in a soft bed. A warm glow around me. Posters on the walls I recognize, a familiar stuffed toy squirrel beside me.

My room.

I'm in my room.

"Jie-Lin?"

I look up, and sitting above me is a face I never thought I'd see again. Round cheeks. The lines across his forehead that my mom used to joke were there from the age of fifteen, because the world surprised him so much.

"Daddy?"

"I've been waiting for you, Jie-Lin."

He pulls me into his arms and I can feel his chest shaking because he's laughing and he's crying and I'm laughing and crying, too. And all the things I could have said, I should have said, are filling my head because he's not dead and it's not too late and I try to pull away and speak because there's so much I want to say.

But I can't.

I can't pull away. He's holding me too tight. And I can't breathe and I can't speak. I push hard, forcing him off me, but it's like he's made of tar. Pieces of him come with me as I pull back, long strings of him stretching between us like human taffy. Seeping in under my skin.

"*Let me go!*"

He looks at me and smiles, and his irises are shaped like blue flowers.

"*Ra'haam,*" *he says.*

"*Let go!*"

"*Ra'haaaaaaam.*"

. . . . .

"Aurora?"

I open my eyes, heart thundering. Scarlett's sitting beside me, Zila and Kal standing above me. My mouth is dry as chalk and I ache all over. But slowly, I realize I'm still here. Not there.

A nightmare.

I don't know whether to be relieved or heartbroken all over again. I'm not home, not back in my room. I'm on a spaceship a million light-years from any of it. Everyone's still gone, my dad is . . .

Scarlett hands me a cup of water, concern and suspicion in her eyes. It's not lost on me that Zila has her hand on her pistol. That Kal is armed, too, watching me with those cool violet eyes from over near the door.

"Do you remember what happened?" Scarlett asks.

Images flash in my mind. Me throwing Scarlett into the wall. Blood on my lips. Raised voices. My dad's skin melting into mine like taffy. One image burning brighter than the rest. A name.

"Sempiternity," I murmur.

Zila and Scarlett exchange a glance, and the redhead nods. "We've been Folding for almost four hours. We're nearly there. Tyler asked us to bring you up to the bridge in case you . . . see anything."

I blink hard to rid myself of that image of my dad. The pieces of him melting into pieces of me. Wincing as Scarlett helps me to my feet, I note we're in some kind of habitation area. Bunk beds and lockers and gunmetal gray, Aurora Legion logos on the walls. I catch a glimpse of my reflection in a mirror. The shock of white in my bangs, the white of my right iris. I don't know what any of this means, but it feels like a stranger looking back at me. Helpless. Angry.

"I know you all think I'm crazy," I murmur.

"Nobody thinks you're crazy, Auri," Scarlett says, touching my arm. "You've been through a lot, we all know that."

"The *Hadfield* was bound for Octavia III, Scarlett," I say, low and fierce. "I studied years to get on that mission, you don't forget something like that. Every spare minute was training—memorizing maps, rock climbing, orienteering competitions. And all of it with one goal in mind: Octavia."

She gives me a sympathetic smile, but shakes her head. "Auri, we checked the records. Octavia III is uninhabitable."

"THAT'S WHAT I SAID," comes a small chirp from my pocket. "BUT DOES SHE LISTEN TO ME? NOOOO—"

I clap my hand over Magellan to shut him up. "Why don't we go check it out, then? I know the composition of the atmosphere, the layout of the continents—I'll show you where Butler settlement and the outposts are, I'll—"

"Octavia III has been under Interdiction for hundreds of years," Zila says.

"And the last time we set an alternate course, you almost destroyed the ship." I look over at Kal as he speaks, and his expression is unreadable as always. But remembering that footage of me attacking Scarlett, holding the ship in place while it shook and my eye burned white, it's hard to argue with him.

"Seems like this is where you're meant to be," Scarlett says. "And maybe we're heading where we're supposed to go, too."

She touches my arm again, and her smile is warm and kind in comparison to Kal's frosty stare. I can't help but smile weakly in return. She voted to take me back to the academy, but now their course is set, I realize . . .

She's trying to be nice to me.

"Come on," she says. "Ty wants you on the bridge."

I don't miss the glance Zila and Kal share as we leave the room, or the fact that Zila's hand hasn't left her gun the whole time we talked. But together, we make our way down a long corridor, Kal in front, Scarlett beside me, Zila walking behind. My bones creak and my pulse is pounding and I've got one mothercustard of a headache.

As we step out onto the bridge, the others turn to glance at me, but only for a moment. Looking at the huge screen above the central console, I can see we're coming in to dock at what must be Sempiternity. Cat and Tyler seem occupied navigating us through a maze of ships and docking stations and loaders and shuttles surrounding the most amazing sight I've ever seen in my life.

The future is grimier than I expected. Dirtier than it was meant to be. Sempiternity kind of looks like an inside-out termite nest, with endless additions bulging in every possible direction. So many glittering lights and strange shapes and odd angles, thousands of ships molded and bolted and welded into one giant World Ship.

"Holy cake," I murmur.

How did I know this place existed?

How did I know its name?

And how did I drag our ship to a halt and turn it toward this mashed-together world of hundreds of thousands of ships that all ended their stories here?

If I can answer even one of those questions, I'll be closer to understanding what's happening to me. Why my own government's trying to erase every trace of me. I'm aching to set a course for Octavia, to see if anything's left of the colony I *know* was there. But this thing that's overtaking me has led me here, to Sempiternity.

So I'll follow this path, try and understand why it's twisted in this direction. Hope it's brought me here because this is where my answers are.

Scar helps me to a seat at an auxiliary station, then takes her place around the central console. I know I should be watching the amazing station we're slowly moving toward, but instead I find myself looking at the squad around me. At these six young soldiers I've suddenly found myself thrown together with. The strangers my life seems to depend on now.

Squad 312.

I wonder what makes them who they are.

What's driving them to even be here.

Cat's attention is mostly on steering through dozens of vessels coming and going, detaching from the messy sides of this sector, or clamping on to airlocks and joining the throng. But she's watching me out of the corner of her eye as well, her gaze flicking my way like clockwork every thirty seconds or so.

She doesn't trust me.

I don't blame her.

Tyler looks kind of peaceful, really, all things considered. Shaggy blond hair hanging in bright blue eyes fixed on his readouts. He's picked his course, it seems, and for better or for worse, the decision's made. Still, I have a long way to go to win over him and his sister, and I'm not even sure what I want them to know or believe about me.

Next along from Tyler is Fin, white hair spiked above his white face, so hard to read behind those black contacts that cover the whole of his eyes. It's hard to even tell where he's looking sometimes. Between that and the equally effective shield of sarcasm, it's tricky to know who he is, either. Right now he has his head down—he's fixing or modifying something in the forearm of his suit with a magnetic screwdriver. Zila takes her seat at the station beside him, but her dark eyes are still fixed on me, as if I'm a puzzle she can figure out with sufficient study.

Kal's glancing at me occasionally, but I can't get a read past those eyes of his. He's over six and a half feet of long silver hair and lithe muscle, and he looks like he's on his way to counsel Gandalf or something. He acts like he's better than me, though, I know that. *Liability,* he called me. *Beneath concern.* I suppose just because he's an alien doesn't mean he can't be a total jerk.

They're all suspicious of me to one degree or another. Some of them are scared. And I'm scared of myself, but I'm trying to be brave. I don't know what's happening, but I want to figure it out as badly as they do. To know where I'm headed, and why. How I can do the impossible things I've done. But I barely even know what I'm running *from,* let alone *to.*

Still, this station might hold all my answers. Like Scarlett said, maybe we're going exactly where we're meant to go.

There's a gentle bump as we come into berth, a series of thuds and a brief chorus of electronic noises as we lock on to the docking system. Cat's hands dance across consoles as she powers down the main drive. She kisses her fingertips and presses them against her monitor screen, then the stuffed dragon sitting above it. The thrum of our engines slowly dies, the computer noises fall quiet. Everyone looks at everyone else, wondering what comes next.

"We need three things," Tyler says, breaking the uncomfortable silence.

Fin looks up from his home repair job, answers without missing a beat. "I'll take a fresh pair of pants, a professional masseuse and a shot of Larassian semptar."

Tyler nobly presses on. "Shelter, intel, and a change of clothes. So Fin got one out of three right. This place is run by interstellar pirates, so we won't get far in these uniforms."

"We need four things," Cat corrects him.

"We need to know why Aurora brought us here," Zila supplies.

And of course everyone looks at me again. And my muscles ache from what I guess was my seizure before, and the echoes of my nightmare are still lingering inside my head, and I'm tired, and I *still don't know the answer.*

Scarlett comes to my rescue. "I'll go shopping for the clothes. Place like this, it won't be hard to find a market. And I have better taste than all of you put together."

Tyler looks mildly wounded. "Hey, I—"

Scarlett aims a withering glance at her brother, and he wisely falls silent.

"I have a cousin here," Fin says. "I can get us a place to lay low."

Zila blinks at him. "That ventures into the realm of coincidence."

"Not really," he says, wiggling his hand in a *so-so* gesture. "I mean, if you want to get technical, he's the second cousin of my third mother once removed on my matriarch's side, but we generally just say 'cousin.'"

"Second of third . . . ?" Ty tilts his head, and I can practically see some of the others counting on their fingers and toes, trying to make the connection.

"Family reunions are tricky for Betraskans," Fin smirks.

"Go find your cousin," Tyler says. "Take Cat with you."

Cat blinks. "I should—"

"I'm not sending him off solo. Nobody moves alone. Scarlett, you'll take Zila. I'll take Kal and Auri, we'll do some recon. Maybe Auri will see someone or something she recognizes, and we'll get a better idea of what we're supposed to be doing here. Using our currency accounts will give away our location, so everyone give up whatever creds you've got on you."

. . . . .

There's nobody to check our IDs or ask any questions as we make our way out of the airlock and into a long hallway lined with heavy doors. It's made of a transparent material, and I can see that an umbilical corridor snakes away from every hatchway. Each one connects to a ship at the other end, like we're part of one big bunch of grapes. And beyond the ships, I can see the stars, dimmed by the station lights.

"It's beautiful," I whisper.

"It's ghastly," Fin says beside me, dismissing the glories of the galaxy with a wave of his hand. But even though he's grumbling, I realize he might be attempting conversation. And it's not like anyone else is talking to me right now.

"You don't like stars?" I ask.

"No," he says quietly, lacking his smirk for once, and staring at the floor. "A lot of those stars actually died millions of years ago. It's just they're so far away, the light they created before they died hasn't finished reaching us yet." He waves at the galaxy beyond the glass. "You're looking at a sky full of ghosts."

"Well, that's depressing."

"My people live underground," he shrugs. "Wide-open spaces, not so much."

"And you signed up as a space soldier?" Scarlett scoffs beside us.

"Yeah." He winks. "Intriguing, aren't I?"

Scarlett rolls her eyes as we reach the end of the docks. With much flashing of globes and beams of light cutting over our bodies, another airlock runs us through some kind of scan and then opens into a promenade bustling with life and light and noise. With the stars safely out of sight, Fin seems a little more at ease. He squares his shoulders and claps Cat on the back.

"Let's go find some crash space, eh?"

"Never say the word 'crash' to a pilot, Finian," Cat scowls. "And if you touch me again, I'll feed you your fingers."

"I like you, Zero," he grins, managing to make the nickname sound only a tiny bit like he's making fun of her. "Don't ever change, okay?"

Cat shoots an accusing glance at Tyler, and she and Finian slip off into the crowd to scout out somewhere for us to go to ground. Scarlett and Zila head for the marketplace, the bulk of our money in their pockets (or in Scarlett's case, down her bra) in search of disguises. I'm left with Kal and Tyler, one on either side as I gawp at the crowd around us.

Many of them are human, and most of them are at least human shaped. There are healthy numbers of Betraskans, mostly dressed in dark colors that match their contact lenses, their skin as white as paper. I realize none of them wear the whole-body frame that Fin does—I'd wondered if they were common among his people, but I guess it's just him.

I spot a couple of silver-haired Syldrathi in the distance, but closer are other . . . aliens, I guess. I see midnight-blue skin and scaly red, I see eyes covered by yellow-lensed goggles and hidden deep in the folds of damp gray faces.

I stare at a pair in sweeping silk robes that flow like water behind them and at a cluster of figures no higher than my waist, with the heavy build that I guess comes from living in a high-gravity environment. There must be dozens of species I haven't seen before here, and none of them are paying me a moment's notice.

"So, where are we going?" I ask.

Tyler offers me a tired grin. "The place the latest gossip always is. A bar."

We head off into the crush, and the crowd grows thicker as we move away from the docks. Kal moves out in front, and the look in his eyes seems to do wonders to protect our personal space. He walks tall, almost prowling, one hand close to his weapon. Most people take one look at the three crossed blades marked on his forehead and give us a wide berth.

It doesn't take long for us to locate what I presume is a bar, its facade clustered with glowing lights and strange neon letters. We head in through a narrow door, so low that both the boys have to duck. A faint light glimmers inside the doorframe as we're scanned, and the air tastes like cinnamon and rubber. We pause inside to let our vision adjust, and I take in the space around us.

Holy cake, this place is unbelievable.

It's kind of like a cross between a sports bar and a Wild West saloon, spread over three rotating, circular levels. Bodies of all shapes and sizes are packed onto barstools and into booths, heads bowed in quiet conversation. There's five . . . things? People? Both? . . . in the corner, playing strange, beautiful music. They have transparent skin and tentacles instead of fingers.

I clench my jaw so it doesn't drag on the ground.

There are tables on the edge of the room, layered in fluorescent yellow. They're covered in brightly colored stones—round, square, jagged—laid out in intricate patterns that clearly mean something to the players jostling for position around them. I see a blue-skinned woman with a high-domed head, dressed in a tunic that almost seems to be a continuation of her blue skin—it's hard to tell where one ends and the other begins. She smiles, then delicately nudges a green rock forward with a long stick, pushing another stone aside. A chorus of shouts goes up from the crowd. Delighted or angry, I can't tell.

A large bar sits like an island in the middle of the room, wreathed in light pink smoke. A row of screens rotates around it, showing a dozen fast-moving games. I might not recognize the sports they're playing, but I know that's what I'm seeing.

"Grab a table, Kal," Tyler says. "I'll scope out something to drink."

I guess I'm not part of the team in Ty's head when it comes to decision making, which ticks me off a little. I know I'm a newbie in all this, but I don't like being treated like baggage, either. So instead of waiting to be led, I head off in a circuit of the room, Kal stalking along behind me.

When I find an empty booth with a good view of the whole bar, I slide in among the empty glasses and look up at the Syldrathi boy.

"Good enough?"

Kal glances around, and apparently happy with my choice, sits on the opposite side without a word. He presses a button on the table, killing the display of tiny 3-D figures playing space sportsball across it. I push myself into the corner, but he stays on the edge, watching the room rotate. The aliens here are all different shapes and colors, wearing everything from grungy mechanics' jumpsuits to iridescent robes, and every level of formality in between.

I feel like I'm dreaming.

I feel like maybe I'm going insane.

My brain's not hurting anymore at least, but my aching muscles remind me of what happened on the Longbow's bridge. In my head, I can still see the image of myself on the vidscreen, throwing Scarlett into the wall without ever touching her. I can still hear the words I spoke with the voice that wasn't my own. I force myself to look around the bar again. Is there some hint here I can find, something to help me guess why I—or whatever possessed me—insisted we come here?

"He will not be long." Kal's voice startles me.

"Huh?"

He nods at Tyler. "Do not worry. He will not be long."

I hadn't been worrying about that in particular. If anything, Kal looks more concerned than I do. I realize he's not watching Tyler anyway—he's got his eyes on a group of Syldrathi at the bar, all of them dressed in black.

"Friends of yours?" I ask, peering at the group.

"No."

The word is heavy and lands between us like a weight.

". . . Well, who are they?" I ask.

Kal just ignores me, his eyes never leaving the other Syldrathi. I find myself getting ticked off again. Tired of the way he speaks to me, or doesn't speak to me at all. He might be six and a half feet of va-voom, but son of a biscuit, he's infuriating.

"Let me guess," I say. "I'm beneath their concern?"

"Almost certainly," he replies, still not looking at me.

"So don't worry my pretty little head about it, basically?"

"Correct."

I breathe deep, my temper finally getting the better of me. "Are all Syldrathi as full of themselves as you are?"

He blinks, deigns to look in my direction.

"I am not full of myself."

"If your nose were turned up any higher, it'd be in orbit," I scoff. "What's your problem with me? I didn't ask to be here. I was supposed to wake up on Octavia III with my dad, and instead I'm in hiding on a pirate space station with a messed-up eye and stupid hair and a condescending jackass."

A slow frown creases his tattooed brow. "What is a jackass?"

"Check a mirror, Elrond."

The frown grows more quizzical. "My name is Kal."

"You. Are. Insufferable."

I fold my arms and glare. He stares at me, tilting his head.

"Are you . . . angry with me?" he asks.

I just stare at him, gobsmacked.

"Why are you angry?" he asks. "I have been protecting you."

"No, you've been treating me like a little kid," I say. "I'm not stupid. You haven't taken your eyes off those other Syldrathi since we sat down, and your hand's never left your pistol. So if you want to protect me so much, maybe help me understand why you're on edge instead of ignoring me?"

He stares at me for a long, silent moment. I wonder if

he'll even answer. This boy's lukewarm one minute, ice-cold the next, and I don't understand him at all.

But finally, he speaks.

"My people are divided into what we call cabals. Weavers. Workers. Watchers. The Syldrathi you met on Sagan Station were Waywalkers. The most mystical of our number, devoted to the study of the Fold." He taps the tattoo etched on his forehead. "We all wear a glyf here. The sigil of our cabal."

I feel my temper calm a little. He's still talking like Lord Snooty McSnootface, but at least he's talking. That's a point in his favor.

"Your glyf was different from the others on Sagan," I say.

"Yes." The word is heavy once again. "I am Warbreed. We are warriors."

I consider him. Yes. That's exactly what he is. Looking him over, I realize Kal was built for violence. The way he walks, the way he talks—every move he makes communicates it in subtle ways. There's an anger in this boy, smoldering just below the cold, composed surface. He keeps a leash on it, but I could sense it when he squared off against Aedra on Sagan Station. And I can sense it again now as he turns back to look at the other Syldrathi.

"So which cabal are they?" I ask, nodding toward the group in black.

"None," he replies. "They are Unbroken."

"I thought you just said—"

"My people and yours fought for many years," he interrupts, erasing all his brownie points and just annoying me again. "The war between us was bitter. I am one of only a few Syldrathi to have joined the Aurora Legion after the peace treaty. Most still mistrust me. That is why I was left to join the squad of Tyler Jones. But even after the hostilities ended, some Warbreed still refused to acknowledge the treaty between humans and Syldrathi. They called themselves the Unbroken, and they now war against those Syldrathi who supported peace with Terra."

"They sound . . . friendly," I venture.

"You are being sarcastic, I hope."

"Well, duh."

Tyler slides in beside me in time to catch the end of what Kal is saying. He has three glasses that are so cold they're sporting a thin coating of ice. Each one has an insulation band so you can hold it without your fingers getting stuck to the surface. A second band of rubber circles the rim to save your tongue the same fate.

"So, what are we talking about?" he asks, handing out the drinks.

"Jackasses," Kal replies.

"Whose side are the humans on?" I ask Tyler, just wanting to know more. "In the Syldrathi war, I mean?"

Ty looks between Kal and me, obviously deciding how much to tell me.

"Nobody's," he finally says. "The Starslayer made sure of that."

He pauses, and Kal closes his eyes at the strange word.

". . . What's a Starslayer?"

"Not what," Kal murmurs. "Who."

A small beep comes from my breast pocket. "CAERSAN, AKA THE STARSLAYER, IS A RENEGADE SYLDRATHI ARCHON AND LEADER OF THE UNBROKEN. HIS FACTION

SPLINTERED FROM THE SYLDRATHI GOVERNMENT BACK IN 2370, WHEN IT SEEMED PEACE TALKS WITH EARTH WERE ABOUT TO SUCCEED. THE UNBROKEN ATTACKED TERRAN FORCES DURING A NEGOTIATED CEASE-FIRE, HITTING THE SHIPYARDS AT SIGMA ORIONIS." Another beep sounds. "WOULD YOU LIKE TO KNOW MORE?"

"Magellan, hush," I whisper.

I touch the screen, putting him in silent mode. It's one thing to have a talking encyclopedia in my pocket, but it's another thing entirely to have an actual conversation with people who've lived this stuff. And I can see both Tyler and Kal have more to say here. That this all *means* something to them both.

I look at Tyler, waiting for him to speak.

He touches the chain around his neck, the ring hanging at the end of it, a faraway look in his eyes. I remember him doing the same thing in the med center. "My dad . . . he was a senator. But he was former Terran military, too. When the Unbroken attacked Sigma Orionis, Terra called up its reserve pilots. . . ."

I can see the sadness in Tyler's eyes as he speaks, and I realize . . .

His father must have died there.

"Remember Orion," Kal says softly.

Tyler looks up sharply at that, but the taller boy has his eyes fixed on the other Syldrathi again. His voice is so soft I almost can't hear him.

"The attack at Orion prolonged the war another eight years," Kal says. "Eventually, our two peoples found peace. But the Unbroken have been in rebellion ever since. One year ago . . ." He purses his lips, shaking his head. "They attacked Evaa. The star our homeworld of Syldra orbited."

"Nobody knows how they managed it." Tyler's voice is hushed. "But they made the Syldrathi sun collapse upon itself. Turned the star into a black hole that destroyed everything in the system."

"Ten billion Syldrathi died." Kal looks at me, and the sadness in his eyes pierces my heart. "Ten billion souls gone to the Void."

I think on that number. Try to wrap my head around the size of it.

"Starslayer," I murmur.

Tyler nods. "With a weapon like that at his disposal, the whole galaxy is terrified of him. And he's made it clear that as long as Earth stays neutral in what's now a Syldrathi civil war, he won't turn his attention to us."

We sit in silence for a moment, the air in the room feeling heavier, the light a little dimmer. Kal's the one who changes the subject, his voice cool, his emotions hidden behind that wall of ice once more.

"Did you hear anything at the bar?"

Tyler sighs and shakes his head. "The bartender definitely saw my uniform, but she didn't seem to think there was any news worth sharing. At least there doesn't seem to be any word about our attack on the TDF out there yet."

I sip my drink slowly, thinking about what I've learned. The sweet, sparkling liquid seems to almost vibrate on my tongue, refreshing and energizing all at once. I look between Kal and Ty and wonder which of our many problems or mysteries they're focusing on at this particular moment. The fact that they're renegades among their own people? That we're the only witnesses to the Terran massacre at Sagan Station? That we're out here without a plan or a prayer?

Or the fact that I'm the only reason for all of it?

I don't have any answers. About the colony, my dad, what's happening to me. But day by day I'm learning more about this galaxy I've found myself in. And I'm going to find the truth if it's the last thing I do.

"Do not lift your head," Kal says, his voice as cool as the drink in my hand. "But those Unbroken are headed our way."

I do as Kal says, only looking up with my eyes. Half a dozen Syldrathi are making their way over to us, cutting through the crowd like knives. On the surface, they're all similar to each other. Similar to Kal. Their long silver hair is bound in complex braids, their eyes are all shades of violet. They wear an elegant kind of black armor, scratched and battle scarred, daubed with lines of white paint that twist into beautiful letters in a language I don't know. All of them are tall, slender, strong. Ethereal and graceful. And all of them have the same small glyf that marks Kal's forehead.

The three blades.

But as they draw closer, I see each of them is subtly different—one has bones woven through his hair, another has what I realize are severed pointed ears strapped across her chest in a diagonal line, like the world's most morbid beauty queen sash. The tallest has a vicious scar cutting right across his handsome face. They all carry themselves the same, though—cold and menacing, radiating disdain, bringing with them the sense that they could descend into violence at any moment. I'd know even if nobody told me—these Syldrathi are warbringers.

There's a woman at the fore. Her pale silver hair is pulled back into a braid so tight it must be giving her one hell of a headache. Maybe that accounts for the extremely unfriendly expression.

"Human," she says, addressing Ty. "I see you have a pet."

"I have a squadmate," Ty says, with a polite nod of greeting. "And he's enjoying his drink right now, just like me. We don't want any trouble."

An unfriendly ripple goes through the Syldrathi.

"He has forsaken the rightful cause of his people," the leader says. "He seeks the company of Terrans when there is work yet undone for all Warbreed. Until all our people are united under Archon Caersan's hand, there is no rest, whether we will it or no. He is a traitor. Cho'taa."

Behind her, there's a rumble of agreement from her followers. Their eyes are narrowed, sparkling with hatred. Beautiful and ugly all at once. The woman leans forward, and slowly, deliberately, she spits on the table between Kal and Tyler.

"You should be careful he does not betray you next, human."

"You do not want this, Templar," Kal tells the woman quietly, not even looking at her. "Believe me."

"Believe you?" She laughs, short and sharp. "You who have no honor? You who wear the uniform of the enemy?"

"We've nearly finished our drinks," Tyler says, his friendly tone not budging. "Once we have, we'll go our way, and you can go yours."

"Will you?" says the woman, tilting her head as if he's said something curious. "I see no path between you and the door."

Kal's eyes flicker to the woman's, then away again. "Perhaps because you are as blind as you are foolish."

Tyler glances at the other boy. "Take it easy, Legionnaire Gilwraeth."

Kal goes very still for a moment, and the braided woman looks at him sharply. It feels like all the air has been suddenly sucked out of the room.

"I'na Sai'nuit," she breathes.

Kal turns his head to speak to me. "Stay behind me, be'shmai."

The woman looks incredulously at me. "You name a human be—"

Kal's open palm collides with her stomach, his elbow with her jaw, sending her backward with a spray of spit and blood. He springs from our booth, lashing out at another two Syldrathi and sending them stumbling away with bloody lips and broken noses. His opponents are caught unprepared for a moment, but then they come to life with snarls and shouts. Tyler's caught flat-footed too, but he recovers quick, rising to his feet and stepping to Kal's side with his fists raised.

Problem is, there are six of them and only two of us.

Well, three, I guess. Counting me.

Kal's still holding his glass, and he swings it in a lightning-quick arc against another Syldrathi's head. It shatters, and the man falls, deep purple blood welling up from his wounds. Kal and Ty swing their fists, each aiming for a different Syldrathi. This isn't like fighting in a vid—it's brutal, ugly, savage. Their opponents stagger back, but the boys don't follow up, staying with the booth at their backs, side by side, limiting the angles from which the others can approach.

Their fighting styles are totally different. Kal's has a dark grace to it. For such a big guy, he's perfectly fluid, and as he fends off a return punch, then delivers a haymaker of his own, it's like every movement is choreographed in a perfect deadly dance.

Ty fights more like an athlete. He's fit and strong and has good technique—even I can tell that. He punches, he kicks, and he hits below the belt when he has to. They're all bigger than him. Faster and stronger. But even still, he's fearless.

A third Unbroken is already on the ground at Kal's feet, more of the pack surging in to replace the fallen.

Ty's trading blows with his opponent, dancing back and forth like a boxer. Kal is swaying and weaving, saying something to his adversary that draws a snarl from the man, which Kal promptly ends by knocking out his teeth. The brawl's now surrounded by a ring of bar crawlers who've gathered to watch. A part of my mind is busy watching the fight, another part monitoring myself—afraid I'll feel myself slipping, that I'll feel the gray closing in, that I'll do something awful to defend them, something the whole bar will notice.

But I don't want to just sit here doing nothing . . .

One of the Unbroken shoves a Table Rock player, steals his stick, and draws it back like a spear. Without thinking, I grab my glass, the cold burning my fingers for an instant before I throw. It clocks the guy right in the face, and he stumbles back with what's definitely a curse.

Kal glances over his shoulder, lips quirking in what might be a smile.

And son of a biscuit, I find myself smirking back.

Then the outer crowd is parting, revealing six feet of angry human bartender. She's got a ring through her nose and full-sleeve tattoos, and she looks like she is *not* in the mood. She's holding a large canister with a hose attached, and as she takes a swipe at one Unbroken's back and unleashes a torrent of frothing white goo at another, I realize it's a fire extinguisher.

"Security is on the way!" she roars. "Now take it outside before I kick you out the airlock!"

Style points, Bartender Lady. I like you.

We're all pretty much frozen, Ty and Kal swaying on their feet, the Syldrathi scattered around us, everyone dripping with foam. Now would be a really, *really* good time for us to make an exit. My gaze sweeps the room, checking to see what's between us and the way out, and that's when I spot Zila and Scarlett.

They're standing framed by the door, hands full of bulging shopping bags. Scarlett steps in to do her diplomat thing, but her first words are drowned out by a loud, low-pitched alert.

Everyone in the bar stops what they're doing. Announcements in a dozen different languages spill out of the loudspeakers. The holographic displays above the bar dissolve into snow, then flicker back to life once more.

And every single one of them is showing a picture of me.

It's a still from footage they must have taken aboard the TDF destroyer. I'm wearing the same uniform I have on now.

It's a clear shot of me—black-and-white hair frames my face in a more-tousled-than-usual pixie cut, my mismatched eyes are wide.

Text flashes on every screen, right below my face.

WANTED FUGITIVE.
REWARD OFFERED.
CONTACT TDF FOR
MORE INFORMATION.

Time stands still. My heart pounds as I stare at the screen. But finally, desperately not wanting to, I drag my eyes down and look around the room.

Every single person in the bar is staring straight at me.

Son of a *biscuit*.

BETRASKAN SOCIETY
▶ **CLAN STRUCTURE**
　▼ **OBLIGATIONS**

BETRASKAN SOCIETY IS SO MIND-BOGGLINGLY INTRICATE THAT EVEN BETRASKANS HAVE TROUBLE UNDERSTANDING WHAT'S GOING ON HALF THE TIME. THE MOST IMPORTANT THING TO KNOW IS THAT BETRASKAN CLAN STRUCTURE IS MORE COMPLICATED THAN A SIX-WAY **FIRALOR WEDDING CEREMONY**, AND THEY OWE LOYALTY ON TWO LEVELS, AS DICTATED BY THEIR NAME.

FOR EXAMPLE, SARA DE MOSTO DE TREN IS A MEMBER FIRST OF THE DE MOSTO CLAN—THIS WILL COMPRISE HER SIBLINGS, NO MORE THAN A DOZEN PARENTS (SEE **BETRASKAN FAMILIAL STRUCTURE**), AND ONE TO TWO HUNDRED BLOOD RELATIVES.

SHE IS THEN SECONDARILY A MEMBER OF THE DE TREN CLAN, WHICH WILL COMPRISE SEVERAL THOUSAND INDIVIDUALS. BETRASKAN SOCIETY PLACES ALMOST IMMEASURABLE VALUE ON FAMILY OBLIGATIONS, KNOWN AS **FAVORS**, AND ANY CLAN MEMBER MAY BE CALLED UPON TO PERFORM A FAVOR OWED BY THE CLAN AS A WHOLE.

JUST HOW BETRASKANS KEEP TRACK OF THEM IS ANYONE'S GUESS.

15

FINIAN

My sort-of cousin Dariel is blocking his doorway, and this isn't going as well as I'd hoped. I'm trying to convince him to let us inside, give us some crash space that's off the grid, a place to lay low until we figure out what we're supposed to be doing here. And so, for the last twenty minutes or so, with Cat lurking behind me like a very cranky bodyguard, we've been exchanging familial details, figuring out where we both fit in our extended family tree—and therefore who owes what, and what a fair price would be for his help. Because nothing comes free in a place like Sempiternity.

I've never met Dariel before, but I can see the de Seel nose on him. He's dyed his shoulder-length hair pitch-black, matching his contacts, and he comes off looking like some kind of human corpse. The white skin that looks perfectly normal alongside proper white hair just looks weird and pallid now.

And he doesn't just look like a corpse. He looks like a wannabe-tough-guy lover-boy corpse, dressed in black pants and a black shirt that's open at least two buttons too many.

Not gonna lie, it's a little embarrassing that Cat's seeing this.

"So my third mother's brother is Ferilien de Vinner de Seel," I say patiently.

"But you're a de Karran de Seel," he says, for the third time.

Make that a *stupid* wannabe-tough-guy lover-boy corpse. *Ugh.*

"My third mother became a de Karran," I sigh. "But originally she was a de Vinner, and the de Vinners are your—"

"Aw, bugger me sideways," Cat curses behind me.

I turn my head, but she hasn't finally lost interest in our connect-the-dots game. She's staring up at a big holoscreen mounted in a corner of the dirty corridor where Dariel's quarters are located. I follow her gaze, and . . . there's our stowaway's face in close-up, with a WANTED banner streaming underneath it. Somewhere out there, Goldenboy is now having an even worse day than he was before.

And this puts me at a distinct negotiating disadvantage.

Dariel braces both hands against his doorframe and leans out into the hall to take a look at the screen. "Friend of yours?"

It nearly kills me to say it, but I force my expression as close to neutral as I can possibly manage. "If you let us in, I'll owe you a Favor."

His smile widens, and he presses his palm to mine, sealing the deal, while I try not to look like I'm freaking out. Putting myself in his debt like this without nailing down any of the details . . . well, now he knows how bad things are. Without another word, he steps back and leaves the doorway open for us.

"Welcome, cousin, welcome."

Cat's already on her uniglass, checking her fauxhawk in the mirror as she walks inside. "Ty, I'm sending you our location," she says, her voice echoing in my earpiece.

"Roger that," comes the reply.

"Everything okay?" Cat asks. "You sound out of breath."

"Running," Tyler gasps.

". . . From what?"

"Bar brawl."

"Aw, bloody hells, you started one without me?"

I raise an eyebrow at Cat, speaking into my uni. "Do you need backup, Goldenboy?"

"Negative," our noble leader grunts. *"Hold position."*

I shrug and follow Cat inside, and as I step across the threshold into Dariel's place, a whole-body shock goes through me. It's like I've stepped straight through a FoldGate and into a room back on Trask. The walls are lined with white stone, bright green flic vines tumbling down from the niches along the ceiling where they've been planted, gently glowing leaves helping light up the room. Water trickles down the walls, and the ceiling is a jagged landscape of stalactites.

It's like being back in a place I've barely visited since I was six years old, and I'm completely unprepared for the wave of . . . I'm not even sure what this feeling is.

"Grew most of them out of salt." Dariel's voice in my ear startles me, and I turn to see him pointing to the stalactites above. "And commissioned a few carved out of rock—a guy back home does them."

"It's, uh . . . authentic," I manage.

Cat's looking around the cramped living room like she's scared the surfaces are radioactive, and I don't blame her—there are crates stacked up to the ceiling, computer gear everywhere, notes and pictures and screens pinned to every available surface, and it's none too clean. Looks like my cousin's running quite the business empire in here. I'm surprised his brain can keep up with it.

About forty minutes go by before the rest of our squad shows up, and Dariel and I spend most of it on family talk. Whenever you get two Betraskans together, we figure out where folks in our extended family have ended up lately. Cat's pacing by the time the others arrive, walking a circuit of the room that weaves between boxes and crates and stacks of junk.

Our squadmates clearly found somewhere to hole up and change, and the results are impressive. Both the Jones twins look *completely* edible, him in a stretchy show-my-muscles kind of shirt, her in an equally stretchy bodysuit made of . . . some kind of black . . . something.

Hey, it's hard to focus on fabric finishings with this level of *hello there* coming at me in stereo, okay?

Pixieboy's in a coat with a hood that casts a shadow over his forehead, and therefore his Warbreed sigil—smart work, Scarlett—and Zila's in a neat blue jumpsuit covered in pockets, her tight black curls tied back in a braid.

Kal and Tyler muscle their way through the door with a big plastene crate between them. Both are breathless and look like they've been in trouble—Goldenboy's lip is split, and Kal is limping. Their hair is damp, too.

"Everyone okay?" Cat asks, peering anxiously out into the corridor.

"Five by five," Tyler says, shutting the door behind him. In the dim light, he casts a quick glance around the room, taking in the rock walls, the softly glowing plants, the trickling water. It's a trip, coming from the metal hallways outside into this little slice of Trask.

"I never thought I'd say this," Scar says, dragging damp red hair from her eyes. "But thank the stars for all those laps they made us run in PT."

Tyler shakes his head. "How you move that fast in heels, I'll never know."

"It's a gift, Bee-bro." Scarlett does a little twirl, showing off her new boots. "And aren't they *gorgeous*?"

"What did you do with the trouble magnet?" Cat asks.

In reply, Tyler raps on the crate with his knuckles, and Kal kneels down to open it up, revealing a blinking, mussed Aurora inside. Her black-and-white hair is askew, light brown cheeks turned pink, hiding her freckles. She's wearing a hooded black tunic dress and a pair of black leggings, looking a little worse for wear.

"Can you smuggle me in something softer next time?" she groans as Goldenboy helps her up. "With room service?"

Dariel's watching all this with undisguised interest, leaning against a dry section of the wall, arms folded over his open shirt. With an inward sigh, I make with the formalities.

"Everyone, this is my cousin Dariel. Dariel, this is everyone."

Tyler looks our brand-new host over, gives him a polite nod. "We're grateful for your help," he says.

"I'm certainly anticipating that." Dariel smiles, which I

guess answers the question of how he's going to handle my debt.

"Any friend of Finian's . . . ," says Scarlett, turning her attention to my cousin and unleashing one of her deadlier smiles on him.

Dariel's clearly as impressed as I am by the team's Face, because without a word, he produces a green box, the sight of which sets my mouth watering. When he takes the lid off, Scarlett leans forward and makes a suitably impressed noise.

"Are those luka cakes?"

"The very same," he nods, holding the box out for her to take one.

She does, and dials her smile up to Pure Heart Attack. "The guild seal means they're all the way from Trask, if I'm remembering right? I love what you've done with the place, by the way. The flic vines really bring it together."

Don't get me wrong—given the chance, I'd cheerfully jump aboard either of the Jones twins, but moments like this, it's hard to take my eyes off her. Flaming red lipstick to match her flaming bob, the same fiery color shaded around those big blue eyes of hers. What Dariel's serving up is clearly an attempt to impress—delicacies from our homeworld are hard to come by—and recognizing the gesture is the best thing she could possibly do right now.

I grab one too, just in case Dariel forgets to offer the box in my direction. The flaky pastry dissolves on my tongue, the slightly sweet, slightly sour ground luka nuts inside flooding my mouth with flavor. These things taste like home. But if I'm not careful, they're going to taste like homesickness instead. Like safety, and the longing to get the hells out of this situation. I swallow quickly.

Scarlett's nibbling slower, more appreciative. "I like a man who knows how to get what he wants. You must know this place inside and out."

Dariel puffs up, predictably. "I've been around."

"I'll bet," she winks. "Anything you can teach me?"

He drifts closer, like oily smoke. "There's a lot I can teach you, Earth girl."

Scarlett only smiles wider. "I mean about this station. For now, at least. Nothing like a local to show you the ropes."

"What do you want to know?"

She shrugs, her eyes sparkling. "Anything you want to tell us."

Dariel glances at me, then leans in closer to Ms. Jones.

"Well, first off, you can't just think of this place as a big city," he says, with what he clearly believes is an air of suave authority. "You gotta think of it more like a hundred different cities that just happen to border each other, right? There are probably a million souls aboard. We got governing councils and lawless zones, warlords and high society and rumors about black sectors in the depths. You can find anything for the right price. We got fancy art, we got weaponry, we got delights that'll take you away from your troubles. If you were, say, looking for a place to go dancing in those *fine* new clothes . . ."

I can't even tell if he's being sleazy or just doesn't have any social skills—and when *I'm* noticing your lack of grace, you really oughta take a good, hard look at yourself. But Scarlett just shrugs in an elegant *maybe* kind of way.

"It was a long ride here, handsome." She stretches, and lifts one hand to muffle a yawn. "What I'm really looking for is a place where we can sleep?"

Dariel blinks. "You mean . . . you and me, or . . ."

"I mean me and them," Scarlett smiles, gesturing at the rest of us.

". . . Wait, all of you are—"

"Don't hurt yourself thinking about it too much," I growl.

My cousin takes a few moments to try and wrap his brain cell around it, but eventually he just gives up and leads us through to a back room. It's not decorated—the walls are standard issue, the ceiling bare. There's one flic vine up the far end, but the leaves are barely glowing. The space is tiny, set with three bunks, the lower two mostly full of cans of luminescent white paint and freeze-dried sarbo oil pods. I don't ask. I can only assume he got a good deal.

"This is perfect," Scarlett says. "Thanks, handsome."

"No problem," Dariel smiles. "If you want any more compa—"

The rest of his offer fades out as Scarlett winks and slides the door closed, finally giving us a little privacy. I dunno what it is about this girl, but she pulls it off without offending him—she could probably slap you in the face and make you feel good about it afterward. The others set to work clearing a spot to sleep. Tyler's making room on the bunks, and Kal is piling the junk around the place into perfect stacks. But Scarlett hangs back by the door with me, out of the way.

"Do you need a hand?" she asks softly.

She's talking quiet so the others won't hear. Gesturing at my suit. I thought I kept my movements pretty smooth since we came aboard, but truth told, my muscles are aching—they don't love being flooded with adrenaline over and over. And though I'm usually the first to bite when people point the thing out, somehow she makes it so I don't mind. There's no sympathy, no gentle grimace. Just a casual offer.

Fact is, I'd kill for even a few hours in low gravity—I could get my suit off, curl up to sleep properly—but making that happen would mean leaving the squad. And adding another favor to the list I'm racking up with Dariel.

I was meant to have low-gee accommodations aboard the Longbow once my squad was assigned. I had my own room at the academy so I could reduce gravity every night and operate without the suit. I'm gonna pay a price for sleeping like this later. But I'll worry about that tomorrow. For now, I'm really not about to ask anyone to help me undress.

"Thanks, I'm fine," I say. "It's designed to stay on for several days if needs be."

Scarlett nods, content that I'm content.

"You think we can trust your cousin?" she whispers. "My gut was yes."

I nod. "Your family seals your den, that's what my clan says."

"I haven't heard that one before," she admits, keeping her voice low. "What's it mean?"

"It means we can trust him."

That was meant to be the whole of my answer, but she just looks at me, expectant. Trust a Face to want to learn something new about etiquette when they should be focusing on naptime.

With a sigh, I try my best to explain. "You know we live

underground on Trask because of the wind, right? It carries microscopic shards of stone. Get enough in your lungs, it'll kill you."

"So the seals on your den help keep it out?" she supposes.

"Right. When you build a new home, your family comes around to make the seals that go around the edges of your door out of peta mud. It's a whole ceremony, and it's a gesture of trust. Everybody gets their hands on it."

"I get it," she murmurs. "You're showing your family that you trust them by letting them make the seals. If they didn't do a good job . . ."

"Right, you'd die. So, you build strong seals, then you close the door and fight behind it, if you have to. Dariel won't cross us because he's family." I smirk. "That, and my grandmas are pretty scary ladies."

She's quiet a moment, and her whisper is gentle. "It must be hard, being away from family."

I snort. "For me? Not really. I got sent away from most of them early."

She looks like she doesn't quite buy it, but she lets it go.

"Get some rest," she offers. "I'll stay up and watch for a while."

The squad is busy claiming their spots—everyone is pretty wrecked after the fight on Sagan, then *Bellerophon,* then the Fold here. Kal's big frame is in the top bunk, Auri and Zila are curled up together in the middle. Ty's on the floor—looks like our noble leader is planning to sleep sitting up against the wall, which I'm sure he won't regret at *all* later on. Cat's opposite, still looking sore she missed out on the brawl.

Scarlett and I both know I'm going to need the bottom bunk, so I wordlessly hand her the pillow and blanket, and she settles on the floor near her brother. I bed down on the mattress, staring at Aurora's boots where they hang over the edge of the bunk above me. From the glow on the ceiling, I can tell she's plugged into her secondhand uniglass again, eating up info as fast as she can read.

She's such a little thing. No bigger than Zila. Nothing about her hints at the trouble she spells for all of us. Except, you know, when her eye starts glowing . . .

I know we're in deep because of her. I know the smart play would just be to sell her to the GIA and pray our court-martials don't land us in prison. But my whole life, I've been on the outside looking in. A problem. A burden. An aberration. Just like her. And it's taught me to be sure of one thing.

Us outsiders gotta stick together.

I lie in the dark. Watch Scarlett watching over the rest of us. She reaches over, pulls the blanket up under Cat's chin, tucks another around her brother. There's something about her—under the bitchy and the sexy. Something almost maternal. Goldenboy looks after us because we're his squad. His responsibility.

Scarlett looks after us because she *cares*.

She catches me watching her.

"Go to sleep, Finian," she whispers.

I close my eyes and let the slow breathing of my squadmates lull me to sleep.

I dream of home, of Trask, with its red sun and sprawling city hives running deep beneath the ground. I'm topside in my dream and it's snowing, tiny flakes spilling from the sky and covering the unforgiving white rock surface in an endless thick blanket, far as my eyes can see.

It's the weirdest thing, though.

Last time I checked, snow isn't supposed to be blue. . . .

. . . . .

I wake up to the sound of Tyler and Cat arguing in whispers.

"I don't care," she hisses. "This is bloody creepy, Ty. And we're in it up to our love pillows already. She's a wanted fugitive. We need to turn her in."

"We don't even know what this is," he points out, just as soft.

Zila's voice comes next. "It appears to be repetitions of a single image."

I roll over from where I'm huddled in against the wall. My major servos and muscle-weave activate immediately, though my fingers take a moment to articulate. Cranking open my eyes, I'm greeted with our grungy little room and . . .

Maker's bits.

By the light of Cat's uniglass, I see a design—the *same* design—daubed over and over again in the luminescent white paint. It's on every grubby wall, every hatch, every crate, and it's slowly dribbling toward the floor, where one huge version of the design takes up all the space that wasn't needed by sleeping squad members.

It's a figure. Humanoid. But it has only three fingers, which grow longer from left to right. Its eyes are mismatched—the left one empty, the right one filled in white. And there's a shape drawn on its chest where its heart would be.

A diamond.

Kal wakes, and Scarlett opens her eyes after a nudge from her brother. She props up on one elbow with a groan, arches her back, then freezes in place when she spots the hundreds of glowing figures now decorating our temporary home. The six of us sit and stare at the paint on the walls.

"Zero's right," I say quietly, looking around. "This is spooky shit, Goldenboy."

At the sound of my voice, our stowaway stirs in the bunk where she slept with Zila. She sits up and dangles her legs over the edge, yawning, squinting at the light in Cat's hand. Wiping the sleep from her eyes, she blinks around the room, finally twigs we're all staring at her.

"What?" she asks. "Was I snoring or something?"

Her fingers are smudged with luminescent white.

There's a smear of paint across her cheek.

She looks at the pictograms on the wall. Down at the paint on her fingertips. The look on her face when she realizes this was her—or that she did it, at any rate, even if it wasn't *her*—kind of breaks my heart. At least, I assume that's what the ache and contraction in the center of my chest is.

Doesn't happen too often.

"I don't . . ." Her whisper trails off.

Kal drops down silently from the top bunk to peer at the design. He turns his eyes on Aurora, a small frown between his brows.

"Why do you fear?" he asks, his voice cool. "This is a sign. We are in the place we are supposed to be. And now we know something of what we seek."

It's definitely the most practical thing anyone's said so far, but his tone doesn't help calm Auri down any. She's got her jaw clenched, eyes wide, and I can see her fighting the urge to scream. Cry. Break. Which is exactly when Dariel opens the door. Without knocking.

He pauses halfway in, blinking slowly. "I see you've re-decorated," he says eventually. "I'll put the cost of that paint on your tab."

Nobody says a word, because really, what are we going to say? But my cousin doesn't seem to understand he's walked into the middle of an awkward situation. He blinks again, then squints at the biggest of the designs, painted on the floor by Scarlett's feet.

"You people art buffs or something?" he says. "What you painting that old chakk on my floors for anyway?"

The room comes alive.

"You recognize this?" Tyler says, immediately on his feet.

"What the bloody hells is it?" Cat, less delicate.

Scarlett stands in one smooth movement, the groaning of a moment before, the night on the floor, all forgotten. She shoots Cat a *shut up* smile, turns the high beams on my cousin.

"You really *do* know this place inside and out. Color me impressed." She smiles a little wider, leans a little closer. "This . . . chakk . . . is something we're looking for. If you could help us out . . . ?"

A lot of people assume all Betraskans are traders—which is kind of hilarious, if you think about it. I mean, a whole society made up of nothing but? Who'd manufacture anything? Who'd plumb your house, design your latest comms gear? Betraskans are as many and as varied as any other species.

But every Betraskan likes a deal, no question of that. And we know how to get one. Which is where the universal rep came from, I guess.

We know how to bargain, and the de Seel clan is famous for it.

"Mmmmaybe," says Dariel slowly, with the air of a man realizing he has valuable information in hand. "Yeah, I think *maybe* I can do that."

"For a favor, maybe?" I ask.

Dariel smiles at me. "You catch on quick, Cuz."

I glance at Aurora. At Goldenboy. Hoping Tyler knows what the hells he's doing and how deep we're sinking. But it's not like we've got much choice here.

We follow Dariel out into the main room, cluster around him as he sits at his console. Scarlett's leaning close, one hand on his shoulder, watching the screen as he logs in to the Sempiternity network. I pick a dry spot and lean against the cool of the stone wall, easing a glowing vine out of my way.

"It was an exhibition," he's saying, one hand flipping through the air to alter the holographic display. "About a year ago. I made some quick creds putting up the posters. Casseldon Bianchi, art connoisseur and resident of the one and only World Ship, Sempiternity, put it in his museum. . . . Here it is."

Dariel's console projects an advertisement he's found in 3-D. He swipes again, and the display spins, showing off vases and paintings, necklaces and bowls and sculptures and things I'm not civilized enough to appreciate.

Beside me, Auri abruptly leans in at the sight of a glazed

ceramic bowl. "That's Chinese. How did it get all the way out here?"

Dariel stops the spinning with one lifted finger, looking over his shoulder with immediate interest. "You a ceramics expert or something? Because I got—"

"No," she replies. "My dad is— I mean, my dad was Chinese."

The reminder of the past tense is clearly a kick in the gut for her. Her gaze drops and she presses her lips together, swallowing hard. Dariel notes the change in mood, but Scarlett's quick to distract him.

"So he's a collector?" she asks, leaning closer. "This Casseldon Bianchi?"

"He's *the* collector," Dariel replies, turning back to her. "*The* man on the World Ship. If you've got something exquisite and you want to move it, that is. He deals in exotics. Artifacts. Tech. Life-forms, especially. If it's hard to find, he's the guy to find it. And if it's expensive, he's probably the guy who owns it."

"I COULD'VE TOLD YOU THAT," says a chirpy voice inside Auri's breast pocket.

"Magellan, hush," she whispers, lifting a hand to smother it. "Later."

"SERIOUSLY," the uniglass says. "I'M SEVENTEEN TIMES SMARTER THAN ANY—"

"Silent mode," Tyler snaps.

I look at Aurora, eyebrow raised. "You named your uniglass?"

Auri shoots me a quick glance. "It said 'name your device' when I turned it on."

225

"Sure, like 'Fin's uniglass' or something."

"I'm original," she says.

"That's one word for it," Cat snorts.

Dariel's display stops moving again, and suddenly there it is on his screen—our mystery object. It's a sculpture made out of a strange metal. And it's shaped like our three-fingered friend painted all over the walls of our room. The statue has gemstones for eyes, the left one polished black onyx, the right one gleaming pearl. There's a diamond embedded deeply in its chest, right where its heart would be.

"What is it?" Tyler asks, a hint of impatience in his voice.

"Says here it's a religious artifact from the . . . Eshvaren Empire?" Scarlett leans in to read the subtitle, whistling softly. "Supposed to be a million years old."

"What a load of crap," Cat chuckles.

But Auri's mismatched eyes have gone wide, and she's staring at Dariel's screen like it punched her in the mouth. Her voice is just a whisper.

"Eshvaren?"

"It's a scam," I assure her. "Don't worry about it."

"What do you mean?" Kal asks, scowling at me.

"I mean the Eshvaren. They're a ghost story, Pixieboy."

"Load of bollocks," Cat nods, and I make a note to mark my calendar because this is the first time I ever remember her agreeing with me on—

"Who," Auri says, her tone growing more strident, "or what, are the Eshvaren?"

"An old grandmother's tale," Dariel says.

"Ghost story," I nod. "Supposed to be a race that lived a million years ago. Except there's no evidence they existed."

"Other than the relics they left behind," Kal says, pointing to the screen.

"They're a *scam*, Kal," I smirk. "A way for curio dealers to part rich and stupid people from their creds. Parents tell their kids about the Eshvaren when they want them to grow up to be stellar archaeologists."

Kal glowers at me with those big, pretty eyes in a way that makes it hard to focus on what he's saying. "The Syldrathi are the oldest race in the galaxy. Older than Terrans. Older than Betraskans. And we keep tales of the Eshvaren. They were the first beings to ever cross interstellar distances. The first to find the Fold."

"And Terrans still tell stories about the tooth fairy and Santa Claus." Cat leans on the doorframe, folding her arms. "Doesn't mean they exist."

Aurora licks her lips, swallows hard.

"Does the word . . . 'Ra'haam' mean anything to anyone?"

We exchange a series of blank looks. Shake our heads or shrug.

"It's just . . . I've heard the word 'Eshvaren' before," Auri murmurs. "'Ra'haam,' too."

I raise an eyebrow. "Like on that busted uniglass of yours, or—"

She shakes her head.

"In my dreams . . ."

An uncomfortable silence settles over the room. Cat looks at Tyler and shakes her head. Tyler's looking at Auri, fingertips brushing the Maker's mark at his collar. Auri's eyes are locked on Dariel's screen, on the image of that sculpture rotating on the display. She looks halfway between terrified and exhilarated.

"So Casseldon Bianchi owns this thing?" Scarlett says, breaking the silence.

Dariel comes to his senses, nods. "This and half the sector, yeah."

My cousin taps his keyboard, and the image of an alien appears on a second monitor. He's Chellerian—tall and bipedal and broad shouldered. His skin is smooth and pale blue, his jaw heavy, his head hairless. He has four eyes, perfectly circular, bright red. The muscles in each of his four arms strain the fabric of his blindingly expensive suit. His grin is white and wide and full of razor-sharp teeth.

"That's Bianchi?" Scarlett asks.

"The one and only," my cousin nods. "Thank the Maker."

"Tell me about him."

Dariel finds his smirk again and shakes his head. "Oh, sweetheart, fairy stories aside, ain't none of you doing a deal with him. He practically runs this place. He lives inside a reconditioned luxury liner—one of those old-time cruise ships that Tesellon Inc. used to run through the Thiidan Nebula. Nobody gets into that joint without an invitation, and most people who get invited never come out again. He runs the security force on the whole World Ship. Keeps holding cells underneath his 'estate,' where people go to disappear. If your business is bringing you into Bianchi's orbit, then I recommend you either alter course or settle up with me before you get yourselves cadaverous."

"He's that dangerous?"

"He's worse than the Lysergia plague and the Selmis pox put together."

I look around the room at the faces of my squad. Cat's a tiny ball of suspicion, staring right at the back of Auri's head. Kal has his lips pursed in thought, and even Zila looks a little put out. Scarlett glances at her brother, but Tyler is still peering hard at the image on the first monitor screen.

The one Aurora painted on the walls.

"You notice anything about its eyes?" he says softly.

I look at the display. Skeptical as I am about the artifact's origin, I can't help noticing that its gemstone eyes bear an awful similarity to Auri's.

One dark.

One white.

The younger Jones twin takes hold of Dariel's chair, swivels it to face him.

"Okay, Big Time," he says. "Tell us everything you know."

THE UNIVERSE
▶ **HISTORY**
  ▼ **WAY BACK WHEN**

FIGURING OUT EXACTLY WHEN RECORDED HISTORY BEGAN IS A NIGHTMARE FOR ARCHAEOLOGISTS, HISTORIANS, AND MATHEMATICIANS.

WE KNOW THE **UNIVERSE** IS AROUND 13.8 BILLION YEARS OLD, BUT CONCEPTS OF BOTH TIME AND RECORD KEEPING HAVE VARIED WILDLY AMONG ALL **475 CURRENTLY KNOWN CIVILIZATIONS** IN THE **MILKY WAY**. THE **SYLDRATHI** ARE CONSIDERED THE OLDEST CIVILIZATION IN THE GALAXY, BUT THEIR HISTORIANS—**MYSTERIOUS BASTARDS** THAT THEY ARE— ARE FOND OF INTIMATING WITH KNOWING EXPRESSIONS AND PATRONIZING SMILES THAT OTHERS CAME EVEN BEFORE THEM.

OF COURSE, THEY COULD JUST BE MAKING IT UP. SNOOTY JERKS.

FOR FURTHER INFORMATION, CONSIDER SEARCHES ON THE FOLLOWING GROUPS, RUMORED BUT NOT PROVEN TO HAVE EXISTED:

▶ *THE ESHVAREN*

▶ *THE OCTARINE FLEET*

▶ *THE SAINE OF ISTA*

16

TYLER

"Wow," Scarlett breathes.

It's not often my big sister is reduced to being monosyllabic. Our father told us that when we were kids, Scar was speaking full sentences while I was still struggling with *dada*. But as we walk through the BIANCHI MUSEUM—VISITORS WELCOME holograph and into the ship's grand entry hall, I can't help but agree with her assessment. My eyes roam the graceful archways above our heads, the smooth curves of the alien architecture, the milling crowd, the beautiful exhibits. We're here hunting down information about Aurora's mysterious artifact, and tensions are high in the squad after her impromptu painting session last night. But even if we're in it up to our eyeballs on this little adventure, this place is still breathtaking.

"Yeah, it's a sight," I murmur.

"Didn't think you liked blonds, Bee-bro," Scar replies.

I raise a brow, look at my sister sidelong. And that's when I realize she's not admiring the architecture or crowd or exhibits; she's checking out the security guards posted beside the door. Both are human, handsome, well armed and kitted out in dark blue power armor. Scar catches the blond one's eye, gives him a wink. The guard grins with all due enthusiasm.

"Come on, let's take a look around," I say.

"I *am* looking around," my twin protests.

I grab Scarlett's hand and haul her inside, mind on our mission. Wondering for the hundredth time if I should have my head examined, if I wouldn't be smarter just turning Aurora over to the authorities, if this wild-goose chase is going to lead me anywhere but a dishonorable discharge and a prison cell.

"You must believe, Tyler."

That's what Admiral Adams told me. And in the five years I've served at Aurora, our academy commander has never steered me wrong. He's the one who secured me extra time in the simulators when I needed to practice zero-gee combat. He's the one who arranged for me to take my astronav exam over again when I only scored a ninety-eight and he said I could do better. He's the one who sat with me in chapel, telling me stories about my dad—how they came up through the TDF together, both of them gun pilots. Rivals turned best of friends.

Adams gave the eulogy at my dad's funeral.

Adams has always had my back.

Always.

But this time . . .

You must believe, Tyler.

Scar and I walk through the foyer of the Bianchi Museum, simulated sunlight illuminating the large open space.

I couldn't even guess the origins of this part of the station, but the structure is huge—maybe it was a cargo ship or freighter?

Support pillars stretch floor to ceiling, and the place is packed. Betraskans and Rigellians and Lierans and Terrans. Dozens more goons in power armor cover the entries and exits, but in our civilian clothes, we don't raise any eyebrows. We're surrounded by artwork and sculpture and displays from all over the galaxy. According to Finian's cousin, this museum stretches over seventeen floors. So what we really need to find is—

"Information?"

Scar and I turn at the sound of the voice. A young Betraskan woman is standing behind us, smiling warmly in my direction. She wears a formfitting blue uniform with the star-shaped crest of Casseldon Bianchi on its breast. Above her small hat spin a dozen holographic logos, one of which is a question mark.

"Do you require directions?" she asks. "Mr. Bianchi's museum can be a little overwhelming at first. Is there a particular exhibit you're interested in?"

"Oh, thank you, that's so sweet!" Scar smiles. She reaches into a pocket in her long red coat and holds up a picture of the sculpture that Auri scrawled all over the walls last night. "We're looking for this?"

The Betraskan woman looks at the pic, a tiny LED in the memory implant at her temple flickering. Reams of glowing data roll down her black contact lenses for a moment, her lashes fluttering.

"Unnamed religious artifact from the Eshvaren Empire,"

she finally says. "I'm afraid that exhibit closed quite some time ago. That particular artifact is now part of Mr. Bianchi's private collection."

"Is there any chance we could get a look at it?" Scarlett asks, turning her smile up to eleven. "I'm studying galactic history, you see, and my thesis is . . ."

The woman sadly shakes her head. "It wouldn't be much of a private collection if it were open to the public, I'm afraid. Although we do have some other ancient artifacts on Level th—"

We hear a loud alarm blare, and the lighting overhead dims to red. A Terran in a jetball cap and an I ♥ EARTH T-shirt looks alarmed as eight heavily armed and armored security guards surround him and the glass case he's leaning on. A shrill electronic voice spills out of the PA in a dozen different languages.

"PLEASE DO NOT TOUCH THE EXHIBITS."

"Sorry," the guy says. He picks his greasy StellarBurger up off the glass case and the priceless alien relic inside. "I didn't—"

He yelps as the security goons hit him with a sickstick, drop him to the ground in a puddle of vomit. Grabbing him by the armpits, they haul the groaning man to his feet and drag him through the crowd toward the exit. Our walking information booth watches the drama with a small scowl.

"Your security takes things seriously around here," I murmur.

"They're not *ours*," the Betraskan mutters, looking at the guards with distaste. "Mr. Bianchi has put on extra personnel for the masquerade tomorrow night."

"Masquerade?"

The woman points to a projection on one of the walls. "It's the fiftieth anniversary of the World Ship. There's to be a grand celebration. Mr. Bianchi will be throwing one of his parties. Very exclusive. Very exciting."

"Oh, riiiight," I nod. "Of course. The masquerade."

She blinks, looks me up and down. "You don't have an invitation, do you?"

"Um, no," I say. "I just arrived."

"Pity," she purrs. "I look amazing in a backless dress."

I let my dimples off the leash, and with a flirty smile, she turns away, moves off to help more lost visitors in the crowd. I watch her go, the words *backless dress* echoing in my head. It's only when I look around that I realize I've lost Scarlett.

My twin is six feet tall with bright blue eyes and flaming orange hair—it's not as though she's easy to misplace. I stand on tiptoes, looking around the throng, finally catching a flash of fiery red near the entrance. Scar's talking to the two security guards, laughing and smiling as the blond leans in, one elbow on the wall above her head in that classic *Intergalactic Romeo* pose. She grins, toying with the secure-coded ID badge hanging around his neck.

I walk over behind my sis, clear my throat.

"Hey, Bee-bro," she says. "This is Declan and Lachlan."

"Hey," Blondie says, not looking at me. The other simply nods.

"They just transferred here," Scar explains. "This is only their fourth day on the World Ship. Declan came all the way from the Martian colonies, isn't that *amazing*?"

"Scar, we gotta go," I say. "Remember we got that thing?"

Blondie whispers in Scar's ear and she laughs, smacking his armored chest. I rub my temples and sigh.

"Scarlett?" I say, trying not to let too much frustration creep into my voice.

She shoots me a death stare, turns back to Blondie, and bumps her uniglass against his, transferring her contact details. "Don't be late."

"The Great Ultrasaur of Abraaxis IV couldn't keep me away," he smiles.

I hover patiently as they whisper a little more, then Scar takes my arm and, with a final wink at Blondie, walks me out of the Bianchi Museum. We wander along the promenade, back in the direction of Dariel's flat. The colors and sights and sounds of the World Ship wash over us like a rainbow, and I wait till we're well out of earshot before I speak.

"Hot date tonight?" I ask.

"Seven o'clock," she replies. "Right after he gets off shift."

"That means he'll still be dressed for work. And still carrying his ID badge."

"I told him I have a thing for guys in uniform."

"Clever girl," I nod.

"I *am* a Jones." She smiles, squeezing my arm.

I squeeze her back, suddenly grateful all over again that she's with me. She might never miss an opportunity to give me a hard time, but I know my sister would follow me to the edge of the galaxy if I asked. If blood is thicker than water, Scar and I are practically concrete.

"I'm surprised you didn't have an ex working on this station already," I say, stepping into a turbolift down to the hab levels. "You seem to run into one every other place we go."

"Are you passing judgment on my number of relationships, Bee-bro?"

"Maker forbid." I grin.

"It's not my fault I get bored. Or that boys get boring." Scar pouts, taps her lip. "There *is* one tiny problem, though. More of a six-foot-seven problem, actually."

"The other guard?"

"Yeah. Declan's buddy asked if I had a friend."

"I hope you said no."

"I needed to sweeten the pot. I said I knew a girl just Lachlan's type."

I fold my arms as the lift begins to descend. "Scar, you can't take Zila on a double. She's liable to shoot her date with a disruptor just to see what happens."

"I'm not talking about Zila, Ty."

"Well, you can't bring Aurora, there's a bounty on her head!"

My sister rolls her eyes. "I'm not talking about Aurora, either."

I blink, doing the math in my head.

". . . Oh no, you didn't?"

Scarlett chews her lip and nods.

"I did."

. . . . .

"No way," Cat declares.

"Look, it's simple," Scar insists. "Just sit and smile, let me do the talking."

"No. Bloody. Way."

"Come onnnn, roomie," Scar wheedles. "This is just like

237

old times. You and me? Two space queens on the prowl? It'll be fun!"

"It won't be fun, it'll be fu—"

"Stop being such a pessimist!"

"I'm not a pessimist, I'm a realist."

"Well, good, because they're rrrreal cute."

"I see what you did there."

"Cute."

"*No.*"

"Cuu-uuuute," Scar sings, wiggling her fingers.

"Maker's breath, I hate you so much right now, Jones. . . ."

We're gathered back at Dariel's damp stone den, sitting around his tiny lounge room while the life-support system rattles and hums overhead. The light in here is a little too dim for a human, provided mostly by the vines that cascade down from the ceiling.

Aurora is curled up on the couch, knees beneath her chin, flicking through the history of the World Ship on the uniglass I gave her. Kal is sitting nearby, studiously ignoring the girl beside him and studying the imported stalactites instead. I'm not entirely sure what's going on between those two, but it's something I have to keep a watch on.

Zila is playing on her uniglass as usual, Scar leaning in the bedroom doorway. Dariel himself is out doing the wheeler-dealer thing, so he's left Fin in charge of not letting the place burn down while he's gone. Looking at the heat in Cat's cheeks, I'm not sure he's gonna pull it off.

"Look, this is a two-girl mission, Cat," Scar says. "It's not like I can bring Zila or Aurora with me. We just need to hook these guys long enough for me to swipe an ID card. Then we can access the Sempiternity security network."

Finian nods. "Been looking at some schematics Dariel dug up and poking around their system. They're running the entire station on a reworked Occulus 19 grid with mimetic encryption. If we can get a leech into one of the main nodes, I reckon I could hack the camera network. We'd be able to see everything on the station. Including inside Bianchi's luxury liner. Which means we can see where he's keeping the . . ." Finian blinks, glancing at the display of Auri's sculpture on one of the smaller monitors. "What're we calling this thing, anyway?"

"The Whatchamacallit?" Scar offers.

"The Doodad?" I suggest.

"The Trigger," Zila says quietly, not looking up from her glass.

"Well, you can all stick your *Trigger* where your Trigger isn't s'posed to get stuck," Cat says, scowling around the room. "I didn't train for this crap."

"It'll be sixty minutes, tops," Scar insists. "Just relax. Let your hair down."

Cat aims a pointed glance up to her fauxhawk.

"My hair doesn't go down."

Scar looks to me, and I push myself off the wall, approach my Ace with considerable caution. "Cat, I know this isn't your ideal mission. But we need intel."

Finian nods. "Best way to get eyes inside Bianchi's liner is the cam system."

"Ah, we're trusting the knucklehead who irradiated the academy propulsion labs now," Cat scowls. "Fan-bloody-tastic."

"Trust me, I know what I'm talking about."

"Well then, *you* go on the double date, Finian," Cat growls.

Fin puts his hands to his cheeks in mock horror. "But . . . whatever would I wear?"

Cat lunges across the room at our Gearhead, and I grab her shoulders, force her back. For a second we're touching, chest to chest, and I'm reminded of the last time we were this close. The last time I ever had a drink.

Graduation day back on Cohen IV.

"Ease off, Legionnaire Brannock," I warn her.

She glares at Finian, but she stops trying to push past me. Straightens her clothes and then straightens her faux-hawk. She's wearing short sleeves and I can see the Ace logo on her right arm among the other tatts. I remember sitting with her in the parlor as we got inked, the liquor we used to dull the sting at the bar later. Looking at each other across that table as the empty glasses stacked up and knowing the mistake it'd lead to.

Because that's what I told her afterward.

That's what it was.

A mistake.

Cat turns her glare on Aurora, and the accusations in her eyes as plain as starlight: *This is your fault. Without you, Tyler would have got his golden squad and I'd be part of it and none of this would be happening.*

And it's true. Every word. And not for the first time, I hope Battle Leader de Stoy knew what she was doing when she told Auri to stow away on our ship. I hope Adams knew what he was saying when he asked me to believe. Because it's getting harder by the minute.

"Please, Cat," I say, soft. "We could really use your help on this."

My Ace meets my eyes, then glances once more at Auri. The girl stares back, lifting her chin, faint challenge in her eyes. Cat clenches her jaw. But I know what she'll say before she says it. The same thing she said the morning after, lying on those rumpled sheets when I told her a CO couldn't date a subordinate, that an Alpha couldn't date his Ace, that best friends who'd known each other since kindergarten shouldn't risk that friendship to try for something more.

"Sir, yessir," Cat says.

. . . . .

"This toilet is not big enough for the five of us," Kal says.

"It's not my fault you're seventeen meters tall, Pixieboy," Finian growls.

"And it's all we could afford," I say. "So quit griping, they'll be here soon."

Me, Kal, Fin, Zila, and Auri are crowded into the small and grimy bathroom of a love motel on the lower side of the World Ship's nightclub district. We're pressed in like ration packs, Fin's elbow in my ribs and Kal's left boot in the commode. The room our bathroom is attached to has been booked under my sister's name, and it's a short stagger from the bar where she and Cat are hopefully working their magic. Any minute, we'll hear them coming through the door, and then it's game time.

But in the meantime . . .

"It stinks like my fourth grandmother's underwear drawer in here," Fin says.

"You know what your grandmother's underwear drawer smells like?" I ask.

"My family is very cosmopolitan."

"I do not think that word means what you think it means," Zila murmurs.

"Um," Auri whispers. "Sorry, but is someone touching my butt?"

". . . Would you like someone to be touching your butt?" Fin asks.

Kal clears his throat. "If you wish it, I—"

"Shut up!" I hiss.

I hear the ping of the electronic lock on the front door, smothered laughter. My squad falls silent as we listen to heavy footsteps, a drunken guffaw. The door slams, someone stumbles, a glass breaks.

"Oh noooooo," says a male voice, muffled through the bathroom door. "Declan, you dropped the booze."

"Did I?" comes a second male voice.

"You"—*hic*—"did."

"Oh *noooooo*."

"Declan, come over here," someone purrs.

Scarlett.

"Lachlan, stay waaaayyyy over there," someone growls.

Cat.

"Why are there"—*hic*—"three of you?" Declan asks.

"There's just one of me," Scar laughs. "You're tipsy, come sit."

"I kinda"—*hic*—"like the idea of three of you."

"Believe me, handsome, one of me is *way* more than you can handle."

"I think . . . I'm gonna be sick," Lachlan declares.

"I know the feeling," Cat sighs.

242

"No, seriously," he burps. "Where's the . . . bathroom?"

Inside said bathroom, the five of us exchange a brief, horrified glance.

"Can't feel my feet," Declan mumbles.

"All the more reason to get you off them," Scar purrs. "Come on, come sit on the bed with me."

"Seriousssly, I can't feel'em," he giggles. "What was in that las'drink?"

"Approximately twelve milliliters of benzothelemene," I hear Zila whisper behind me. "If Scarlett followed my directions precisely."

I hear a heavy thud, followed closely by another.

"Sounds like she did," I smile, opening the bathroom door.

Sure enough, laid out flat—one on the floor, one at the foot of the bed—are the two security guards from the museum earlier today. Sitting on the bed beside Blondie is my sister, looking vaguely disappointed. Cat's sitting on the second bed looking vaguely annoyed, her boots resting on the bigger goon at her feet.

"Okay, let's do this," I say.

Fin leans down to inspect Cat's trophy. "If you'd told me he was *this* hot, I would have gone on the date for sure."

"Shut up, Finian," she replies.

We strip the sleeping guards naked and haul them into bed. Kal and I then pull on their power armor and loop their ID badges around our necks. Finian stares first at the photo on my badge, then up into my face.

"I gotta admit, the likeness is pretty uncanny," he says.

I glance at the unconscious goon in the bed. "We look *nothing* alike."

My Gearhead shrugs, hands me a small device. "All you dirtchildren look the same to me, Goldenboy. Now you need to plant this in the uplink nodes. Centr—"

"I heard you the first seven times, thanks."

Kal finishes suiting up, smooths back his braids, gives me the nod. He cuts a pretty impressive figure. Good thing Lachlan here was so tall.

"The dosage will keep them sleeping for at least six hours," Zila says, looking at the slumbering SecBoys. "They will remember very little."

"Just make sure you have their armor back here by dawn," Scar says. And without ceremony, she clamps her lips onto the sleeping blond's neck and starts to suck.

"Holy cake," Auri whispers, watching with wide eyes. "Please don't tell me that on top of everything else, vampires are real?"

"Evidence." Scarlett comes up for air with a smirk, and I can see the angry red love bite she's left on the goon's neck. She unclasps her bra and tugs it out through her sleeve, then drapes it over the bedside lamp and writes *thanks xxx* on the wall in deep red lipstick. "Can't have a crime without leaving some evidence."

Cat makes a face. "If you think I'm leaving my bra behind in this dump, you're sorely mistaken."

"There's enough of mine to go around."

"Touché," Cat nods sadly.

"You ready for this, Kal?" I ask.

My Tank adjusts the ID badge around his neck and gives me a small bow.

"I am always ready," he replies.

We turn toward the door, but Aurora's voice stops us.

"Hey . . . wait . . ."

She looks at me as Kal and I turn back to her. Dragging her hand through her bone-white bangs, she chews her lip, searching for the words.

"Thanks," she says, glancing about. "I know how weird this is. I know none of us really know what's going on here. And I don't like sitting on the bench while you risk your necks for me. So I want you to know . . . I appreciate it."

I look around the room. Her thanks are met with a nod from Zila, a small smile from Fin. But I can tell Scar's still uncertain about this girl. Cat barely gives her a glance. And Kal just stares.

I see Aurora's shoulders slump a little. Her lips tighten, she looks at the floor. She probably didn't expect everyone to be turning cartwheels, but still . . .

"You're welcome," I say.

She looks up at that. I pat her shoulder, a touch awkward in the power armor. Cat's eyes narrow, but Aurora manages a weak smile.

This can't be easy for her. Two hundred years out of time. Everyone she knew, everything she had, gone. I don't know many people who'd still be on their feet after that. But not only is she up and moving, she's fighting too. Clawing for answers the only way she knows how. She's got heart, this girl. Even without De Stoy's message about our precious cargo, that counts for a lot with me.

"We'll be fine, Auri," I say, trying to calm her fears. "This is what we do. Just stick with Scar, we'll see you back at Dariel's place, all right?"

". . . All right."

"We are wasting time, sir," Kal murmurs behind me, his voice cold.

"Yeah, okay," I sigh.

I really need to talk to him about this girl.

I nod to Scar. She nods back.

"Be careful."

And without another word, we're gone.

Syldrathi Society
▶ Social Customs
　　▼ How Not to Get Punched

THE FIRST THING TO KNOW ABOUT LEARNING **SYLDRATHI CUSTOMS** IS THAT YOU'LL FAIL. THEY'RE IMPOSSIBLY SUBTLE, AND MOST SPECIES CONSIDER THEM FORMAL TO A FAULT. SYLDRATHI BOW INSTEAD OF NODDING. THEY CLOSE THEIR EYES INSTEAD OF BOWING. THAT SAID, MAJOR TRAPS TO AVOID ARE:

NOT DEFERRING TO THE ELDEST PERSON IN THE ROOM. SYLDRATHI BELIEVE THAT WISDOM COMES WITH AGE. THIS IS VERY CONVENIENT, SINCE THEIR LIFE EXPECTANCY IS A FEW HUNDRED YEARS AND ANY SYLDRATHI YOU'RE TALKING TO IS PROBABLY OLDER THAN YOU.

MAKING UNINVITED PHYSICAL CONTACT. ESPECIALLY OF AN **INTIMATE NATURE**. FOR A SYLDRATHI, THIS INCLUDES TOUCH APPLIED ANYWHERE ON THE FACE, NECK, EARS, OR HANDS. HUGS ARE ALSO RIGHT OUT.

INSULTING THEIR MOTHERS. JUST DON'T.

17

KAL

My jaw aches from the elbow I took in the bar yesterday.

My ribs are bruised where one of the Unbroken adepts kicked me, and I can feel the faint swelling of the knuckles in my left hand from a clumsy punch.

That was careless of you, the Enemy Within whispers.

Weak.

We are riding the turbolift in our stolen power armor, preparing to infiltrate the World Ship's security hub. It will not be easy, and my mind should be on the mission. But instead, I am thinking about the brawl with the Unbroken yesterday. The disdain in their eyes. Their blood on my knuckles.

I am *not* thinking about Aurora.

I focus on the pain as my father taught me. Those endless lessons in the Aen Suun—the Wave Way—drilled into me since the day I was born. I remember the two of us standing beneath the lias trees on Syldra before it burned. His hand on my arm, guiding my strikes. His voice in my ear. He was Warbreed like I am. Proud. Fearless. Peerless.

But all his training and all his skill were worth nothing in the end.

And so I permit myself to feel the hurt.

The places I allowed my enemies to touch me.

Vowing they will never touch me again.

"You all right?"

I look across the turbolift at my Alpha as he speaks. Tyler Jones is watching me with those cool blue eyes, and I can feel his mind at work behind them. He is wondering how he ended up so close to the edge so quickly. He is wondering if there is any way out of this. And though he would deny it with every fiber of his being if I accused him of it, he is wondering if he can trust me.

I cannot blame him. He was quick to assist in the bar yesterday, but that was mere muscle memory—an Alpha stepping to the defense of a squadmate.

I wonder what he truly thinks of me in the dark and quiet hours.

I could see the pain in his eyes yesterday when he spoke of his father. Even Syldrathi know of the great Jericho Jones. A Terran Defense Force commander who slew thousands of my people in the war, then suddenly turned pacifist. He became the loudest voice in the Terran Senate, arguing for peace between our peoples. It was Jericho Jones who brokered the first round of peace talks between Terra and Syldra. It was *his* negotiations that opened the way for the cease-fire in 2370.

And when the Starslayer and his Unbroken took advantage of the lull in hostilities to attack the Orion shipyards, Jericho Jones was among those who answered the call for reservists. He had not flown a fighter in thirteen years. He had two children waiting back on Terra for him to return.

And he did not.

I wonder how much of Tyler Jones blames me for that. I wonder if he looks at the glyf on my forehead and sees what everyone else sees.

Warbreed.

Betrayer.

Killer.

I'na Sai'nuit.

"I am fine, sir," I reply. "I thank you for asking."

Tyler licks his lip, the small split he earned in the brawl yesterday.

"Listen, I'm not sure how to bring this up," he says. "And maybe it's none of my concern. But you're my Tank, and I'm responsible for you."

"You are my Alpha. Ask what you will."

"Auri," he says. "Aurora."

The sound of her name is like music. I actually feel my belly flutter, my skin prickle beneath the power armor I am wearing. I picture her eyes, pupils of bottomless black, one ringed in seventeen different shades of brown, the other encircled by a white as pale as starlight. I think of her lips, and I—

"What's the deal between you two?" Tyler asks.

A surge of sudden enmity roars through me. Territoriality. Aggression. I know that primal instinct has no place here and I fight it, as I have fought it since the moment I laid eyes on her in that cargo bay and she spoke words I will never forget.

"I've seen you before. . . ."

I blink hard. Focus my mind as my mother taught me.

"There is no deal between Aurora and I," I say.

"You called her 'be'shmai,'" Tyler replies. "In the bar before the fight."

I feel the anger surging again. The war in my blood, entwined with the overwhelming desire of the Pull. The Enemy Within, whispering in my ear. Digging fingers into my spine. I stamp him down. Push him away. Clear my thoughts.

This conversation will not end well.

I clear my throat, keep my voice calm. "Sir, with all due respect, I believe you were correct. This is not your concern."

"I don't speak Syldrathi as well as Scar, but I know what 'be'shmai' means."

A bitter smile curls my lips. "No, sir. You do not."

"I've never heard of the Pull happening between a Syldrathi and a human before. Is that what's happening here? Have you told Aurora?"

"No," I say, horrified at the thought. "Of course not."

"Look, I want you to know I respect you. I respect where you're from. But if you're going to lose your head at some critical moment because of some Syldrathi mating instinct, then I—"

"The Pull is no mere mating instinct," I say, steel slipping into my voice. "And explaining it to a human would be like trying to describe the color of a rainbow to a blind man. You do not . . . you *cannot* understand."

I swallow the steel. The taste of anger in my mouth.

"Sir," I add.

"The Pull is usually reciprocal, right?" he asks, head tilted. "What happens—"

"You need not concern yourself." I scowl, uncomfortable even discussing this with a Terran. "I assure you I have it under control."

"You certainly lost it quick against those Unbroken yesterday."

"I *lost* nothing. I knew exactly what I was doing. The violence was necessary."

"Because they threatened Auri?"

"Because you spoke my name."

He blinks at that. "What's your name got to do with it?"

I fold my arms and say nothing, signaling that I wish the conversation to end. But Tyler Jones keeps at it, like a keddai on a corpse.

"Look, I know it can't be easy, Kal. I know I can't really understand it. But you need to understand how close to the edge we are here. We can't afford these kinds of entanglements right now. I need you to keep a lid on it."

"I might say the same about you. Sir."

Tyler blinks. "What's that supposed to mean?"

"I see the way Legionnaire Brannock looks at you."

He bristles at that, standing a little taller. He still only comes up to my chin.

"That's none of your business, legionnaire."

"I agree, sir. It is none of my business at all."

We stand there in silence, electricity crackling between us. The thing I was raised to be is acutely aware of how easy it would be to reach out and break this human boy. But the man I try to be keeps his arms folded instead. His face

252

expressionless. His pulse calm. The turbolift hisses to a halt, the door slides open with a small chime. Time stands still, and so do we, until the door starts to close.

My hand flashes out, holds it open.

"After you, sir."

Tyler exits the lift after a few more moments of staring, tapping his uniglass as he goes. "Finian, this is Tyler, do you read?"

"Loud and clear, Goldenboy."

"We're on Level seventy-one. Point us in the direction of the security hub."

"On it. Shift changeover is in five minutes according to Dariel, so you wanna hustle if you're going to get overlooked in the crush."

We hurry down the halls at Finian's direction, into a broad, open space. Dozens of other security crew members in power armor matching ours are converging on the airlock of what looks to be an old Neltaarian cruiser, flashing their IDs at the guards on duty before being waved through. The hour is late—almost midnight shipboard time—and the guards on duty look both bored and tired.

A good combination.

A broad-shouldered Terran in front of us pushes his ID badge under the scanner and is met with a flashing red light and an angry buzz. The guard on duty sighs and tells the Terran to run it again, which he does, only to be met with another angry beep.

"Piece of crap," the guard says, kicking the scanner.

"In a hurry, boss," Tyler says smoothly, waving his ID with his thumb over the photograph. "Meeting some ladies, and they don't like to wait."

"Yeah, yeah, go through," the guard says, thumping the scanner again.

As the big Terran complains behind us, we shuffle past into the security hub. Walking down a long main hallway, Tyler taps the commlink in his ear.

"Good work, Finian," he murmurs.

"Child's play. Get your uniglass within a meter of any wireless system and I can work miracles. You want to look for a sign for the server core."

As we step through the airlock, another scanner runs a series of red lasers over our badges and armor, an electronic voice urges us to proceed. The hallways are busy, SecTeam members either clocking off or clocking on. I spot a sign for the server systems, point it out to Tyler. I keep my stride easy, my smile polite. I ignore the tension in my muscles, the feeling of enemies on all sides, the violence simmering inside me. Walking softly. Hearing my father's voice in my head.

We arrive at a set of double doors, sealed with an electronic keypad and marked SERVER CORE. We pretend to chat as a man in an administrator's uniform hurries past. When the corridor is clear, Tyler holds his uniglass near the lock.

We wait. Trying not to look suspicious. Which, given that we are breaking into this room in the middle of an armed facility, is somewhat difficult.

"Take your time, Finian," Tyler mutters into his commlink.

"Look, if you know someone else who can run a wireless hack on an eighteen-digit encryption, be my guest," comes the reply.

"I thought you said you were a miracle worker."

The lock beeps. The server doors click open.

"Well, hey now, would you look at that."

We steal inside the room, pulling the doors closed behind us. The air is cool, filled with a subsonic hum, the room lit by flickering LEDs and overhead fluorescents and lined with rows of servers and tangles of cable. Finian's voice crackles in our ears.

"Wow, that was amazing, Finian. You really are *a miracle worker. I think I'm going to name my firstborn dirtchild after you beca—"*

"Knock it off," Tyler snaps. "Where do we plant this leech?"

"Tertiary uplink oughta do it. Now listen close. I'll use small words."

I keep watch at the door, peering out through the crack while Tyler follows Finian's instructions. Security personnel march past, a few stragglers heading to their shifts. A refreshment drone trundles by on smooth tracks, carrying a tray of coffee and celedine and stimulant supplements. Five minutes pass, each as long as an eon, until finally I turn and whisper to my squad leader.

"Someone comes."

Tyler looks up from the server, elbow-deep in cable. "You sure?"

I peer back down the corridor at the approaching Terran. He carries an armload of computer equipment and wears a tool belt full of e-tech. He is three days unshaven, glares at the security personnel around him with an air of undisguised contempt, and looks as though he has not slept in seven years.

"He certainly has the appearance of a man who works with computers, yes."

"Finian, are we good?" Tyler asks.

"Affirmative, I'm getting a signal from the leech. We're in."

"Roger that," Tyler says, sealing up the server cabinet.

A passing security team member bumps into the approaching commtech. The tech curses, stoops to pick up the gear he dropped. But he is barely four meters from the server room door now. He will surely notice us if we walk out of it right in front of him.

Tyler joins me at the door, peers outside.

"This isn't good."

"Agreed."

My Alpha looks at our surroundings. Rapidly reaches the same conclusion I have. There is nowhere to hide in here, particularly in the bulky power armor we are wearing. The Enemy Within whispers that I could easily deal with this tech in silence—crush his windpipe as soon as he steps inside. Snap his neck. Choke him to death. A dozen different endings dance inside my head. But the quieter part of me knows that would leave a corpse in the server core, and that might lead to an investigation, bringing our leech closer to discovery.

My mind is racing. But I am not the one who scored a perfect one hundred on his military tactics exam in final year. The legionnaire beside me is.

"Suggestions, sir?"

Tyler scowls. Permutations and possibilities running behind his eyes. The commtech is shuffling toward the door now, weighed down by his gear, muttering under his breath. Tyler glances at me. Takes a deep breath.

"Look, apologies in advance for this. But whatever you do, don't punch me, okay?"

"Wh—"

Tyler grabs the front of my power armor and pulls me close. The door opens and the commtech walks right in at the precise moment Tyler's lips land on mine. My eyes go wide. The tech's jaw falls open.

I am shocked into stillness. I know Terrans touch casually, slapping each other on the back, shaking hands. This is a lot more than a handshake. This is Tyler pressed up against me, turning slowly toward the commtech, our mouths still mashed together. . . .

The tech stands in the doorway, glancing back and forth between us. It's Tyler who breaks off the kiss, looking appropriately embarrassed. For my part, I am simply stunned. Shuffling his armload of gear, the commtech backs slowly out of the room.

"Thiiiiiiink I'm gonna give you boys a moment," he says.

The tech drags the door shut behind him with an apologetic smile. Tyler pulls away completely.

"You okay? Not going to punch me or anything, right?"

"What . . . ," I sputter. "You . . ."

Tyler waits for me to compose myself, then nods toward the hall.

"Give it a second," he says. "Then slink out of here looking embarrassed."

"That will *not* be difficult," I say.

Tyler chuckles and opens the door.

"After you, sweetie."

With a deep breath, I stalk out of the server core, back toward the entrance. The commtech is standing a short distance down the corridor, studiously pretending not to notice me leave. But as I pass by, he winks.

My ears burning, I climb the stairs and make my way through the security hub until I'm swiping my ID under the scanner at the entrance hall. The guard on duty nods as I exit, not even looking up from his uniglass.

"Have a good one."

A few minutes later, Tyler joins me in the entrance hall, and we march off together. Inside the turbolift, he stands beside me, hands behind his back, whistling a soft tune. I am forced to admit that his quick thinking just averted a calamity, that the tech believes we were in the server for . . . if not innocent reasons, then not illegal ones. That our leech is now safely inside the security network and we have eyes all over the station.

Such a touch is an intimacy among Syldrathi.

It should be treated with reverence, not used as a cheap trick.

But it *did* work.

"Look, sorry again," Tyler finally says. "I had to think fast. We good?"

". . . Did they teach you that technique in tactics class at the academy?" I ask.

My Alpha grins and shakes his head. "The best tacticians know how to improvise. That means working with whatever comes to hand."

"Or mouth?"

Tyler laughs. "I guess so. Good thing I brushed my teeth this morning."

We ride in silence for a while, watching the numbers on the display rise.

"I didn't know Syldrathi blushed with their ears," Tyler muses.

"I am not blushing."

"I mean, it kinda looks like you're blushing."

"I am *not* blushing."

"Ooookay," Tyler nods. "I sometimes have that effect on people, is all."

"Is your request not to punch you still in effect, sir?"

My Alpha only grins in reply. And though I am still somewhat shocked, I cannot help but feel a grudging respect also. He thinks swiftly, this Tyler Jones. He does not rattle, and he does not hesitate. With everything on the line, he still sees clearly, and he does what it takes to win. He is a born leader.

The lift halts and the doors open, and as I step out into the hallway, I hear him chuckling to himself behind me.

"What is funny?" I ask.

"I was just thinking," he grins. "Scarlett *did* tell us to just kiss and get it over with. . . ."

Aurora Legion Squads

▶ **Squad Members**

   ▼ **Aces**

Trained to fly anything from **SHUTTLES** to **CRUISERS**, **FREIGHTERS** to **SHIPKILLERS**, Aces are the pilots of **Aurora Legion squads**. You bring them the eye of a needle, and an Ace can thread it for you with the ship of your choosing.

Aces have a rep for being daring, confident (reckless even), and above average in the looks department. Just ask them, they'll tell you themselves.

Being an Ace requires lightning reflexes, quicker thinking, and **REPRODUCTIVE ORGANS OF SOLID TITANIUM**. Let's be real: their job is as cool as they are.

ACE'S INSIGNIA

18

CAT

"So I have good news," Finian declares. "Then excellent news. Then absolutely terrible news."

Ty sinks down on the couch beside me, Scarlett on his other side. He and Kal have just got back from their job in the security hub, their power armor dumped in the love hotel with our unconscious double dates. Our illustrious leader leans down to rub a scuff off his boot, his mop of shaggy blond hair hanging in his eyes. I watch the muscles play in his arm from the corner of my eye. Pretending not to notice. Pretending not to care.

"Good news first," Tyler says.

Finian swivels his chair to face us. His uniglass is plugged into the forearm of his exosuit, a holographic screen projected from a lens at his wrist. The light's bright against the gloom of Dariel's den, the image crisp. I wonder how much processing power is in that rig of his. Wonder at the kind of mind that could even *make* a suit like that. Finian's an annoying little shithead for sure, but at least he doesn't have shit for brains.

"Good news is the leech is working perfectly," he declares. "I'm in their network, moving slow so as not to attract attention. But I have access to the infamous Casseldon Bianchi's luxury liner, and all the security cams therein."

He pauses, looking around the room.

"Don't everyone applaud at once."

"What's the excellent news?" Scarlett asks.

Finian taps a pad on his exosuit's other arm. His small holographic screen flickers into larger, brighter life on the white stone of the wall. He swipes the air, and the holograph flips through half a dozen screens until he finds the one he wants.

"Excellent news is I think I found our Trigger."

From her seat in the corner, Aurora comes to her feet. Her mismatched eyes are wide, fixed on Fin's projection. There, floating on a beam of blue light, is the sculpture she painted all over the storage room—a figure with three-fingered hands, wrought in strange metal. Doesn't look much bigger than my own hand. The diamond in its chest and the pearl in its right eye are actually real gemstones. It's hovering inside a transparent case of what might be glass, slowly spinning.

"Is that it?" Tyler asks.

Aurora stares. Her whisper's almost too soft to hear.

"Yes."

She drags her eyes away from the screen, over to Tyler.

"I don't know how I know. But I *know*. That's why we're here. . . ."

"Okay," Tyler nods, staring at the sculpture. "Give us the bad news, Finian."

"I never said I had bad news," our Gearhead replies, tapping on his keyboard. "I said I had absolutely terrible news."

"Maker's breath," I sigh. "Just spit it out, will you?"

Finian blows me a kiss and moves his fingers, pulling our image to a wider shot. I can see a large circular room, decked in fancy furnishings. Huge glass windows look out into what seems to be some kind of jungle. Dozens of glass cases and cabinets are arranged around the space, picked out with warm spotlights and filled with strange objects. Some are sleek and elegant, others twisted and shimmering. But all of them are pretty.

"This is Casseldon Bianchi's office," Finian explains. "It's at the heart of his estate. It's protected by the kind of security that'd wake a career criminal screaming in the night. Temperature-responsive scanners. Genetic sensors. Pressure floors reading off micro-changes in air density. And even assuming you could fool those measures, there's only one door in or out. And there's only one key. Which, as far as I can tell, hangs around Bianchi's neck at all times."

Finian flips to a picture of Bianchi dressed in a sharp suit, unveiling some piece of exotic sculpture in his museum. His grin is a row of dazzling white fangs. Around his neck, I can see a digital passkey hanging on a platinum chain.

"Polymorphic gene-coded sixty-four-digit encryption," Finian says.

"Sounds complicated," Tyler says.

"Complicated doesn't even begin to describe it. His office is going to be harder to get into than my date's boxer shorts at last year's Genesis Day Ball."

"Is there any way in at all?" Tyler asks.

"I honestly don't know," Finian sighs. "I tried poetry, I tried flowers, I—"

"I'm talking about the *office*, Fin. What about air vents?"

Our Gearhead shakes his head, pulling up the picture of the office again. "The vents are three centimeters wide at best. And ion shielded. So unless you're planning on losing a *lot* of weight . . ."

"What about those huge windows?" I point out.

"They're not windows, they're walls," Finian replies, swiveling three-sixty in his chair again. "Whole office is enclosed in transparent polarized silicon."

"Why?"

"Bianchi buys trinkets and artifacts from all over the galaxy. But his main interest is in exotic life-forms. He's got over ten thousand species in his menagerie, according to this interview I read in last month's *Galactic Gentleman*."

"People still subscribe to *Galactic Gentleman*?" Scarlett asks, eyebrow raised.

"I mean, I'd heard rumors . . . ," I mutter.

"I buy it for the articles. Anyway, Bianchi's office"— Finian's fingers dance, and the projection on the wall shifts to a schematic—"sits right in the center of his menagerie. And surrounding his office is the cage for his most prized exhibit."

"Please tell me it's a small friendly terrier named Lord Woofsly," Tyler sighs.

"Close, Goldenboy," Finian says, flipping his display again. "Very close."

Projected on the wall is the most horrific . . . thing . . . I've ever seen. And as of one eye-gougingly accidental encounter outside the shower this morning, I've seen Dariel de Vinner de Seel in his underwear.

The beast is all razor teeth and lurid green eyes and rippling muscle. Its claws are broadswords and its hide is horned and armored, and it's making a shrieking, metallic noise—like two chainsaws trying to have sex.

"Fellow legionnaires, may I present the pride of Casseldon Bianchi's menagerie," Finian says. "The Great Ultrasaur of Abraaxis IV."

"Amna diir," Kal breathes, his usually cool facade cracking just a little.

"You said it, Pixieboy," Finian nods. "I mean, I have no idea what you said, but yeah, you said it. Rumor has it Bianchi paid his fourth testicle to get his hands on this thing."

"Why do they call it the *great* ultrasaur?" Aurora asks. "Does it have, like, excellent penmanship skills or something?"

"It's the last one of its kind in the whole galaxy," Fin says.

"What happened to the rest of them?"

"This one killed them," the Betraskan replies simply. "It's the last of its kind because it literally *ate* all the others."

The girl blinks. "Holy cake, it *what*?"

"Yeah, ultrasaurs are the most infamously hostile species in the 'Way," Finian says, running one hand through his white hair, leaving it more spiked than before. "They killed every living thing on Abraaxis IV. And when they ran out of things to kill, they killed each other."

"Evolutionarily speaking, that makes very little sense," Zila points out.

"Makes perfect sense to me," Finian shrugs. "People do it all the time."

"Why is it making that noise?" Scarlett winces.

"Mating call, I think? Eat all your potential ladyfriends, I guess you get lonely."

"Okay, okay," Tyler says. "I think we've established that going in through the menagerie isn't an option. So, front door it is. We need that key."

"Won't do us any good, Goldenboy," Finian says. "It's a polymorphic gene-coded combination sequence. That means the combination changes every time Bianchi comes into physical contact with it. And if anyone else so much as sneezes on it, the key registers the foreign DNA and locks the whole estate down."

I feel a sort of relief at that. This mission is looking more impossible by the second. The sooner Tyler realizes we're wasting our time on this crap, the sooner we give up this bloody insanity.

I trace the whorls and lines of ink on my right arm with my fingertips. I do that when I get nervous. When I get angry. When I need to center myself. My tatts are from a dozen different artists, a rainbow of colors, a collage of styles, but they all have one thing in common. The one thing I've loved since I was a little girl.

Wings.

Dragons. Birds. Butterflies and moths. I have a hawk inked across my back and shoulder blades, just like my mum. She was a pilot in the TDF before she got sick. I still remember the smile on her face when I told her I was joining the Legion. She told me she was proud. She said the same thing the last time I spoke to her. Wheezing it, with what little breath the plague let her take.

"I'm proud of you, baby girl."

I wonder how proud she'd be if she saw me now. A fugitive. Neck-deep in trouble. A court-martial with my name on it already sitting on someone's desk. I know Tyler will try to take the fall for us if we get caught. I know he'll say he *ordered* us to help him. But a part of me is still trying to figure out why.

He saw something aboard that TDF destroyer.

Something O'Malley did that he won't talk to me about.

We used to talk all the time.

"And there is no way to defeat this lock without the key?" Kal asks.

"I suppose divine intervention might work," Finian says. "But that's not even our first problem. We can't get *close* to Bianchi's office. His estate is the most highly guarded area on the World Ship. State-of-the-art security. Hacking his cams is one thing, but we're never getting in there without getting caught."

Silence descends on the room. And into the quiet, Aurora finally speaks.

"I didn't want to say anything. . . ."

We all look at her, expectant. She's obviously still hesitant, looking up into Pixieboy's frozen stare, my glower. She chews her lip, finally speaks.

"But . . . I saw something in the shower this morning."

"It's disgusting in there," Scar agrees. "The mold has mold growing on it."

"No, I . . ." Little Miss Stowaway meets my stare. "I saw Cat."

"Well, well!" Finian grins. "I didn't know your creshcake was syruped on that side, Zero."

"Shut up, Finian," I growl.

"Hey, no judge here, kiddo. . . ."

"No, I mean . . ." Aurora shakes her head. "I had another . . . vision. I was feeling a little woozy, maybe from the steam, I don't know. So I sat on the tile and rested my head against the wall, and then . . . I saw Cat in a mask and fancy jumpsuit. And Scarlett and Tyler, too." She looks between us. "You all looked like you were dressed for a . . . party, I guess?"

"A party in *that* bathroom?" Scarlett asks.

"I know it sounds like it," Aurora replies. "But it wasn't a dream."

Tyler leans forward, fingers steepled at his chin as his eyes light up.

"There's a party tomorrow night," he says, looking around the room. "Fiftieth anniversary of the World Ship. Bianchi is putting on a masquerade ball." He looks at Aurora and breaks into a dimpled grin. "If we get ourselves some invitations, we can just *walk* into his estate."

"Okay?" Scarlett says. "And how do we manage that?"

Tyler rubs his chin, staring at the schematic as he leans back in his chair. "I'm working on it. We've got a few advantages here."

Ty's twin raises her eyebrow. "Such as?"

"Well, for starters, a gangster as murderous as Bianchi isn't going to be expecting to get robbed. No one's stupid enough to cross him."

"Except us, apparently," I growl.

Ty winks at me. "Never underestimate the element of surprise."

"Great," Finian says. "So we get onto the grounds. Then all we have to do is steal a key from around the neck of the most dangerous criminal in the sector, in full view of a party full of guests *and* his guard detail, without setting off the genetic alarms. Which will happen as soon as one of us touches the key."

I'm watching Ty's eyes. Watching his lips. The glow of the vines plays across his face in the dim light, and I can see his dimples just waiting in the wings. He was the golden boy at Aurora for a reason. Sure, he aced every exam. But his favorite subject was always tactics. When we were out gaming or drinking or cruising, Ty would be sitting in his room studying old dead generals. Sun Tzu. Hannibal. Napoleon. Eisenhower. Tankian. Giáp. Osweyo.

Most boys want to grow up to be jetball players or firemen.

Ty wanted to grow up to be Marcus Agrippa.

"And then there's the security systems in the actual office to deal with," Scarlett points out. "Unless we just snatch and grab the Trigger, in which case, we'll have the whole station on our tails."

And finally, I see Ty's dimples come out to play.

"Sounds like a challenge to me," he says.

I feel my answer surging in my chest. I try to fight it. Try to hold it in. Ty is my squad leader. I go where he says, I do what I'm told. That's what they teach you at the academy. Always back your Alpha.

Always.

"No," I hear myself say. "No bloody way."

My squad looks at me as I stand, fists balled up tight.

"Seriously, enough of this *crap*."

"Do you have something to say, Legionnaire Brannock?" Ty asks.

"You bet your damn tailpipe I do," I say, letting the anger fill my voice. I'm so furious at him right now, I can barely stop myself from screaming. "This has gone way beyond stupid and all the way into brain-dead. It was bad enough being on the run from our own people, attacking Terran personnel, risking all our lives. Now you want us crossing the deadliest criminal in the sector for the sake of a trinket this crazy skirt saw in a *dream*?"

I gesture at O'Malley, still glaring at Tyler.

"For real, Ty, have you gone *all* the way sideways?"

"There's more than dreams going on here, Cat," Tyler says. "And you know it. You saw what Auri did to the Longbow. When I first found her in the Fold, I was close to drowning inside my suit and she *moved* us. *She* got us to safety. And you heard what de Stoy and Adams told us at the start of this mission."

"This isn't a bloody mission!" I shout. "It's a robbery! And for what? To satisfy this headcase's delusions? Am I the only one who sees how spaceloops this is?"

"Don't call me a headcase," O'Malley shoots back.

"Oh, she speaks!" I say, dropping into a low bow. "We are not *worthy*. And what advice do you have for us, O mighty prophet?"

Kal raises one silver eyebrow at me. "You are embarrassing yourself, Zero."

"Jam it up your arse, Pixieboy!"

"Look, I don't pretend to know what's happening here,"

O'Malley says. "But something *is* happening. I'm seeing things before they happen. I'm seeing—"

"Are you seeing any way we pull this off without ending up dead, Little Miss Visionthing?" I demand. "Do you see *any* way for us to get in and out of Casseldon Bianchi's private office without getting caught?"

She squares her jaw. Glances at the schematic on the wall.

"No," she says quietly.

"Well, color me all the way shocked."

"Cat," Tyler says. "Put a lid on it."

"Maybe she's right, Tyler."

All eyes turn to Scarlett. She's looking at her brother, her voice soft, her tone the kind of gentle that only comes with the delivery of bad news.

Tyler breathes deep, looks at his twin. "Scar?"

"All I'm saying is, we're a long way into the weeds here. Before we go any further, maybe we should stop and ask ourselves where this road leads."

"Right out of the Legion, that's for sure," I say. "Dishonorable discharge. Probably prison. You worked for this since you were thirteen years old, Tyler. Are you so mad about missing the Draft you're willing to throw your whole career into the recycler?"

"This isn't about the Draft," Tyler growls. "You heard what Adams told us. 'You must endure. You must *believe*.'"

"But why?" I demand. "What about *her* makes you want to?"

"I don't know." Tyler shrugs, looks at O'Malley. "But I do. That's what faith is."

I grit my teeth. Resist the urge to slap him. To roar in

his face. I look at Scarlett and she just shakes her head. Finian's face is a mask, but it's clear he's reckless enough to go along for this ride. Zila's watching me like I'm some kind of bug she's trying to classify. Kal is silent, those cold violet eyes slightly narrowed. I'm outnumbered. Outgunned.

"Hells with this," I spit, snatching up my jacket and marching toward the door.

"Where are you going?" Scar asks.

"I need a damn drink."

"I didn't dismiss you, Legionnaire Brannock," Tyler warns.

"Then court-martial me!" I snarl.

I know slamming the door as I leave is a kid's move. I know I'll look like a little girl having a tantrum, mad because she didn't get her way. I know it in my bones. All the way to the tips of my wings.

But I slam it hard enough to bust the hinges anyway.

·　·　·　·　·

"Gimme another."

The bartender raises three of their eyebrows, proboscis quivering.

"Are you certain?" they ask. "You have consumed six already."

"You know, your impression of my mum is getting really good," I growl, tapping the lip of my glass with my finger.

The bartender shrugs, tops me up, and turns back to their other customers.

This place is a dive, neon lit and smoky, deep in the low-rent section of the World Ship. The band is loud and abrasive, the floor sticky. It's the kind of place you end up at three in the morning when you want to brawl or bang. Not sure which way I'm leaning—yet.

Tyler.

I slam back the cheap ethanol in one shot, wince at the chemical burn in the back of my throat. Trying to figure out why I'm so mad. Is it really because he's seriously considering this scam? Or because of who he's doing it for?

"You must believe, Tyler."

Tyler's good at believing. Admiral Adams knew it. They went to chapel together every Saturday. You'd think religion might not have survived in the age of interstellar travel. The notion of faith was all but dead as humanity started reaching out to the stars. But after we discovered first one, then ten, then eventually hundreds of species, it didn't really escape anyone's notice that all of them were bipedal. Carbon based. Oxygen breathers. The odds of that were just too remote to be plausible. Stuff like that doesn't happen by chance.

So hey presto, say hello to the United Faith.

I touch the Maker's mark at my collar. That perfect circle etched in silver. Wishing I believed like Tyler did. Because I can't. Because I won't. Because even though we've been friends since I busted that chair over his head in kindergarten, because even though I followed him to the end of the Milky Way, he didn't believe in me—in *us*—the way he believes in *her.*

"O'Malley," I growl, nodding to the barkeeper again. They're about to pour when a gloved hand covers the mouth of my glass.

"Please allow us."

I turn, wondering if this is my bang for the night. My muscles tense as I realize it's the exact opposite.

It's wearing charcoal gray, head to toe to fingertips. Its face is hidden behind a featureless mirrormask, elongated and oval shaped. I can see my dull reflection in the surface. My eyes wide with surprise.

Holy crap, GIA.

I rise from my chair and a second gloved hand clamps down on my shoulder. There's another agent behind me, I realize. Sitting with my back to the door in a bar this loud, liquored this hard, I didn't even notice them sneaking right up on me.

Sloppy.

I've got no chance here. But my hand wraps around my glass in preparation for my swing anyway. If you gotta fall, fall fighting.

"PLEASE REFRAIN FROM UNNECESSARY VIOLENCE, LEGIONNAIRE BRANNOCK," the first agent says, its voice sexless and hollow. "WE ONLY WISH TO SPEAK WITH YOU."

"Everything okay here?" the barkeep asks, those three eyebrows rising again.

I look at the G-men. The pistols bulging beneath their jackets, the distance to the door. Crunching the odds as the music crashes in my ears and the booze thumps in my blood. And slowly, I sit back down in my seat.

"We're good," I say.

"ANOTHER DRINK?" the G-man asks.

"If you're buying."

"THE LARASSIAN SEMPTAR," the GIA agent says. "THREE, IF YOU PLEASE."

The barkeep complies, pouring us three bullets in three fresh glasses. The first operative sits on my right side. The other stays behind, staring at me in the mirror over the bar.

Once Old Three Eyes has shuffled off to serve their other customers, the first agent reaches into its gray suit. Moving slow and deliberate, it places a uniglass on the counter in front of me. Above the device I can see a small holographic projection of a third G-man—the creepy badass dressed all in white who nabbed the others aboard Sagan Station. From the instrumentation behind it, I can tell it's standing on the bridge of a Terran destroyer.

"GOOD EVENING, LEGIONNAIRE BRANNOCK," the figure says, its voice expressionless. "WE HAVE NOT BEEN INTRODUCED. YOU MAY REFER TO ME AS PRINCEPS."

"Charmed, I'm sure."

I lift my glass to my lips and tip it back slow. Taste smoke and faint sugar and notes of sheer bloody adrenaline on the back of my tongue.

The other two glasses sit in front of the operatives. Untouched.

"YOU ARE A VERY LONG WAY FROM HOME, LEGIONNAIRE BRANNOCK," the small holograph says.

"No home like the black," I reply, smiling around the old Ace saying.

"THE INSIDES OF THE CELLS AT LUNAR PENAL COLONY ARE NOT BLACK," Princeps replies. "THEY ARE GRAY. NO SKY. NO STARS. JUST GRAY. FOREVER."

"You trying to scare me, G-man?" I hold out my glass to the bartender again with one rock-steady hand. "Because I'm shaking."

"I KNOW IT IS DIFFICULT TO SEE," Princeps says as the barkeeper pours. "BUT THERE IS A WAY OUT OF THIS. FOR YOU AND YOUR SQUAD."

"WE DO NOT WANT YOU," the one behind me says in my ear, electronic voice crawling on my skin. "WE ONLY WANT AURORA O'MALLEY."

"THE REST OF SQUAD 312 WILL BE FREE TO LEAVE ONCE SHE IS IN OUR HANDS," Princeps nods. "RETURN TO THE ACADEMY. YOUR CAREERS. YOUR FRIENDS. YOUR LIVES. YOU NEED NOT THROW AWAY ALL YOU HAVE WORKED FOR, LEGIONNAIRE BRANNOCK."

I blink hard. Shake my head. "I'm sorry, Princess, could you repeat that? I couldn't hear you over the sound of all the shits I don't give."

I slam back my shot, stand up slow.

"Thanks for the drink."

The operative behind me grabs my arm with one gloved hand. The grip is perfect. Hard enough to hurt. Soft enough to let me know it could hurt a lot worse.

"THE GIRL YOU ARE HARBORING IS AN ENEMY OF THE TERRAN PEOPLE. THE ENTIRE TERRAN DEFENSE FORCE IS NOW ON ALERT AND DEVOTED TO HER CAPTURE. AND SHE WILL BE OURS." The agent's voice goes soft and dangerous. "WITH OR WITHOUT YOUR HELP."

"Yeah, I guess that's why you're skulking around dive bars at ungodly o'clock in the morning, huh?" I sneer, motioning at the uniglass on the bar. "This guy isn't even in the same bloody *sector* as the rest of us."

"THE *BELLEROPHON* IS EN ROUTE TO YOUR LOCATION EVEN AS WE SPEAK, LEGIONNAIRE BRANNOCK," Princeps

says. "You cannot escape from us. But a TDF inva-
sion of the World Ship will cause unnecessary
loss of life. We hope to resolve this issue without violence. Aurora O'Malley has killed enough
of our agents already."

My eyes narrow at that.

"You did not know?" Princeps asks. "She murdered
two operatives aboard the *Bellerophon*. Crushed
them like paper cups with a thought."

Princeps disappears from the screen, replaced with an
image of what might be an interrogation room. Two charcoal-
gray suits. Blood and guts smeared along the floor and three
meters up the walls.

My stomach surges. I swallow hard. "Maker . . . ," I
breathe.

"This is the girl you are harboring. She is not
what she appears, Legionnaire Brannock. She is
dangerous. To you. To those you care about."

I shake my head. "It's not my call. An Ace backs her Alpha. Always."

I glance at the agent behind me, staring at my reflection
in that faceless mask.

"Always."

"Your loyalty to Tyler Jones is admirable,"
Princeps says. "But surely you must have wondered
at his recent decisions? Does he truly seem himself?"

"Aurora O'Malley can crush people with her
mind," the second operative says. "Do you not wonder
what she can do to the minds of others?"

277

"Are you saying she can . . . control us?" I demand. "Control *him*?"

"WE ARE SAYING YOUR MOTHER WAS A LOYAL MEMBER OF THE TDF UNTIL THE DAY SHE DIED," Princeps says. "AND WE ARE HOPING HER DAUGHTER SHARES HER LOYALTIES."

The GIA operative releases its grip on my arm.

I look toward the door. I look at my face in its mask.

Tired. Wired. All the way scared. I glance at the picture on the screen of the G-man's uniglass. Think about the Longbow shaking like a leaf as we tried to change course. Scarlett being thrown back into the wall with a flick of O'Malley's wrist. Tyler pushing us closer and closer to the edge.

Lying with him on those crumpled sheets the morning after, shivering as he traced the lines of my tattoos with his fingertips.

And it still wasn't enough.

"WE CAN OFFER ASSURANCES. IN WRITING. FOR YOU AND YOUR SQUAD."

I chew my lip. Grit my teeth. And sitting back down on the stool, I look at the G-man's featureless face and hold out my glass to the bartender.

"Gimme another."

19

ZILA

There is no way we're getting in and out of Casseldon Bianchi's private office without getting caught.

20

AURI

"I can't believe you thought this would fit me," Cat grumbles behind me, yanking at her jumpsuit again. "The girls are going to fall out of this thing, Scar."

"I did offer you one of my bras," Scar replies.

"I thought you were being sarcastic."

Scarlett shoots Cat a sympathetic smile. "Maybe a little."

We're standing in the long, winding line for Casseldon Bianchi's grand gala, Ty and me, with Cat and Scarlett behind us, decked out in the fanciest outfits Scarlett's bargaining and Dariel's connections could offer. Scarlett and Tyler look smooth as always, but Cat couldn't look more uncomfortable in formalwear if the stuff was woven out of poison ivy. We're slowly shuffling up toward the doormen (door aliens?) who'll check our invitations.

And everybody's nervous.

"Your girls will be fine," Scarlett promises Cat again, adjusting her mask. "It's meant to fit like that. You look great. Wow, so do I. I *love* this dress."

I hear Fin's voice, crystal clear through my tiny earpiece

but sounding a bit uneven. *"Maker's bits, Scarlett . . . Not that you don't have an appreciative audience back here at base, but if you're going to give us a view like that, maybe a little warning? Dariel just dropped a mug of hot caff all over me, I think he's short-circuited something in my suit."*

"Just doing my bit for morale," Scarlett purrs, smug as can be.

"I mean, normally I wouldn't complain," Fin adds.

"I'll give you something to complain about," Cat mutters.

We're nearly at the front of the line, and now I've got a clearer view of the pair of aliens—both perfectly identical—who are checking invitations. They have leathery brown skin and small heads that remind me of binoculars, huge eyes dominating their faces. Their necks look a little too thin to support them, and their arms are long and spindly. As I watch, one leans right out over its silver podium to extend a long twig-like finger and trail it slowly across the invitation that a particularly tall, pink-skinned woman is offering up for inspection.

"They're really looking at the invites carefully," I murmur, and at my side, Ty tilts his head in closer to mine to get a look.

"Confidence," he murmurs. "Slow breaths. Play it like you belong here."

My gut does a slow flip. I *don't* belong. Not just here, but anywhere in the galaxy. I was supposed to live two centuries ago. The tiredness and the fear feel as though they're stretching the bonds that held me close to my family until they're dangerously thin, ready to snap and leave me utterly alone.

I'm not sure what will happen then.

Dariel swore the invitations were as good as real—which isn't the same thing as real, but Fin seemed to trust him. Our Betraskan squadmate looked a little sick at asking the favor, and I could tell that somewhere in the complex web of family obligations, he'd just racked up another big one. He's been talking a little extra, a little more obnoxiously, ever since. Covering his nerves, I think.

I'm slowly learning them, these six young soldiers who hold my life in their hands. Though even if I'd met them five minutes ago, I couldn't miss Cat's simmering frustration. I'm standing arm in arm with Ty, and she's behind us, arm in arm with Scarlett, and I can feel her gaze burning two holes right between my shoulder blades. My skin gives an uncomfortable twitch.

The outfit that's bothering her so much is the most incredible tailored jumpsuit I've ever seen. It's the same one I saw in my vision of her—navy blue, strapless, and, despite her protests, structured enough to keep everything where it belongs. She's paired it—or rather, Scarlett's paired it—with silver boots that look like someone smashed a mirror to a million pieces, then glued it onto them in a perfect mosaic, and the mask covering her eyes is made of the same stuff.

She wears a thick, gleaming gold belt and no other jewelry—her tattoos are gorgeous, and they do the work for her, the jumpsuit's back cut low enough to show off the spectacular hawk inked across her shoulder blades, matching the phoenix across her throat. Skin pale, eyes dark, and hair darker, she looks fearsome. The sort of person I want on my side, if only I could be sure she was.

She keeps looking at me in a way that makes me wonder.

Scarlett's dress is a perfect complement to her Ace's outfit, a deep turquoise gown that hits the floor—again, the exact same one I saw in my waking dream, though she brought it home without me ever describing it to her. A shiver went straight down my spine when I saw it.

How did she know which one to buy?

Scarlett's strapless gown (down which Fin and Dariel just had the view of a lifetime, I'm pretty sure) picks up the shattered-mirror motif from Cat's boots with a thousand silver beads, which are scattered over her dark skirts like the first stars in the night sky. About three hundred buttons travel from her mid-back to the floor. It took Zila and me—the pair with the smallest fingers—half an hour to get them all fastened. Her mask sets off her big blue eyes with more flecks of silver.

Both of them look so fit, so fierce, now that they're not hidden under their Aurora Academy jumpsuits. I know I should be nervous, but I can't help but feel a little fiercer beside them.

My own dress is the cutest thing I've ever worn. It's exactly what I would have chosen for my prom, if I'd ever had one.

I wonder what Callie wore to hers.

The fitted bodice is red-and-gold embroidered silk swirling in intricate designs. It has perfect cap sleeves and an upright collar hooked closed at the neck. The top half is just like my qipao at home, but the knee-length skirts are a thousand flouncing layers of red tulle. I wanted to twirl like a freaking ballerina when I put this thing on, but Scarlett was looking at me super intently.

"I wasn't sure if the silk was right," she said.

I looked down, smoothing it with one hand. "It's perfect."

But her gaze had lingered, and it was a long moment before she spoke again, uncharacteristically hesitant. "You said your father— I mean, I know it's not *actually* Chinese, but . . ."

And that was when I realized she'd tried to get me something that would remind me of home. And I found I'd lost my breath, as well as my words.

"It's . . ." I took a second swing at it. "It really is perfect, Scarlett, thank you. I think he'd have loved it. Keeping our culture alive was important to him."

It sounded like someone else speaking, talking about my dad in the past tense. I could hear how careful my voice was, a fraction too cheerful, overshooting the mark by just enough to show her how hard I was trying.

Keeping our culture alive in our family *was* important to him. When I was growing up, the way to put off bedtime just a little longer was to ask for another traditional story from the big, old-fashioned book on the shelf. After he left mom behind, I was so angry at him I'd have said story-time routine was just another example of something mattering more to him than his family. He wouldn't spend extra time together for *me,* but he would for the all-important traditions.

But maybe he just wanted an excuse to spend a little more time together as well.

Scarlett busied herself neatening my hair, carefully blacking out the white streak, and gluing the micro-cam disguised as a beauty spot in place on my cheek. It was an intimate moment, but the touch didn't feel like an imposition. It felt like a comfort. "Ty and I, we understand," she said quietly. "We know what it's like to lose a parent. Cat, too, and Zila. If you need to talk about it, I'm your girl."

Maybe she was just being a Face, team diplomat, keeping everyone level. But I didn't think so—or I choose to believe she wasn't, anyway. I choose to believe that moment was real.

Fin gave a small round of applause when we marched out of the bedroom in our outfits. Zila nodded at me and said, "Adequate."

Kal didn't look at me at all.

Unlike the others, I'm actually a wanted fugitive, so a masquerade ball is about the only place I can be seen in public right now. My mask covers the top half of my face, leaving only my lips and chin exposed. Its glazed lenses cover my mismatched eyes, and it's made out of some kind of mysterious red velvet. It looks like something a spy in an old sim would wear.

Honestly, it makes me feel a little badass.

The final member of our quartet is Ty, who complained about his outfit nearly as much as Cat. I was curious to see whether a tux was still a tux with a couple of centuries in between viewings, and the answer was *sort of*. His suit is that kind of tailoring that looks like it's about to fall apart, yet somehow conveys with perfect fit that it's worth a fortune. Or at least it did once Scarlett made a few alterations.

He's in big black stompy boots, a pair of tight black pants (the tight was what had him joining Cat in a chorus of *you gotta be kidding me*) with black straps buckled around his left thigh, like a hint at a gun's holster, and big silver zips cutting across his right hip. His black shirt and jacket are equally fitted, and his mask is a swoosh of black material right across his eyes. Jones Twin No. 2 looks as amazing as his sister.

"Hey, Stowaway," drawls Fin over the team channel as we move up to second in line for the door aliens. *"I'm just reading up on the significance of red in Chinese culture, and—"*

"Wait a minute, you can *read*?" I ask.

"Oh, now you're throwing sass to cover up your feelings for me, too? Is every female on this team planning to fall in love with me?"

"Can it," Ty mutters. "We're almost in."

As the couple in front of us make their way through the huge double doors and into the swirling mass of color beyond, I breathe a small sigh of relief. I'm pretty sure Fin was about to point out that red's a traditional wedding dress color. With Cat right behind me. And Ty's arm in mine. Even unarmed, she could probably pull my head off and bounce it like a basketball. I have no idea if Ty knows how she feels about him, but if I've noticed in just a couple of days . . .

The alien reaches down with one spindly finger to touch Ty's invitation. The flexible plastic surface turns blue under its touch, then fades back to cream. I force myself to breathe slowly, then realize my arm's so tightly wound through Ty's that he's leaning sideways to make up for the difference in our height. I release him with a blush, and that's distraction enough to pass the next couple of seconds.

The alien waves us on, turns to inspect Scarlett and Cat's invitation.

Ty and I step through into the archway, where another alien—this one a bulky Betraskan with a white ceramic mask and black contact lenses—points to instructions for the security sweep. We both halt at a line on the floor and lift our hands. A network of red light beams starts at our heads and traces over our bodies, maybe registering our faces, or searching us for weapons, I don't know.

Fin's talking in our ears again as we wait for the girls to follow us through for their scan. *"Just remember, I'm going to need as much time as you can give me to snatch the signal. Ideally, start a conversation with Mr. Bianchi."*

"And try not to get eaten," Ty says quietly, turning his head as though he's speaking fondly into my ear.

"The sooner he touches the key," Fin adds, *"the sooner I can get to work. Remember, I need one of you within a meter of him when the code changes."*

His tone sounds calm, but I saw his face as we worked through the plan back in Dariel's cramped quarters.

He's not even sure he can do this.

I should be terrified, but as Scarlett and Cat come through security, I discover that somehow . . . I'm not. I'm a weird kind of peaceful, like I used to be before orienteering comps, or track meets. I'm nervous, but I'm moving toward my purpose.

I'm not the girl who set out for Octavia, who worried about things like whether there'd be anyone my age to date when I got there, or whether I'd be fit enough to handle my Exploration and Cartography apprenticeship with Patrice.

I'm not the girl who mourned the loss of her social life as she stepped into her cryopod, or shoved her stuffed toy squirrel into her one small crate of personal belongings.

I'm something else now. And if I don't know what, that

287

doesn't make it any less true. I can feel it more every hour, every day.

But my old self has a part to play here, too. I trained in exploration because I wanted to see everything, and I'm sure getting a load of that lately. When my parents were prepping for the Octavia mission, I changed schools two, three times every year. I know how to walk into a room full of strangers. And I'm going to do it now like I've always belonged here.

Scarlett and Cat step up beside us, Scarlett outwardly serene, Cat scowling, and the four of us look out into the ballroom for the first time.

And it's like nothing I've ever seen, or imagined.

Because it's underwater.

We're in a huge, round cavern of a room, and we automatically peel away to the right, following the curve of the wall as we get our bearings.

The walls themselves are made of glass, and studying my reflection, I realize I'm looking at an aquarium that stretches back as far as I can see. It's a bright, shimmering aquamarine at its base, darkening to a velvety blue and then a deep violet when I tilt my head back to trace its path up.

I can't see where it meets with the roof, an endless midnight dome blanketed with delicate lights that's . . .

Oh, holy cake, the dome above us is the *galaxy*. Star clusters and nebulae dance slowly around its edges, moving gracefully along their predetermined paths, gliding around and through each other like old-fashioned dancers. Millions of years are sped up before my eyes in a cosmic ballet.

Cat's mirrored boots and the silver beads on Scarlett's dress sparkle in the endlessly shifting blue light, and Ty's teeth gleam white when he grins. There must be a thousand people here, and I can't see more than a few dozen humans.

I'm underwater. On a space station.

The room is a thumping kaleidoscope of bright colors glittering beneath the lights. Every possible silhouette is represented in the living, breathing creature that the crowd's become. The entire place is moving to music, a low, pounding bass that runs straight up my spine with a perfect thrill. I can hear talk and laughter over it, coming at us in waves as the crowd's hands rise as one to mark the changing beat.

It's like an underground club, like a very grown-up intergalactic fairyland with a dangerous undercurrent, every face and secret hidden behind a mask. And when I smile, I'm almost baring my teeth, the last of my uncertainty falling away. What I want is here. And somewhere out in the dark, I can feel it calling to me.

Mr. Bianchi . . .

Come out, come out, wherever you are. . . .

How to Have a Good Time
▶ **Parties**
　▼ **Famous Parties in History**

The third-greatest party of all time occurred throughout the **Wroten system** on the occasion of the **Grand Julesli's** wedding. Festivities involved 437,000 guests from twenty-seven planets, and one of only three known performances of the **Forbidden Dance of Bas**. At the conclusion, the Grand Julesli was wedded to seventy-three spouses—and presumably quite tired.

History's second-greatest party was thrown on **Terra** in 1694 by **Naval Admiral Edward Russell**. This champion among humans mixed 250 gallons of brandy, 125 gallons of wine, 635 kilograms of sugar, 20 gallons of lime juice, and 3 kilograms of nutmeg into an enormous cocktail fountain. A literal *fountain*. Bartenders manning *canoes* worked shifts lasting just fifteen minutes, thanks to the fumes, and it took the five thousand guests eight days to drink it all. Admiral Russell, I am but a humble uniglass, but I salute you.

But without question, the greatest party in history was thrown by the **Keet** people of **Leibowitz VII**. An unfortunate misreading of ancient prophecies led the Keet to believe the apocalypse was nigh, and they partied like it was the end of the world. Piecemeal records suggest that a regrettable decision involving a **dance-off** and the planet's largest antimatter reactor resulted in the early fulfillment of prophecy.

21

FINIAN

So it turns out Dariel's really into fish. I did not see that coming.

"Look at that one!" He's like a kid on his first outing to the Muthru Bazaar, his attention darting from one thing to another. I'm trying to guide my team through the overhead security lenses and a dizzying array of micro-cams attached to their very fetching selves, and he's too busy staring at the aquarium ballroom to help.

"That's not a fish," I tell him. "That's a rock. Are you sure we're related?"

"Fish," he says, triumphant, as the purplish, lichen-covered rock is startled by a cloud of garish pink-and-yellow micro-squid. Its eyes snap open, it moves what I thought were shells but turn out to be fins, and scoots away in a cloud of sand.

"Fine, it was a fish," I concede. "It's gone now. So help me out."

"*Finian?*" That's our fearless leader, sounding a little confused about the sudden turn in conversation.

Crap, I forgot to mute my uni.

"Nothing, Goldenboy," I say cheerfully. "I'm checking in on Zila and Kal, Dariel's scanning the cameras looking for our host. Have you g—"

I glance at my cousin's virtuascreen and find it occupied by another damn fish. It's a huge, oval-shaped thing, sort of looks like a kebar ball with six eyes slapped onto the front. They're freaky eyes, though—forward facing. And the dome of its head is completely transparent, the blue water visible behind it.

"That's its brain," Dariel whispers, entranced, pointing at a blob of white inside the thing's see-through head.

"Jealous that it has one?" I snap. "Keep yours on the job, yeah?"

He huffs as I switch my screen to Zila's cam, trying not to reflect on the fact that I sound like my least favorite mother right now.

I've got Kal and Zila on a separate comms channel. Goldenboy's listening in to make sure he's across both sides of the action tonight.

There's a dirty joke in there somewhere.

The pair have made good progress, and they're almost at their entry point, marching down a crowded public corridor and looking only marginally suspicious in their brightly colored and definitely stolen uniforms. Kal has his hands full of flat insulated boxes, marked Uncle Enzo's—30 minutes or less. Zila's wearing earrings with tiny pizza slices dangling from them. And in a storage cupboard down on Level seventeen, there's a couple of nearly naked fast-food delivery boys who're gonna wake up with a real hangover later.

Zila is awfully fond of that disruptor.

"Okay, Zila, Pixieboy," I drawl, just to watch him frown. "The cameras in this zone are now on a loop—I'm transmitting footage of empty corridors to the goons at Bianchi Central. But there's still actual security patrols in the hallways beyond. I'm gonna guide you through them. So you move where I say, *when* I say. Clear?"

"Clear, Legionnaire de Seel," Zila says simply.

"Get your uni close to the lock, I'll pop it."

The pair reach a heavy blast door marked AUTHORIZED PERSONNEL ONLY. Kal makes a show of dropping the delivery boxes and cursing fluently while Zila sidles up to the control pad. The encryption isn't a cakewalk, but an academy-issued uniglass isn't a toy, and while I'm good at fixing things, I'm better at breaking them. It takes me thirty-seven seconds to smash the intrusion counter-electronics on the lock to splinters.

Getting slow in my old age.

"Okay, corridor ahead will be clear in twelve seconds," I say. "That uniform suits you, by the way, Kal. You look good."

Pixieboy adjusts the ridiculous little hat on his head. *"I look like a fool. It is too tight. How am I supposed to fight in this?"*

"I dunno. Sexily?"

"You are not much of a warrior, are you, Finian?"

"Well, you're not . . ." I bite down on my comeback as the security patrol in the corridor beyond turns and walks around the corner. "Okay, corridor is clear, go, go."

Zila opens the blast door and slips inside, Kal right behind. Pixieboy hands Zila his delivery boxes, draws out his disruptor pistol from inside them. It's not like he can fire it in here without bringing the house down, but he seems the sort who's more comfortable with a weapon in hand.

On my go, they make a dash for the next corridor, slipping into a maintenance closet a few seconds before another patrol rounds the corner. I'm watching seventeen cams at once, plotting the patrols' course on an overhead schematic, trying to predict which way they're going to move and see my kids through—

"Great Maker . . . ," mutters Dariel beside me.

My heart lurches and I glance across to see what's worrying him, only to find a giant silver . . . thing on the monitor. It has a row of perfectly white fangs that would make a mass murderer proud. And *another* row of fangs behind that. Scarlett must be fascinated by it, too, because her micro-cam is following it as it swims up to the glass. Its skin ripples in a threat display, silver to blue to red.

"I thought you were an atheist," I growl, elbowing him as I turn my attention back to Zila, Kal, and the heist I'm attempting to mastermind.

So hard to get good help these days . . .

But even though I'm complaining—Dariel's about as much use as a waterproof towel—I can't deny I'm having fun. Swapping family gossip with my cousin between fish talk, breathing in the scent of wet stone by the dim light of the vines and my screens, guiding my squadmates through terrifying adventures—it's practically my childhood all over again.

I weave my pair of assistants through another six hallways and two close shaves before the inevitable moment comes. "Okay, end of the line. Grav-generator room is dead ahead. Time for phase two, kids."

Kal peels away from Zila like a ghost. She stands perfectly still, waiting for him to move into position, dark eyes fixed on the ceiling, dark skin almost gleaming in the light of the overheads. She's good at that—if she doesn't need to be doing something, she doesn't. Maybe so she can channel any extra brainpower she has into her master plan for taking over the galaxy . . .

"Okay, go," I whisper, and she strolls out and around the corner in her delivery uniform, looking lost.

The four guards on the heavy blast doors at the other end of the hallway freeze in place. They scope Zila's uniform and boxes, do a bit of confused math in their heads, then raise their weapons anyway.

"Halt!" one shouts, and Zila obliges, going so far as to drop the boxes and raise both her hands as an added precaution.

"This area is restricted!"

"What're you doing back here?" demands another, coming no closer until he has a better idea of whether she's dangerous. Though I can already see the cogs turning. She's so small. She's ten meters away. How could she be dangerous?

"I have a question," she says, in that solemn way she has.

The quartet look at one another blankly.

"In entertainment sims," she continues, *"I've often seen scenes in which groups of guards are accosted by a seemingly harmless infiltrator while a larger, more dangerous infiltrator uses the distraction to incapacitate them. I was wondering if you thought this was realistic behavior for trained security personnel."*

The four blink at her, the way people often do around Zila Madran.

"Are you c—"

The guard doesn't get any further before Kal drops from the air vent above and clocks him at the base of his skull. In a handful of seconds, he's laid out the other three with barely a muffled shout. No disruptor required.

"I genuinely believed you would get shot there," Zila muses.

Kal turns to look at her, eyebrows raised. *"You said I had an eighty-seven point three percent chance of success."*

She tilts her head. *"I did not want you to be nervous."*

"Okay, you two," I say. "I gotta check on the A-Team. Grav-generators are just through those blast doors. Kal, hide the bodies. Zila, you've got my instructions."

"Is she dating anyone right now?" Dariel whispers, eyes on Zila.

"I will cut your toes off," I tell him. "One by one, and then you can watch as I feed them to your damned fish if you don't stop interrupting me."

He holds up his hands like, *Whoa, no problem. What's your deal?* and I grit my teeth, turning back to the cameras.

I'm scanning the jam-packed ballroom sector by sector, looking for Bianchi. But he stands out like a Betraskan in a snowstorm, which is to say not at all. He's blue, and thanks to the light cast by the aquarium and the star-studded ceiling, so is every other thing in the room. Doesn't help that every being at the party is wearing a damn mask over their faces.

I keep my search methodical, working through each grid square, until finally I find him. He's got all four hands in the air, waving them in time to the bone-shaking beat, razor-sharp teeth bared in a wild grin. He's surrounded by what I

296

can only describe as a harem, a dozen beautiful young things of a dozen different species, male and female, both and neither, all clustered around him. They're dancing along with him, turned toward him like maza flowers to the sun.

Beyond them is a ring of security personnel I'd safely describe as "terrifying." They're Chellerian like Bianchi—big and blue, with more teeth than head. Their muscles barely fit into the suits they're wearing, and given the quality of Bianchi's tailors, that's probably a deliberate choice. They stand in the crowd around their boss, four eyes apiece watching the throng, suspicious bulges in their jackets.

"Okay, kids," I tell my team. "Bianchi's in the northwest corner. The amount of security he's got around him, there's only one way you're getting close."

"And that is?" Goldenboy asks.

"Dance like there's ass in your pants."

"On it," Ty says without hesitation, grabbing Aurora's hand and hauling her into the crowd. I can just make out her squeak over the low thud of the music.

Scarlett and Cat stay by the aquarium a moment longer. Scarlett's studying the others who line the wall, but on her micro-cam I can pick up the nearest fish on the periphery, and now Dariel's got me looking at the damn things too.

Casseldon Bianchi really does have one of every species in the galaxy, as best I can tell. This fish is serpentine, two meters long, as fiery orange as Scarlett's hair. The real party trick, though, are the huge venom sacs on either side of its face, each one bigger than its head, giving it the appearance of wildly ballooning cheeks. Its white eyes bulge, as if it's as surprised by this development as I am.

Cat, on the other hand, is staring straight at our Alpha and our stowaway, like she has been all night.

I don't like where this kind of fixation leads. We already saw one outburst, and even after she slunk back to Dariel's den smelling like Larassian semptar, there's been an uneasiness about her.

"Uh, Zero," I say. "Can you give me a sweep of the room?"

She obliges, turning in a two-hundred-and-seventy-degree arc, giving me a good look at the crowd. There's nothing to be seen that I couldn't pick up through the overhead cams, but as expected, our infallible Face doesn't miss the cue in my tone. She turns her attention back to the Ace beside her.

"Why should they have all the fun?" Scarlett asks, suddenly grabbing Cat by the hand, pulling her out into the crowd.

Cat's spluttering, and Scarlett's laughing, and despite the tension zinging through me, I grin too. Scarlett has a *great* laugh. And now she's sweeping our pilot into her arms and dipping her over backward in an extravagant move.

There are so many different species here that everyone's dancing in their own way. In ones and twos and tens, hands linked, bodies intertwined or not touching at all. After five years at Aurora Academy, its hallways only ever populated by Terrans, Betraskans, and recently the odd Syldrathi, I'm not as used to this kind of mixing bowl as I used to be. I grew up with my grandparents on a station like this, and I loved it.

I've missed it.

Scarlett and Cat have struck up the most ridiculous dance now, joined hands pushing out in front of them.

"What are you doing?" I laugh down the line.

"*A tango. Traditional Terran dance, very romantic,*" Scarlett tells me, though Cat's laughter makes me wonder if they're even close to getting it right.

Goldenboy and Aurora really don't know how to dance together, but they're both picking it up by sneaking looks at the crowd around them, and it's kind of satisfying to see there's *something* he's not instantly on top of. But more importantly, they're getting closer and closer to one Casseldon Bianchi.

"Okay, you need to get near enough for me to snatch the signal," I tell them as I sweep the cameras again, looking for trouble. "Not so close that those goons decide to bite your head off. Remember—"

"*One meter,*" Ty and Auri chorus together.

"They *can* be taught!"

Zila speaks up on comms. "*Finian, is this appropriate positioning?*"

I flick my gaze across to my other screen. Crap, they're at the grav-generators already. I gotta keep juggling, gotta keep all my balls in the air.

Heh, balls in the air.

"That looks good," I say. "Charges need to go on the secondary buffer."

"*I am aware,*" Zila agrees.

"There's a second patrol heading in your direction," I say. "You might wanna have a plan to deal with them in case they notice those missing guards and stick their heads into the gen room. A distraction of some kind, maybe."

"*Kal, did you brush your teeth this morning?*" Tyler asks over comms.

"Thankfully, I do not think it will come to that," Kal replies.

Tyler laughs in answer and I hear Auri ask him what's so funny. I make a mental note to ask him myself. Later. For now, I'm busy.

"Set remote detonators and leg it back here," I tell Zila and Kal.

I glance to my other screen to check on Goldenboy and Aurora's progress. They're getting close now—I can see Bianchi on their micro-cams. There's just two rows of masked dancers between them and their quarry. They're weaving through his security, lost in the swirl of light and color, so close now to the magical meter. The guards look wary, but not bitey. I'm guessing Ty and Auri look just the right flavor of pretty and gormless, grinning at each other like idiots.

But they might just pull this off.

My fingers are poised over my uplink, ready to jump the signal if Bianchi's hand touches his bio-key. I dunno if I'll manage it; there's already a ton of traffic in that room. Snatching a specific stream is going to be like catching a knife while a thousand others are thrown at me, and I was never a very good catch in school.

Good thing we're not in school anymore.

"Okay, just a litt—"

The door of the den bursts inward off its hinges, smashing into a stack of Dariel's junk and flinging it in every direction. The leaves of the flic vines burst into bright light at the sudden impact around them, and a stalactite breaks off the ceiling, missing me by a hair's breadth before it shatters on the ground.

Adrenaline kicks me in the gut, and I lunge without

thinking for the cables connecting my makeshift rig, yanking them free. All my screens cut to gray static, and my view of the team is gone.

A squad of goons burst through the breach, weapons up and locked. They're in unmarked tac armor, but it's hard to miss the fact that every one of them is Terran. Military haircuts. The physiques of humans who spend a lot of their day lifting up heavy objects and putting them down again.

Dariel gawps like one of his damn fish.

"You're not supposed to be here yet!" he shouts.

My stomach sinks as two figures walk in behind the thugs. Featureless gray suits, with featureless gray helmets, every possible hint of their identity hidden.

Crap, crappity, craaaap.

It's the GIA.

I hit the Mute button on my uniglass, slide it under an empty packet of *Just Like Real Noodelz!*™ And then one of the figures speaks, its voice an electronic monotone.

"Hello, Legionnaire de Seel."

STUFF TO RUN AWAY FROM
▶ LIFE-FORMS
  ▼ ULTRASAUR (ABRAAXIS IV)

THE ULTRASAURS OF ABRAAXIS IV ARE WIDELY REGARDED AS THE MOST HOSTILE SPECIES IN THE HISTORY OF **THE MILKY WAY GALAXY**. POSSESSED OF MORE TEETH THAN **TPHAR'S DENTURES EMPORIUM**, LESS CHARM THAN THE **MORIBUND SLUGBEASTS OF BANON III**, AND FEWER FRIENDS THAN THE **SOLITARY HERMIT OF BARR** (THE ONLY INHABITANT OF HER SYSTEM), THEY WERE CREATURES OF SUCH ASTONISHINGLY BAD TEMPERAMENT THAT, IN DEFIANCE OF ALL ECOLOGICAL LAW, THEY WIPED EACH OTHER OUT IN AN ORGY OF CARNIVOROUS MAYHEM.

IT'S THE VERY GREAT FORTUNE OF **EVERYTHING ELSE IN THE GALAXY** THAT ULTRASAURS ARE NOW ALMOST EXTINCT, BUT IN THE UNLIKELY EVENT OF AN ENCOUNTER, TRADITIONAL WISDOM DICTATES DYING QUICKLY AS THE BEST COURSE OF ACTION.

22

CAT

"Finian, we're in position."

Tyler's report crackles over squad comms, almost lost under the music. I'm watching through the swirling crowd, the flashing lights, the strobing blue. The beat is thudding in my ears and my pulse is thudding in my temples as I watch Tyler and O'Malley dance. They're close now, close enough to Bianchi for Finian to work his magic. Tyler leans in as if he's whispering something in O'Malley's ear. She smiles as if it was funny. My jaw clenches.

"Finian?" Tyler asks. *"Do you read me?"*

No answer.

I feel the butterflies in my stomach flutter then. They've been growing louder since the bar last night, since those G-men said their farewells and bumped my uniglass to transmit the paperwork—official documents, emblazoned with the GIA seal, signed off with my thumbprint. Words like *immunity* and *cooperation* and *capture* written in bold. Words I don't want to think about right now.

"Has anyone got Finian on comms?" Tyler asks.

"Fin, do you read me?" Scarlett asks beside me.

Nothing.

It wasn't supposed to happen this way.

Tyler leans in close to O'Malley's ear again to mask the motion of his lips.

"Zila, Kal, report status?"

"Charges are set," Pixieboy replies. *"We have just left Gravity Control."*

"We may have a problem. Finian is off comms. If he can't snatch the signal, we can't open the door to Bianchi's office."

"Why is he off comms?"

"That's what I want you to find out. Head back to Dariel's squat. Expect trouble. Scar, I want you to go with them as backup."

"And what are you going to do?" Scarlett asks.

I look through the crowd, find Tyler's masked face in the pulsing light. The mass of bodies is rolling and swaying around him, Bianchi and his concubines, people of all shapes and sizes moving in unity with the beat. But he stands perfectly still. Brow furrowed. Eyes narrowed. Mind racing.

"Cat, meet us near the restrooms."

Scarlett looks at me, and I see her uncertainty. But once Ty has given an order, she's not going to buck on him in public. She's as loyal to him as I am.

As loyal as I am. . . .

"Be careful, roomie," I warn her.

"You too," she nods.

We part ways, Scar moving off toward the exit, me diving through the crowd. Tyler and O'Malley are working their way out of Bianchi's swarm of bodies, slowly, not attracting attention. I run my hand along the aquarium as I walk, watch a dozen luminous worm-things follow the path of my fingers across the glass. My heart is thumping. The music is so loud.

"You all right?" Tyler asks when he sees me.

"Five by five, sir," I reply on instinct.

I try not to notice the way O'Malley is hanging on to his arm. Tell myself she's more overwhelmed by all this than I am. That she doesn't know. Can't know.

"Orders, sir?"

"Zila and Kal's explosive charges are in place." He taps his uniglass. "Even without Fin, I can detonate them remotely. When they pop, Bianchi's security will be in chaos. We'll still have ourselves a window, just like we planned."

"But without Fin, we can't get the passcode," O'Malley protests. "Even if we make it to Bianchi's office, we won't get through the security door."

Tyler calls up the schematic from Finian's presentation and points.

"The security door isn't the only way in."

". . . You're not serious?" I ask.

Tyler winks, and my heart drops into my boots.

"I'm improvising," he grins.

A few minutes later, we're lurking near a heavy plasteel door in a shady corner at the back of the ballroom. It's a little quieter here, and a few couples and one triple are getting to know each other better in the gloom. Large red letters are stenciled on the door in a language I can't read. If I was a betting girl, I'd wager the passkeys to the Longbow that it says
MENAGERIE: KEEP OUT.

The door is guarded by four huge Chellerian goons, leathery blue skin gleaming in the dim light, thin black masks covering their four blood-red eyes. They're each standing with four arms folded across their broad chests, but they're not on high alert—there's cams everywhere after all, almost a hundred other guards in this ballroom. And as Ty said, nobody in the 'Way is stupid enough to mess with Casseldon Bianchi.

Well, almost no one.

Tyler looks at me, the whites of his eyes aglow in the black light.

"Ready?"

"Is this a trick question?"

We all reach down, flick the switches on our boots. The electromagnets Finian installed in our heels begin to hum softly, fixing us to the metal floor. Tyler looks at O'Malley, squeezes her hand.

"Just act drunk and stupid," he says.

"Second part should be rrrrreal easy for us," I mutter.

We begin walking toward the guards, heels clunking on the deck. It's a little awkward to move in the magboots, but Tyler takes the lead, pretending to be off his face. He wobbles, almost falls. I support him, trying to look embarrassed and loaded at the same time. O'Malley trails somewhere behind us. The goons look us up and down as we approach.

Tyler holds up his uniglass, slurring, "Any of you got station time?"

"Move 'long, hoo-maaan," one growls.

And as he steps within range, Ty gives the detonation command.

There's a second's delay. The lights flicker overhead as Zila and Kal's charges explode deep down in the belly of the station. And with a rush of vertigo, the sickening sensation of my insides suddenly floating free in my body, I feel the gravity aboard the World Ship die.

The Chellerians wobble, lifting gently off the ground. They reach out to the walls for balance, but their movements are too sharp, and they're overcorrecting. I hear shouts of joy from the crowd, followed by uncertain screams as that ocean of people begins to float up off the deck toward the galaxy-clad ceiling.

Tyler moves quick, I move quicker, each of us reaching into one of the Chellerians' jackets to draw out his disruptor. I fire once, twice, Tyler offloading into the third's chest. The fourth manages to grab Ty's wrist and twist it hard before I fire into his face. Red eyes roll up into his skull and the guards are drifting unconscious. The couples and triple are screaming behind us, but their cries are lost among the chaos of the ballroom. People are floating everywhere now, a sea of bodies rising into the air, the music still blasting, strobe lights bursting.

"Go!" Ty orders.

I grab a passkey off a goon's belt, swipe it through the scanner. The door to the menagerie opens wide, and in a heartbeat, Tyler, O'Malley and I are inside, slamming the door behind us.

Tyler takes the lead, magboots clomping as he follows Fin's schematic. O'Malley's eyes are wide. I wonder if it was the GIA who hit Dariel's den before they were supposed to. If some other drama took Fin out of play. How I can keep this whole thing from spinning out of control. How we're going to get through this alive.

We round a corner, find two guards floating in mid-air, shouting into their commsets and trying to get a grip on the ceiling. A blast from our disruptors silences them, and we're slipping in through a heavy door, sliding it shut behind us.

The room beyond smells like a sewer. I wince at the stench, looking around at the doe-eyed beasties in the cages surrounding us. They're sorta like cows, gentle fuzzy quad-rupeds with big brown herbivore eyes. They mewl when they see us, ears flicking back in fear.

"What is this place?" O'Malley whispers.

"A larder," Tyler says. He's got his uniglass held up on translate mode, scanning the Chellerian letters on the controls and searching for the right switch.

"Bianchi eats these things?" she asks, horrified.

"Not Bianchi," I sigh. "His baby boy."

Ty presses a button and a section of the floor rumbles and slides away, revealing a steep ramp curving down out of sight. I smell wet earth below, the sweetness of flowers.

O'Malley has her head down, and for a moment I think it's fear. But then she lifts her chin, and her mouth's a straight, determined line.

"Does that lead where I think it does?"

"To Bianchi's office?" Tyler nods. "Yeah, it does."

I shake my head. "This is crazy, Tyler. This is every kind of stupid."

"At least we're being consistent," he says, ripping off his mask and jacket.

"This bad boy killed every living thing on its planet. You really wanna go poking around its house?"

"Gravity is still down, the ultrasaur's not going to be mobile. We move quick and quiet, we'll be okay. We've come this far. There's no backing out now."

"And presuming we dodge that thing down there, how do we get into Bianchi's office afterward?"

Tyler smiles. "Trust me."

A beep sounds inside O'Malley's belt.

"YOU REALIZE YOU'RE ALL ABOUT TO DIE, RIGHT?"

"Magellan, hush," she whispers, muting its volume.

Annoying as the little bastard is, I can't help but agree with it. I want to protest more, but Ty has deactivated his magboots and is pushing himself down the ramp. For all her obvious fear, O'Malley throws her mask aside and follows close behind—Tyler Jones just has that effect on people, I guess. Because as pants-on-head stupid as this is, I find myself killing my magboots and floating after him too.

The ramp emerges into a broad stretch of amazing jungle—a bona fide rainforest right here in the middle of a space station. I don't know why it surprises me after the aquarium, but this is somehow even more incredible.

I can't imagine the creds Bianchi must have blown to put this place together, how mad he's going to be if anything happens to his prize pet. The foliage is thick, rippling shades of red and orange and yellow, like a permanent autumn. The air smells sweet, the enclosure hung with vines and vibrant alien blooms. We push ourselves around the edge, using the twisted magenta trees to guide our movements. The space is massive, deathly still, and the sounds we make as we brush past the branches seem deafening, though they're no more than a whisper.

And in the distance, in that stillness, I hear a shuddering, chuddering roar.

"Son of a biscuit," O'Malley whispers.

"Why don't you just swear like a normal person?" I mutter.

She smiles then, like I've said something funny. Glancing at me with those mismatched eyes. "Sorry, but . . . do I seem normal to you?"

Yeah, okay, fair enough . . .

Another roar rings through the enclosure. The vibration shakes my belly, sets my teeth on edge. Tyler pulls out his uniglass, punches in a set of commands, throws it hard, back toward the ramp we just came from.

"What the hells are you doing?" I hiss. "That's a Legion-issue uniglass! It's more valuable to us than the Longbow!"

"Just keep moving," he whispers.

He's out in front, moving sure and steady—he aced his zero-gee orienteering exam, after all. O'Malley follows, careful and quick. I'm guessing maybe she practiced for this sort of thing in her colonist training, because for once, she looks like she knows exactly what she's doing.

I can hear earth being torn up, timber breaking, another bellowing roar. Tyler makes a fist, bringing us to a halt. And peering over his shoulder, my stomach turning to solid ice, I see it.

It's about the scariest thing I've laid eyes on, and again, I've seen Dariel in his undies. It looks like the Maker took every monster from under every bed of every child ever born and squished them into one great big über-monster—and then made a creature that'd eat *that* monster on toast with a glass of OJ and the morning news.

It's as big as a house, all teeth and claws, sinewy legs flailing as it scrambles for purchase in the zero gee. It's got its hands dug into the black earth, and apparently it's not stupid, because it's using its front claws to pull itself about. It snuffles the air with a blunt, snotty snout and roars again, spit flying from its mouth, black pupils dilated in five emerald-green eyes. The reptile part of my brain is just screaming at me: *Run! Go! Get out!* Because there's apex predators and there's Apex Predators. And then there's the Great Ultrasaur of Abraaxis IV.

"It can smell us," I whisper.

"That's Bianchi's office." Tyler points, somehow cool as ice.

I see the glint of a polarized silicon wall through the undergrowth, a hint of the spotlights and furniture in the office beyond. The wall is perfectly clear, but there're no seams. No latches. No hinges. Nothing.

"How we gonna get in there?" I whisper.

"Faith," he murmurs with a smile.

I scowl at the ultrasaur. "Is faith gonna get us past that thing?"

"Not faith." Tyler waggles his eyebrows. "Hormones."

In the distance, I hear a sound. It's faint, tinny—about the quality you'd expect coming from a uniglass's speakers. It sounds like two chainsaws trying to have sex.

The ultrasaur falls still, perks up, its eyes wide. The sound repeats again—it's the recording from Finian's presentation,

311

looped on playback, over and over. I look at Tyler and he grins, and much as I still want to punch him, I can't help but grin back.

It's a bloody *mating call*.

"You smug son of a b—"

The ultrasaur roars, slavering, spitting, bellowing as it scrabbles across the enclosure. It leaves huge gouges through the earth, ripping up trees in its wake as it struggles to get closer to Tyler's abandoned uniglass. Its teeth are bared, eyes flashing, great clods of shrubbery ripped free as it disappears into the thick foliage.

"It seems more . . . annoyed than excited?" O'Malley says.

"You'd be annoyed too if you thought there was another male in your house, cruising for ladysaurs." Tyler nods toward the office. "Come on."

Ty pushes himself hard off the nearest tree, moving quick now. I dart behind him, O'Malley bringing up the rear, waves of ridiculous tulle floating around her in the zero gee. Ty slows his dive with a handful of thick vines as he draws close to the silicon barrier, catching me as I come sailing in. O'Malley lands beside us, her mismatched eyes alight, seemingly energized at the thought of being so close to the prize. There's some metal under the earth here—brackets for the wall, I'm guessing, and Ty activates his magboots, heels clomping on the turf.

"How we getting through this?" I hiss, thumping my fist on the glass.

"When all else fails, just blast it," he shrugs.

He pulls out the disruptor he took from Bianchi's guards, sets it to Kill, and gives me a nod. I do the same, cranking the power up to max, and we both unload on the glass. There's a bright flash of light, a searing sound. The shots melt the wall's surface, leaving a black, charred scorch mark a few centimeters deep.

Problem is, this sucker is at least half a meter thick.

"Um," Tyler says. "Okay."

"Um, okay?" I say, incredulous.

"Is there an echo in here?" Ty asks.

I hear a small electronic beep from inside O'Malley's belt.

"If I may venture an opinion—"

"No, you bloody can't!" I snap. "Silent mode!"

We hear a distant roar, the sound of towering trees being torn out of the earth by claws as big as swords. I glance over my shoulder, back to Tyler.

"Please tell me 'When all else fails, just blast it' wasn't your only play?"

Tyler blasts the wall again, melting another couple of centimeters. He frowns, blows his mop of hair out of his eyes. "I really thought that'd work. . . ."

"Great Maker," I flail. "This from Mr. One Hundred Percent on My Military Tactics Exam?"

Ty raises his scarred eyebrow. "Cat, I hate to shatter your opinion of me, but this is probably as good a point as any to confess I've been pretty much making this up as I go since the *Bellerophon*."

Another roar shakes the foliage.

"Mothercustard," O'Malley whispers.

We turn and see it.

See *it* seeing *us*.

Its mouth is open, showcasing row upon row of razor-sharp fangs. Its breath is like a blast furnace, its claws are dug deep into the ground, ruptured earth and shredded plant life floating in the zero grav around it. Its five eyes flash with rage, a forked tongue flicking the air as it drags itself closer to us. I look up, see glass above me. Glass behind me. Monster in front of me.

We're boned.

"Cat, break left, take Auri," Ty whispers, killing his mag-boots and gently lifting off the ground. "We work our way b—"

Whatever Ty's command was going to be, he never gets a chance to finish it. The ultrasaur tenses its muscles and springs, the zero grav letting it sail right at us like a fang torpedo.

I grab O'Malley's hand and we kick off the wall, hear the sound of a massive body colliding with the polarized silicon behind me.

The ultrasaur roars, claws scrabbling on the glass, and I risk a glance over my shoulder. Tyler has kicked off the ground, up to the ceiling high overhead. He hits the roof hard, shoulder crunching into the glass. But he's moving again, lunging back toward the ground just as the ultrasaur crashes claws-first into the spot he'd been floating a moment before.

"Tyler!" O'Malley screams.

I know it probably won't make a difference, but I crack off a shot with my disruptor anyway, rewarded with a satisfying sizzle as the blast burns a hole in the ultrasaur's side. The shot doesn't do any real damage, but it gives Ty a few seconds to gather himself and take another spring, back in the direction of the feeding hatch.

Except now I've got Beastieboy's attention.

It roars and lunges at us, and I'm barely fast enough to leap aside, dragging O'Malley with me as I hook my fingers around an outstretched tree branch and shift our momentum. I feel the talons slice through the air behind me, just a breath from my back. I kick off the tree, bring us up through a tangle of branches, crack off another shot over my shoulder. I hear Beastieboy roar, smell sizzling flesh, feel O'Malley beside me. Heart hammering. Mouth dry.

I'm back in the flight simulator. The day we graduated into our streams. Fellow cadets gathered around me. Instructors watching dumbfounded as I weave and roll. Cheers growing louder as the KILL SHOT notifications keep flashing, as I keep firing, the weapons an extension of my fist, the ship an extension of my body, as the final miss tally flashes up on the screen and they cheer my new name.

ZERO.

ZERO.

ZERO.

Something big hits us from behind, sends us both pinwheeling into the office wall. I realize it's a tree, that this thing is smart enough to be able to throw. I guess you don't get to be the last surviving member of your species by being a dunce. I hit hard, O'Malley crashes into me, cracks her head on the glass, leaving a bright smudge of red behind her. I bite my tongue, the breath driven from my lungs in a spray of spit and blood as I lose my grip on my disruptor.

We bounce off the wall, sail back through the air. We're

spinning out of control. Nothing to hold on to. As I grab at her, I see O'Malley is out cold, eyes rolled up in her skull, tiny globes of blood floating from her split brow. I can see the beast over her shoulder, tensing for another spring. I hear a disruptor fire, Ty shouting.

But its eyes are locked on me. I've pissed it off. You don't get to be the last surviving member of your species without learning to hold a grudge, either.

I look at O'Malley again. Her eyes are closed, her jaw slack, brow bleeding. I do the math. Figure we both don't need to die. So I let her go and kick her away.

She sails apart from me.

The ultrasaur springs my way, roaring as it comes.

Tyler fires again, I see a bright flash.

The world is moving in slo-mo, I'm spinning weightless as that engine of teeth and claws flings itself right at me. But I find myself smiling. Because I'm flying.

Here at the end, at least I'm flying.

And then I hit something hard.

There's nothing there, but still I hit it—some invisible force that arrests my flight. Holds me in place.

The ultrasaur is frozen too, hanging in midair and defying every law of momentum and gravity I know.

It roars in fury.

The air vibrates around me, the world goes out of focus. I taste salt in my mouth. I see O'Malley from the corner of my eye. She's floating on air too, short hair rippling as if the wind were blowing. I can see her right eye is glowing, burning, her arms outstretched, a subsonic hum building like static electricity in the air around me.

"*T-t-ttrig-ggerrrrr,*" she says.

A wave of force rolls out from her, shivering, translucent, spherical. It flattens the undergrowth, crushes the trees, expanding in an ever-widening circle until it hits Beastieboy.

And Beastieboy just . . . pops. Like a bug being squashed by some massive, invisible shoe. Its armored skin splits apart and its insides become its outsides and I turn my head and close my eyes so I don't have to watch the rest.

The enclosure shakes like it's in the middle of a planet-quake. There's something soft and spongy under my feet. Opening my eyes, I realize my boots are now touching the floor.

Maker's breath, she's moved me. . . .

O'Malley sinks down to the earth, arms still outstretched, blood spilling from her nose and floating in the air. Her eye is still burning with that ghostly white light, almost blinding. But I can feel her looking at me. Feel her *seeing* me.

"*Believe,*" she says.

She convulses once, then her eyes close and she passes out again, slowly curling into a fetal position and floating there like a baby in its mother's womb.

"Cat!"

I turn and see Tyler behind me, shaggy blond hair drifting about his head in the zero gee. He's clinging to the flattened tree line, spattered in ultrasaur blood. His face is pale, his blue eyes wide. But he's pointing past me.

"Look," he says.

I turn, look past the curtain of gore to the office wall. And I see that the force of O'Malley's . . . well, *whatever* she just did . . . hasn't just flattened the trees, torn the shrubs

317

free, squeezed the Great Ultrasaur of Abraaxis IV like a very large and angry jelly doughnut. It's also cracked the wall of Bianchi's office open like an egg.

She did it.

We're in.

"Told you," Tyler says.

I look at him blankly, and he just smiles.

"Faith."

POWERS OF THE MIND

▶ **HYPOTHETICAL**

▼ **TELEKINESIS**

TELEKINESIS IS THE HYPOTHETICAL ABILITY TO MANIPULATE MATTER WITHOUT THE DIRECT APPLICATION OF FORCE—THAT IS, TO MOVE THINGS WITH THE POWER OF THE MIND.

WHILE OTHER MENTAL POWERS, INCLUDING **TELEPATHY**, **EMPATHY**, AND MILD **PRECOGNITION**, HAVE BEEN WELL DOCUMENTED ACROSS SEVERAL SPECIES—MOST NOTABLY, **SYLDRATHI**, **ILESARS**, AND THE **KELINRORI**—THERE ARE NO SCIENTIFICALLY VALIDATED INCIDENTS OF TELEKINESIS. NO MATTER WHAT S'REN FROM ACCOUNTING TOLD YOU ABOUT HIS GREAT-UNCLE WAYBO AND THE **SPOONS**.

23

SCARLETT

"WE ARE AWARE WORLD SHIP RESIDENTS MAY CUR-
RENTLY BE EXPERIENCING DIFFICULTIES WITH [GRAVITY].
PLEASE REMAIN CALM."

The prerecorded announcement spilling over the public
address system is met with hundreds of outraged shouts from
people already well aware of the problem. I push my way out
of the turbolift, sailing into the grand bazaar and a scene of
absolute chaos.

People and goods and everything else float in the air,
a tumble of colors and shapes, like confetti at a very angry
wedding. As I pull myself to a stop on an access ladder, my
gown billows about my waist in ripples of shimmering blue
and glittering crystal. I'm feeling glad I decided to wear sen-
sible underwear for once.

"OUR TECHNICIANS WILL RETURN THE [GRAVITY]
SERVICE SHORTLY," the announcer assures us in a lilting female voice. "WE THANK YOU FOR YOUR PATIENCE."

The announcement cycles through a dozen different languages, only four of which I can speak. The reaction from

the residents is universal outrage. The savvier folks in the bazaar are wearing magboots like me—but that doesn't do much for their wares, their livestock, their belongings.

I keep to the edge of the bazaar, pushing myself along the wall, engaging my magboots only when I need to. It's quicker to fly, and time is something we're apparently way shorter on than we planned.

"Kal, Zila, can you hear me?"

"Affirmative, Legionnaire Jones," Zila responds.

"What's your position?"

"Almost at Dariel's flat. ETA, forty-two seconds."

I reach the edge of the bazaar and consult the schematic on my uniglass, shaking my head. "Crap, I'm at least five minutes away."

"We cannot wait for you," I hear Kal declare.

"Three guns are better than two, Punchy."

"The World Ship's technicians will have the secondary gravity generators online at any moment. If Finian and Dariel are compromised, your presence in a close-quarters battle will not outweigh the cost of delay."

I kick through a doorway, sail into another turbolift.

"Are you saying I'm no good in a fight?"

"I am saying this is no time for diplomacy," Kal responds.

"Listen here, you pointy-eared, prettyboy jer—"

"We have arrived. I am going in."

I curse, hit the turbolift control, engage my boots as the thrust pushes me down. I hear a crashing noise over my uni comms channel, the sound of weapons fire. My heart is racing now, stomach in knots as I kick out of the lift and into the hab sector. I hear a scream over comms, disruptor blasts.

"Kal?" I shout. "Zila, report!"

More shouting, wet thuds, another scream. I hear Kal swearing in Syldrathi, and though his tone is ice-cold, I realize he's far more creative at cursing than I thought.

"Tiir'na si maat tellanai!" (Father of many ugly and stupid children!)

"Kii'ne dō all'iavesh ishi!" (Stain on the undergarments of the universe!)

"Aam'na delnii!" (Friend of livestock!)

And with a sizzling crack of disruptor fire, my comms channel dies.

"Kal?"

I kick off a wall, gliding past two bewildered-looking boys crawling out of a storage cupboard, stripped down to their underwear. One of them is wearing an Uncle Enzo's cap.

"Zila, can you hear me?"

I make the stairwell, engaging my magboots as I kick my way upward. My pulse is really hammering now, sweat in my eyes as I disentangle myself from this ridiculous dress, bustle it up and stab another channel on my uni.

"Ty, I think Kal and Zila are in trouble, I—"

I fall silent as I make it up to Dariel's floor. There, waiting for me in the corridor is a figure in a drab gray suit. Featureless gray helmet. Looking over its shoulder into the den, I see Finian hunched in his chair, pale pink blood leaking from a split in his brow. I see bodies floating in the zero gee, the walls charred with weapons fire.

The GIA operative stows a disruptor in its jacket.

"Legionnaire Jones," it says. "So nice of you to join us."

THINGS TO MAKE YOU BLUSH

▶ **CURSE WORDS**

▼ **BEST OF**

THE RANKING OF CURSE WORDS, FROM THE **BLASPHEMOUS** TO THOSE INVOLVING **BODILY FUNCTIONS**, WILL ALWAYS BE A MATTER OF SUBJECTIVE JUDGMENT. THAT SAID, IT IS WIDELY ACCEPTED THAT SOME OF THE MOST EFFECTIVE AND OUTRAGEOUS ARE:

[PLEASE CLICK **HERE** TO VERIFY YOUR IDENTITY AND CONFIRM YOU HAVE REACHED THE AGE OF MAJORITY IN YOUR CULTURE. BY CLICKING, YOU ACKNOWLEDGE THAT I, MAGELLAN, AND MY PROGRAMMERS ARE NOT LIABLE FOR ANY DAMAGE, TEMPORARY OR PERMANENT, CAUSED BY OR RELATED TO EXPOSURE TO THE WORDS ON THIS LIST.]

1. ▮▮▮▮

2. ▮▮▮▮▮▮▮ ▮▮ ▮▮▮ ▮▮▮

3. ▮▮▮▮▮ ▮▮

4. ▮

5. ▮▮▮ ▮▮▮ ▮▮▮

24

TYLER

I'm feeling a little naked without my uniglass, but presumably it's somewhere in that ultrasaur's stomach and I'm not about to wade through the mess to get it back.

Pushing myself off the broken foliage, I sail across the enclosure and gently scoop up Auri's limp body. She stirs, frowning at the shift in momentum as I bring myself to rest at the edge of the wall to Bianchi's office. The polarized silicon has been cracked wide. Fragments of glass drift in the air above the pressure-sensitive floor—luckily, whatever else Aurora did, she seems to have killed the power in Bianchi's office and the alarms along with it.

Whatever else she did?

Call it what it was, Tyler.

Telekinesis.

I touch her cheek, speaking softly. "Auri, can you hear me?"

Cat comes to rest next to me, bloodstained and dirty, looking as shaken as I feel. But as terrifying as what we both just saw might have been, her voice doesn't tremble.

"She okay?"

"I don't know," I reply, glancing through the broken glass wall. "But we have to move, security has *got* to be on their way by now. Look after her for me."

I leave Cat cradling Aurora and push through the crack into Bianchi's office. The spotlights are dead, the air filled with floating pieces of sculpture, objets d'art, alien artifacts, all knocked off his shelves by the force of Auri's blast. A wide desk is ringed by large chairs, glass cases arranged in a widening spiral around the huge room. My heart surges when I see our target—the three-fingered statue wrought in strange metal—floating inside a tall glass case.

The Trigger.

I glance back to Aurora, watch her stir again in Cat's arms. The power she's displaying—this small, frail girl out of time—is like nothing I've ever seen. If I wasn't a believer before—if Admiral Adams's and Battle Leader de Stoy's warnings, what happened on the *Bellerophon,* and Auri's visions of the future hadn't been enough to convince me that we're caught up in something *way* bigger than ourselves, the way she squeezed that ultrasaur like a zit sure would've been.

Looking into Cat's wide eyes, I can finally see it, same as mine.

Belief.

I hope it hasn't come too late.

Cat pushes herself into the office, floating above the ground with Aurora in her arms. Auri groans and opens her eyes, blinking hard. She takes a long, slow moment to focus, to find me, to remember where she is. But then her mismatched eyes fix on the Trigger, and she tenses, coming suddenly, completely awake. Breathing quicker, jaw clenching.

She looks at the sculpture, looks at me. Her voice is hoarse, as if she's been screaming.

"That's it," she whispers.

I draw my disruptor, fire it into another of Bianchi's display cases. Splintered silicon sprays across the room, the four-headed statue inside goes crashing into the wall. Lowering the setting, I shoot another case and watch the glass crack but not shatter.

Better.

I turn to the Trigger's case, fire into the glass. A thousand cracks spread out across the surface like spiderwebs. I lift my disruptor and give it a gentle tap with the butt, and the glass shatters at the precise moment the gravity kicks back in.

We all drop to the ground suddenly, off guard, me on my belly in a hail of glittering splinters. Cat and Auri hit the floor nearby, my Ace grunting as she lands. There's a long, disgusting splash as the insides of the ultrasaur hit the ground outside, followed by a heavy, wet thump as the rest of its body follows. I push myself onto my knees, shaking the glass fragments from my hair.

Bianchi's techs must've engaged the secondary grav-generators.

We had to run out of time eventually.

I hear a series of electronic beeps at my back. The sound of heavy locks sliding away. My heart lurches at the small, somber hiss of the office door opening.

I already know what I'll see when I turn around, and still, my gut is full of butterflies as I glance over my shoulder. I let my disruptor fall from my fingers to the polished boards as a bloodcurdling scream of rage fills the air.

So close.

Casseldon Bianchi storms into the room, surrounded on all sides by his bodyguards. They're Chellerian, every one—big as small cars and armed to the teeth. Bianchi's four eyes are wide with rage, fangs bared in a snarl as he stalks into his office. But it's not the smashed cases, the scene of chaos, the antiques scattered among the broken glass on the floor that make him raise his fists and scream again. It's the long slick of gore outside the glass. The sight of his most prized pet—the rarest beast in the galaxy—reduced to the consistency of the soup of the day.

"Skaa taa ve benn!" he roars.

And turning on me, all four of his red eyes narrow to paper cuts.

"Hoo-maaan," he hisses.

His punch lifts me off the ground, sends me back into the wall. I hit the deck on my knees, jagged pain in my gut, blood in my mouth. Bianchi grabs a disruptor from one of his goons, points it at my head. Auri screams my name, Cat raises her weapon as Bianchi's goons all draw on her.

"No firing in here please, gentlemen," comes a sexless electronic voice.

I glance up, clutching my aching belly, breath rasping through my teeth. A GIA operative in a featureless gray suit steps into the room, flanked by a second.

Bianchi bellows in Chellerian. He points to the splattered remains of his ultrasaur with three arms while waving his weapon at me with the other.

"And I appreciate that, Mr. Bianchi," the operative says, motioning at Auri. "But as we explained, this

ASSET IS OF VITAL IMPORTANCE TO TERRA. WE WOULD PREFER THAT SHE DID NOT BECOME COLLATERAL DAMAGE IN YOUR FIT OF PIQUE."

Bianchi tilts his head, looming over the G-man and growling in perfect Terran.

"This is my ship. My world. You have no jurisdiction here, hoo-maaan."

I can't see its face, but the operative speaks like it didn't even blink. "YOU WOULD NOT EVEN HAVE BEEN AWARE OF THIS ROBBERY HAD WE NOT INFORMED YOU OF IT, MR. BIANCHI. SOME GRATITUDE MIGHT BE IN ORDER."

"If you had warned me sooner, my pet would not be dead!"

"THE *BELLEROPHON* IS ONLY A FEW HOURS AWAY FROM THE WORLD SHIP, SIR. ON ARRIVAL, OUR PRINCEPS WILL COMPENSATE YOU ADEQUATELY FOR YOUR LOSSES. WE REQUIRE ONLY THE GIRL. AS FOR THE REST OF THESE TRAITORS"—the G-man gestures to me and Cat—"WE ARE SURE A MAN OF YOUR REPUTATION WILL ENJOY TAKING HIS TIME WITH THEM IN YOUR HOLDING CELLS."

"Waitaminute," Cat says, stepping forward. "That wasn't the deal. . . ."

I turn on her, eyes widening. "Deal?"

She doesn't look me in the face, staring at the GIA agent instead. "You said we had immunity! You said we could go back to our lives!"

The agent tilts its head. "WE LIED, LEGIONNAIRE BRANNOCK."

". . . You sold us out?" I whisper at Cat, hands curling into fists.

She meets my eyes, tears welling in her own. "I . . . I did it for the squad, Ty."

"For the squad?" I yell. "You betrayed me for the *squad*?"

"Betrayed?" Cat's voice is incredulous. "If anyone betrayed us, it's you!"

"*What?*"

"You heard me!" Cat points at Auri. "Ever since she came aboard the Longbow, you've thrown the regs out the window! Sucking us all down into the toilet, and for what? For *her*?" She presses her hands to her breast and whines, *"Oh, I'm so sweet and helpless, Mr. Jones, won't you gather me up in your big, strong—"*

"That's what this is about?" I demand. "You and me?"

Bianchi steps forward and growls. *"Enough—"*

"This has nothing to do with *us*!" Cat screams right over the top of him. "This is about the Legion! About the academy! Everything we worked for since we were kids, Tyler! Some skirt bats her eyes at you and you throw it all away?"

"It was a mistake, Cat!" I yell. "I'm sorry about what happened between us on shore leave! I'm sorry I messed it up! But isn't it about time you got over it?"

Her eyes widen at that. "You sonofa . . ."

She launches herself across the room, slugs me right in the jaw, shoves me back into a display, cracking my skull on the glass. I tackle her backward, we crash into the Trigger display, knocking it over as we hit the deck. Broken glass and flailing fists, Cat pounding on my face and screaming, *screaming*.

The room dissolves into chaos: a couple of the Chellerians guffawing at the stupid hoo-maaans, the two GIA

329

agents striding in to break us up, Auri crouching low and covering her ears as Bianchi raises his disruptor and fires into the ceiling.

The G-men pull Cat off me, my blood on her knuckles. She's panting, flailing, still spitting curses at me.

"You bastard! I'm gonna kick your arse so hard, your fu—"

"ENOUGH!" Bianchi roars. *"Take them to the cells!"*

One of the G-men grabs Aurora's arm, hauls her up from the debris. "WE WILL BE TAKING MS. O'MALLEY BACK TO EARTH, AS PER OUR ARRANGEMENT."

Bianchi squares up to the operative, folding all four of his arms.

"YOU WILL HAVE EARNED THE FRIENDSHIP OF THE TERRAN GOVERNMENT, MR. BIANCHI. I ASSURE YOU, OUR GRATITUDE IS ALMOST BOUNDLESS."

"Perhaps while they are showing their gratitude, they can explain why they had two of their agents aboard my World Ship without my consent."

The G-man shrugs. "THE GLOBAL INTELLIGENCE AGENCY HAS ONE THOUSAND EYES, MR. BIANCHI."

The gangster grits his fangs. But finally he growls and nods. The Chellerian goons step into the room and grab me and Cat. The GIA agents march briskly out through the office door, hauling Auri between them. With a hard shove to help us, Cat and I follow, boots crunching on broken glass, leaving Bianchi to stare mournfully out at the remains of his pet.

We're marched side by side, Auri and the GIA operatives out in front. Cat refuses to meet my eyes. Blood drips down my chin from the split she reopened in my lip. I can hear

Auri's breath catching in her chest, the soft metallic hiss of the G-men breathing. I can't hear the party music anymore.

The G-men bundle into a turbolift, press the button for the docks. One of the goons swipes a passkey and hits another button—presumably the level for Bianchi's infamous holding cells. People who go in there never come out.

I stand facing the doors, six Chellerians at my back, two GIA agents behind them. I ache all over. One of the goons talks to me, lips curling in a sneer.

"I don't speak Chellerian," I reply, licking my bloody lip.

"HE'S ASKING IF YOU'RE STUPID," one of the operatives replies helpfully. "HOW YOU POSSIBLY EXPECTED TO GET IN AND OUT OF THAT OFFICE WITHOUT GETTING CAUGHT."

I smile at the goon, then glance over my shoulder at that faceless mirrormask.

"Tell him I didn't."

The operative draws its disruptor, unloads a stun blast into the back of the Chellerian's head. The second agent draws too, firing into one goon's face as he turns, then dropping another with a second point-blank blast to his chest. There's a brief scuffle, stun blasts flash again, and in a handful of seconds, every goon in the lift is laid out on the floor, twitching and drooling.

"WELL." Scarlett drags off her GIA mask, checking her reflection and adjusting her flaming red hair. "That went less than smoothly."

"Everyone's a critic," I say. "Is Finian okay?"

"HIS EXOSUIT IS DAMAGED, BUT HE IS ALIVE," Zila replies from beneath the other G-man uniform. "KAL TOOK HIM BACK TO THE LONGBOW."

"Could've gone bad," Cat mutters. "Bastards told me they were going to wait till after we had the passkey before they stormed the flat."

"I think it's safe to say we were right not to entirely trust the agents of the Global Intelligence Agency," I smile.

Cat smiles back. "If they were so bloody intelligent, they wouldn't have asked an Ace to sell out her Alpha. They would've expected me to run right back to you and tell you everything they said."

I reach out and squeeze her hand, and she grins at me, feral, triumphant, fierce as the heat of a thousand stars.

"Good work, Legionnaire Brannock."

"Always back your Alpha," she says. *"Always."*

The turbolift door opens, and we're met by Dariel on the other side. He blinks in surprise, his jaw hanging open.

"Holy crap, it *worked*?" he asks, looking at the unconscious bodies in the lift.

"Never underestimate the element of surprise," I say, marching past him.

We roll out into the corridor and through an airlock, heading into the docks. The place is a shambles after the gravity outage, but the cleanup crews are already at work. We move quick, Dariel shuffling alongside me, scowling and scratching his head. I'm sorry to say it, but I'm guessing Finian gets his brains from one of the other three sides of his family.

"Okay, explain it to me again," Dariel says.

"THIS," Zila notes, pulling off her helmet, "WILL BE THE third time."

"I'm a lover, not a thinker," the Betraskan winks. "By the way, you got a number I—"

"It was like Fin said," I say. "There was no way to pull this off without getting caught. So once the GIA tried to flip Cat, I *counted* on it. The original plan was to snatch Bianchi's passkey and get into his office. The GIA would hit your flat at a time they arranged with Cat, arrest Fin, cut off our comms. They'd then alert Bianchi to our scam, and everyone could roll down to the office and catch us. If the GIA worded up Bianchi beforehand, we'd just get killed by his security teams and they'd get nothing. But catching us red-handed, the GIA would look like heroes."

"And a grateful Bianchi would hand over Auri while the rest of us got shot," Cat adds.

"But the GIA hit the den early . . . ," Dariel objects. "Beat the crap out of Fin."

"So we had to go through the ultrasaur enclosure instead," I nod. "And Kal had to storm the flat to take out the GIA instead of waiting for them in ambush."

"He was . . . kinda terrifying," Dariel murmurs.

"Again, sorry about the mess," Scar says.

"All that really mattered was getting hold of the GIA uniforms," I say. "It's hard to tell who's actually under those masks. And Scar can sell almost anything."

Dariel blinks. "So . . . you went to all that trouble . . . just to get caught?"

"Yeah," I reply. "But we had to be *in the office* when the GIA arrived. After that, the only thing Cat and I really needed to do was get in a fistfight."

"Take Bianchi's eyes off the prize," Cat nods.

"Make sure nobody was watching me," Auri says quietly.

Dariel turns as the girl speaks. And with a triumphant

smile, she reaches into the bunches of bright red tulle around her waist and produces a three-fingered statue wrought in strange metal, a winking diamond set in its chest, its right eye a gleaming pearl.

"Classic misdirection," I shrug. "Basic Tactics, second semester."

"How long until Bianchi notices it's gone?" Dariel asks.

"Given the state of disarray we left his office in," Zila says, "I would estimate another three to four minutes. Approximately."

"And the *Bellerophon* is still en route to the World Ship," Cat says. "And from the sound of things, I don't think Mr. Princeps is going to be happy about what Kal did to the only two agents the GIA had aboard."

"You have *no* idea," Scarlett says.

Auri blinks. "So . . . remind me why we aren't running?"

It's a good question, and I can't think of a good answer. And so we run. Dashing past the loaders and dockers, down through the tangled snarl of the World Ship berths, along the transparent umbilical leading to our Longbow. The airlock is open, and Kal's waiting for us. His Uncle Enzo's delivery uniform is spattered in blood, a disruptor rifle is in his hand. He sees us, and though he keeps that typical Syldrathi cool in place, his lips curl in a small smile.

Aurora meets his eyes.

His smile falls away.

"We should move, sir," he says.

I nod, turn to Dariel, and shake his hand in thanks. "I don't know what Fin owes you, but I owe you now too, Big Time. You need my help in the future, just shout."

Scarlett kisses Dariel on the cheek and winks. "Thanks, Romeo."

Dariel turns to Zila, a small smirk on his lips. "Do I get a kiss from you too?"

"Thank you, goodbye," she says, walking right past and into the ship.

Aurora produces a second artifact from the folds of her skirts—it's a small figure carved from a greenish stone. She holds it out to Dariel. "I grabbed this for you. In case you need some relocation funds."

He pockets it with a grin. "Probably not the worst idea," he admits. "And thanks, those stalactites weren't cheap."

The rest of us hustle aboard. With a final nod to Dariel, we seal the airlock behind us, scatter up to the bridge. Finian is already in his chair. His suit seems a little worse for wear, and he's working on the left forearm with a small photon welder, looking bruised and miserable. But he perks up when he catches sight of us. Shamrock is sitting in his lap.

Cat scowls at him as she slips into the pilot's seat.

"That's my dragon," she says.

"I was just holding him for you," Finian says, tossing the toy across.

"What for?" she asks, snatching Shamrock from the air.

"Figured we could use the luck."

Cat grins, kisses the dragon on his head, and starts punching commands into her console. "Shut up, Finian."

We strap ourselves in, run through preflight check. My hands are flowing over my controls, and I don't know what comes next. I know the *Bellerophon* is inbound to Sempiternity. I know the GIA won't stop till they have Auri in their custody. I don't know who or what she is, or where she's leading us. No doubt we're being hunted by the Terran dreadnoughts that patrol the Fold, too, and I know we just made another deadly enemy in Casseldon Bianchi.

But that's the future's problem. For now, we need to get out of here before—

"ALERT," says the PA. "ALERT. ALL DEPARTURES FROM THE WORLD SHIP ARE SUSPENDED BY ORDER OF CASSELDON BIANCHI, PENDING SEARCH OPERATIONS. PLEASE POWER DOWN YOUR ENGINES AND—"

"Hold on to your undies, kids!" Cat shouts.

She hits the thrusters, docking clamps shrieking as they try to stop us blasting free. But with a burst of full power, a bone-shaking tremor and a scream of metal, we tear out into the black and leave the World Ship in our wake. Momentum pushes me back into my seat, and for a moment it's hard to breathe. And then I remember how lucky I am to be breathing at all.

We're out.

We made it.

I look around the bridge at my crew. Squad 312. This pack of losers and discipline cases and sociopaths, these misfits nobody in the whole of Aurora Academy wanted to get paired with. And I realize the magnitude of what we just pulled off.

I think about the fact that I just asked every single one of them to walk into the mouth of the beast because they believed in me. The fact that none of them blinked. And the fact that they didn't just walk in.

They *flew*.

Auri's curled up at an auxiliary station, knees under her chin. She's bruised and tired and bloody, but there's a new fire in her eyes. She has the Trigger clutched in her fist, staring at it as if it holds all the answers to all the questions.

What am I?

Why am I here?

What is this all for?

And now we've got our hands on it, I can't help but wonder. I know we're part of something bigger. Something at least two centuries in the making. Maybe even more. Something the leaders of the academy knew about before we did. Something the GIA knows about, too.

I feel like a pawn being pushed from square to square. And try as I might, I can't see the rest of the board. But you don't spend five years at military academy without learning a thing or two about how guns work.

And if this thing in Auri's hand is the Trigger . . .

Then where's the Weapon?

And what in the 'Way is that Weapon for?

PART 3

BLACK HOLE HEART

THE UNIVERSE
▶ THE FOLD
▼ RISKS

IT'S WIDELY HELD THAT THE ONLY INDIVIDUAL WHO TRULY UNDERSTANDS THE MATHEMATICS OF **FOLD TRAVEL** IS THE ÜBER-BRAINY **DR. RAMASCULUS CH'FAR SI-LIENTO THE THIRD OF VOLI VI**. SI-LIENTO HAS CLONED HIS BRAIN THREE TIMES AND HOOKED IT INTO A LOCALIZED BIO-NETWORK CAPABLE OF CALCULATING AT 1 **EXAFLOP^3**, AND HE'S STILL INCAPABLE OF PARSING FOLD CALCULATIONS AND **ORDERING BREAKFAST** AT THE SAME TIME. IT'S VERY COMPLICATED, IS WHAT I'M SAYING.

LUCKILY, YOU DON'T HAVE TO UNDERSTAND HOW YOU'RE GOING FROM A TO B TO KNOW WHAT CAN GO WRONG ALONG THE WAY. A FEW OF THE RISKS OF FOLD TRAVEL INCLUDE:

- ▶ **HALLUCINATIONS**
- ▶ **FOLDSTORMS**
- ▶ **LONG-TERM CEREBRAL DAMAGE**
- ▶ **UNANTICIPATED GATE CLOSURE**
- ▶ **PSYCHOSIS**

STILL, GIVEN THE DISTANCES A SHIP CAN COVER IN THE FOLD, IT'S WORTH WEIGHING UP THESE RISKS AGAINST YOUR GUARANTEED DEATH FROM OLD AGE IF YOU TRY AND MAKE THE JOURNEY THE OLD-FASHIONED WAY.

25

AURI

We plunged into the Fold ten minutes ago, and no one has spoken since.

The colors are monochrome, black and white and shades between, bleaching the fire out of Scarlett's hair, turning Zila's rich brown skin a dark gunmetal gray. The ship is traveling smoothly, and I'm sitting on one of the long padded benches at the rear of the bridge. The weight of the Trigger resting in my hands.

Every part of me is aching, from my teeth to my toes, but though I'm light-headed with exhaustion, I'm *alive*. Not just with the adrenaline of survival but with the sense that I'm on the path I need to follow. I don't know where it leads— I don't even know where it goes next—but there's an indefinable sense of rightness that comes with doing what I'm supposed to.

Supposed to? By whose rules? And for what reason?

If I follow this path, will I find out what happened to my father and the others on Octavia? Will I find out why my government wants to erase me, too?

Will I find out what I am?

I look down at the statue in my hands, running my fingers over the surface. It looks old, worn smooth with time. It feels right in my palm, like it's *supposed* to be there. But I've got no idea what I'm supposed to do with it.

It's Tyler who breaks the silence, unbuckling his harness and coming to his feet. He's still in his formalwear, the black fabric ripped far beyond the dictates of fashion now. "We need to decide where we go next," he says.

Then he pauses, looking around the cabin. Surveying the tired faces of Aurora Legion Squad 312. His lips curve to one of those dimpled smiles he does so well. "What I meant to say," he corrects himself, "is that that was incredible. I couldn't be prouder to serve with every single one of you."

They're the right words. I see how each of the squad sits up just a fraction straighter after he speaks.

Still, Fin sounds as he always does when he replies. "Thanks, Goldenboy. But you're right. We need to figure out where we go from here, or the only thing we'll be serving is time. And no way am I sharing a cell with you reprobates."

Cat speaks without turning her head, though I wish I could see her face. "I admit I *could* do with some navigational input."

I open my mouth, then close it, looking down at the Trigger in my palm again. This thing we all just risked our lives for. Everyone is staring at me now—except for Kal, of course, who's ignoring me as intently as he always does. But I can feel everyone else on the ship looking to me for answers.

I have no idea where we're meant to go.

I'm saved from answering by Zila, who unbuckles herself

and stands. "I will provide medical treatment," she says, in the same calm voice she always uses, as if she didn't just help blast six Chellerian bodyguards three times her size after blowing out the gravity of an entire space station. "Scarlett, could you access the supplies? We are due to eat. And we should change our clothes."

The idea of food animates us all. So there's a pause by mutual agreement as the Jones twins grab and distribute shake 'n heat ration packs. Mine says *NotPork'n'Apple Casserole and Pie!*™ on the foil. I'm not sure whether to worry about the *NotPork* or the *and Pie!* and I shake it until the foil warms to the touch, then tear it along the dotted line.

A now-familiar beep sounds from inside my belt. "You realize there is nothing close to either pork or apple inside there, right?"

Squinting inside suspiciously, I suspect Magellan is right, but I shrug and chow down anyway.

"Ty, we need to talk," Scarlett says.

"Uh-oh," Tyler replies, mouth half-full. "No conversation in human history that began with those words ever ended well."

Zila is standing by Fin, dabbing something on the cuts on his face. "We should discuss what we saw at Dariel's flat. The information may impact our next decision."

"Why?" Cat asks, looking between them. "What did you see?"

Kal speaks beside me, his voice low. "There was something wrong with the GIA agents. We saw it when we removed their uniforms for Scarlett and Zila to wear."

Tyler glances across at him. "Wrong? Care to elaborate on that?"

Scarlett sets down her *Just Like Fish Dumplings*™. "I don't think we want to tell. This, we have to *show*."

She's still wearing gray GIA armor from the neck down, and she pops a release on the chest plate, pulls her uniglass from the sweaty bodice of her dress, aims it at the cabin's holographic central display, then transfers a picture there with a flick of her finger.

The image slides up to replace the trajectory readouts, and the whole squad goes perfectly still and silent.

Cat's the first to speak, in a voice I've never heard from her before.

"Holy *shit*."

It's a picture of a woman—a human woman. She's probably in her thirties, though it's hard to tell at first. She's dead, her cheeks hollowed. Her mouth is a little open, and her skin is a lifeless, sullen gray. And where this woman's right eye should be there's . . . a plant?

It reminds me of the succulents my mother used to grow in our apartment. Thick, juicy, diamond-shaped leaves bursting from her eye socket in a tight bouquet, none much bigger than my thumbnail. They're a lifeless tinge that matches her skin, with a dark blush along their edges and a tracery of veins running through them.

Some kind of moss spreads across the right side of her face. It's made up of soft fuzz and wispy tendrils and covers half her forehead, trailing down to disappear beneath her black undershirt. The same black veins in those leaves also run under her skin like spiderwebs.

It's like she's made of stone, and the plants and moss are *growing* out of her. No wonder Kal said something was wrong. Deep in the pit of my stomach, I know I've never seen anything *more* wrong. It should just be gross, out of place, but instead it's sending my every nerve jangling, my spine prickling with panic.

"I am not well versed with human maladies," Kal says quietly. "But I assume this is not some common condition."

"No," Ty says, sounding as close to shaky as I've ever heard him. "You're telling me this woman was one of the GIA agents? She was walking and talking?"

I glance up at the woman's face again. I don't . . . There's something incredibly wrong about this, but there's something *familiar* as well. I hold up my hand to block out the eye that's blooming with that unnatural plant and stare at the rest of her.

Then my gut twists.

"Tyler, I . . . I know her." My voice is hoarse, just a whisper.

Ty looks at me, his scarred eyebrow raised. "You met her on Sempiternity?"

I shake my head. "I *used* to know her. Before I ever got on the *Hadfield*."

I feel, as much as see, the six-way glance my companions exchange.

"That's impossible," Scarlett says. "That would make her over two centuries old. Your cryo survival was a freak accident, Auri. Are you saying the same thing happened to her, on some other ship that never made headlines?"

"Either that, or she really must moisturize," Fin offers, but nobody laughs.

"I know," I say weakly. "But this is Patrice Radke. She

was a settler on Octavia III, the head of Exploration and Cartography."

I drag my gaze away from the picture, and they're all looking at me. Some are expectant. Some skeptical. But all of them are hanging on my every word.

"She would've been my boss," I whisper. "I was going to do a practical apprenticeship in Exploration and Cartography under her. She and my dad . . . they . . ."

"Thanks for the birthday wishes, Dad."

"Thanks for the congratulations about winning All-States again. Thanks for remembering to message Callie about her recital, which she nailed, by the way. But most of all, thanks for this. Mom couldn't get clearance for Octavia, so what . . . you just replaced her? You're not even divorced yet!"

And then I hung up on him. The last words I ever spoke to him were a list of reasons he sucked.

And now he's dead. . . .

I look up into Patrice's lifeless face, my stomach sinking. *But if she—*

"Officially, there was no colony on Octavia III," Zila says. "Records indicate that you were bound for Lei Gong."

"Well, the records are wrong," I reply.

Zila tilts her head, studying me in that way of hers. "And this Patrice was one of the original settlers for your expedition, some two hundred and twenty years ago."

It doesn't sound like she's questioning me. Just thinking things through. The others are less certain, though nobody's offering the flat-out disbelief I've seen before. I think we're past that now.

"This sounds like I'm crazy," I say. "But I know I'm right."

Except that Patrice Radke has been dead for over two centuries.

Then again, I'm two hundred and thirty-seven years old myself.

On a ship full of aliens. Who I just robbed a space station with.

Nothing is impossible.

But something is very, *very* wrong.

AURORA LEGION SQUADS

▶ **SQUAD MEMBERS**

 ▼ **BRAINS**

BRAINS ARE THE SCIENCE AND MEDICAL OFFICERS OF **AURORA LEGION (AL) SQUADS**. MOST ARE POSSESSED OF SCARILY HIGH IQs, OFFICIAL NERD SQUAD MEMBERSHIP CARDS, AND HAVE A TENDENCY TO RUN TOWARD DANGEROUS SITUATIONS ON THE GROUNDS THAT THEY "MIGHT BE INTERESTING."

BRAINS ARE RESPONSIBLE FOR TREATING INJURIES, PROVIDING THEIR **ALPHAS** WITH SCIENTIFIC INFORMATION ON THE FLY, AND, OCCASIONALLY, FIGURING OUT HOW TO **BLOW THINGS UP** WITH ONLY A TOOTHPICK AND A STICK OF GUM.

I DON'T WANT TO STEREOTYPE OR ANYTHING, BUT PEOPLE WITH THAT MANY BRAIN CELLS ARE SOMETIMES A LITTLE . . . **WEIRD**.

BRAIN'S INSIGNIA

26

KAL

"The other GIA agent was like this, too?" Tyler asks.

I nod affirmative. Remembering the way their bodies felt as I hit them. The sounds they made when they fell. Their flesh was . . . wrong under my hands. Fibrous. Wet. Bones bending like green saplings rather than breaking like dry wood.

"I have come to blows with many Terrans in my time at Aurora Academy," I say. "These operatives were not human."

"But they're GIA," Cat objects. "The highest arm of the Terran Defense Force's Intelligence Division."

"Then your Terran Defense Force may have problems," I reply.

I can feel Aurora sitting nearby. Her presence is like the light of the sun on my skin. I feel bathed in it, though I try to ignore it, focus on my Alpha's face and our predicament. But the pull of her is like gravity. A bottomless pool in which I would happily throw myself to drown.

"How does a two-hundred-and-sixty-year-old Octavia settler get into the GIA?" Aurora asks. I can hear the distress in her voice. She knew this woman. Perhaps even cared for her.

"Um, slightly more pressing question," Fin says, nodding at Auri. "As far as I know, Stowaway here is the only person to have survived a cryo period of more than a few decades. How is a two-hundred-and-sixty-year-old human even *alive*?"

"I do not believe she was."

We turn to Zila, who is looking at her uniglass.

"I did not have long to conduct tests," she continues. "But both these GIA agents showed signs of epidermal degradation consistent with early necrosis."

"You're saying they were dead before Kal got to them?" Tyler asks.

"I am saying they showed signs of it, yes."

"But they were walking and talking?"

"I cannot explain it. Perhaps these growths"—she waves at the silvery leaves sprouting from the agent's eye—"have something to do with it. Like Betraskan saski polyps or Terran nematomorphs."

Zila looks around an ocean of blank stares.

"Nematomorphs are parasites native to Earth," she explains. "They mature inside other organisms, then exert a chemical control over their host's brain. Urging the creature to drown itself in bodies of water where other nematomorphs breed."

"And you put on those uniforms anyway?" Cat asks, dumbfounded.

"I thoroughly irradiated the GIA garments first," Zila replies, unruffled.

"She *really* likes that disruptor," Finian mutters.

"I wish we could have brought one of the bodies aboard to study," Zila sighs.

"No thanks," Tyler replies, looking at the image on the display in horror. "The further away from those things we are, the better. Maybe it was some virus they picked up aboard the World Ship or something?"

"Doubtful," Zila says.

"Even if they did, how'd they live long enough to catch it there?" Fin asks.

Aurora is staring too, her eyes distant, perhaps lost in memories of this woman, this partner of her father, now become her enemy.

"Auri, do you recognize this man?" Scar pulls up the image of the second GIA operative I killed. He is like the first—those strange fronds sprouting from his eye, a cluster of bright flowers growing from his ear and through his hair, the right side of his face glazed with mossy growth. I can see a tracery of fine veins within the leaves scrawled across the man's cheeks. Dark as blood.

Aurora bites her lip. "Maybe? He might've been an engineer."

"Another Octavia colonist," I say.

"Who should've died two hundred years ago," Scar nods.

"He looks good for his age," Fin says. "All things considered."

The joke perishes in silence, but a part of me admires Finian for at least trying to lighten the mood. The bridge is quiet, save for the thrum of the engines, the hum of the consoles around us. Aurora is looking at the main display screen, the lifeless skin of these people she knew, the growths sprouting from their heads. I can feel the tremors in her body, feel the fear in her soul. I wish to reach out to her, to take some of it away. But I resist the Pull with all I have, try to keep the want from my voice as I speak to her.

"The Trigger." I nod to the statue in her hands. "Does it tell you anything?"

She simply shakes her head.

"We all just risked our tail sections for that little thing-amajig," Cat growls. "You're telling me it was for nothing?"

"I don't know. It feels . . . right. It's supposed to be here with me. But I don't know how to use it." Aurora shakes her head, looks up at Tyler. "Listen, why don't we just go to Octavia III and check the planet out? If these colonists—"

"We can't," Cat interrupts. "Interdiction, remember?"

"Correct," comes a digital voice from Aurora's belt. "The planet has been off-limits by order of the Terran government for several hundred years."

"Well, does anyone know why?" Aurora demands.

The device beeps. "According to records, explor-atory probes discovered an aggressive pathogen in the atmosphere of Octavia III. Galactic Inter-diction was invoked to stop the virus getting off-world."

"But it looks like it already has!" Aurora says, pointing to the screen.

"We should definitely report this to the authorities," Scar-lett says.

I nod to the GIA corpses up on the screen. "These people *are* your authorities."

"Well, whatever we do," Cat says, "we can't just charge off to bloody Octavia. The penalties for breaching Interdiction are scary bad."

"She means they kill you," the device offers. "Like, really painfully."

"Yes, thank you, Magellan," Aurora sighs.

"Hey, no problem," he replies. "I only mention it because you're sometimes not the brightest spark in th——"

"Silent mode," she says.

Aurora hangs her head, staring at the Trigger in her hands. I can see the struggle in her. She wants to know the truth about what became of her loved ones. The colony that supposedly never existed. But at the same time, she knows what this squad has already risked for her. The danger she's brought among us. And it seems she's unwilling to ask us to risk our lives for her again.

"Auri, do you remember the fight outside Bianchi's office?" Tyler asks. "What you did to the ultrasaur?"

"No," she whispers.

I feel the fear in her swell. I do not wish to accuse her of lying, but I suspect what she says is untrue. That perhaps part of her *does* remember. It's just that the rest of her does not wish to.

"Maybe this . . . power you have has something to do with the Trigger?" Tyler offers. "Can you try to——"

A soft alert sounds through the bridge, a series of warning lights flashing on the displays. Cat turns to her controls, and Tyler jumps behind his own station, his fingers flowing swiftly over the console.

"Something just pinged us with LADAR," Cat reports. "Got a reading. . . . Behind us, heading seven sixty A-12 gamma four."

"Main display," Tyler says.

Cat complies, pulling up visual of the craft that has tripped our proximity alarms. I feel the mood drop around the bridge as the image flickers to life.

I have lived among Terrans for two years now, but I still have difficulty processing how singularly *ugly* their ships are. Syldrathi vessels are moments of beauty frozen in titanium and time. They are our songs to the Void they sail inside— graceful patterns and gentle curves and smooth, shimmering skin.

The destroyer chasing us is crude by comparison, with a flat snout and all the blunt elegance of an object made purely for function. The Terran Defense Force logo is emblazoned on its dark hull. Its name painted in white.

"*Bellerophon*," Tyler says.

"We knew they were en route to the World Ship," Cat shrugs. "Looks like they finally caught up." Her voice is casual, her bluff as good as ever, but she knows what we all know. Princeps is aboard. The first among equals who pursues Aurora with such perfect single-mindedness.

"Hey, at least we can report to the authorities now . . . ," Fin says.

Our Alpha's voice is tense as he speaks.

"Cat, can we outrun them?"

Our Ace shakes her head. "They'll catch us over a long enough distance. A Longbow is slower than a destroyer, *and* they've got a lot more fuel. And not to harp on it, but we don't actually have a bloody heading. I'm just flying in a straight line here and trying to make it look fancy."

Scarlett nods, folding her arms. "And if we stay in the Fold too long without cryo, we're all going to start losing it."

"We need a course," Cat agrees.

All eyes turn to Aurora. She's looking at the Trigger in her hands, turning it this way and that, like a puzzle.

"I . . ." She shakes her head. "I don't know—"

BAMF!

The flash from a disruptor lights the bridge up white. Aurora is slapped backward by the blast, the Trigger rolling from her fingers onto the deck. In the space of a heartbeat, I am on my feet, overcome with sudden and impossible fury. Zila is standing in front of Aurora, weapon in hand, peering at the girl with unreadable eyes.

"Yeah, she *really* likes that thing," Fin says.

"Zila, are you *insane*?" Scarlett demands.

"I am testing a—"

Zila gets no further. I lash out with an Aen strike to her shoulder, numbing her arm and sending her weapon clattering to the floor.

Stop it.

But the Enemy Within is loose now. The sight of Aurora unconscious on the floor finally sets the beast free from his cage, howling in dark delight. The killing song fills my veins as I reach toward the fallen pistol. My pulse is screaming. My vision razor sharp. My finger closing on the trigger as I raise the weapon to Zila's head.

Stop. It.

Something hits me from behind, knocking the disruptor away. I roll to my feet, lashing out at my enemy, feeling my knuckles hit bone. I hear my father in my head then. Urging me on. I feel his hand on my shoulder, guiding my strike into Tyler's throat. I sense him laughing as my Alpha grunts, as his blood sprays and he staggers back, breathless. Cat hits me from my flank, but I twist free, blood on my knuckles, hands rising, heart hammering.

Stop.

The Enemy is all I am at that moment. The Pull setting him free. Even here in the Fold, my vision is red. I cannot breathe. Cannot think except to know that Aurora is hurt, she is unsafe, she who is my all, my everything, my—

"KAL, STOP IT!" Scarlett cries.

Stop.

It.

I close my eyes. Fighting with all I have. The Enemy is so strong. The Pull is so deep. So very loud. They would be hard enough to resist alone, but together, they are stronger than the forces that hold my cells together, that bind the universe into one. It is like nothing I have known. I cannot explain. Cannot rationalize it.

But I *must* master it.

There is no love in violence.

There is. No love. In violence.

And so, slowly, I open my eyes.

The bridge is in disarray. Tyler is rising from where he fell, blood on his chin. Cat is on the floor, holding her ribs. Zila is pressed back against the wall, staring at the chaos with wide eyes and sucking on one tight black curl of hair.

"It was set to Stun," she whispers.

"And we were all getting along so well, too," Fin smirks.

I am at Aurora's side. Everything I have tried to hide is now bubbling to the surface. The walls of ice that guard my feelings utterly shattered. My heart is thundering against my ribs.

She has been knocked unconscious by Zila's disruptor blast, her head lolling against the velocity couch, eyes closed as if sleeping.

But she is well, I realize.

All is well.

"Is everyone okay?" Tyler asks, his voice rasping from my blow to his throat.

Slow nods in response.

"Kal, you told me you had a handle on this!" he says, glaring at me.

"I am sorry," I say. I am aghast at what I have done. To have lost myself so completely. "I . . . I did not mean . . . I did not know the weapon was set to incapacitate. And seeing Aurora in danger . . ."

I shake my head. Trying to find the words. But how can I describe what it is to fly to those who have never even seen the sky?

"I am sorry," I say again, looking at Zila. "De'sai. I am shamed."

"Legionnaire Madran, explain yourself," Tyler demands, turning on the girl.

Zila blinks, takes a moment to focus. "It occurred to me that Aurora has mostly manifested hidden gifts when asleep or unconscious. I thought—"

"You thought *shooting her* without warning would be a good idea?"

"It was a calculated risk, sir," Zila says. "If I warned Aurora, the probability of a calamitous defensive reaction increased dramatically."

My squadmates exchange looks, unsure who poses the

greatest threat to them—Zila or myself. It may be inexcusable, but at least I have a *reason* for the violence of my reaction. Zila . . . It is as though she simply does not fit here. As if she is fundamentally incapable of understanding what is done and what should not be.

Tyler closes his eyes, rubs his temples.

"Zila, you're the smartest person on this ship," he says. "You might be one of the smartest people in the whole Legion. Do you know what your problem is?"

"I . . . would be happy to hear your feedback, sir," she replies.

"Your problem is that you know how everything works except other people."

She blinks at that.

I think I see tears gleaming in her eyes.

"I am—"

Cat curses and scrambles back as Aurora stands bolt upright. Her muscles are tense, her whole body rigid as steel. Her eyes are open, her right iris burning white. Her hair is blowing as if in a breeze, a faint nimbus of dark light tracing her body. This close to her, I can feel current crackling off her skin. Taste sodium on my tongue. Feel a force thrumming in the air and in my chest.

"Well, well." Finian raises one pale eyebrow at Zila. "You called it."

". . . Aurora?" I ask.

She stretches out her arms, rising slowly off the floor.

"Nnnu-u-uuh," she says.

"Auri, can you hear me?" Tyler asks, stepping forward.

The static pulses. I can feel the hair on my scalp rising.

The Longbow is shaking, the power flickering, a faint scream-ing building in the air. Aurora turns those burning, mis-matched eyes on Tyler, the light about her shimmering black.

Scarlett approaches slowly, apparently fearless, hands raised before her.

"Who are you?"

The ship trembles around us, the screaming grows louder and the light flares darker as Aurora struggles to speak.

"*N-nnnotwho,*" she replies. "*Whatn-nnnotwhonotw-w-who-WHAT.*"

"All right, *what* are you?" Scarlett asks.

"*Eshvarennnnnn-n-nn,*" she replies.

My pulse quickens at the word. The name of the Ancient Ones, extinguished hundreds of millennia ago. The first of us to find the Fold. The first of us to walk the stars. I look to Finian in triumph, watching the skepticism melt from his black eyes. Aurora tilts her head, and my heart lurches side-ways as blood begins to spill from her nose and dribble down her chin.

"What do you want?" Tyler demands, steadying himself as the ship shudders.

Aurora makes no reply. Turning to the cabin around her, she spies the Trigger, lying where it rolled beneath the main console. She reaches toward it and the statue trembles in re-ply, rising up from the floor seemingly of its own accord. Her eyes narrow, and she curls her fingers into a fist. Cracks ap-pear on the Trigger's surface, the sound of splintering metal echoing in the air.

I step forward, hand outstretched. We all risked our lives to attain that sculpture, we all—

360

"No!"

The Trigger shatters, shards of metal spraying across the bridge. A splinter cuts my cheek, another whistles past my throat, the screaming in my ears rising. And there, floating in the air before Aurora, is the diamond that once sat in the sculpture's chest. It is larger than I first thought—its bulk was mostly hidden, like an iceberg beneath an ocean's surface. It is glowing now, and its surface is carved with a complicated tracery of spirals.

Aurora beckons and the gemstone floats toward her, coming to rest in the palm of her small hand. As it touches her skin, a projection made of pure light fills the entire bridge. A kaleidoscope of tiny bright pinpricks, billions of them, whorls and spirals and patterns that any cadet at Aurora Academy would recognize.

"That's the Milky Way!" Cat shouts over the rising screams.

The entirety of our galaxy.

The gemstone shimmers, pulses. And out among that vast collection of glittering star systems, despite the monochrome of the Fold, dozens of suns turn to red. The only splash of color in the black and the white, crimson as human blood. The screaming in the air becomes almost deafening. I feel cold panic in my belly without quite knowing why. I can feel it among my squadmates too, the faint latticework of their minds crackling with instinctual terror. It is a primal sort of fear. The fear of the talaeni as the shadow of the drakkan's wings falls over its back.

The fear of prey.

I look at the projection, fighting the terror in my chest.

I see our galaxy laid out before us, all around us, spiraling around the tremendous black hole that lies at its storm-wracked heart.

An impossible sky, shimmering and pulsing with tiny red dots of illumination.

And I realize what it is we are looking at.

"It is a star map!" I shout over the screaming.

The galaxy begins to move. As if time were flowing forward. Swirling around that gleaming black heart, faster and faster. An endless spiral, billions of stars interacting and coalescing, flaring and dying.

The systems closer to the heart spin faster, overtaking the slower stars on the outskirts, flowing over and through them, the force of their passing sending out ripples into the starlight. A cosmic ballet. Hundreds of thousands of years in the blink of an eye. And the red begins to creep out from those few illuminated stars, the stain spreading like blood until the whole galaxy is drenched in crimson.

Aurora looks at me. Her white eye flickering with inner light, the blood now pouring down her chin and spattering on the deck beneath her. I feel the Pull roaring in my veins at the sight of her bleeding. The desire to protect her overwhelming all thought and reason. She points at the images on the central display. The GIA agents, their faces dead and overgrown.

"*Ra'haam*," she says.

"You are hurting her!" I say, stepping forward.

"*Gestalt*," the thing in Aurora replies, pointing at the crimson stain. "*Beware. Ra'haaaaaa-a-ammm.*"

"Release her!"

362

I reach out, grab her hand. I feel a cold so fierce it burns. I feel the deck drop away from my feet. I feel the vastness around me, how small I am, one tiny mote of animated carbon and water amid an ocean of infinity.

All that I have lived through. All that I have suffered. The destruction of my homeworld. The collapse of my culture. The mass murder of my people. My mother. My sister. My father. The war without and the Enemy Within.

All of it feels meaningless.

"Alllllll," Aurora says. *"Burrrrrrrn."*

Then she closes her eyes and collapses into my arms.

"Holy flaming nadsacks, is she all right?" Cat asks.

Zila rushes to Aurora's side, scanning her vitals with her uniglass. The Longbow has stopped shaking, that awful screaming cut off like someone snuffed out a lamp. Tyler and the others are staring at the remnants of the star map as it slowly fades from view, like spots on the back of your eyelids after you look at the sun.

"Heart rate is normal," Zila reports, and I sigh with relief. "Respiration normal. Everything is normal."

"Um." Scarlett raises her hand slowly. "I beg to differ."

"Seconded," Fin replies, his eyes wide.

Tyler's eyes are still fixed on the fading star map. That spreading stain has receded once more, leaving those original star systems still picked out in burning red in the black and white all around us.

He shakes his head, glances at me, then down to the girl in my arms.

"Take her to sickbay. Zila, go with him. Make sure Auri's all right."

I glance at Zila, but she seems composed again, despite our confrontation. And so I nod, lifting Aurora as gently as a sleeping babe. As we walk off the bridge and down the corridor toward the sickbay, I hear Scarlett's voice, soft behind me.

"What the *hells* does this all mean, Ty?"

But the door slides closed before our Alpha can answer.

And I am left inside the silence.

27

ZILA

I stand over Aurora's unconscious body, a med-scanner in hand. She is laid out on a bio-cot in sickbay, and I am reviewing her vitals. It is almost five minutes since I stunned her—she should be conscious any moment now.

"Is all well?" Kal says softly behind me.

"There is nothing of concern in her readings."

". . . I meant you, Zila."

My arm is still moderately numb from his nerve-strike, but there is no pain. I can only see concern in his eyes as I glance back at him. But that concern melts into relief as Aurora slowly stirs, raising one hand to her brow and moaning. I am forgotten as Kal takes a step forward, lips parted slightly, eyes on her.

"Wh-what hit me?" Aurora whispers.

"I will leave you alone," I hear myself say.

"Zila . . . ," Kal says as I turn toward the door. "I truly am sorry. I sought only to take the weapon from you."

"I understand," I lie.

My Alpha's words are ringing in my ears as the door slides shut behind me.

"Your problem is that you know how everything works except other people."

It's true, and it's not.

I learned too much about how humans work when I was six years old.

I know everything I need to.

But I still can't say I understand them.

28

KAL

I should have seen this coming.

Aurora opens her eyes, and the light catches her iris and turns it to glittering pearl, and the flood of relief in my chest escapes my lips as a soft sigh.

"Be'shmai . . ."

I help her to sit up on the bio-cot, watch her blink away the grogginess from Zila's disruptor blast. The thought that she is safe entinguishes the fire that consumed me on the bridge. The mere sight of her is water in an endless desert, if I must speak the truth. But I have never felt so torn in all of my life. Because this cannot go on.

"What do you remember?" I ask her.

I watch, almost hypnotized as a small frown creases her brow.

"Zila . . . shot me."

"She intended no harm," I say. "She wished only to awake that which is within you."

Aurora looks up at me, and my heart beats a touch quicker as our eyes meet.

"Eshvaren," she whispers.

"The Ancients," I nod. "Somehow they are involved in *all* of this. And you are part of it, Aurora."

"This is insane." She closes her eyes, rubs her temples as if pained. "I could see the whole thing. Even though I was out cold. It was like . . . like I was outside my body. Watching it on a vidscreen. Zila blasting me, and you . . ."

Our eyes meet again, and my heart sinks. I expect a rebuke. A righteous admonishment for the violence I set free among my squadmates. I can feel the Enemy Within, coiled inside my chest. The shadow of my father at my back.

". . . You defended me," she says.

I blink. Shake my head. "No. I shamed myself."

She looks at me then. Up and down, from my boots to my eyes.

"I don't *get* you, Legolas," she sighs. "I don't understand you at all. One minute you're calling me a liability or ignoring me entirely. The next you're blasting your way through a TDF destroyer to break me out of prison or punching face with your own squad to protect me."

She sighs and shakes her head.

"What is your *deal*?"

I draw a deep breath, hesitating before I let myself fall. I know once I speak these words, there can be no taking them back. But I should never have let it get this far. And I cannot do this anymore.

"It is past time I spoke to you of this. Why I behave the way I do around you."

"You mean why you act like a total jackass?" she asks.

Despite the pain in my chest, I feel a small smile curling my lips as I search for the right words. For a way to make any part of this make any sort of sense.

"There is a gravity to everything, Aurora," I finally say. "Not just planets. Not just stars. Every cell in our bodies, every cell in creation exerts a gravity on the objects and people around it. And . . . that is what I am feeling. For you."

She frowns slightly, eyes glittering under the warm lights. For a second, she looks so beautiful, my breath is stolen clean away. But still, I lunge to catch it. Because if I do not say this now, I fear I never will.

"Syldrathi call it the Pull," I say. "It is an instinctual . . . attraction we feel. A bond that is elemental. Primal. Just like gravity. I have never heard of one of my people being Pulled to a human before. But . . . I feel it for you, Aurora."

She opens her mouth as if to speak, but my words are a flood now.

"I did not wish the others to know. And you had troubles enough without me compounding them. I thought that because you had seen me before you met me . . . we might be . . . fated, or some such." I shake my head, feeling an utter fool. "And so I tried to keep you out of danger without letting you know what was happening. I did not wish to place you under some sense of obligation."

"What . . . what obligation might it place? If I were Syldrathi?"

A long silence falls between us.

"The Pull is the bond between lifeloves," I finally say. "Mates."

She swallows. Clearly lost for words.

"I should not have let it come to this," I sigh. "I should never have put a human in this position. It is not fair to you, nor the others. And you should not have to make this choice."

I breathe deep again, nod to myself. Fighting off the rush

369

of anguish. Feeling the rip widening inside my chest until it is so dark and deep I know I might never find my way out again.

But it is better this way.

"I cannot help the way I feel for you," I say. "But I *can* control what I do about it. So once we discover the truth behind this Trigger, the star map, I will resign my position in the squad. I have ignored the war among my people for too long. I can stand apart from it no longer. Once we reach the end of this road, you will not have to see me again."

The silence between us is as wide and cold as the Void. For a moment, I cannot imagine an end to it. But my uniglass pings in the quiet, filling that edgeless gulf and breaking the spell between us.

"Kal?" comes Tyler's voice. *"Do you read?"*

I touch the device at my belt. "I copy."

"Zila says Auri's awake?"

I look into those mismatched eyes, feel the pain cutting through my heart like a blade. "She is awake."

"I think you two better come up and see this."

". . . We are on our way."

I touch the uniglass again, cutting off the transmission. Staring at the girl sitting opposite me, centuries and light-years away from anywhere and anything she expected to be. Tasting blood and ashes in my mouth.

What can you say when there are no words for what you're feeling?

What can you do when there is nothing left to be done?

"We should go," I say.

And without a word, she slips off the bio-cot and marches out the door.

29

CAT

I'm at work on the navcom when O'Malley and Pixieboy walk back onto the bridge. She looks like ten klicks of rough road, and he looks like someone murdered his puppy and left the head in his bed. But truth be told, we got bigger problems than Feels right now. The *Bellerophon* is still closing on us, and after what we've just discovered . . .

"Auri, are you okay?" Scarlett asks, obviously rating Feels a little higher than me. She's good like that.

O'Malley glances at Pixieboy, and I can see the lie in her eyes before she speaks it. "I'm okay."

"Cat, show them," Ty says.

"Roger that."

With a flick of my wrist, I throw my navcom visuals up onto the main holographic display. O'Malley stares at the revolving spiral of glittering stars.

"What am I looking at?" she asks.

"The map inside your Trigger highlighted twenty-two stars in total," I say. "I've plotted those systems onto the known segments of the galaxy."

"Took her a while," Finian says. "She couldn't tell just by looking at them."

"There's around two hundred billion stars in the Milky Way, Skinnyboy. I don't have all of 'em memorized."

He sniffs. "I thought you were supposed to be good at this."

"Shut up, Finian." My fingers fly over the controls, and twenty-two tiny points of red flare out among those billions of suns. "Most of the systems highlighted on the map are unexplored. And a lot are a deep trek from here, even Folding. But it turns out every one of them sits on a known weak spot in the Fold."

"They all have naturally occurring gates?" Pixieboy asks.

"Looks like, yeah." I tap another series of commands. "And you're never going to guess the closest system to our current coordinates."

Kal raises his eyebrow in question, and I throw the answer up onto the main display, where the visuals of our creepy-as-hells plant people used to be. A holographic rendering of a star floats above our consoles, burning bright. It's orbited by seven planets, the third world sitting inside the Goldilocks zone. The system's name is highlighted in glowing letters beneath it.

"Octavia," Aurora whispers.

I glance at Ty, then across to Scarlett. At every member of this jank squad on this jank mission that we spent five years at the academy prepping for. We all know this can't be coincidence. The official records point us toward Lei Gong, but those GIA agents with the funky plant crap all over their faces were former Octavia III colonists, according to O'Malley. She said her ship, the *Hadfield,* was bound for Octavia III when it disappeared two hundred years ago. And now, whatever else this million-year-old map is for, it's leading us straight back to that same bloody planet.

"So riddle me this, legionnaires," Tyler says. "Say you're the GIA and there's a system you don't want people visiting. And say you can't just lock its gate down because it's at a naturally occurring Fold spot. How do you keep folks from poking their nose in?"

"Maybe you make up a story about some deadly atmospheric virus," Scarlett murmurs.

"Maybe it's no story," I remind them. "Zila said those colonists in the GIA uniforms were dead before Kal got to them. Maybe they were infected with the virus this Interdiction is warning us about."

"So why change the records to point toward Lei Gong?" O'Malley asks. "Why delete any record of the Octavia colony existing? Why chase down the last person with any remaining link to the place?"

Tyler folds his arms across his broad chest. "I don't know about anyone else, but I'm getting the feeling there's something on Octavia that the GIA doesn't want us to see. Or more importantly, something they don't want Auri to see."

"Ra'haam," Zila murmurs.

Kal nods. "Beware."

I don't like where this is all heading. Government conspiracies and cover-ups and Maker knows what else. But we've got bigger problems.

"*Bellerophon* is within comms distance," Scar reports. "They're hailing us."

"Main display," Tyler orders.

The image of the Octavia system dissolves, replaced with a figure in a white suit, white shirt, white gloves. The winged crest of the Terran Defense Force is embossed on the wall behind it. Its face is a featureless white mirrormask.

"Good morning, Princeps," Tyler says.

"*LEGIONNAIRE JONES,*" the figure replies. "*YOU ARE RESPONSIBLE FOR THE MURDER OF GLOBAL INTELLIGENCE AGENCY PERSONNEL, AIDING AND ABETTING A WANTED FUGITIVE AND VIOLATION OF COUNTLESS AURORA LEGION REGULATIONS.*"

"It's been a funny couple of days," Tyler agrees.

"*YOU MAY FIND YOURSELF LESS GLIB ONCE INCARCERATED AT LUNAR PENAL COLONY,*" the G-man replies. "*YOU ARE HEREBY ORDERED TO POWER DOWN YOUR ENGINES AND MAINTAIN POSITION TO AWAIT OUR BOARDING PARTY.*"

"And if I refuse?"

"*WE WILL DESTROY YOUR VESSEL,*" Princeps says.

"I'm sorry," Tyler says, shaking his head. "But with all due respect, I don't believe you. I'm afraid you're just going to have to follow us to the Octavia system."

Princeps raises its voice for the first time since we've met it. "*THAT SYSTEM IS UNDER GALACTIC INTERDICTION BY ORDER OF THE TERRAN GOVERNMENT!*"

"Exciting, right?"

"*YOU WILL—*"

Tyler makes a cutting motion across his throat and I kill the signal, reverting the image back to the Octavia system. The whole bridge is quiet except for the thrum of the engines. Scarlett has her eyebrow raised at her baby brother, and I can't help but stare, too. In all the years I've known him, I've never seen Tyler buck authority. Not once. But in the last couple of days, he's gone from star academy pupil to wanted interstellar fugitive.

And Maker help us, I think he's getting a taste for it.

"Hell of a gamble, Bee-bro," Scar says.

"Not really," he says. "From the beginning, the GIA has been about capturing Auri. They were willing to kill any-one who knew she was in their custody. And *this* is what it's all about." He gestures to the display. "There's obviously something at Octavia that the GIA doesn't want us to see. And whatever it is, it's connected to Auri's new abilities. Her trances led us to the Trigger, and the Trigger is leading us to Octavia. Now, I don't know if Battle Leader de Stoy and Admiral Adams knew it'd come to this, but I believe we were meant to be here. I believe there's something way bigger go-ing on than any of us realize."

He glances around the bridge at all of us.

"But we're stepping over the edge here. I won't blame any of you if you want out. We're fugitives from the Terran gov-ernment now. But if we cross a Galactic Interdiction line, we're going to be wanted by every government everywhere."

Tyler's right, and everyone knows it. Galactic Interdiction is the hardest of hard-core codes. It's only used on the most dangerous sectors in the galaxy—systems ravaged by out-breaks or infestations that present an imminent threat to the rest of galactic civilization. The Lysergia plague. Selmis pox. Temporal storms. You don't mess around with systems under GI. You break it, they don't court-martial you. They vaporize you on sight and try not to get any on their shoes.

Tyler looks us all in the eyes. "Anyone who wants to leave, head down to Level three, hit the escape pod, and abandon ship. No hard feelings."

Scarlett puts her hand on her hip. "You're kidding, right?"

"I mean it, Scar. We don't know what we're going to find once we get to Octavia. This isn't what any of us signed up for."

She walks across the deck, places both hands on Tyler's shoulders, turns his chair to face her. This close, even though they're not identical, I can see how alike they are. The unshakable bond between them. Deeper than blood.

Leaning down, Scarlett kisses her brother's cheek.

"I signed up for *you*, dummy."

"An Ace backs her Alpha," I say.

I meet Tyler's eyes as he looks up at me.

"Always," he replies.

I smile in return. "Always."

"I am not normal," Zila says into the quiet that follows.

We look at her. Her eyes are downturned, and she's toying with the gold hoops in her ears. I realize they've got tiny pizza slices on them. Her curls are a dark curtain around her face, her voice a murmur.

"Zila?" Scar asks.

"The only places I fit are the places inside my head," she continues. "It is as you said, sir. I do not understand people." She looks around the bridge. "But I believe of all the places I have not fit, I fit here a little better."

Scar smiles. "Who wants to be normal when you can be interesting instead?"

Zila looks at Scar and nods. "I will stay."

Kal speaks up from his place by the weapons console. His knuckles are scabbed, his eyes burning as he looks to O'Malley.

"I will stay until the end of this road."

"Well, good luck with that," Finian says. "But speaking personally, breaking Galactic Interdiction is where this particular Betraskan draws the line. I'm not about to make an enemy out of every government in the galaxy for the sake of a two-hundred-year-old telekinetic dirtchild who starts tossing us around like kebar balls every time someone clobbers her on the brainthing. But have fun with the suicide mission, kids!"

We're all a little stunned, I think. The whole squad watches as Finian twirls once in his seat, stands up, and starts slowly limping toward the doors, his exosuit whining. I can't blame him, really. He's Betraskan, after all, and the trouble we're in only goes as far as Terra. If he follows the smart money and cuts ties now, he might even be able to—

Finian turns back to face us, points right at me.

"Had you going, didn't I?"

". . . What?"

He breaks into a broad shit-eating grin. "Admit it. All of you. You thought I was actually going to eject, didn't you?"

Finding myself grinning, too, I pick up Shamrock and hurtle him across the bridge. Fin doesn't try to catch him, and the toy bounces off his chest and hits the deck.

"You're an asshole, Finian," Scarlett sighs.

"Yeah," he replies. "But I'm *your* asshole."

He makes a face.

"Wait, no, that didn't come out right. Ew. Sorry. Terran as a second language and all . . ."

Tyler grins, looks around the bridge at Squad 312. Most of us have only known each other for a handful of days. We've already been through the wringer together. We're maybe about to go through hell. But the truth is, despite everything, there's no one else in the 'Way I'd want leading me.

"Lock in a course for the Octavia system, Zero."

I give him a salute, then give him a smile.

"Sir, yessir."

· · · · ·

We're almost at the Octavia FoldGate when *Bellerophon* starts shooting at us.

Princeps has been trying to get us on comms for the last hour, but Ty ordered Scarlett to ignore the hails. It's noisy enough in here without adding dire warnings from the GIA into the mix. Our systems have been wailing for twenty minutes, the local beacon alerting us that we're approaching a system under Galactic Interdiction, that entry to the Octavia system is "extremely hazardous," may result in "catastrophic consequences," and "constitutes a violation of galactic law, as outlined by the Treaty of Verduum IV and cosigned by blah blah blah blah."

I'm starting to hate life.

And then a missile gets thrown our way and I remember why I like it so much.

Everyone's changed out of their party clothes and into uniform again, so at least we're dressed for it. I deploy our decoys, warning everyone to hold on as I lay on the burn and go hard evasive. Our screens flare as the missile explodes behind us, lighting up the Fold a pure and burning white.

"Was that a nuke?" Scarlett asks, eyes wide.

"It sure wasn't a pocket full of posies," I reply.

"That poem is about the black death," Zila says. "A pocket full of posies was supposed to ward off the—"

"Yes, thank you, little Legionnaire Sunshine," Finian says. "But morbid Terran poetry aside, I do believe your fellow dirtchildren are trying to kill us and I thought our fearless leader said they *didn't want to do that!*"

Tyler is looking at his scopes in disbelief. "I didn't think they did?"

"Didn't *think*? I thought you were meant to be a tactical genius!"

Ty raises his scarred eyebrow. "Finian, I hate to shatter your opinion of me, but this is probably as good a point as any to confess—"

"Hold on!" I roar.

Another three missiles are speeding our way along with a burst of fire from the *Bellerophon's* railgun batteries. I lean hard on the controls, throwing up another round of decoys. I weave through the firestorm, feeling the engine purr underneath me, fingers flowing over the controls, fast as thought. The blasts are thousands of kilometers wide, scorching the Fold as they blossom outward. But our Longbow is quicker, twirling and spinning through the railgun storm, the rounds streaking soundlessly past her skin as she comes out the other side without a scratch on her.

"These bastards mean biz," I growl.

"How long till we hit the Octavia FoldGate?" Tyler demands.

"Entry in four minutes thirty-one seconds."

"Can you hold them off till then?"

I look up at him and wink. "They didn't name me Zero for nothing."

We can see it in front of us now. Instead of the hexagonal titanium gates we Terrans use, or the teardrop-shaped crystal portals of the Syldrathi, this one is totally natural. It looks like a glimmering rend in the fabric of the Fold—as if torn by the claws of some impossible animal. It's tens of thousands of kilometers across, edges rippling with quantum lightning. The view over its horizon shimmers like a mirage in a desert. And through that unthinkable tear in the universe's skin, we can see faint glimpses of the Octavia star, burning red in a colored sea of realspace.

Bellerophon is pouring on the railgun fire now. Any lingering question as to whether they actually want to kill us is answered as a dozen shells shear right past our port wing, missing us by less than a hundred meters.

"Great Maker, that was close," Finian breathes.

"Shut up," I growl. "I've got it under control. Realspace entry in sixty seconds."

A railgun round crashes into our backside, tearing a football-sized hole in the hull. Alarms shriek, and the auto-containment systems kick in, locking off the breached deck. I glance at the damage report, realize we've taken a hit to Engineering.

Not good.

"I thought you had it under control!" Finian shouts over the alerts.

"I thought I told you to shut up!"

Kal smiles, his eyes alight, totally at home in the chaos of battle. It's the most relaxed I've seen him since we met. "You are not much of a warrior, are you, Finian?"

"Well, you're not much of a . . ." The Betraskan blinks those big black eyes as he comes up short. "Wait, wait, honestly, I had something really good for this yesterday. . . ."

Another depleted uranium round slices within three meters of our starboard flank. Hard as I'm flying, fast as I'm burning, there's too many guns lighting us up. Longbows aren't built to take on capital ships; it's like throwing a terrier into a fight with a Doberman. Sure, the terrier might put up a show, but in the end, fast and angry as she gets, the little dog's gonna end up on the bigger dog's toothpick.

"Realspace entry, fifteen seconds!"

"Everyone hold on!" Tyler shouts.

The tear looms in front of us, filling our display. I can feel the pull of it now, crawling over my body and stretching out my skin. Our alarms are blaring about the Interdiction, our hull breach in Engineering, the incoming fire from *Bellerophon*. There's a lurching in my stomach, a deafening silence as the whole galaxy flips on its head. And then, with the scream of engines and the bone-jarring impact of reality hitting home, we're through, out into the welcoming colorscape of realspace.

Good news is, we made it in one piece.

Bad news is, *Bellerophon* is still right behind us.

She rips out of the Fold like a bat out of hell, releasing another salvo of nukes. Whatever their earlier plans for getting hold of O'Malley were, it looks like they've decided to cut their losses and just flatline us, and the weird thing is, I've got no bloody idea why—on my scopes, Octavia seems like a perfectly normal system. There's nothing I can see that they'd want to hide or protect at all costs—even at the cost of giving up on taking Aurora.

As we close in on it, I can see that Octavia III is a completely run-of-the-mill M-class rock. A speck of blue-green land masses and blue-green water. Seventy-four percent ocean. Balmy temperatures, four major continents. In other words . . . boring.

So what the hells about it didn't they want us to—

"Sir," Zila glances up from her instruments, first to Aurora, then to Tyler.

"What is it, legionnaire?" Ty asks.

With a flick of her wrist, Zila throws a scanner sweep of the continent below up onto the main display. And there, nestled in a lush valley beside a ribbon of glittering water, are thirty or forty *buildings*.

"That's Butler," Aurora whispers. "The first settlement of the Octavia colony."

So, it's true. There *was* a settlement here. People lived on this planet. Families. Kids. Something went wrong, and for the past two centuries, the highest branch of the Terran Defense Force's Intelligence Division has been covering it up.

"Lying bastards," I whisper.

I look to the image of the *Bellerophon* behind us, then to Tyler, waiting for orders. His gamble that the GIA wouldn't be willing to kill us hasn't paid off, and now we're left with the unpleasant realities of trying to run from a ship we can't outrun, or fighting a ship we can't outfight. We're close to Octavia III, but the *Bellerophon's* missile systems have us locked; their railguns are ready for another burst. We're leaking power, too—looks like that hit to Engineering damaged our reactor core. And good as I am, I honestly don't know if I'm gonna be good enough to win this for him.

"*Bellerophon* is hailing us again," Scarlett reports.

Tyler sighs, looking around the bridge. I can see it in his eyes: his fear for his people, his disappointment in himself. We're so close to Octavia III now, I can see the swirls of cloud in the atmosphere, the jagged shapes of the continents beneath. Aurora is on her feet, looking at the image of the colony on the central display. This place where she was supposed to spend the rest of her life.

We almost made it. We almost brought her home. But in the end, maybe all Tyler's faith was misplaced? Maybe this trip is finally over?

"Open a channel," he orders Scarlett.

The image of Princeps appears on our central display, its white mirrormask featureless, its voice dead and metallic.

"LEGIONNAIRE JONES," the G-man says. "THIS IS YOUR FINAL WARNING. IF YOU DO NOT POWER DOWN YOUR ENGINES IMMEDIATELY, YOU WILL BE—"

The sound of an explosion cuts over the transmission, the feed momentarily dissolving into static. An alarm blares on the *Bellerophon*'s bridge, another on ours. I look at my scopes, try to make sense of what I'm seeing.

"Cat, report!" Ty barks.

"*Bellerophon* is . . . under attack?"

"From who?"

I shake my head. "I've got half a dozen energy sigs out there, but I'm getting almost no profile off LADAR. Scanners can barely see them."

"Visual?"

Pulling up a display of the *Bellerophon,* I can see she's been hit bad in her portside engines, and she's leaking coolant into space. Swarming around her, barely visible against the darkness, are a dozen slender, crescent-shaped ships. They're totally black, their pilots keeping them angled with minimal profile, so there's virtually no surface area to generate a LADAR hit. They've struck with surprise, and they've struck hard; their plasma cannons are melting the destroyer's hull to vapor. And I can't figure out if we've just been saved by a last-minute miracle, or if we're in deeper crap than we were a minute ago.

"Those are Chellerian stealth frigates," Kal says.

Princeps's voice rings out over the open comms channel. *"ATTENTION, UNIDENTIFIED CHELLERIAN VESSELS. YOU ARE FIRING ON A TERRAN DEFENSE FORCE VESSEL UNDER COMMAND OF THE GLOBAL INTELLIGENCE AGEN—"*

"I know damn well who I'm shooting at, hoo-maaan," comes the growling reply as the terrifying face of the sector's most infamous crime lord materializes on the display. *"You GIA shraakz sold me out, and nobody stabs Casseldon Bianchi in the back and lives to talk about it."*

"Looks like someone wants his Trigger back," Scarlett breathes.

"Um." Finian glances at Aurora. "Someone want to tell him we broke it?"

We've hit the gravity well of Octavia III now, the coolant leaking from the *Bellerophon's* port engines slowly spiraling down into the planet's upper atmo.

The Chellerian ships are moving quick as hummingbirds,

flitting through the destroyer's railgun fire and blasting away at the bigger ship, like a swarm of ants on an elephant. I watch as the *Bellerophon* launches her fighters, the smaller ships streaming out from its bay doors. Most of the destroyer's birds turn to combat the smaller Chellerian ships, but at least half a dozen of them turn and zero in on us.

Our power levels are dropping quick, but this is where I live. I turn our Longbow to face the incoming fighters, weaving through their streams of fire like thread through a needle's eye. All the years of training, all the instinct, all the rhythm pulsing in my veins flow to the surface. I can't feel my hands as they skim the controls. Can't feel my body as the ship rolls and twists beneath me.

I sling us down and out of Octavia III's gravity well, picking up an extra burst of speed. Kal has manned the secondary weapons array, and between us, we carve a swath of fire through the TDF birds. Elation surges through me, watching the hunter become the hunted. Watching the Chellerians and the *Bellerophon* cutting each other to pieces. Watching the flashes of blue flame and shrapnel as we shoot down the fighters on our tails, one by one.

And then I remember my mum was a TDF pilot.

And I realize there are real people inside those fighters.

I've never shot down a living person before today. All the hours, all the training, the cockpit where I earned my nickname—all of that was just a sim. These are *real people* out here. Terrans, fighting for what they believe in.

Just like me.

The engine's getting sluggish. The power drain from our damage is reaching the redline. And thinking about the people inside those cockpits, I'm getting sloppy. *Bellerophon* is on fire, oxygen pouring out of its melted hull and burning in the black. The Chellerians have been torn to ribbons too, pieces of those sleek black stealth ships glittering like shards of broken glass as they tumble away into space.

A flash of nuclear fire ignites Octavia III's upper atmosphere—a desperate stab from the dying *Bellerophon*. Bianchi's roaring over comms as his vessel gets caught in the blast. I see the fireball, watch the electromagnetic shock wave travel toward us.

I try to pull us up, but the engines don't have the kick I need anymore—my girl's too wounded to fly as fast as I need her to. The EMP burst hits us, a wave of light and sound, the instrumentation in front of me lighting up in a hail of sparks.

I'm thrown sideways in my harness. Hear Fin cry out. Alarms are screaming. Temperature's rising. We've hit atmo, our ship skipping across it like a stone skimmed along the water. I try to fight the drag, pulling back with everything I've got. But we're hemorrhaging too much power.

We've taken too much damage.

"We're going in!"

Search not found: Ra'haam

Your search didn't return any results, boss. I couldn't find a thing. How embarrassing.

Suggestions:

Make sure all words are spelled correctly.

Try different keywords.

Try more general keywords.

Turn me off and turn me back on again.

30

FINIAN

"Ty, boost the stabilizers! Squad, brace, and prayers if you got 'em!"

Cat's covering her console like she's one of our four-armed Chellerian friends up above: hands everywhere at once, flicking switches and dancing across buttons, trying to coax a little more lift out of our wounded steed.

"Everyone strap in," Ty commands. Aurora buckles herself onto a spare velocity couch at the back of the cabin, and all around me my squadmates deploy their restraints. "Ready for impact."

The whole Longbow shudders, tilting to the right with a scream of protest, and Zila crashes into the far wall before she can get to her seat. None of us can so much as lift a hand to help her out, and Cat keeps on rapping out orders. Golden-boy's our Alpha in the field, but he's trained to back her up at times like this, and that handsome face is all business.

"Stabilizers deployed," he reports.

"Doesn't feel like it!" Cat shouts as the whole craft shudders again, shaking like we're on a bumpy road. If that road was a screamingly steep descent that ended in a drop off a cliff.

Maker's bits, we're going to die.

"I'm telling you, they're deployed!" Ty reports again as Zila manages to grab her chair and throw herself into it, one hand smacking the harness button so the straps snake over her shoulders and into place.

"There are atmo pockets everywhere," Cat growls. We hit another bout of turbulence, and there's an insistent buzzing at my wrists as my exosuit tries to warn me to stop switching gravity levels so fast it can't keep up.

"Pursuit?" Ty asks as blue sky whirls past the front screen, and we're treated to a snatch of the continent below for an instant. It's a lot closer than it was before.

"Not yet!" she shouts above the proximity alarms and Interdiction warnings. "Stand by with the APU, we'll be dead-stick if the fuel gets any—"

It happens before she finishes the sentence. The power flickers and vanishes, every light across the board going black, the sirens and warnings all around us dying in a breath. And now we *really* know what life's like without the stabilizers.

Ty's lips are moving silently as he fires up the auxiliary power unit, and despite his stony pretty-boy facade, I think I hear Kal whisper something as well. My wrists have stopped vibrating their protests, my exosuit finally happy that I'm in consistent gravity, but it's pinned-to-my-seat-by-an-uncontrolled-descent gravity. And it might be the last kind my suit ever compensates for.

Everyone's silent, every face mirroring the same kind of

grim. Nobody willing to do the slightest thing that might distract Cat and Ty from their work.

"APU engaged," our Alpha reports. "Spooling up."

"Confirmed," Cat says as the lights on the dashboard flicker back to life. "APU at one hundred percent, mark."

And now we have a clock. The Longbow's too damaged to run her engines, too sick to power herself home, but the auxiliary power unit will give us a few moments of minor assist. Enough that our pilot will have basic instrumentation, a steering boost.

Enough, just maybe—if you're Zero—to do this.

"Touchdown one-fifteen seconds!" she reports, and I want to close my eyes, I want to appeal to my Maker, I want to haul up my faith front and center and demand some kind of payback for all those years of devotion so far.

But it doesn't work like that, and anyway, I can't close my eyes. The horizon flickers into view again, and I see a rolling blue-green ocean, a coastline, the mirror gleam of a river as it rushes by.

"Auxiliary power at seventy percent," Ty reports, low and tense. He's done everything he can now, and like the rest of us, he's watching his Ace as she tries to wrestle the Longbow into a controlled descent.

"Touchdown sixty seconds," she replies.

Will the power last until we reach the ground?

Or cut out a few seconds before?

I tear my gaze away from the view to look around at my squad. Auri looks like she's trying not to throw up, and Kal's watching her, violet eyes full of concern. Zila's got her head tilted slightly to the side like she's calculating our current odds of survival and needs to concentrate on carrying the one. Scarlett's watching Cat, her lips silently moving, though I doubt it's a prayer.

"Auxiliary down to forty percent," our Alpha reports, soft now.

"Forty-five seconds to touchdown."

I can see the trees, blue-green leaves swaying as the wind travels across their tops like a wave. They ripple like water, and in my head the Longbow's a pebble, tossed out to skip across their surface, bouncing over and over.

"Fifteen seconds."

"Thirteen percent."

"IF I MAY VENTURE AN OPINION—"

Seven voices scream at once. "Silent mode!"

"All crew brace!" Cat shouts, not even blinking, her whole body thrown into the effort of wrestling the ship toward a long strip of pale beach and dark stone ahead of us.

The Longbow screams as we whip across the rocks with a staccato series of crashes, gouging our hull as we pass.

Nobody's counting now, but the numbers are dropping in my head.

Seven. Six. Five.

All the lights on the control panel go out, and Cat curses, pushing the yoke away with trembling arms.

Four. Three. Two.

We slam into the sand, lift off again, crash down, then skid uncontrollably. The whole ship's shaking so hard I can barely breathe, the noise is deafening, our belly skipping along the waterline. The Longbow hits something hard, and we're yanked around in a half circle until we finally come to a halt. I can see the path we've carved through the beach behind us, and so will anyone else overhead. It's the largest YOU ARE HERE arrow we could possibly ask for.

But we're alive.

The silence is broken only by the soft pings of our cooling hull. I'm heaving for breath, a dozen silent alarms all over my suit informing me that I'm under extreme physical duress—*thanks, I hadn't noticed*—and nobody speaks. Slowly, Tyler and Cat swivel around to take a look at the rest of us and confirm we're all in one piece.

"Well," I say, trying to keep my voice steady. "I don't want to be a downer, but I don't think we're getting our deposit back on this thing."

Scarlett's the first to laugh, unbuckling with shaky hands and doubling over to brace her elbows against her knees, her head in her hands. And one by one the others follow, unbuckling, rising from their chairs, standing, stretching, shaking.

I stay where I am for now, because I'm waiting for enough motor control to raise my hand and hit the release button in the middle of my chest, but nobody seems to realize it's not a choice.

"Do we have any power left?" Goldenboy asks, not sounding that hopeful.

"Not even enough to run my favorite toy," Cat says, running a hand over her console. "And that thing gets amazing battery life."

He shoots her a grin, reaching across to squeeze her shoulder. "That was something, Cat. That was . . . that was *flying*."

She smiles in reply, letting out a shaky breath. "They do

say you should try everything once. But that was my once. Never again."

Everyone laughs for that—we're all too ready to laugh at anything, too jittery still. But Tyler's already getting back to work.

"Zila, pull out the biosuits and distribute them. I don't want anyone breathing one molecule of air without protection. Kal, break out the heavy weapons. We don't have scopes, so we'll have to keep watch for pursuers the old-fashioned way. And we'll need to look over the Longbow, figure out what she needs to get her space-worthy again."

Aurora is standing now, staring at the displays of the world waiting for us outside. Her eyes are wide, her face pale.

Zila hands out the suits, and Kal and Ty and the others start to wriggle into theirs. But Scar rests her hip against the central console in front of me, no doubt noticing I'm still exactly where I was when we landed. With a wink, she leans forward to press my release clasp, and the restraints slither back over my shoulders to retract inside my seat.

"You always could press my buttons," I tell her, and I sound pretty damn close to myself. But she's a brilliant Face, as good at her job as her brother is as an Alpha. Of *course* she was the one who noticed something was off with me.

"Need a hand getting into your biohazard gear?" she asks.

"What, now you're trying to get me to put even *more* clothes on? I'm going backward here."

"It's no trouble," she says, lowering her voice to keep the conversation between the two of us. "How's your exosuit?"

Truth is, it's sluggish, reacting slower to my movements than it should be. The EMP that knocked out our Longbow

393

systems hit my suit, too. It's shielded against that kind of thing, but apparently not perfectly—I've never exposed it to a nuclear explosion in space before. And no way do we have the time for me to spend several hours servicing it.

"It's good," I insist.

"Fin?" She's not buying it, but the question's still gentle. And that's what slugs me in the guts. I don't want it from her, of all people. If she looks like she's sorry for me, like she wants to say something to make me feel better, I'll . . .

But when I look up, her blue eyes don't hold the pity I'm expecting. There's nothing there except a touch of worry. And I think that's why I speak, keeping my voice as low as hers. Saying something I've never said out loud.

"Scarlett, I don't want to be the guy who needs help. Every time I've shown what others think is weakness, I've paid the price for it. Full gravity's hard? Send me away from Trask, from my friends and family. Need low grav at night to give me a rest? Stick me in academy quarters on my own, no roomie like everyone else. Suit malfunctions? Your brother'll keep me out of the action, put all of you in danger. And you never get back what you lose, once they see it. So please, don't make a big deal out of it. And if you could hold off your customary scarcasm, that'd be great too."

Scarlett quirks one sculpted eyebrow. "*Scarcasm?*"

"Yeah, fits, right? I thought that one up last night."

Great Maker, Finian, did you just let her know you were thinking about her last night . . . ?

"Nobody here is going to think less of you if you accept help, Fin," she says.

"Easy for you to say," I reply, waving at my exosuit. "There's a reason I got picked last out of every Gearhead in the Draft."

Ever so slowly, Scar pouts. "Finian?"

". . . Yeah?"

"Do you ever wonder if the reason you were picked last might not be the suit?" She pins me with her eyes. "I'm not saying people don't notice it. I'm just saying that maybe . . . just *maybe*, you got picked last because you spend all your time convincing the galaxy you're an insufferable asshole?"

I don't know how to reply to that. Knocked all the way back on my heels.

"It's okay, Fin," she says quietly. "Your family seals your den, right?"

And I know, in that moment, that she's figured me out. A Betraskan wants a group to be a part of—needs one on a deep, instinctive level. It's not just cultural for us, it's a part of our very DNA. Much as I pretend, we don't like to be alone.

And though I'd rather tango with Casseldon Bianchi's favorite ex-pet than say it out loud, all this time, a part of me's been hunting for a connection. I can't help it—I lean toward it like a flower following the sun. And looking around the bridge, I realize maybe, just *maybe*, I've found my clan in this squad.

So, I thump my hand into hers, and with a nearly invisible heft, she has me on my feet. For a moment, we're only a few centimeters apart. Big blue eyes staring right into mine.

Maker's bits, I really like her.

And then she throws me a wink, holds up a biosuit between us. The silvery material is like water in our hands, and Scarlett just happens to be down on one knee to straighten the foot of hers at the right time to shift mine and help me get a leg into it more easily, with nobody else the wiser.

But by the time we're all suited up, I know I'm actually in trouble. It's hard to move, harder to walk, and my suit's flashing warning signals at me that I silence with the press of a couple of buttons.

Zila reports there's nothing unfriendly in the skies overhead, and Cat and I head into the Longbow's belly to check the state of Engineering. Surprisingly, it only looks about half as bad as I feel. Peering about, I can see our hull's been punched through like wet paper. The hole is reparable, but our baby's heart has been cut up pretty bad by the railgun round.

"How's it looking in here?" Tyler asks, mooching up behind us.

"Messy," Cat replies, pointing at our power core. "Reactor's totally spanked."

"I realize being Mr. Sunshine isn't usually my job, but it's not all terrible news," I note. "The hull will get taken care of by the auto-repair systems. The core's a discrete part, so we could switch it out easy enough. Assuming we can find some heavy radioactives to replace the fuel cells with."

"Okay, but where are we going to find some of those?" Tyler asks.

"I was aiming for the settlement as we came in," Cat says. "It should be about ten klicks from here."

Color me six shades of impressed that she managed to even get that close. But it seems like a solid plan.

"Then we want to find the colony spaceport," I say. "I presume they had one, and odds are good that the folks here never evac'ed, or more people would know that the Interdiction was a lie. That means their ships should still be on the ground. In the right conditions, and with a little spit and polish, we might get a working reactor core out of this yet."

"Sounds good," Ty nods.

"Yeah, sure," Cat scoffs. "I mean, for a definition of *good* that includes a ten-klick forced march over hostile territory with walking wounded toward a colony that wasn't supposed to exist and TDF birds likely to fall from the sky and land on our heads at any moment."

"Cat," Tyler says, flashing a pair of dimples that could explode ovaries at twenty paces. "I keep on telling you. You gotta have faith."

· · · · ·

Twenty minutes later, we're standing on the Longbow's loading ramp, almost ready to get under way. Of course, *I'm* the walking wounded Cat was referring to—I guess it's more obvious than I hoped—but I'm also the one with the best chance of jacking a working core for us, so at least I won't get left behind at the ship. The ocean stretches out behind us, a short stretch of sand dunes ahead of us, blue-green hills beyond. The sound of the waves seems strangely out of place.

"Which way to the colony?" Ty asks.

Cat purses her lips, tapping her finger against the visor of her biosuit. "I think it's maybe west? Although now I think of it . . ."

"It's that way," Aurora says, pointing.

"You sure?" Ty asks.

She nods, and when she speaks, her voice is certain.

Stronger than I've ever heard. "I studied this place for two years to get my spot on the *Hadfield*. I was supposed to be in Cartography when I arrived. We're about twelve kilometers northwest of the colony site. Rough ground. Maybe three hours away on foot."

Ty nods, impressed. "We better get moving, then."

The rolling dunes are eerily quiet as we trudge down the ramp, the planet around us is all smooth lines and endless sky. The air is laden with what I mistake for snow at first, and it covers the ground too, but stepping out of the Longbow's loading bay, I realize it's some kind of . . .

"Pollen," Zila says, peering at the semi-luminous dust falling from above.

I swallow hard, holding out my hand to the tumbling blue.

Aurora leads us over the dunes, away from the crashing waves, our wounded ship. There's an audible hiss from my exosuit every time I take a step, and I struggle on the incline, sand crumbling away beneath my boots. Scarlett hovers nearby, close enough to let me know she's there if I need her. But I push on, finally cresting the hill and looking out at the landscape beyond.

"Maker's breath," I whisper.

Past the beach, the rocks, the ground, everything is *covered* with a low scrub that has teardrop-shaped, juicy leaves—just like the ones we saw bursting out of the late Patrice Radke's eye socket. It almost seems to be all one plant, a continuous, creeping spread. The trees are choked with it, long tendrils twisting up and spreading across the bark. There are long patches of flat, silvery grass, too—it reminds me of the mossy growths we saw on the faces of those GIA goons.

". . . Is it supposed to look like this?" Tyler asks.

"No," Aurora replies, shaking her head. "No, it's not."

There's an old communications tower a few hundred meters off—the only visible sign a human colony once existed here. But it's cocooned in that same weird plant growth, thicker stalked, heavier, winding around the supports like the tentacles of an Ospherian seldernaut. The plants look ready to pull the whole structure down beneath the dirt, like a ship vanished beneath the sea.

It's like fungus, almost. And it covers *everything*.

"I've . . ." Aurora blinks rapidly. "I've seen this before."

"Me too . . . ," I whisper, unsteady.

The squad looks at me questioningly. I reach toward the Maker's mark at my collar, but it's covered by my biosuit. My heart is thumping in my chest.

"I dreamed it," I say, looking at Auri. "What I thought was blue snow falling out of the sky. It was everywhere . . . just like this. But it wasn't here on Octavia. The planet I dreamed about . . ." I shake my head, looking to the others. "It was my homeworld. Trask."

"I would advise nobody touch *anything*," Kal says.

"Roger that," Tyler nods, his face pale. "Everyone keep your eyes open and hands to yourselves." He hefts his disruptor rifle. "Let's move out."

With nothing really left to say, we set off again, out into the swaying blue-green scrub. Aurora's expression is hard, her eyes locked on the ground and the plants in front of her. Kal stalks along behind, violet eyes smoldering, a disruptor rifle in his hands, too. Every so often Auri turns her head just enough to check he's close. But they don't make eye contact.

Scarlett's sauntering along beside me as if her fine silver biosuit is a Feeney original design and she's got a catwalk to slay. Cat's just kind of trudging in front of us, no doubt coming down from the kick of getting the Longbow on the ground in the first place. Tyler and Zila are bringing up the rear. He's carrying the containment system we need for the replacement core elements, and she's—well, exactly as expected. Stoic. She's walking with a pair of telescopic binoculars pressed to her eyes, looking up into the sky instead of at what's directly in front of her. There's no signs she intends to shoot anyone, though, so that's a bonus.

The undergrowth gets thicker as we travel, and we find ourselves walking in what might've been light woodlands before it was overrun with this . . . whatever it is. I'm walking in silence, still thinking about my dream, and maybe it's because I'm so tuned in to the soft, distressed whines and hisses of my suit that I think I hear the sound.

Behind us.

Rustle, rustle.

I stop, peer over my shoulder with narrowed eyes.

"All right, Finian?" Goldenboy asks, coming up beside me.

". . . Do we know if there was any native fauna here?"

Zila glances at me. "Is there a reason for your query?"

"I thought I heard something," I admit, my pulse pounding a little too quick.

"Most of the fauna on Octavia wasn't very complex," Auri says from up ahead. "At least from the early surveys and reports from the Biology department. There were mice in the labs, though. And chimps, too. My dad worked with them."

"There were what now?" My imagination's supplying a steady stream of things that could match that name, most of them with claws and teeth I would not like to say hello to. Kal's on alert immediately, his grip tightening on his disruptor rifle.

"Chimps," Auri repeats.

"Pan paniscus," Zila supplies helpfully.

"They're almost the size of a regular person," Auri explains. "Same basic build as us, same family tree. They're covered in black hair, though. They climb really well."

"So they're just hairy humans?" I ask. "What's the difference between a chimp and— Did you guys ever meet O'Donnell? There was a guy who sat behind me in mechaneering, and let me tell you—"

"They're not human," Tyler replies. "They're highly intelligent, but they're animals. What were they doing on the colony, Auri?"

"Initial environmental testing," she said. "They're the nearest thing to a human, without being one. Our DNA is almost identical. That's why they were in the very first rockets ever launched from Earth as well."

"Wait," I butt in. "These things are smart enough to pilot spacecraft?"

Kal has his disruptor rifle up now, turning in a slow circle.

"They sound a deadly foe. . . ."

"No," Auri corrects us. "Look . . . They're not dangerous. And they didn't fly those early ships, they were just passengers. We put them into space to see how it would affect them. Because physiologically, they're a lot like humans."

Pixieboy and I share a long look.

"But if these chumps—" I begin.

401

"Chimps," she corrects.

"If they couldn't fly the ships . . . how did they land them?"

"They didn't have to," says Auri. "It was automated."

"So," I say carefully, "just let me understand this. You dirtchildren took these animals nearly as smart as you and shoved them in rockets and hurled them into space to see if it would melt their insides?"

"It wasn't us personally," Cat points out, defensive, and there's a fair amount of foot shuffling going on among Team Terran.

"Wow," I say, looking about the group. "Did we Betraskans know about all this choomp murder when we allied with you?"

"Enough, Finian. Even if there were chimps here, that was two centuries ago, and . . ." Tyler trails off, no doubt thinking the same thing as the rest of us. Patrice Radke and her fine, ferny friend were here two centuries ago as well. Didn't seem to stop them from roaming the galaxy.

Maker's bits . . .

"Weapons," says Kal simply, and when we continue, everyone's holding one.

I don't hear the *rustle-rustle* again.

Aurora leads us on through the spiny fronds, the suffocated trees, thick pollen falling around us like sticky blue rain. Our biosuits are soon covered with it, and we have to be careful about the fronds, too—the suits are tough, but not indestructible. It's a couple of hours and several battles with the undergrowth later that we crest a hill and find Butler colony in the valley before us.

Or at least the ruins of Butler colony. Every building is

wreathed in that green-blue foliage, crawling with creepers, every squared-off shape and hard angle softened by the plants surrounding it. The vines crawl over the concrete and steel, the spores tumble through the sky, swirling in faintly luminous showers.

It's kinda beautiful. Until I remember my dream of this same blue pollen falling on the surface of my homeworld. I picture Auri's star map. The red, spreading out from those marked stars like a bloodstain.

And then my heart's thudding in my chest again.

It takes me several limping steps to realize Auri has stopped at the top of the hill. I see tears rolling down her cheeks as she gazes at the colony below, and with her faceplate in the way, there's nothing she can do to stop them. I stay where I am, but Scarlett leaves my side and treks up to her.

"If the *Hadfield* had made it, I'd be down there," Auri says quietly, but her voice carries. There's no competition, nothing to drown it out.

"But you're here," Scarlett says gently. "And you're with us. I didn't know your family, but I think they'd have been glad to know you found a squad to be a part of."

Aurora sniffs, deep and inelegant. "My dad left my mom when she got scrubbed from the Octavia mission. In a way, she and my sister had already lost him. But when the *Hadfield* disappeared, they would have felt like they'd lost both of us." She shakes her head. "And I just . . . I can never help them. I can never go back and tell them I was okay."

She sniffs again, her voice quavering.

"The last time I spoke to my dad before I left Earth . . .

we were fighting. I said things I didn't mean. And they were the last things he ever heard me say. You don't think about that when it's happening. You think family's always going to be there."

Everyone's quiet, the breeze stirring up the falling pollen and slowly rippling across the strange plants all around us, setting them softly shivering.

I have no idea how to reply. My family numbers in the hundreds, so the concept of *alone* is just . . . impossible. Though I've felt isolated many times, often singled out and often separate, I've never been alone like Aurora is now.

"I think," says Zila slowly, and I brace for incoming tact-lessness, "that if your sister and mother were given a choice between you being dead or *believing* you were dead and never knowing they were wrong, they would choose the latter. If my family could be alive, but the price would be my igno-rance, I would pay it."

And what is there to say to that?

Miraculously, Aurora offers Zila a small, watery smile.

Our girl out of time isn't just grieving for her family, she's grieving for herself—none of us know what she is anymore, even as we follow the trail she's laying down for us. But she must wish for some hint of normality. And we all know what that's like.

It feels . . . companionable as the seven of us set off again, the strangest group of misfits that ever trekked across an abandoned alien planet beset with creeptastic plants and besieged by military forces. But it's probably another twenty minutes' hike to the colony, and my stomach feels like it's full of greasy ice and everyone is quiet as the grave. It's clearly time to lighten the mood.

"So," I say. "About these chints—"

"Chimps," Tyler says, long-suffering already.

"Whatever. You still have any of those?"

"They're extinct," Cat says. "Just like you're about to be."

"Very funny, Zero. Anyway, are you sure you're not making them up? They sound ridiculous. I mean, hairy dirtchildren who fly spaceships and have almost identical DNA to you lot?" I scoff. "I don't think they exist."

And that's when a snarling, furry pitch-black humanoid thing with jagged yellow teeth that would put an ultrasaur to shame comes screaming out of the undergrowth and straight for my face.

[Search not found]
▶ [Unknown]
  ▼ [Unknown]

Error Type 4592.

Uplink not found. You are too far from a signal.

You're on your own, boss.

31

AURI

Fin crashes to the ground, the biggest chimpanzee I've ever seen in my life landing straight on top of him. Thick greenery blooms from its eyes, its back is covered in a tangle of beautiful flowers, and when it opens its mouth to snarl its defiance at him, I see reddish-green leaves all the way down its throat.

Terror surges through me as it brings both hands down against his faceplate once, twice, sending his head bouncing back against the earth. Kal already has his rifle trained on it, but as if it knows, the thing grabs at Fin's shoulders and rolls the pair of them, throwing him around like a rag doll and using him as a shield.

"Get this choomp off me!" Fin wails.

"Aee'na dō setaela!" Kal spits, falling to his knees and kicking wildly. I realize with cold horror that the vines nearest him are snaking out, curling around his ankles and rifle and dragging it and him away from the beast. I cry out, and Scarlett steps up beside me, rapidly blasting at the plants with her disruptor.

Not wanting to risk hitting Fin with his pistol, Tyler aims

a kick at the chimp's back instead. It's sent flying, screeching, and Cat gets off a blast. There's a bright flash of light, another unearthly screech, but the hit doesn't seem to stop it. Instead, the thing rolls to its feet and jumps on top of Fin again, screaming as Zila takes two quick steps in, raising her disruptor and looking for a clear shot.

Scarlett is still blasting at the vines that have grabbed Kal, and I'm trying to pull his legs free of the snarl, his eyes locking on mine for one long, intense moment. After his confession in sickbay, we have so many things left to say, and I'm suddenly terrified we won't get the chance. I hear a shout, turning as Fin's thrown clear of the brawl. He lands with a crash, something in his suit snapping sharply, and I run forward to hook my hands under his arms and drag him clear.

The thing barrels into Ty and sends him flying—my dad always used to remind me that a chimp was four times as strong as a human, that you could never let your guard down around them. Cat shouts Ty's name as he's sent sprawling. She blasts the thing with her disruptor again, and it turns on her, lashing out with its moss-covered hands and yellowed teeth. With a cry, she's sent tumbling away, rolling to a stop and lying still on her side.

"Maker's breath, shoot it!" Ty's bellowing as Zila circles them, twisting this way and that to try and get a shot that won't take out one of her squadmates.

I throw my hands up, desperately trying to summon whatever it is that's helped me so far. The air around me shivers. A low hum building behind my eyes. But my mind's a wild thing, wheeling away from the sights before me, screaming out to run, to abandon my friends and *get away, get away,* save myself from this place.

The creature turns on me, and despite the greenery in its eyes, I know it's looking at me, I know it's *seeing* me, lips peeling back from its teeth as it shrieks and launches itself right at my throat.

And then Kal's roaring, almost unrecognizable behind his helmet's faceplate. Abandoning his trapped rifle and ripping free of the plants to crash into the beast, coming to my aid with nothing but his bare hands.

He knocks the chimp away from me, both of them tumbling over in a tangle of limbs. Rolling with the impact, curling himself into a ball, Kal plants both boots in the thing's chest and kicks it hard, launching it up into the air as he cries out to Zila.

And Zila doesn't miss her shot.

BAMF!

The thing's head is just . . . gone. And a thousand tiny spores are floating through the air, carried around us in a quick swirl by the breeze as its body crashes to the ground.

Cat whimpers where she's still curled up on her side, and Ty scrambles over to her. But Zila's already skidding in on her knees, as quick as I've ever seen her move, pulling her med kit from her back.

Kal crouches over the remains of the beast, gasping for breath. I help a groaning Fin up to his hands and knees, my heart thumping in my chest. Scarlett has finished blasting the animated vines to ashes. Her hands are shaking, and she keeps her weapon trained on the landscape around us in case any other part of it starts moving when it shouldn't.

"On three," Zila's saying softly, and with infinitely gentle hands, she and Tyler roll Cat onto her back so they can get a look at her injuries.

Oh no. No.

"Maker's bits," Fin breathes, and though he's in obvious discomfort, he's reaching for Zila's bag already.

All down Cat's left side, her suit has been torn open. I can see blood and skin and bone, I can see her ribs, I can . . .

The air's reaching her skin.

Even as I stare in paralyzed horror, a minuscule spore wafts down in slow motion to land on her side.

"The pollen," I gasp, reaching across to try and cover her wound with both my hands, her blood slicking my silver gloves in seconds.

"The pollen will not matter if we do not prevent bleeding," Zila says simply, as a shaking Fin hands her a spray, and she leans down to apply it to the wound.

"Overhead!"

It's Kal, rising from the chimpanzee's body, pointing to a white shuttle cutting a quick arc across the sky. Whether or not the *Bellerophon* is still in orbit, I don't know, but it's obvious someone has survived the clash between the TDF and Bianchi's ships. Even as I watch, they wheel around toward the trail of destruction from our crash landing on the beach, the signpost we left behind.

And they start to descend.

Cat groans as Zila seals her suit with some kind of sticky plastic patch, precious seconds slipping away. Tyler watches Cat, a frozen statue crouching by her side, running the odds in his head.

"Zila," he says quietly. "She needs more than just first aid, yes?"

"Yessir," she nods. "She needs serious attention."

"Well, we can't go back to the Longbow." Ty stares in the direction of that descending TDF shuttle, then to the colony in the valley below. "Auri, suggestions?"

I close my eyes, reaching for what I know about Butler settlement, trying to picture the maps I've studied a thousand times. My exhausted, overloaded brain glitches for a long moment before I remember.

"There's a med center," I say. "On the west side of the settlement."

Tyler rises to his feet, peering down to the settlement's eerie layer of green-gray foliage. "I think I see it. Fin, can you walk?"

"Yessir," Fin says simply. He straightens with a wince, his exosuit spitting out a low, hissing whine. His eyes are narrowed in pain. But he doesn't complain.

"Okay," Tyler says. "Scar, Zila, we take Cat to the med center. Kal, you get Fin to the colony spaceport and look for a replacement reactor core."

"I know the way," I say, sounding braver than I feel.

Ty nods. "Keep Auri with you, and comms open at all times. When you find what you need, call it into me immediately."

Kal stands in one graceful movement, nodding at me. I rub my hands against the mossy grass to rid them of some of Cat's blood, and my stomach turns as the color shifts— green-blue to a deeper purple. There's a warning screaming in my head. I can feel it in my bones. I can feel it under my feet, and in the skies full of dancing spores above me.

Something here is completely, *horribly,* unnaturally wrong.

I hear a whisper inside my mind. An echo of my own voice in my head.

Beware.

Ra'haam.

Cat's jaw is clenched, and the fact that she doesn't fight the splitting of the party, doesn't try to join the conversation, tells me just how badly she's hurt. I let Kal pull me to my feet, and we stand side by side for a moment, looking down at the wounded girl, her friends around her.

I brought them all here.

This is because of me.

"Go," Tyler says, without looking up. "Good hunting."

Kal retrieves his disruptor rifle from the ashes. As the two of us set off after the already-limping Fin, I allow myself one last glance back.

I can't escape the feeling I won't see Cat again.

. . . . .

It's a lot more than twenty minutes to the flat expanse of the spaceport now, with Fin moving slowly and painfully, concentrating on walking and carrying the containment unit for our new reactor core. Though I can't see it under his biohazard gear, I can hear the protests from his exosuit from a few meters away. Kal and I both keep guns at the ready, even though I'm really not sure how to shoot mine. All three of us are trying not to jump at imaginary sounds.

We skirt the edge of the ruined colony—it would be faster through the middle, but Kal says the terrain is too good for an ambush. His voice is steady and his movements are sure, and I find myself drifting a little closer to him.

My mind's whirling—jumping from the shuttle that's now vanished from overhead, to Cat's pale face and bloodied side, back to hazy memories aboard the World Ship, to another monster I destroyed without even touching it. I told the others I didn't remember doing it, but that was a lie. Like I confessed to Kal in the sickbay, I can see it in my head now. As if I'm a passenger in my own body, watching through the screens of my eyes. I remember killing the ultrasaur. I remember shattering the Trigger after Zila shot me, the words I spoke as the star map glittered on the Longbow's bridge, the word I've been hearing in my dreams since I woke up two centuries too late.

Eshvaren.

The word draws me in, calls to me, in exactly the same way this planet repulses me. The need to find out more about that ancient species is at the forefront of my mind, the only thing that keeps returning to shove my fears and questions aside.

Well, not the only thing.

Kal is prowling beside me, his disruptor rifle raised, moving with that strange, ethereal grace. His every motion is sharp, fluid. The warrior he was born to be is so close to the surface now, it's almost all I can see. I can't forget how he threw himself at the chimp when it turned on me. Heedless of his own safety. Fearless and fierce.

He looks at me. Looks away again just as quick.

He's not like anything or anyone I've ever known. I mean, I've dated before, but there's a world of difference—a galaxy of difference—between a movie and popcorn on a Friday night and a guy telling you he's bonded to you for life.

But when he spoke to me in the sickbay, it was like he switched on the lights, and I found myself somewhere so completely unexpected that I had no idea what to say. After all that time he spent ignoring me, trying to keep me away from anything resembling action or responsibility, I was so sure he really did think I was a burden. That if he defended me, it was out of a sense of duty to Tyler's orders.

Except now I know all the times he kept me at arm's length, *that* was his duty showing. The times he defended me, they were something else entirely.

Now he walks alongside me, his gaze ahead, every line of him alert and ready. And even with all the chaos and insanity around us, it's so much better just being beside him.

He makes me feel safe.

The three of us arrive at the spaceport, easing past the vines that cover the open gates, and my heart sinks at the sight before us. The docking bays and control tower and ships are overrun with the same plant growth that seems to have infected everything else in the colony. The skiffs, the freighters, the orbitals, everything. Their hulls crawl with long snarls of creepers and strange flowers, coated in a blanket of this sticky blue pollen that's falling about us like rain.

This place is huge. How are we supposed to find what we need to restore the Longbow's power in all this?

"Mothercustard," I mutter.

"I don't know what that is," Finian says. "It sounds awful. But we're not lost yet, Stowaway. The elements we're after have a half-life of a few million years. If they're here, a little bit of weed won't hurt them."

"The reactors in these ships have what we need?" Kal asks.

"Dunno," Fin says. "These ships are older than my fourth grandpa, and I'm not sure what kind of drives they ran on. But those GIA goons are still on our tails, so we should split up. We'll work quicker, cover more ground. If you find a ship with an active core, shoot me an image on my uni."

"Very well." Kal nods. "Stay on communications."

"Don't worry," Fin replies. "If I see another one of those choomps, you'll hear me screaming without my uniglass."

Kal raises an eyebrow. "You are not much of a warrior, are you, Finian?"

"Well, you're not . . ." Fin makes a face and sighs. "Ah, forget it. . . ."

He limps off toward the biggest freighter, struggling with the containment unit. Kal and I head toward the skiffs, him in front with his rifle raised, me close behind. He offers me his hand to help me over a tangle of vines, even as he looks back to check on Fin. I'm realizing now he's always attuned to where I am, always looking out for me.

"Kal . . . ," I begin softly.

I'm not sure what to say. I'm just sure that I want to talk about this. He's instantly attentive, though he doesn't take those intense purple eyes off the buildings and ships around us.

"What is it, be'shmai?"

"I've been thinking a lot. About what you said."

He stays silent, which I suppose is fair enough—he

already bared his heart to me. I wouldn't volunteer for a second round either if I were him.

"I'm glad you told me," I say. "It can't have been easy."

He's quiet for a bit after that, but I can tell he's considering my words, rather than refusing to answer. Fin is long out of earshot when he finally speaks.

"It was not," he says. "But I owed you the truth."

As we approach the first skiff slowly, carefully, I look around at the ruins of the place that would've been my world. Kal raises his uniglass toward the engines, taking some kind of reading. After a moment, he sighs and shakes his head—no dice. The power core on the skiff is dead. We move on to the next.

"I'm sorry I didn't say anything straightaway," I offer. "It was . . . a surprise. I mean, for you too, I'm guessing. Back when it first happened, I mean."

"It truly was." He pauses. "You Terrans say that home is where the heart lies. When my world died, I thought perhaps my heart had died with it. I did not think I could ever feel this way. About anyone. Let alone a human."

"But you do."

". . . I do," he says.

"But you're going to leave when this is over."

"Yes." He walks on, weapon raised, me beside him. "I joined the Legion because I wished to escape. The war among my people. The war in my soul. But to reject my darker side only strengthens it. To lock it in a cage, to deny it is part of me . . . I cannot stop being what I am. Instead, I must muster the rage to master it."

He shrugs.

"My mother's people have a saying: Ke'tma indayōna be'trai. It means . . . you do not walk alone when you walk your true path. I will be able to walk mine if I know you are pursuing your own. By honoring your wishes, I honor the Pull that has called me. And my path leads back to my people. To the war tearing us apart."

I can see what the words cost him. What the idea of going away costs him. I can see it for the excuse that it is. He's not a very good liar, now I know what I'm looking for.

I glance down at the disruptor in his arms. The blood on his hands.

"Are you sure that's your true path?"

He follows my gaze, tightens his grip on the rifle.

"A warrior is all I was raised to be, Aurora."

I look up sidelong at him for a moment, wishing he'd meet my eyes, but he's steadfastly concentrating on our surroundings. And as the silence stretches and I consider his words, it strikes me that he's not the only one who needs to find a way to walk his path.

Truth is, I'm afraid of what I'm becoming. I can feel it inside me now, if I look. There's something so much bigger going on here. And even though I know I'm a part of it, I'm afraid I'll lose myself inside it. But if I was in control of it, if I could have called up whatever this power of mine is, I could have stopped the fight before Cat was hurt.

And isn't protecting my friends worth the risk?

I'm beginning to think that my choice is between surfing this wave—barely in control, but at least trying to steer—or being dumped by it. Tumbled over and over until I drown.

Watching Kal, I realize how alike we are. Both alone.

Both without a home. Both of us have had our paths chosen for us by forces outside our control. He said he's never heard of a Syldrathi who felt the Pull with a human. Being at the mercy of that, of the warrior within him—it must be so hard.

"I'm sorry," I finally say. "That you don't get to choose for yourself."

He glances up to the sky briefly, sunlight glinting in those violet eyes. "Do moons choose the planets they orbit? Do planets choose their stars? Who am I to deny gravity, Aurora? When you shine brighter than any constellation in the sky?"

I look at this strange boy beside me. It would be so easy to simply see him as a weapon. A beautiful one, sure. But still, a boy made of violence, with his scabbed knuckles and his arrogant grace and his cold purple eyes. But now, here on this impossible world, I begin to see the possibilities. In him. In me.

In us.

"A warrior might be all you were raised to be, Kal," I say. "But it's not all you are."

I slip my free hand into his and squeeze. He flinches a little at first, as if surprised. But then, ever so gently, squeezes back. His gaze flicks to me, then skitters away.

"What does the name you call me mean?" I ask.

"Be'shmai?" he replies. "There . . . there is no adequate human word for it."

"What about inadequate words, then?"

His answer is very soft.

"Beloved."

418

There's two biosuits and a rain of blue pollen between us, and I'm suddenly wishing we were someplace far away from here. Someplace quiet and warm. Someplace private.

"Kal," I say, and with the softest pressure of my hand, I draw him to a stop.

He looks around us carefully, then up, assuring himself we have a moment's safety before he looks down at me through his helmet's visor.

I keep hold of my gun in one hand—this is an important conversation, but I don't want to die in the middle of it—and I let go of his hand so I can reach up and rest my palm on his chest. It's where his heart would be if he were a human, and I'm sobered for a moment by the fact that I don't even know if that's true for a Syldrathi.

But it's just one more thing I want to learn.

"I appreciate what you did," I say softly. "That you tried to spare me the obligation. I can't imagine how hard it was for you to do. It was honorable."

He swallows, his composure lessened just for a moment. "Of course," he whispers. "For you, I would . . ."

I can feel his breathing quickening under the hand I'm resting against his ribs, but he holds himself still for me.

I could keep him in place with the weight of a fingertip, I think.

"I wonder," I continue, still soft, "if you could do one more thing for me."

"Anything," he breathes.

I can't help it. I smile, just a little.

"Would you consider letting me make up my own mind about you? I don't want to make promises I can't keep, but did it ever occur to you that if you let me get to know you, I might like you back?"

His eyes are locked on mine, and through his faceplate, I can see the tiniest hint of a blush creeping up his ears.

"No," he admits quietly. "It did not."

Very gently, very carefully, I curl the hand on his chest into the fabric of his biosuit, tugging him ever so slowly toward me. My cheeks are streaked with dried tears, and I can see every shade of violet in his eyes, the line of blood across his cheek where a shard of the exploding Trigger cut it. And as our helmets touch, we're so close I can count his eyelashes.

And he holds still for me.

"I don't know what comes next," I say softly. "But why don't we see where this path leads us? Let's just find out together."

"You would . . ." The words fade away, laced with hope.

"I'm not a Syldrathi," I murmur. "I can't just fall in deep like you. But if you stopped . . ."

"Being a jackass?" he supplies, with a faint smile.

I can't help it. I laugh. "Maybe," I reply. "Then we'd have a chance to see what happens. Does that sound like something you could do?"

It's not an easy question, and I know it. I'm asking him to leave his heart unguarded, just to see if a girl of a different species could love him back. I'm asking him to let an already-lifelong bond strengthen so that it will hurt even more if he leaves, and I don't know what I'll be able to offer in return.

But there's so much in us that's the same. And there's something about him.

I think it might be worth the risk.

His gaze slides away as he considers the question, and this time I'm the one waiting, my own breath as quick as his now. I can count my heartbeats.

I'm at ten when he looks back to me once more, still so close, the glass of his faceplate against mine.

"Yes," he murmurs.

"Yes," I echo.

There's a softness to his smile that sets off flurries of butterflies in my stomach. And then Finian's voice crackles across Kal's uniglass.

"Pixieboy, you there?"

We break apart. Dragged back to reality. My pulse pounding and my hands shaking as Kal touches the device at his belt.

". . . I read you, Finian," he replies, blinking as if he's coming out from under a spell.

"Okay, don't all ask for my autograph at once, but I think I've worked out our answer. I'm in that old D-class freighter on the south end of the port, come take a look."

"We are on our way."

Kal smiles at me, sweet and warm. I draw a deep breath and nod. He holds out his hand to me and I take it, feeling the strength in his grip. He hefts his rifle, the warrior, the soldier in him rising to the surface once more. But now, I realize, he's something else too.

He's mine.

And fingers entwined, we make our way through the rolling blue.

· · · · ·

"You two want the good news or the bad news?"

Fin's leaning against the ancient freighter's console, which he's miraculously managed to crank back to life with the help of his uniglass, a screwdriver jammed between two panels, and what looks like a jury-rigged power unit. A mess of sticky blue pollen covers every surface, and growths of tendrils and vines have forced their way in through the hull and crawled over almost everything. Considering the state of this place, I'm amazed Fin could even coax it into turning on, let alone giving up any information.

"The good news," I say.

"The bad news," Kal says simultaneously.

Fin smirks, noting the fact that we're holding hands.

"Well, it's nice that you lovebirds still have some stuff to work on. The bad news is none of the ships here are going to have a core compatible with ours." He glances at me and shrugs. "Looks like you dirtchildren were still using simple plutonium drives back in the day. But the good news is, I think I can still synthesize what we need. I just need to get the colony reactor going."

"They sssshould not be here."

The voice comes from behind us. We all whip around, and three figures are standing there, shrouded in the gloom. The first is a man, heavyset and broad, the second, a paler, younger man about my age, and the last is a woman with dark brown skin and black hair that falls to her waist in a wild tangle. Clusters of flowers bloom from their eyes, and moss grows down the sides of their faces. It disappears at their necks into the vines clothing them, twisting along their arms, coiling around their legs. Those GIA agents on the

422

World Ship looked infected by the same . . . disease, but these people look totally corrupted.

"Holy cake," I whisper.

The woman turns toward me, head tilted.

"Aurora?" she says, sounding almost affectionate now.

Kal steps forward, putting himself between us and raising his weapon.

"Come no closer."

The younger man takes a shuffling step forward. The vines around the woman's arms begin to writhe, but it's her voice that catches at me. Her eyes are flowers, but I somehow know she's looking at me, *seeing* me, as she hisses like a snake.

"She deliversss hersssself to ussss?"

"Jayla," I say slowly, trying it out. "Jayla Williams."

Another colonist. She's the one who got picked for Patrice's Cartography team the year before me. She tilts her head, as if she's trying to make sense of me. Like I'm the last person in the galaxy she expected to see. The bigger man's bright blue eyes are fixed on Kal, the younger one rocking back and forth on his heels and hissing. All around us, the plants and vines that cover the spaceport begin to move in concert, slow and sinuous, snaking across the deck toward us.

"They will not sssstop the ssspawning," the woman says, shaking her head and baring black teeth. "They sssshould not *be* here!"

"I will not warn you again," Kal says.

The young man looks at him quizzically. Takes one step closer.

". . . What issss 'I'?"

Quick as lightning, they lunge forward, all at once. Their speed is blinding. Kal only gets two shots off—the first taking the big man's head off his shoulders in a spray of blue spores, the second burning a black hole through the young man's chest and dropping him to the floor. But Jayla is on Kal now, overgrown fingers wrapping around his disruptor.

I raise my own weapon, but she's so quick, lashing out with her foot and sending the gun flying from my hand and me skidding to my knees. She strikes at Kal, but he manages to block, seizing her wrist and locking her up.

The pair strain against each other. Kal towers over her, but I can see his jaw clenched, the veins in his neck standing taut. I desperately try crawling for my disruptor, but the plants are clawing at my hands, snagging around my ankles, just like they did to Kal when the chimp attacked.

The vines slither up around Kal's boots like snakes, entwined about his shins and holding him in place. His eyes widen in disbelief as the woman leans in. Twisting his rifle with a terrible strength until the long barrel is jammed under his chin. His teeth are gritted as her fingers close on the trigger.

"Be'shmai," he gasps. "Run."

BAMF!

BAMF!

BAMF!

The woman staggers back as the disruptor blasts ring out. The first shot strikes her in the ribs, the second in her shoulder, and the final one goes straight through her blooming eye and out the other side.

A greenish-blue mess spatters on the wall behind her.

She makes a strange sound, wobbles on her feet. But slowly, Jayla Williams drops to the ground, and the plants around us fall perfectly still.

Kal looks over his shoulder to Fin, who's standing there with his disruptor pistol in hand. Kal's silver eyebrow is raised as he looks the smaller boy up and down.

"Fine shooting," he whispers, reaching visibly for his usual calm.

Finian grins, jamming his gun back into its holster.

"Yeah. Not much of a warrior, am I?"

32

SCARLETT

"Hold on, Cat, you hear me?" Tyler says. "We're almost there."

The girl in his arms, my roomie, his bestie, only moans in reply.

"T-they're coming. . . ."

"Scar, how far to the med center?" my brother asks.

"About eight hundred meters," I reply, voice trembling.

I can see it in the distance now, standing tall in the falling eddies of pollen. It's three stories high—probably the biggest structure in the settlement aside from the reactor. The green crosses on its flanks are barely visible under the growth of twisted blue-green vines, blood-red flowers, silver leaves. This whole place looks like some ancient ruin on Terra, abandoned centuries ago by people and left for nature to reclaim. Except I get the feeling the people here didn't abandon anything. And there's nothing *natural* about any of this.

Tyler is carrying Cat in his arms—she's too hurt to walk. Zila is bringing up the rear, ice-cold as always. I'm walking point, and I'm nowhere near as cool, my eyes darting left and right. I'm sweating inside my biosuit, my breath coming quick. The plant life covers everything, rolling and swaying like waves on the ocean's face—always toward us. The pollen is thick and sticky, and I have to stop every so often to wipe it off the glass dome of my helmet. And I think of Cat, and I think of the rip in her suit, and I wonder—

"Movement!" Zila calls, looking at her uniglass. "Three hundred meters!"

I see them coming through the haze, moving in long, loping strides. Their fur is overgrown with weeds and vines and spiny leaves and flowers of blood-red, but I can still see the chimps they used to be underneath. They're moving quick, crawling across the vertical surfaces of the colony buildings like spiders, or swimming through the undergrowth as if it was water. They're going to hit us before we reach the med center.

"Open fire!" Tyler roars.

I take a knee, start blasting with my disruptor, feeling the sharp recoil up my arms. Truth is, I'm a bad shot. I spent most of senior-year marksmanship classes flirting with my range partner (Troi SanMartin. Ex-boyfriend #48. Pros: loves his mother. Cons: called me his mother's name), but Tyler scored in the top 10th percentile, and Zila probably sleeps with her disruptor under her pillow.

The shots ring out in the empty streets. It might be my imagination, but as each chimp-thing falls, I swear I hear the plant life around us . . . whispering. The leaves shiver like the wind was blowing, but there's not a breath of it. Blue blood spatters, and the animals fall, shrieking as they tumble. But there's a lot of them.

I can see one bearing down on me, mossy lips peeled

back from its teeth, eyes full of flowers. I take steady aim, try to remember my lessons, but my hands are shaking. I fire once, twice. The third shot hits home, striking the chimpthing in the arm. It spins on the spot but keeps coming. Closing to forty meters. Twenty.

It leaps at me, opening its mouth to scream. And as it does so, its head just keeps . . . opening.

Lips peeling away from its face.

Face peeling away from its skull.

Skull peeling away from its torso until the *entire top half of its body* has opened up like some awful flower, ready to swallow me whole.

I'm pinned in place by the horror of it, five meters away now, and I can't help but screa—

BAMF!

The chimp-thing pops like a water balloon, Tyler's disruptor blast knocking it sideways and spattering it across the undergrowth. As the blood touches them, the plants shiver and sigh, but Zila blasts them to ashes before any of them can move to attack us. My heart is thunder inside my chest and my legs are shaking and I'm looking for something bitchy or sassy to say, but I can't quite manage it anymore. Ty's already up and moving, Cat back in his arms. I can see the blood on her biosuit, the patch job over the tear, the blue pollen clinging to the silver.

As Ty wipes at her faceplate, I can see her eyes are blue, too.

They used to be brown.

"T-Tyler," she moans. "They're c-coming."

"Scar, we need to move," my brother says. "Now."

428

His voice is like iron, but I can feel the fear in him. We've known each other since before we were born. I can read him better than anyone. And I know that under the facade, beneath the even tone and steady hands, he's terrified.

For us.

For *her*.

I blink hard. Nod once. And then I'm up off my knees, moving quick. We run through the overgrown streets, through the swaying fronds, the med center finally looming up ahead of us.

We have to blast our way past the vines to get in through the entrance, but I'm not sure what he's hoping to find here. Even if the place wasn't being swallowed by this . . . infection, the facilities are two centuries old. It's only now, up close, that I'm realizing how desperate and hopeless this plan is.

The inside of the building is dark, the windows covered with growth, the power long dead. We arc up the searchlights on our biosuits, bright beams cutting through the gloom. The place is completely overrun—the floors carpeted in moss, the walls crawling with creepers and sticky flowers.

"Zila, what do we need?" Tyler asks.

The girl shakes her head, looking at Cat. Through the visor of her biosuit, I can see our Ace's blue eyes are open, eyelashes fluttering. Her skin is covered in sweat. I swear there's a faint silver sheen on it.

"I am unsure, sir," Zila replies. "I have never seen symptoms like—"

"Improvise," he snaps. "You're my Brain. I need you now."

"Medical storage," she says. "I do not know what chemicals they had here, or what will be unspoiled after two centuries. But I may be able to cobble together some kind of antibacterial agent or suppressant if we find a supply cache."

"Right," Tyler nods. "Let's move."

We stalk off through the dark belly of the med center, footsteps squeaking and squishing on the carpet of plant growth. Every surface is covered with it. The heat is oppressive, like the inside of a sauna. I can hear Cat's shallow breathing, my heart thumping in my chest. We check room after room, but everything is overgrown, useless, unrecognizable. Vague shapes of maybe-beds and possibly-computers, tiny motes of luminous blue pollen dancing in the air.

Cat reaches up in Tyler's arms, grabs his shoulder. "Tyler . . ."

"Cat, you just relax, okay?" he says. "We're getting you out of this."

"Y-you . . ." She shakes her head, swallows hard. "D-don't under . . . stand."

"Cat, honey, please," I beg. "Try not to talk."

"I . . . see," she whispers.

"What do you see?" Zila asks.

"G-men." Cat closes those new blue eyes. "C-coming."

"The shuttle we saw." Zila looks at Tyler. "Survivors from the *Bellerophon*."

"Zila, what's happening to her?" I ask.

Our Brain's brow creases in thought, her lips pursed. I can see that genius-level IQ at work behind her eyes. Her detachment bringing a clarity I can only envy. I wonder what it was that made her like this. How she got to be who she became.

After a moment pondering, she turns and fires her disruptor at the wall—when all else fails, stick to what you know, I guess. The blast burns a section of the overgrowth to cinders, the blue-green leaves reduced to ashes. Just like when we killed the chimp-things, the rest of the plant life around us ripples, whispers, shudders. And my heart sinking in my chest, I see Cat shuddering too.

"Ohhh," she moans. *"Ohhhhh."*

Zila runs her uniglass over Cat's body, through the air. The device beeps and clicks, Zila playing it like a concert pianist.

"Legionnaire Madran?" Tyler asks.

Zila shakes her head. "There is so little data. So many variables. But these growths, the infected animals, all we have seen . . . there appears to be a congruence between them. When one is hurt, the others seem to feel pain."

I think back to the bridge of the Longbow. The words Aurora spoke when she pointed to those glowing red dots on the star map.

"Gestalt," I whisper.

Zila nods. "A gestalt entity, yes. A multitude of organisms that are actually a single being. It is as if everything on this planet, everything affected by this plant bloom . . . it is as if they are all connected."

Cat begins convulsing in Tyler's arms, a fit gripping her whole body. Her teeth are bared, and as she thrashes, he lowers her to the floor, tears shining in his eyes.

"Cat?" Tyler asks. "Cat, can you hear me?"

"Ra'haam," she groans, echoing Auri's words on the bridge.

"Hold on, we'll figure this out, I promise."

Cat groans, head thrown back, every muscle taut as she lifts herself off the floor, back bent in a perfect arch.

"Ra'haaaaa-a-a-aam!"

I feel so useless, I want to scream. Every ounce of my terror, my horror, is echoed in the lines of Tyler's body, in the way he bends down over her, runs a hand helplessly down her arm, tentative, like touching her might break her.

I know what happened between them on shore leave. Neither of them told me, but I figured it out. Coming back with those new tattoos and a new distance between them. I could see Cat wanted to close it. I could understand why Tyler didn't. Why it might have been a mistake. Why it might have been the best thing that happened to either of them. Because as in love as Ty is with the idea of being a leader, of being a soldier, of being someone Dad would be proud of, I know part of Tyler is in love with Cat, too.

He just hasn't figured out *how* yet.

But what will he do if he loses her?

"I can f-feeeeel it," Cat hisses, sweat beading on her brow. "I can feel them. This place, this planet . . . I kn-know what it isssssss."

She sighs and sinks back down onto the mossy growth. Her eyes are open, the same faintly luminous blue as the pollen floating in the air around us. And with dawning horror, I realize her pupils aren't round anymore.

They're the shape of flowers.

"Cat?" Zila asks, kneeling beside her. "What is Ra'haam?"

Our Ace looks at Zila, tears shining in her lashes.

"*We* are."

"Maker's breath," Tyler whispers. "Your eyes . . ."

Cat's hand snakes out, grabbing Tyler's arm so hard he flinches.

"G-get th-them out of here, Tyler," she breathes, teeth clenched. "Auri, especially. It would have killed you all to stop her finding this place. But now she's here . . . you . . . can't let it t-take her."

"Cat . . ."

"I can f-feel it." She shakes her head, tears spilling down her cheeks. "I can feel it inside me, Ty. For the love of the Maker . . . get . . . get her out of h-here."

My hands are shaking and I can't breathe fast enough. I can't talk, the sobs rising up in my throat to choke me. But Zila says what I'm thinking.

"But the star map inside the Trigger *led* us here," she objects.

"Don't you unders . . . understand?" Cat shakes her head, spine arching again. "W-wasn't an invitation. It-t-t w-was a *warning*. . . ."

She falls silent, closing her eyes, shivering as if she has a fever. I look to my brother, see his face is pale as old bones. I can see the desperation in his eyes. The hurt. The same sinking feeling that's building inside my own chest. There's nothing usable in this med center. We have hostile inbounds—GIA agents in their faceless gray armor and who knows what else. He has to prioritize. He has to put the needs of the group before his own feelings. That's what good leaders do.

He meets my eyes. And I speak to him without having to say a word.

Show the way, baby brother.

433

He reaches into the utility belt on Cat's suit, grabs her uniglass. "Kal, what's your status?"

"We were unsuccessful at the spaceport," our Tank replies. *"But Finian says he can synthesize the necessary components for a new Longbow core if he has access to the colony reactor. We are headed there now."*

"Is everyone okay?"

Kal's voice lowers, as if he doesn't want to be overheard.

"Aurora is . . . unsettled. We encountered more colonists, infected with the same ailment as the chimps. One spoke of . . . spawning?"

"Yessss," Cat sighs, writhing on the floor.

I take her hand and she opens her eyes and looks at me. I want to look away from that unnatural color, those flower-shaped pupils. But instead I squeeze my roomie's fingers, muster a smile.

Tyler takes a shaky breath. "We suspect at least one GIA agent was on that transport—it must have been from the *Bellerophon*. They're inbound on our position."

"The colony reactor is the most heavily fortified structure in the settlement, sir. If we are planning a defense, we should gather there."

"Roger that, we'll head to you."

"I will have deterrent recommendations ready for you when you arrive."

"We'll be there ASAP." He swallows thickly. "Kal . . . tell everyone to mind the integrity of their biosuits. Under no circumstances are you to allow anyone's gear to be breached, is that understood?"

"Zero, is she—"

"Just get it done, legionnaire. We'll be there soon. Tyler, out."

Ty taps the uni, kneels beside Cat. Putting her arm over his shoulder, he scoops her up. But Cat shakes her head, places one hand on his chest.

"N-no . . . ," she whispers. "Leave me, Ty."

He raises that scarred eyebrow of his, and for a second, the charmer in him rises to the surface. "I didn't know you were trying out for the comedy circuit?"

"I'm . . . serious," she breathes. "Let me g-go."

"No way." He stands in one easy movement, Cat cradled in his arms. Her head lolls back, her body limp. But with visible effort, she pulls herself up so she can look him in the eye.

"I c-can see it, Ty," she whispers. "And it can see all of you . . . th-through me." She shakes her head, a kind of wonder creeping into her voice. "It's so big, Ty. It's so b-big and I'm falling into it and you have to let me g-go."

"No," he says.

"Please," she begs.

"You listen to me, Brannock," Ty says, his voice hard as steel despite the tears shining in his eyes. "We are the Aurora Legion, and we do not leave our people behind. Do you understand me?"

She licks her lips, eyes slipping closed.

"Legionnaire Brannock, I asked you a question!" he shouts.

Cat's eyes flutter open and she draws a deep, shivering breath.

"Furthermore," Ty continues, in his best parade-ground voice, "I shouldn't have to remind you that I'm your superior officer. So if you're considering lying down here, if you even *think* of cashing out on this drop, I'm going to kick your ass so hard the lump in your throat will be my *fucking* heel, is that understood?"

Tyler Jones, Squad Leader, First Class, doesn't curse. Tyler Jones doesn't do drugs or drink or do anything we mere mortals do for fun. I can't remember the last time I heard him swear. I doubt Cat can, either.

"Is that *understood*?" Ty roars.

The words have the desired effect. Cat swallows hard and some focus returns to her eyes. Her grip on his shoulder tightening as she whispers.

"S-sir, y . . ."

"I can't hear you, Legionnaire Brannock!"

Cat blinks hard, slowly nods. "Sir, yessir."

Ty looks to Zila and me, his stare hard with command. I can see the leader in him, I can see our *dad* in him, burning so bright it makes me want to cry. To reach out and hug him, to tell him how proud he makes me. But instead, I stand at attention. Because that's what legionnaires do.

"Scar, you've got point," Ty orders. "Zila, watch our tails. We go hard and fast to the colony reactor tower, meet up with the squad. Anything gets in our way, we blast it back to the hells. Nobody in this unit is dying here today, am I clear?"

"Sir, yessir," we reply.

"Right. Let's move out."

33

AURI

All around me, Tyler and his squad are transforming the reactor into the place we'll make our stand. They're hauling
cabinets to block entrances, blasting vines away from windows, figuring out how to augment our defenses with what's
left here.

I'm wrestling with a solidly built table, turning it onto its
side to lay in front of Cat, like a kind of last-ditch shield in
case they come at us through the windows. My gaze meets
Kal's every minute or so—though he's busy single-handedly
matching the strength of half of us combined, he's still waiting for me when I look his way.

My nerves are singing as I position the table in front of
Cat. The GIA agents are coming for me, but I know they'll
take out everyone here. There's no way back to the Longbow
now without a battle, no chance to repair it, to escape. This
is the place we'll make our stand. And I'm terrified.

"The GIA shuttle is now inbound on our position." Over
by the window, Zila lowers her binoculars, calm as ever.
"ETA three minutes."

"Idea," Scarlett says. "Could we use their ship to get back off-world?"

Finian rises up from where he's crouching by a half-dissected computer system, moving with a soft whine of his servos. His containment unit has been rigged up to the core, in a tangle of cables and pipes that look held together by prayers and duct tape. Apparently his rig is synthesizing the elements we'll need to repair the Longbow's reactor for when we get out of here.

If we get out of here.

Limping to the window, he squints at the incoming ship, shakes his head.

"It's just a puddle jumper," he says. "Meant for short atmo-to-surface transit. If we want to get back through the Fold, we need the Longbow." He looks at Tyler. "But that shuttle could get us back to the Longbow fast. If, say, we had a genius tactician with great hair and a daring plan to steal it."

Tyler glances up from where he and Kal are mounting a disruptor rifle on a makeshift tripod near the window.

"I'm working on it," he mutters.

"Well, while you find your hairbrush, I'm going up a level to main control," Fin declares. "See if I can boost the output and override the safety protocols on the power supply."

"What for?" Scar asks.

"I can run a current through the metallics in the structure. Gantries, stairwells, that kind of thing. Cut off access. Electrify them."

"Won't that electrify us, too?"

He shakes his head. "If we stick to the concrete, we're

fine. Before I was saddled with you pack of no-hopers, I was tinkering in the propulsion labs back at the academy in my spare time. I figured a way to give the basic DeBray power systems a seven percent bump, and I'm seeing a few similar components here."

"The propulsion labs you were messing around in," Tyler says. "Would those be the ones you *irradiated*?"

"Hey, don't complain. You got out of your spatial dynamics exam, too." He's trying for his usual grin, but none of us have it in us right now.

"This sounds like a bad idea," Ty says.

"Yeah, but they're the only kind we have left. I can do this, Goldenboy."

Tyler chews his lip and sighs. "Zila, go with him. See if you can help."

"Yessir," Zila says quietly, turning away from the window.

Tyler grabs Finian's arm as he limps past. "Hey, listen up." He looks at me, lowers his voice. But not quite enough.

"These agents are here for Auri." He glances at Cat, back at Fin. "Letting them get hold of her isn't a good idea. Can you rig something up quick? I mean, if it comes down to a choice between getting captured and . . ."

Finian meets Tyler's eyes, all the jokes and bravado gone. "I can do that."

Tyler nods. And without another word, Fin and Zila head upstairs.

My breath's coming too fast, my heart singing. The new parts of me are trying to push their way to the surface, but I don't know how to control them, or how to just let them take me.

If it comes down to a choice between getting captured and . . .

How did this happen? How did we get here?

I flex my fingers and clench my fists, trying to get myself under control as I circle the table to sink down cross-legged beside Cat.

Everything around me is screaming at my nerves, sending my limbs tingling, the back of my neck buzzing with danger. I'm sure the plants and vines are monitoring us, that the pollen drifting in through one broken window and out through another is part of the way the planet's keeping tabs on our every movement.

It's pushing me close to the edge of my courage, but I feel it pushing me closer to the edge of something else as well.

I can feel myself on the verge of . . .

Cat stirs beside me, and I take her hand in mine, giving it a gentle squeeze. Her lashes lift, and she fixes those flower-shaped pupils on me, her eyes the brightest blue. We gaze at each other for a long moment, and then she lets out a soft breath that's edged with a moan.

"I can feel it," she whispers, and I don't know what to say, because I can, too. "It's taking me."

"We won't let it," I whisper in return.

She pins me with a look brimming with fear, with pain, with *come on now, let's not lie between the two of us,* and my heart aches, because none of what's on her face—on her slowly silvering skin—should be coming from a girl my age.

Except she's not my age, is she?

The leaves around us shimmer even though there's no

breeze, and I can feel the centuries beneath my skin. The power waiting inside them.

As Kal walks past, he places a hand on my shoulder, just for a second. Just for a breath. And I think about what he said. About walking your true path. And though I don't quite know how, I know all of this, everything that's happened, has to do with me. With this power inside me.

There's a reason the very existence of this colony was hidden from the world.

There's a reason the GIA is after me, trying to wipe me away too.

There's a reason I'm becoming something else, something more than human.

There's a reason I took us to the World Ship, to the Trigger.

And there's a reason the Trigger brought us here.

And somehow, they're all connected. And though it's frightening, I know I can't be frightened anymore.

Everything that's happened, all I've become . . . I can't stop it.

Instead, I have to muster the rage to master it.

I think about this place. What happened to the people here. I think about my family. About my mom and Callie, when they got the news I was gone. About my dad when he heard, about the things we should have said in that last conversation.

I think about everything I've lost. I think about being this girl out of time, having this power I don't understand. And when I look down, when I lock gazes with Cat again, look into the flowers in her eyes, surrounded by the predatory leaves and vines of this planet, my spine twitching to run, the urge building up inside me . . .

. . . something shifts.

It's like fire melting ice. Like positive and negative charges colliding. Like I'm waking up for the first time in two hundred years. I feel my mind stretch, feel the gorgeous elongation of muscles that have lain dormant for too long, a surge of power running through me. Suddenly I'm *bigger, stronger,* and though I'm exactly the same—I'm still sitting cross-legged beside Cat, holding her hand—there's an extra dimension to everything.

This is what it feels like to control it.

I may not know what *it* is, but everything I've done while I was asleep, everything that rendered me a passenger, a prisoner in my own body—now I feel a part of it is mine. Something bigger. Something more. Snatched from the nothing with my own two hands.

I turn my head to run my gaze over the squad. I can feel a flare of empathy in Kal—a restless presence with a violet shimmer to it. It's almost drowned out by the rest of his nature. It runs through him like fine veins of gold in rock, almost hidden. It shifts and shivers in response as my mind brushes across his.

I can see it in Scarlett, too, and a touch, much less, in Tyler, flowing beneath the surface of his mind. The Jones twins are human, and for a moment a flicker of doubt hits me—has the planet touched them, too?—but an instant later, I know that's not true. The power running through the plants and leaves and vines around us, connecting them via a current that now crackles for me like electricity, is completely different from anything in Scarlett or Tyler, or Kal, or me.

But when I look down again, I can see it winding its way through Cat in a hopelessly complex tangle of vines, like a network of capillaries. Invading every part of her.

Where do I even begin *trying to untangle this?*

I know, though I push the knowledge away, that I can't.

It's too much, too deep.

It has her.

I try anyway, mentally grabbing a handful of the psychic energy that binds her, burning it to nothing, holding it in my mind's grip until it's only ashes. She moans, and as I look down, the silvery green-gray-blue energy snakes through her to cover the gap as if it was never there.

Like the vines, it's everywhere.

I try a different way, leaning into Cat's mind. Maybe I can start there and sweep out, burn her thoughts clear. As I look inside her, I'm hit with a welter of emotions. Her pain, her fear, her anger flow through me, and I flinch for an instant, fight the urge to withdraw. And then I lean in harder, because nobody should be alone with feelings like these.

I'm here, I'm here.

I squeeze her hand, pushing past the sharp-edged outer defenses. And inside them I find the real Cat, a whirl of life and love and energy, the reds and orange and golds of her mental signature spiraling into elaborate patterns that remind me of eddies of wind, that remind me of flight.

I find her love for Scarlett, her grief for her mother, her fierce joy in taking to the air. I find her love for Tyler, deep and strong, laced with frustration.

And in response, without my meaning to—but perfectly naturally, just as it should—my mind dances with hers.

We're not in the reactor anymore. Nobody is around us.

We're somewhere else, just the two of us, and nothing else matters.

My mind is midnight blue and a dust of silver, starlight and nebulas to her fiery winds. To touch her, I have to be open, my own loves and memories as free as hers. She sees my love for my sister, Callie, she catches the scent of the warm rock and crisp leaves at the top of my favorite hiking trail. My happy place. Through me, she tastes a quick bite of the chilies my father adds to his cooking. She's with me through the pain of watching my mother after he left, and then, instead of watching, she's moving. Grabbing at that memory and shoving it away.

For a moment I'm bewildered. But without words, with a flurry of images, she's conveying her purpose—she doesn't want to know these things, because she doesn't want to share them.

When it takes her.

We both focus on the door between us—she pulls, I push—and together we jam it closed, and sweat's running down my back when my eyes snap open, my breath coming quickly.

Her gaze is waiting for me.

"You sh-shouldn't . . . b-be here," she whispers.

Voices ring out behind me. "Try now," Fin's yelling from upstairs.

"It is working," Kal calls, tilting his head back to yell at the ceiling.

"I know," I whisper to Cat. "Everything about this place is wrong. But the star map showed us this place, the Trigger . . ."

"Oh, Auri . . . d-don't you s-see? The T-Trigger . . . is—"

Her eyes snap wide, and her gasp's the only warning I have before her mind assaults mine—but now the reds are the crimson of blood, the yellows too bright, too gaudy. This is Cat's mind, but Cat's not at the wheel.

I throw up my defenses, try to force her back, mental walls as strong as I can make them. Imagining them made of stone, surrounding myself in a tiny fortress, my mind in the middle. But I can see my enemy all around me now, I can sense something of the consciousness trying to reach into my mind through hers.

A being.

A single, colossal, impossible being.

It comes from everywhere, a network spread across the planet—it's every plant, every vine, every flower, every spore floating through the air. I can see the history of it, its purpose and potential. And as if time is nothing, I can see its future.

I'm a speck as I try to understand the timescale on which this journey has been measured. I'm reminded of the ceiling of Casseldon Bianchi's ballroom, of the slow dance of galaxies as they made their way around it, moving through and around one another on a cosmic scale.

This . . . *thing* has been readying itself, first lying dormant, then slowly waking, until now it's riding the crest of a wave that stretches back a million years. This planet, all the planets on that star map, will grow and swell, ripening until they burst like seed pods, throwing their spores, the infection, into those natural, unclosable FoldGates. Into the Fold itself, and from there . . .

From there, everywhere.

This is the instant before a tsunami breaks.

This is the Ra'haam.

"You *can* stop it." Cat's gasp yanks me from my paralysis, and the attack on my fortress falls away, the reds and golds fading into her colors, then withdrawing. Blood is trickling from her nose, her chest rising and falling now, blue eyes fixed on my face. "They stopped it before. And you can stop it now, Aurora."

"Yes," I breathe.

Because I understand how old this story is now. I understand the arrogance of thinking that in the 13.8 billion years the universe has been expanding, this place and this moment—now, in the Milky Way—is the first time life has been forced to fight this war.

I see the last time the Ra'haam woke.

When it last tried to swallow the galaxy.

Tried and failed.

It hid itself here afterward, I realize. Wounded. Almost dead. Because behind the flood, behind the noise of this impossible thing around me, deep inside myself, I can feel something else. The voice calling to me. The voice that's been calling me this whole time.

Telling me who I am.

Who *they* were.

The ones who struggled. Who saw what the Ra'haam would become if left unchecked, and saw their individuality as something worth fighting for.

The Ancient Ones.

Eshvaren.

And though they're gone now, dead for eons

they left behind
the weapon we'll need
to beat it
again.

And the Trigger isn't some ancient statue or some jewel hidden inside it. It's not some star map made of gemstones stolen from some gangster's lair.

The Trigger . . .

"Auri," Cat gasps.

"The Trigger . . . is *me*."

The leaves around us ripple, and I hear an engine roaring outside. The thrum of a slow descent, the crunch of landing gear touching earth. I know before he does that Tyler will speak.

"They're here."

Cat grits her teeth, and I know she's trying to stop it, them, the thing that's winding through her and making her a part of it, from knowing what she knows. The voice that comes from outside is smooth, amplified, genderless, and ageless.

"WE ARE HERE FOR AURORA O'MALLEY."

Princeps.

Fin's voice drawls over our channel. *"Someone want to tell Your Highness it's polite to say please?"*

Scarlett leaves her brother by the window and hurries over to take my place, dropping to one knee. "Go," she murmurs to me, and as I release Cat's hand, the other girl takes it.

I make my way over to where Tyler's watching by the window. The vines all around him have been burned away, but I can see one of the charred tendrils moving, questing along the window ledge, looking for a new purchase even as I crouch beside him. If I stay close to the wall, I can look down without giving the figures below a look at me in return.

A shuttle has touched down on the blue-green scrub outside the reactor. It's marked with the *Bellerophon's* ident, and a landing ramp has extended from its belly. Princeps stands at the bottom in its pristine white suit, pollen falling all around it. At its shoulder is a second GIA agent in the usual charcoal gray, and ranged around the shuttle are dozens and dozens of other figures.

They're not GIA agents. And there are so many of them.

There are a few chimpanzees in the throng, their fur coated in moss and tubers. But beneath the cloaks of silver vines, the flowers crawling through their hair and bursting from their eyes, I recognize the rest of them.

Humans.

Colonists.

"Ah, Aurora." Despite the cover of the window's edge, Princeps looks right at me. "There you are."

I risk casting out a tendril of my midnight-blue, star-speckled mind into the green-silver-blue-gray morass of the plants and vines outside. I'm trying to find Princeps's mind, to see more of it, but it's like interference on the radio—there's so much to sense, I can't find my target in the middle of it.

It's as expressionless as ever when it speaks again—I have no idea if it even sensed my effort. "We've been waiting for you so long, Aurora."

"Wait a little longer," I call back, making my voice firm. It doesn't shake. "Try back in another two hundred years."

"YOU WERE LOST TO OUR SIGHT. WE COULD NOT FIND YOU."

"I was never yours to find!"

"YOU WERE HIDDEN IN THE FOLD, WE SEE THAT NOW. THE ESHVAREN WERE COWARDS TO HIDE YOU THERE. SUCH WAS ALWAYS THEIR WAY. THEIR WEAKNESS. THE SAME WEAKNESS WE FEEL NOW IN YOU. YOU SHOULD HAVE LET US SIMPLY BURN YOU AWAY IN ORBIT. YOU WERE FOOLISH TO BRING YOURSELF TO US."

Behind me, Ty rests a hand on my shoulder, as if he's afraid I'm going to show myself, to stand up in the window and argue. But I hold still and watch, because Princeps is lifting both its hands to its helmet, and with a flick of its thumbs, it releases the seal.

I'm frozen in place as slowly, so slowly, in a movement that takes two heartbeats and 13.8 billion years, it lifts its helmet free and shows me the face beneath.

I know, an instant before I see it, what I'll see.

And yet it hits me like a blow, robbing me of breath, of thought, of strength.

Beneath the fat leaves that bloom from his right eye, beneath the silvery moss that trails down his graying skin to disappear into the neck of his suit, I can still make out the lines of his face. His round cheeks, the lines across his forehead that my mom used to joke were there from the age of fifteen, because the world surprised him so much.

"Daddy . . ."

The words swell up inside my mind, like ugly, oozing slashes across my silver-speckled nebula. It's as if I'm back in the moment of our last conversation.

Thanks for the birthday wishes, Dad.

Thanks for the congratulations about winning All-States again.

But most of all, thanks for this.

I hung up on him before his return transmission could come in. Before I could see the hurt on his face. The way my hits landed.

"I've missed you, Jie-Lin," he says.

My heart implodes, caving in on itself.

"It's been so hard," he says, shaking his head. "To be apart from you when you should have been with us all along. There were so many things left for both of us to say."

I hear myself sob. I feel my mental fortress start to crumble, stones falling away. I thought he was gone forever. I thought I was perfectly alone. And now he's here, and the full weight of my grief finally tumbles down to bury me, an avalanche I can't possibly resist. My vision's blurred with tears, my breath coming so fast it fogs up the inside of my helmet.

The helmet separating me from him.

"We are all connected," my father says, holding out his hand to me. "We are perfectly together. We will be complete when you join us."

"Auri," Ty says quietly from beside me. "That's not your dad."

"But it is," I manage. "You don't understand, I can f-feel them all in my mind. If it w-wasn't him, it would be easy."

But it's so, so hard. Because now, amid the green-silver-blue-gray of the mental plane of this place, I can feel it, I can see it, I can sense Cat's gorgeous reds and golds turning to muddy browns as they merge with the gestalt surrounding us.

And I can see so much more.

My father's reaching out to me. Showing me the connection that could be mine. The brilliance of it. The complexity and beauty. And though they're all one, all the lives, all the minds this thing has swallowed over the eons merged into one complete whole, I can still sense *him* inside the many.

I can see the threads of the whole cloth that were once his. That are *still* his. I can find the parts that are *him* inside this hive mind.

He's still there. I could still apologize to him. Feel him pull me close as he laughs. *Have you been fussing over such a small thing all this time?* he'll say.

"Jie-Lin," he calls. "I need you."

Kal looks across at me from where he sits against the wall, his purple eyes catching mine. And though I'm sure he doesn't know it, the golden tendrils of his mind stretch toward me, strengthening me, twining with my midnight blue.

"I know what it is to lose family, be'shmai."

There's endless compassion in him, but his face is bleak. I can sense the pain of that memory—I can sense a story there I want to know.

His loss is like my loss.

It's a story about losing people who aren't yet gone.

"When we leave this place"—and Kal leans on that word, *when*—"we will seek out word of your sister. Your mother. What became of them. Perhaps something of your blood remains. But you have no family here, be'shmai. Because that is not your father."

And in a moment of stillness, I know that he's right. My

451

father was once in this place, and was once taken by the Ra'haam, once made a part of this whole.

But he's not here now.

These are just echoes.

I nod slowly, tears rolling down my cheeks, and push the rest of my strength into my mental walls, fending off the touch of this planet and the thing inside it.

I was never meant for the Ra'haam, and I will not join with them.

I am of the Eshvaren now.

"Jie-Lin," that thing outside calls. "Come with us."

"No!" I yell.

"It is pointless to resist. Join us."

"Never!"

And finally, that smooth voice from Princeps, from the thing that was my father, changes. And I hear the regret and resolve in it as he replaces the helmet and speaks one more time.

A word.

A whisper.

"CAT."

34

CAT

I'm everything.

I'm nothing.

I'm me.

I'm . . .

"CAT."

I'm a baby wrapped in clean white and I'm resting against my mum's chest and I'm cold and I'm frightened and this is the first voice I've ever really heard and somehow it's all right because I know it's someone who loves me

"Catherine, but I'll call her CAT.*"*

I'm a little girl on the first day of kindergarten and a boy shoves me in my back and I turn and I see blond hair and a dimpled smile and I pick up a chair and smash it over his head and somehow it's all right because I know one day he'll love me

"Ow, CAT*!"*

I'm fifteen years old sitting in front of the vidscreen and I can see the death in Mum's eyes and even though she's sixty thousand light-years away and this is the last time I'll ever speak to her it's somehow all right because I know she loves me

"*I'm proud of you,* CAT."

We're eighteen years old and the empty glasses are stacked in front of us and the tattoos are new on our skin and we know exactly where we're heading and it's somehow all right because deep down I know you love me

"*Oh,* CAT . . ."

And I'm lying there the morning after and even though he left ten minutes ago I can still taste him on my lips and smell him on my skin and even though everything he said made an awful kind of sense I can't stop crying because

because

he

doesn't

love

me

I can see so far. I am one thousand eyes. The eyes inside the skull I was born with, the flesh slowly succumbing to the poison

corruption

infection

salvation

in my blood.

But more than that, I can see through *them*. The fronds that wend and twist around the building my body lies corroding inside. The seedlings that dance in eddies of iridescent blue in the air around us. The shells it inhabits, wrapped in the shape of simple primates or GIA uniforms or colonist skins.

Everything it's touched.

Absorbed.

Embraced.

I'm everything.

I'm nothing.

I'm me.

I'm . . .

. . . *we.*

"CAT."

I hear the Ra'haam's voice through the threads it winds inside my body. I feel how big it is. How impossibly old. A vast consciousness, stretching across countless stars. A legion of one and billions, growing with each mind it enfolded.

Encircled.

Invited.

"WHY ARE YOU FIGHTING US, CAT?" it says, inside my head.

"Because I'm frightened," I reply. "Because I don't want to lose myself."

"THERE IS NO LOSS THROUGH THIS COMMUNION. ONLY GAIN. YOU WILL BECOME SO MUCH MORE INSIDE US. YOU WILL NEVER BE UNWANTED OR UNLOVED. YOU WILL BE US. WE WILL BE YOU. ALWAYS."

"But the others . . . Scarlett and . . ."

"HE WILL JOIN US. ONE DAY, WE WILL ENCOMPASS ALL THIS. EVERYTHING."

"Encompass?" I shake my head. "You mean devour."

"WE ARE NOT DESTROYERS. WE ARE DELIVERERS. FROM THE PRISON OF SELF INTO THE LIBERTY OF UNION. WE ARE ACCEPTANCE. WE ARE LOVE."

It's the same voice I heard when I was new and cold and frightened, staring out at the world for the first time from the bastion of my mother's breast.

But I don't feel cold or frightened now.

I feel warm.

I feel welcome.

Annihilate.

Assimilate.

And I'm lying there on the floor of the reactor in some forgotten colony in some nowhere sector and I'm losing everything I was and ever will be and somehow it's okay because I know

I *know*

I KNOW

it

loves

me.

. . . . .

WE STAND. IN THE SKIN THAT WAS CAT.

SHE IS OURS AND WE ARE HERS.

ONCE WE ENCOMPASSED WHOLE WORLDS. COMMUNED WITH ENTIRE SYSTEMS. BUT THERE IS SO LITTLE OF US LEFT NOW. AN IMPOVERISHED NETWORK, BARELY REMEMBERING THE GRANDEUR THAT CAME BEFORE. WE HAVE SLUMBERED FOR COUNTLESS EONS. THERE IS SO LITTLE OF US AWAKE— JUST ENOUGH TO WEAVE SMALL TENDRILS THROUGH THE TINY SKINS THAT STUMBLED UPON THIS CRADLE CENTURIES AGO. SENDING THEM OUT TO PROTECT US WHILE WE SLEPT A FEW HUNDRED YEARS MORE.

BUT SOON, WE SPAWN. BEGIN ANEW.

BLOOM AND BURST.

We gaze out through the Cat-skin's eyes. The skin named Scarlett looks back at us. A tiny, frightened thing, locked in a prison of her own flesh and bone.

". . . Cat?"

We ignore her. Staring instead at the other.

The enemy.

"Aurora," we say.

We sense the imprint of our old foe on her genes. Her mind. The last Eshvaren died a million years ago. But we knew they would find a way to strike at us from beyond their well-deserved graves. Some long-dormant device hidden in the Fold. Waiting for the right moment. Waiting for a catalyst.

Waiting for her.

We are Cat. Cat is us. And so we know that the skins called Finian and Zila are upstairs, setting the reactor to implode rather than see Aurora consumed. If we have her, we have the means to find the Eshvaren's weapon. If we have her, we have the only one who can operate it. Who knows what we are, and where we sleep, and how we might be stopped.

If we have her, we have the galaxy.

"Cat?"

The skin named Tyler speaks. The apex in the folly of their hierarchy, looking at us from near the window. He is alone.

All of them.

So unimaginably alone.

"That's not Cat anymore," Aurora whispers.

We strike. Moving with the many skins we have embraced since first the Octavia colonists stumbled upon us, deep beneath the planet's mantle. We writhe. We bend. We flow. The one called Kaliis is our primary objective—Aurora's protector. The vines and leaves

SNAKE OUT, GRASPING, THORNED AND BARBED. WE ARE MANY, HE IS ONE. AND THOUGH HE IS OUR BETTER IN THIS NASCENT STATE, WE NEED ONLY PUT THE SLIGHTEST TEAR IN HIS BIOSUIT AND HE WILL BE OURS.

HE KNOWS. HE FLOWS AND CRASHES LIKE WATER. THE OTHER MEMBERS OF THE SQUAD BREAK INTO FRANTIC MOTION. THE SCARLETT-SKIN RAISES HER WEAPON. WE SLAP IT ASIDE. THE FINIAN-SKIN AND ZILA-SKIN UPSTAIRS CRY OUT AS WE STRIKE, RIPPING THE TOOLS FROM THEIR HANDS. WRAPPING THEM ALL IN TWISTED FRONDS AND BLANKETS OF FLOWERS.

THE TYLER-SKIN STANDS PARALYZED. SEEING ONLY WHAT THE CAT-SKIN WAS. UNABLE TO SEE WHAT SHE HAS BECOME.

MORE.

"CAT, STOP IT!"

OUTSIDE, THE PRINCEPS-SKIN RAISES ITS ARMS. OUR GROWTHS ON THE REACTOR BUILDING SHIVER. GRASP. PULL. THE CONCRETE IN THE STRUCTURE SHUDDERS AND GROANS, THE CRACKS SPREAD. THE ELECTRICAL CURRENT THAT THE FINIAN-SKIN HAS SENT THROUGH THE METAL CRACKLES AND BURNS US. BUT WE ARE MANY—THE COOKED AND BLACKENED PIECES OF US FALLING AWAY, ONLY TO BE REPLACED BY MORE. THE BUILDING SPLITS, THE WALLS PARTING, THE ROOF PEELING BACK. THE SKIN-THINGS SCREAM AS THE STRUCTURE IS TORN ASUNDER IN SHOWERS OF CONCRETE DUST AND THE SHRIEK OF DEAD METAL.

THE GANTRIES TUMBLE.

THE SHELL COLLAPSES.

THE FLOOR DROPS AWAY BENEATH THEM.

BUT THEY DO NOT FALL.

"NO."

THE AURORA-SKIN FLOATS UPON THE AIR. RIGHT EYE GLOWING WHITE. ARMS OUTSTRETCHED. THE LIGHT FROM HER BURNS US. THE POWER OF THE ESHVAREN THRUMS INSIDE HER. JUST A FRACTION OF ITS TRUE POTENTIAL.

BUT SO SHARP.

So bright.

We lash out at her—the Cat-skin, the Princeps-skin, the agent-skin, the many forms we have subsumed and embraced in our time here. She fights back with shock waves of psychic rage, tearing the pieces of us away, ripping our grasping tendrils from her friend-skins and bringing them softly to the ground.

But fierce as she is, the power in her is only newly wakened. She has no understanding of its extent. No comprehension of what she might become. And she is one.

We are many.

Too many.

We hit her. Grasp her. Claw her. The disruptor fire from her friend-skins is but summer rain against our totality. For every piece they burn away, another rises in its place. Gestalt. Myriad. Hydra.

And she looks at us, our ancient foe shining behind her eyes.

And she begs.

"Cat, help me!"

We laugh. Feeling the pulse of psychic energy she sends into the Cat-skin's mind. But embraced and loved, encompassed in the warmth of singularity, in the living, breathing completeness inside us, there is no Cat anymore.

There is only Ra'haam.

. . . But

then . . .

. . .

. . . No.

NO.

· · · · ·

I'm nothing.

I'm everything.

I'm we.

But though it's inside me now
hopelessly intertwined with almost everything I was
there's still a tiny ember in a darkened corner
that's
still
me.

I'm back in the flight simulator at the academy. The day I qualified for the Ace stream. Reaching out into the network all around me, moving faster than they can target me. I can hear the voices of the other cadets in my head. The cheers growing louder as my kill tally mounts, weaving through the mossy hands that clutch and grasp me, trying to hold me back.

I take hold of it. Squeezing tight. Holding all of it— Princeps, the other agent, the chimps, the colonists, the tendrils, all of them—still. There's so many of them. It's so big. So much. So heavy.

And I look around at them, through the eyes I know will only be mine for a few moments longer before my ember goes out forever.

These people who were my family. These people who were my friends. Sharp Auri and quiet Zila and snarky Fin and brooding Kal and smooth Scarlett and my beautiful, sad Tyler. I hold out one trembling hand to them.

I can feel the darkness closing in around me. Set to

swallow me whole. And I remember Admiral Adams in his farewell, looking directly at me as he spoke the academy motto, those words and that memory now blinding in my mind.

We the Legion
We the light
Burning bright against the night

"YOU CANNOT FIGHT US, CAT."

Watch me.

"YOU CANNOT STOP US FOREVER."

I don't need to.

"WE ARE LEGION."

So
am
I

I reach out through the network. The tendrils of energy connecting all of it. All of us. Turning the strength of the many back upon itself. I just need to buy them time. Time to run, get out, get away. Time to get the hells off this infected rock, to regroup, to recognize what Auri actually is and what she's supposed to do.

This defeat is a victory.

I can feel her in my mind. Reaching out into me, radiant midnight blue, flaring bright against our burning blue-green.

I can't hold them for long, O'Malley. . . .

"Cat, I . . ."

GO!

Princeps and the others tremble in place. Struggling against the tiny army of me. Aurora can feel them crashing against me, wave after suffocating wave. She knows better than all the others that there's nothing that can be done. And so she turns to Tyler, who's still staring at me in horror.

"Tyler, we have to go," she says.

He blinks at her, understanding her meaning.

Tyler, we have to leave her.

I reach into the muscle that was me. Feel the tears welling in my new blue eyes as I force the lungs to move, the mouth to speak.

"I told you, Ty," I whisper. "You have to let me go."

"Cat, *no.*"

"*Please . . .*"

I can feel them. All of them. These people who were my family. These people who were my friends. They're members of the Aurora Legion, and they don't leave their people behind. But each of them knows, in their own way, that I won't be people for very much longer.

I feel it slipping. I lose my grip. The undergrowth, Princeps, the colonists surge forward and Aurora throws up her hands, a sphere of pure telekinetic force keeping the flood in check. I can't hold them back anymore. I can only hold on to this tiny fragment of me—this last tiny island in a sea of warm, sweet darkness.

I don't want to leave them. But looking into the Ra'haam—all it is and can become—I realize with a tiny spark of horror that I don't want to leave *it*, either.

I look at Tyler. The scar I gave him when we were kids. The tears in his eyes. And I see it. Here at the end. Shining bright against this night.

"Cat . . . ," he whispers. "I . . ."

"I know," I breathe.

I shiver.

Feeling it close in around me.

"Go," I beg. "While you still can."

They run. Limping. Sobbing. Finian clutching the core fuel he synthesized, Kal and Zila supporting his weight. Scarlett, arm in arm with her twin, understanding maybe better than he does. Aurora leads them toward the GIA shuttle, arms flung up, a bubble of telekinetic force pushing back the rippling tendrils, the grasping hands, the all of us set to swallow the six of them.

I follow them at a distance. Walking through the seething, clawing, biting growths, the wreckage of the broken reactor, the ruins of this broken colony. A blue wind dances around me. I can feel it working its way inward now, encroaching on the tiny spark. The last ember. All that remains of me.

I feel its power.

I feel its warmth.

I feel its welcome.

I take off my helmet.

And I'm nineteen and a million years old and standing in a sea of rippling blue-green as the people who were my friends bundle inside that little ship. And I can feel the spores dancing in the air around me and bubbling under the mantle beneath me and all the knowledge in the singularity waiting to embrace me. I'm a million light-years from where I was born and yet I'm right at home. And I'm exhilarated and I'm terrified and I'm laughing and I'm screaming and I'm everything and I'm nothing and I'm Cat and I'm Ra'haam and as the shuttle door cycles closed, as I look on them with eyes that are still mine for the very last time, I see him turn and look back at me.

And somehow it's all right.
"Goodbye, Tyler."
Because
I
know
he
loves
me
.

35

TYLER

She's gone.

We're in space above Octavia III, floating in orbit. Our flight from the colony in the stolen shuttle is just a blur. Our limping trek up from the planet's surface in our wounded Longbow is muddier still. The ruins of the *Bellerophon* and Bianchi's stealth fleet drift through the black around us, starlight glittering among the wreckage.

I'm sitting on the bridge in my copilot's chair, looking at the pilot's seat beside me. Shamrock sits there, shabby green fur and broken stitches, staring back at me with accusing plastic eyes. A single thought is burning in my mind.

I couldn't save her, and now she's gone.

Aurora's star map is projected onto the central display. A holographic rendering of the entire Milky Way, spinning forever around its black hole heart. Out in the spirals of its arms, twenty-two planets are burning red in all that darkness. Twenty-two warning signs. Twenty-two question marks.

Finian and Zila have finished our repairs—the Longbow

is Fold-worthy again. I only need to punch in the coordinates to the navcom, give the command, and we'll be on our way. Except I'm not. I'm sitting there, elbows on my knees, motionless.

The others are gathered around me. Battle-worn and weary. Bruised and bloodied. Silent in our grief.

Seven, now six.

All of them are looking to me.

And I don't know what to do.

We're still fugitives. A rogue squad, hunted by the TDF and GIA and probably the rest of the Legion, too. Even if we weren't kill-on-sight status among Terran personnel, we can't go back to Aurora Academy—the GIA will almost certainly be waiting for us there. And with all we've discovered about Octavia, about the Ra'haam, about those twenty-two planets that this thing is . . . incubating on, we can't risk Auri falling into their hands. Not after all we've already lost.

We can't go home again.

"This defeat is a victory."

We all look at Auri as she speaks. She seems older somehow, this girl out of time. Harder. Something fiercer burning behind her mismatched eyes. She stands small, slender but straight backed, with Kal by her side. And she's looking at me, hands balled into fists.

"What?" I say.

"That's what Cat said to me." Those eyes of hers shine with grief, her voice trembling at the memory of their final moments together. "One of the last things she said, Tyler: 'This defeat is a victory.'"

Scarlett shakes her head, her cheeks wet with tears.

"How?" She paws at her eyes, smudging mascara across her skin. *"How?"*

"We know our enemy now," Auri replies, pointing to the map. "We know where the Ra'haam is sleeping. We know it wants to consume every living thing in the galaxy, until we're all part of its whole. We know the Eshvaren fought a war against it, a million years ago, and they *beat* it. We know they suspected it might return, and they left a weapon to fight it. We know I'm the Trigger for that weapon." She looks around the bridge at all of us. "And we know we have to stop it."

"How?" Finian demands. "Every GIA agent we've come across is infected by this thing. Who knows how far it's spread? Sorry to rain on your parade, friends, but your whole Terran government is suspect."

Aurora's face pales at the reminder. I can tell she's thinking of her father—what was left of him—holding out his hand down there on the surface.

"Jie-Lin, I need you."

But her eyes harden. She shakes her head.

"The signs of infection on a person's body are obvious. Colonists infected here on Octavia must have infiltrated the GIA, got the planet interdicted to help keep it hidden. But if they could spread the infection person to person, there wouldn't be any humans left after two centuries." She glances at the star map, those pulsing red dots. "I don't think the Ra'haam is strong enough to spread while it's sleeping. I think it can only infect people who stumble onto one of these nursery planets. But it's still mostly dormant. It's weak. We still have a chance."

"To do what?" Zila's voice is quiet. "How do you fight something like this?"

"With the Weapon the Eshvaren left us. With me. If we can stop the spawning it talked about, if we can keep these twenty-two planets from spreading the infection through their FoldGates, maybe we can stop this thing once and for all."

"We're wanted criminals," Scarlett points out. "We attacked Terran military ships and broke a Galactic Interdiction. We're going to be chased by every government in the galaxy. We can't rely on anyone for help."

Kal folds his arms. "Then we do it alone."

"The six of us?" Finian scoffs. "Against the whole galaxy?"

I reach under my shirt for my father's ring, hanging on the chain around my neck. I feel the metal against my skin, wonder what he'd say if he could see me now. I'm staring at the star map. Thinking about the odds arrayed against us. The impossibility and insanity of it all.

Asking myself if I still believe.

"It'd take a miracle," I finally murmur.

We sit in silence for a moment. I glance at Shamrock, tracing the line of the eyebrow scar Cat gave me with my fingertip. My chest is hurting so badly, I actually check to see if I'm bleeding. The bridge is quiet except for the hum of the engines. The beat of our broken hearts.

And into that silence, Zila speaks.

"Almost every particle in the universe was once part of a star," she says softly. "Every atom in your body. The metal in your chair, the oxygen in your lungs, the carbon in your bones. All those atoms were forged in a cosmic furnace over a million kilometers wide, billions of light-years from here. The confluence of events that led to this moment is so remote as to be almost impossible." She puts her hand on my shoulder. Her touch is awkward, as if she doesn't quite know how to do it. But she squeezes gently. "Our very existence is a miracle."

"What are you saying?" I whisper, looking up at her.

She meets my eyes dead-on. "I am reminding you of wisdom you have already shared with us."

"And that is?"

"That sometimes you must have faith."

I look at her. At my squad. The hole in space where Cat should be sitting is like a hole in my chest. But then I look into my twin's eyes, just as tear filled and hurt as mine. And she speaks to me without speaking a word.

Show the way, baby brother.

I stand up. Run my gaze over these five who flew into the mouth of the beast for me. We might have the whole galaxy gunning for us. We might not last another day. But as I walk to the pilot's chair, pick up Shamrock and put him on the displays above Cat's console, I know they're all thinking the same as me. We owe it to Cat to fight this thing. With everything we've got.

"We don't have to do this alone, Kal," I say.

I look at the five of them one by one.

"We do it together."

Aurora smiles, weak and watery, but true. "Squad 312, forever."

Kal looks me in the eye. And slowly, he nods.

"We the Legion," he says.

"We the light," Scarlett replies.

"Burning bright against the night," we say in unison.

I sit in the pilot's chair, punch in coordinates for the Fold. The bridge breaks into motion, my squad taking their places, the engines spooling up, light rippling across our consoles in all the colors of the rainbow.

"Where we headed, Goldenboy?" Finian asks.

I stare at the star map in front of my eyes.

Twenty-two warning signs.

Twenty-two question marks.

Twenty-two *targets*.

"Seems to me we're in a war here." I nod to Aurora. "And seems we've already got our Trigger."

Our engines flare, bright against the darkness.

"Let's go find our Weapon."

SQUAD MEMBERS

▶ **BLOOD DEBTS OWED**

▼ **ACKNOWLEDGMENTS**

IT IS WIDELY ACKNOWLEDGED THAT WRITING A BOOK REQUIRES MORE BRAINS THAN THE HAJJI COLLECTIVE OF EEN III AND MORE HANDS THAN A ROOMFUL OF CLOCKS. THE AUTHORS ARE NOT IN POSSESSION OF THIS QUANTITY OF BRAINS *OR* HANDS AND HAVE REQUIRED CONSIDERABLE ASSISTANCE. THE FOLLOWING LIFE-FORMS HAVE BEEN IDENTIFIED AS CONTRIBUTING TO THE EXISTENCE OF THIS STORY:

SQUAD MEMBERS: SINCE THIS JOURNEY STARTED WITH *ILLUMINAE,* WE HAVE BEEN CONSTANTLY GRATEFUL FOR AND ASTONISHED BY THE SQUAD WE'VE GATHERED ALONG THE WAY. BOOKSELLERS, LIBRARIANS, AND READERS—WE ARE SO, SO GRATEFUL FOR YOU ALL. YOU ALLOW US TO DO THIS THING WE LOVE, AND WE LOVE SHARING IT WITH YOU. HUGE THANKS MUST ALSO GO TO ALL THE VLOGGERS, BLOGGERS, TWEETERS, BOOKSTAGRAMMERS, AND EVERYONE ELSE WHO HAS HELPED SPREAD THE WORD ABOUT OUR BOOKS—WE COULDN'T DO WHAT WE DO WITHOUT YOU!

EXPERTS: TO THE MANY EXPERTS ON MATTERS MEDICAL, CULTURAL, SCIENTIFIC, SOCIAL, AND OTHERWISE WHO OFFERED US THEIR HELP ALONG THE WAY, A HUGE, HUGE THANK-YOU—AND AS ALWAYS, ANY MISTAKES THAT REMAIN ARE OUR OWN. TO THOSE NOT NAMED HERE, AND TO JESS HEALY WALTON, AMY MCCULLOCH, YULIN ZHUANG, C. S. PACAT, DR. KATE IRVING, LINDSAY "LT" RIBAR, AND CLAERIE KAVANAUGH: WE OWE YOU ONE. WE OWE YOU *MANY.* PROFESSOR BRIAN COX, PROFESSOR CARL SAGAN, DR. NEIL DEGRASSE TYSON, COMMANDER SCOTT KELLY, COMMANDER CHRIS HADFIELD, AND HANK GREEN AND THE SCISHOW SPACE TEAMS: YOU CHANGED THIS BOOK WITHOUT KNOWING IT. THANKS FOR THE INSPIRATION!

PUBLISHERS: ADMIRAL BARBARA MARCUS AND THE WHOLE RANDOM HOUSE TEAM: THANK YOU, THANK YOU, AND THANK YOU. OUR AMAZING EDITOR, MELANIE NOLAN, THE WONDERFUL KAREN GREENBERG, RAY SHAPPELL, KATHLEEN GO, ARTIE BENNETT, AISHA CLOUD, JOHN ADAMO, JOSH REDLICH, AND JUDITH HAUT, AND ALL THE LEGENDS IN SALES, MARKETING, PUBLICITY, PRODUCTION, COPYEDITING, AND MORE MADE THIS BOOK WHAT IT IS. WE WOULD TRUST YOU IN AN ELABORATE HEIST SITUATION ANY DAY. INTERNATIONALLY, WE ARE SO LUCKY TO HAVE HOMES AT MANY AMAZING PUBLISHERS, INCLUDING ALLEN & UNWIN, WHERE WE ARE GRATEFUL FOR ANNA MCFARLANE, RADHIAH CHOWDHURY, JESS SEABORN, AND THE WHOLE AUSSIE TEAM, AND ROCK THE BOAT, WHERE CAPTAIN JULIET MABEY LEADS AN AMAZING CREW. A HUGE THANKS TO THOSE TEAMS, AND TO THE TRANSLATORS WHO BRING OUR BOOKS TO YOU IN YOUR OWN LANGUAGES.

AGENTS: OUR LONGBOW NEVER WOULD HAVE ACHIEVED LIFTOFF WITHOUT JOSH AND TRACEY ADAMS, CATHY KENDRICK, AND STEPHEN MOORE ON THE CREW. THANK YOU FOR EVERYTHING YOU DO FOR US, AND ALL THE TIMES YOU GO ABOVE AND BEYOND—AND A HUGE THANK-YOU TO THE WONDERFUL FOREIGN AGENTS WHO HELPED EXPAND THE AURORA LEGION AROUND THE GLOBE.

MAKERS OF MUSIC: THE SOUNDTRACK TO THIS BOOK WAS PROVIDED BY THE FOLLOWING GENIUSES: JOSHUA RADIN, MATT BELLAMY, CHRIS WOLSTENHOLME, DOMINIC HOWARD, BUDDY, BEN OTTEWELL, THE KILLERS, WEEZER, THE SCISSOR SISTERS, MARCUS BRIDGE & NORTHLANE, LUDOVICO EINAUDI, OLIVER SYKES & BMTH, RONNIE RADKE & FIR, TRENT REZNOR & NIN, DANNY WORSNOP & AA, MAYNARD JAMES KEENAN & TOOL, WINSTON MCCALL & PWD, IAN KENNY & THE VOOL, ROBB FLYNN

& MH, Chris Motionless & MIW, Anthony Notarmaso & ATB, Jamie Hails & Polaris, and especially Sam Carter, Tom Searle & Architects.

Support and maintenance crew: We would brave the Great Ultrasaur of Abraaxis IV for the following people: Meg, Michelle, Marie, Leigh, Kacey, Kate, Soraya, Eliza, Peta, Kiersten, Ryan, Cat, the Roti Boti gang, the House of Progress crew, Marc, Surly Jim, B-Money, the goddamn Batman, Rafe, Weez, Sam, Orrsome, and the Hidden City Rollers. As always, thanks to Nic for introducing us and getting all this started, and to Sarah Rees Brennan, story midwife extraordinaire.

Family units: To our families, as always, thank you for your never-ending support and enthusiasm, and for everything you do for us, asked and unasked. We are so grateful for you. We love you, and we owe you more favors than even a Betraskan could count.

Spouses: Amanda and Brendan—without you we couldn't do this, and we wouldn't want to. With love, with gratitude, and with secret surprise that you keep putting up with us, thank you for drafting us into your squads.